First published in Great Britain in 2021 by Boldwood Books Ltd.

Copyright © Gemma Rogers, 2021

Cover Design: www.judgebymycovers.com

Cover Photography: Shutterstock

A CIP catalogue record for this book is available from the British Library.

Paperback ISBN 978-1-83889-021-6

BAD GIRLS

GEMMA ROGERS

B
Boldwood

Large Print ISBN 978-1-80048-844-1

Hardback ISBN 978-1-80162-563-0

Ebook ISBN 978-1-83889-022-3

Kindle ISBN 978-1-83889-023-0

Audio CD ISBN 978-1-80048-841-0

MP3 CD ISBN 978-1-83889-019-3

Digital audio download ISBN 978-1-83889-020-9

Boldwood Books Ltd
23 Bowerdean Street
London SW6 3TN
www.boldwoodbooks.com

For every single key worker who risked everything so we could stay safe at home during Lockdown 2020.

PROLOGUE

I stared at my trembling hands, the flesh glowing a radioactive pink. Blood seemed to have worked its way beneath my cuticles and was proving difficult to remove. I'd scrubbed them with bleach, eyes streaming, skin on fire, but still I scraped the brush back and forth, watching rosy specks line the sink.

Karla forced me to stop, resting a cool hand on my arm, her fingertips glacial. She was calm, thinking clearly, whereas my head was spinning like a carousel. What had I done?

'We have to take care of him, Jess,' Karla said as I dried my hands on a paper towel, wiped the sink clean and flushed it down the toilet. She handed me

some latex gloves, retrieved from the large store cupboard, and nodded in the direction of the warehouse, where the industrial machines were housed.

The unit where Bright's Laundry Service was
based was relatively new; a twelve-thousand-square-
foot warehouse in an L-shape on a small industrial
estate on the edge of Croydon. Our closest neigh-
bour was an automotive parts supplier who kept to
themselves; the rest of the units were mostly offices
with a parcel-distribution company taking the
largest warehouse at the entrance to the estate. The
space was open-plan, with the exception of Terry's
office, the toilets and a store cupboard full of detergent and various supplies. It felt like a shell – a cold,
damp space, until all the machines were working
and then it became stifling. It had never felt as claustrophobic before now.

Eyes wide, I glared at Karla.

'We have to call the police,' I said.

'And go back to prison?' she hissed.

Her words were enough. I followed her back to
the office. Where he lay sprawled, half in, half out of
the door. I glanced towards the window; blinds open
a crack to see the sky darkening to a threatening red.

There was a chill evident in the air, not unusual for early February. The lights were on a timer, they came on at four and went off at seven unless turned back on.

'Help me,' Karla gasped as she rolled him over. His face was purple, blood had begun to pool beneath the skin where he'd been lying on his front. She stood, hands upon bony hips, sweat beading on her brow. Her dark glare piercing as she wiped her cheek with her forearm. Wild corkscrew curls pointing in every direction. 'We've got to get him out the back.'

I could see she was getting frustrated with me, and I chewed my lip, willing myself to think clearly. We were both small; around five feet, years of under-nourishment had left my limbs wiry. Was hers for the same reason? The body at our feet had to weigh in excess of thirteen stone. Dead weight.

'We need tape,' I said, eyeing the office chair. If we could get him in the chair, taped in so he wouldn't fall, we could wheel him out between us.

Karla left the office and I wrinkled my nose. It smelt sickly sweet inside; the smell of death lingered in the air. Not helped by him shitting himself as he passed. Bile rose and my chest heaved, but I swallowed it down.

The mobile rang out again, still discarded on the floor where it must have fallen from his pocket. It was the second time it had gone off. Kim, in large capital letters, flashed on the screen. Must be his wife wondering where he was. I glanced at the clock; it was five thirty. No doubt she was expecting him home from work, perhaps wanting him to pick up a pint of milk on the way? What would we do with the phone? I needed time to think. If we got anything wrong, I'd be going back to prison and Karla too, just for helping me.

'Got it.' Karla made me jump as she came back in, a role of silver duct tape on her wrist.

She wrapped tape around the ankles of each trouser leg.

'He's definitely shit himself, don't know about you, but I don't want any of it spilling out when we move him.'

I shook my head, my thumb and forefinger rubbing my earlobe. Trying to concentrate on not being sick.

After ten minutes of struggling, we managed to

get him into the chair. His body flopped forwards and I recoiled as I made contact with damp skin. Drool leaked from his mouth, dripping onto his chest. I turned away so I wouldn't gag. We wrapped tape around his middle, securing him to the back of the chair, and his ankles to the base so his legs wouldn't drag.

'What are we going to do with him?' I asked.

'There's only one thing we can do with him. It's too risky to take him anywhere else. We have to burn him here.'

I shut my eyes for a second, trying to stop my head swimming, until Karla tugged on my arm, bringing me back to the present. There was no time to waste, we had to get on with it.

It wasn't the easiest method of transportation, but between us we managed to push and pull him out to the large red medical waste incinerator. The warehouse contained the industrial machines: the washers, dryers and presses, as well as the incinerator, which was reserved for sheets that couldn't be cleaned.

Bright's would receive a load from a local private hospital Terry had a contract with and some would be stained with blood or faecal matter. These would have to be incinerated and, almost daily, sheets were loaded into the bin tipper at the side, to ensure minimal contact. Using the controls, the bin was raised, sliding the sheets directly into the chamber at the top for incineration.

Unwrapping Terry from the chair, the smell of faeces made me gag. Together, we wrestled him from the chair into the tipping bin, but his dead weight was a struggle. His body, as well as being heavy, was becoming stiffer by the minute as rigor mortis set in. At one point, I was waiting for Karla to suggest removing his legs, as we struggled to fold them in. It would have been the final straw. I'd have given in and called the police. No matter what he'd done, I couldn't hack him to pieces. Dead or not.

Our muscles screaming, we finally sank onto the floor. A joint puddle of sweat and grime. The effort involved in getting him inside the tipping bin had been immense and we were exhausted.

'Come on, we've got to keep going.' Karla sighed, heaving herself up. She squinted, trying to remember the controls of the incinerator, saying she'd only used it a couple of times because Terry liked to operate it, as it was the most expensive piece of kit he owned and he didn't trust anyone else with it. Our speciality was the enormous washing machines that could wash in the region of thirty kilograms of sheets at once.

As she tried to work out which button ignited the cycle, I hurried to the office, ignoring Karla's calls at my retreating back. I had to pull up the carpet tiles. They were old and cheap, a dark blue colour. Most were coming unstuck and beginning to peel back from the concrete. Only two had blood-stains on that I could see, and they needed to go into the incinerator as well. They came away easily with a good tug, the floor beneath looked to be clean.

I surveyed the office, but nothing else looked out of place. The desk was a mess as usual, covered in paperwork, with three coffee-stained mugs on top and a half-full bottle of Gaviscon next to the monitor.

'Good thinking,' Karla said as I returned with the tiles, throwing them in the tipping bin with Terry. She helped me out of my tabard before removing her own and tossed them inside. She hovered at the con-

trols, chewing the inside of her cheek as she de-
liberated.

'Do you know what you're doing?' I asked.

'Fuck no,' she said, slamming her fist on the big
green button. The machine sprang to life, metal
screeching as it lifted the bin and opened the chamber. Terry toppled down inside, landing with a thud.
The tipping bin lowered, the chamber locking, and it
fell silent for a second. Karla and I looked at one another, but before I had a chance to speak, there was a
hiss, a spitting sound and a whoosh of flames from
inside. The deed was done.

1

ONE MONTH EARLIER

I met Karla on my first day at Bright's Laundry Service. My case manager, Barry, at the Community Rehabilitation Company had managed to put a good word in for me. I was relieved there was no prolonged job search involving multiple rejections. The following week of my release I'd secured the position as Laundry Operator with an immediate start.

Based on the outskirts of Croydon, it was only a short bus ride away for me, so the location was good. Barry knew the owner, Terry Bright, well apparently, and I was hired at a little over minimum wage to load and unload the enormous washing machines.

My day was spent wheeling around huge trolleys

of sheets, getting them washed, and moving them to another section to be dried, folded and repacked. It wouldn't have been a job I'd have chosen but I was grateful to be employed at all. I knew my prospects weren't great, my criminal record unappealing to prospective employers. I took a few days to adjust, it was a much more demanding job than my last one as library assistant at HMP Bronzefield.

Bright's, Terry told me proudly during my induction, had contracts with a number of private hospitals and hotels in South London. Bright's were climbing the ranks; Terry was trying to get into the more prestigious hotel chains, but to me it was just a laundry, washing dirty linen.

At the end of each day, my muscles ached from the physical work I wasn't used to. After a week, my clothes were looser, and I rarely consumed enough calories to cover what I was burning. Inside was like a sauna, and some of the girls who'd been there longest said it often hit a hundred degrees on warmer days. The air was stifling, sweat dripped off us and it was easy to get dehydrated. We had to carry water bottles everywhere. The heat was one thing, but the noise took a while to get used to as well, lots of industrial machines, all whirring at once. Sometimes you had to shout to be heard but I was used to that from Bronzefield.

Lots of girls worked at Bright's; although not many were talkative and most, like me, preferred to keep themselves to themselves. I got the impression I wasn't the only one on bail conditions. Everyone had the same look in their eye, all of us just a little bit broken. Stuck in a dead-end job with no prospects there was a general sense of hopelessness that clung to our skin. No one appeared to be much older than twenty-five. We were petite, slim girls, like the Stepford Wives of the laundry world. The conditions weren't great, but beggars couldn't be choosers.

Karla and I met properly when we were thrust together to deal with a large load on my second day which had to be turned around quickly. The machines were out the back, lining the sides and in motion almost constantly. In the centre were long tables laid out for sorting and folding.

'Fag?' Karla asked, as we finished loading two machines side by side and got them going. She rolled her narrow shoulders, collarbones jutting up through her T-shirt.

We had a few minutes before the next load was finished and I was desperate to get out of the stuffy environment. All the air had been sucked out of the atmosphere and into the machines. Sporting yellow underarm stains on our T-shirts became the norm.

I nodded and followed Karla out of the rear of the warehouse, underneath the shutters, where a couple of cars were parked. The fresh air hit like a burst of oxygen to a deep-sea diver and immediately I was light-headed from the temperature dropping so quickly. I took a sharp intake of breath, blowing out foggy air.

'You don't talk much,' she said, seemingly un-fazed by the chill and pulling a packet of Mayfairs out of her pocket to offer me one. I took it and she lit it for me.

'I'm Jess,' I said, fingering the empty piercing on my earlobe. I already knew her name was Karla, I'd heard another girl call after her. We looked about the same age, early twenties, although I was rubbish at guessing. I knew I didn't look twenty-two, more like seventeen at a push.

'How'd you end up here?' she asked, taking a long drag of her cigarette and flicking the ash into the air. Her chin stuck out, exaggerating her pointed features, and she carried an air of confidence I wasn't used to here. I gravitated towards her straight away, like a weaker animal in the pack does towards a stronger one.

'Four years in Bronzefield,' I said, knowing Karla was almost certainly an ex-offender and would know the female prison.

'Send,' she replied. I'd heard of HMP Send, apparently you were lucky if you got sent there.

I nodded and kicked at the gravel with my trainer, spreading the sea of cigarette butts.

We didn't speak much that day, quietly getting on with our work. We stopped for another couple of cigarette breaks and I promised to bring in some tobacco the next day to repay her. At the end of my first week, when our shift finished at five, we walked out of Bright's together and stood awkwardly on the pavement. Karla suggested we went for a cup of tea at a nearby café, sitting outside so we could smoke and not be overheard.

She asked me where I was living, and I explained I had a bedsit a couple of miles away. Stuart, a graphic designer, at the offices where my sister, Helen, was a receptionist, had converted his garage into a large bedsit with a kitchenette, toilet and shower. The garage door had been removed and the space bricked up around a newly installed window and uPVC door. Stuart had put underlay and carpet down, plastered and wallpapered the walls, and boarded the ceiling, but it was still a bit cold and occasionally damp. Although it felt like a palace compared to my cell at Bronzefield. The extractor fan in the tiny bathroom wasn't the best, but I was thrilled to finally be showering alone after four years. I got the impression it had been a cheap renovation, done mostly by Stuart, with the exception of the electrics and plumbing.

I was happy to have my own space, something bigger than the cell I'd shared. Helen had made it pretty clear on my release that I wasn't welcome back with her and Mum. However, she didn't want me living on the streets. I suspect Mum would have pushed her to arrange something for me. Stuart was friendly enough and knew my history. Plus, he was only charging £80 a week, including bills; probably because the place wasn't legally habitable.

We finished our drinks quickly and I bought us

refills, wanting to delay going back to the bedsit. I'd been living in one room for long enough and I loved being outside, even if it was freezing. Karla was sofa-surfing, she said, until she could get a deposit together for her own place. I didn't even own a sofa, well I did, but it was also my bed. I hoped she wasn't tapping me up for lodgings. There was barely enough space for me. Perhaps she couldn't afford to rent anywhere? Money was an automatic problem when you were released. Lack of funds meant no roof over your head and relying on friends and family, difficult if they didn't want to know you any more now you were a convicted criminal. You could earn money inside working, but most of it was spent on tobacco or biscuits. Anything to make your sentence more palatable.

'You had your first meeting with Barry yet?' Karla asked.

I shook my head and used my last chunk of tobacco to roll two cigarettes, passing one to her.

'Not since he got me the job,' I replied. Barry was the community rehabilitation officer assigned to me on release who had put my name forward for Bright's. He saw his probationers every week. Karla said she reported to him too, once a week, but only for another two months, then she was free. I would be seeing him for the next six.

Barry was witty, sharp as a tack and impossible not to like. He was in his mid-thirties, average height with kind eyes, freckles and auburn hair that would curl if allowed to grow. On our first introduction, shortly after I was released, he'd talked easily about Catholicism when I mentioned I went to an all girls' school. I'd remained quiet as his voice boomed around the tiny room. He was a fountain of information on life on the outside and rehabilitation. Not beaten down by the system, like so many others who dealt with us daily, trying to keep us on the straight and narrow. At times, it must have felt like a thankless task.

When he first saw me, he declared I needed feeding up and handed me a lukewarm sausage roll from Greggs. Although rude of him to comment on my stature, I'd munched away, my stomach rumbling gratefully. Pastry crumbs had rained on the table as I watched him complete some forms on my behalf. Together we wrote a rehabilitation plan, how I would go about integrating and adjusting back into society.

When we were done, he took a long look at me, sizing me up and said he knew somewhere that might take me on.

'Can't wait to get the fuck out of here.' Karla sighed, wrapping her hands around her mug. Her nails bitten to the quick.

'You mean Bright's?' I asked.

Karla nodded and took a long drag, squinting as the smoke reached her eyes. Her fingers stained yellow from nicotine. 'Bright's, Croydon, all of it. Once I'm off licence, I'm going to move down the coast, Brighton or somewhere.'

'What about your family?'

'Don't have any now,' Karla said, gazing far into the distance.

'Everyone has parents.'

'I haven't been home since I got released. It's better that way.' She said it so abruptly, I assumed they'd turned their backs on her. It obviously wasn't something she wanted to talk about.

I surveyed her without detection. She was pretty, caramel skin and eyes so dark they could be black, but the circles beneath and hollow cheeks aged her. I couldn't talk, I knew I was a far cry from the girl who had been sent down. My skin no longer glowed, now sallow, and hair like straw. I avoided mirrors, I hated my body, the jutting collar and hip bones. Gone were the soft curves and femininity. I was too angular. Karla and I were the same – pointy and hard.

She grimaced; a shadow crossed her face. I was dying to ask what she'd been in for, but it wasn't the done thing. Most ex-offenders were private and didn't want to talk about their time inside or what had led them to it. I suspected whatever it was; it wasn't as serious as mine.

Although small and fierce, Karla didn't look like she'd killed anybody.

2

Terry Bright's office was a mess, every surface covered in leftover polystyrene food cartons from the 'fat wagon' – the van which came around the industrial estate to feed all the hungry workers. His bin was overflowing with discarded crisp packets and chocolate bar wrappers, but that didn't stop him shovelling the cold fried-egg sandwich into his mouth, licking his fingers one by one. I was amazed to see he had a wedding band on, unable to believe he'd got someone to marry him.

My stomach rolled, throat constricting as I stood in front of the desk, waiting for Terry to speak. He was a short, greasy man with sallow skin and a receding hairline. Although he always appeared to wear fresh clothes, his face had a sheen, like a permanent layer of sweat resided there, and come the afternoon the smell of body odour lingered in his office.

Finally, he spoke, mid-mouthful. His accent reminiscent of an *EastEnders* character. It sounded exaggerated, as though it was what he thought a south Londoner would sound like. 'How did you find your first week, Jess?' Dabbing his mouth with a serviette, missing a splodge of yolk on his cheek entirely.

'Good, thank you,' I said politely. Terry thought he was a big deal, owner of Bright's, master and commander of all in his shitty warehouse. I'd heard him holler at some of the others, he talked to them like dirt, but he paid our wages, so I guessed he believed he was entitled. He gestured for me to sit and I lowered myself into the chair.

'I like to look after my girls, extra hours, bonus schemes, you know.' His eyes twinkled. 'You interested in any of that? Going the extra mile?' He rubbed his crotch provocatively and I chewed the inside of my cheek, my gaze falling upon the expanse of skin where Terry's overhanging belly had stretched his shirt buttons. An icy finger traced its way down my back. He scrutinised me, lingering on my non-existent chest.

I stayed quiet, shrinking inside, contracting smaller and smaller. Trying to shrivel away.

Terry stood and walked over to the blinds, twisting the handle to close them, concealing his office from the warehouse. He stood so close, towering over me, I could smell sweat emanating from his shirt. I sat rigid, biding my time before I intended to open the door and flee, but he returned to his seat behind the desk.

On the wall, I eyed the clock, it was ten past five on Monday afternoon. My second week at Bright's. Most of the workers would have left already. Terry had called me in just as I was taking off my tabard.

'Now, Barry and I are good friends, he likes to keep in touch and see if you're all behaving yourselves,' Terry said, pushing back from the desk, wheeling himself into view, legs spread wide. I swallowed. 'You are behaving yourself, aren't you, Jess? I can tell Barry you're settling in just fine?'

I nodded.

Terry licked his lips, slowly unbuckling his belt,

lowering the zipper and sliding his hand inside. I baulked.

'Your wife?' I said, my voice low, knowing I was clutching at straws.

'What she doesn't know won't hurt her, eh?' He simpered, tapping the framed photo on his desk I hadn't noticed before, and gave me a wink.

A blonde woman holding a gummy toddler smiled out at me and I thought I might be sick. My head swam as I watched him play with himself for a moment, unable to tear my eyes away from the nauseating sight.

'I think we have an understanding, right?' He chuckled, eyes glinting.

My heart pounded in my chest, heat bubbled inside, whooshing upwards like a bottle of fizzy pop. 'Go fuck yourself, Terry,' I spat and pulled open the door, grabbing my rucksack from the side and rushing out of the building. I didn't look back.

At the bedsit, I took a long shower, but I couldn't scrub myself clean. It wasn't the first time I'd been propositioned. Favours were traded for sex on the inside daily with the prison officers, but when I walked out of those gates, I thought I'd be able to put that behind me. Did I go back to Bright's tomorrow, pretend like it never happened? I needed the job, the money. Employment didn't come easily to ex-offenders and I had to keep a roof over my head. I wouldn't survive on the streets.

Agitated and unable to settle, I walked that evening for hours, my stomach tied in knots. Drizzle lit up by the street lamps as I moved between them, the pavements slippery underfoot. It was cold and miserable, not the sort of night to go for a walk, but the bedsit was small, and the walls closed in until I felt I was in my cell again.

I rang Helen's mobile, but she didn't answer. I wasn't surprised, things between us were strained to say the least. I didn't ring the home phone; I didn't want to disturb Mum, not if she didn't want to speak to me either.

Helen had met me outside Bronzefield prison on my release day, with a suitcase full of clothes, an old mobile phone and a bag of groceries. She held the key to Stuart's garage conversion and once she'd driven me there and I was settled in, she'd left. Unbeknownst to me, it had all been arranged while I was inside. Apparently, I wasn't welcome to live back at

Mum's and she'd organised the bedsit to keep me away. I was surprised she was still living there now she was twenty-five; she'd always said she'd move out the first chance she got. Perhaps she'd stuck around to help Mum out or keep her company.

I put the phone back in my pocket, I didn't have anyone else to call, Helen's was the only number I had in my pay-as-you-go phone.

My best friend when I was a teenager, Ashley Parsons, had gone to Portsmouth University. I hadn't spoken to her for four years. She wrote a couple of times while I was inside, apologising for what happened, but I asked her to stop contacting me. Not because I was angry about that night, but I wanted her to move on, forget the past. She had a chance at a real future, and I wasn't going to let this mess drag her down. She'd always been the smartest of us. The one who was going to get off the St Helier estate and make something of herself.

I never thought it was that bad, although everyone said it was overrun by hooligans. Kids on mopeds, dealing drugs on every corner. It was never quiet. Loud music boomed into the night, and no matter what time of day, there would be someone rowing and a baby screaming. The more respectable, hard-working adults moaned about antisocial behaviour and vandalism but nothing ever changed.

Looking back now, I can see we were perceived as the hooligans, although we were only ever having a laugh. The estate was our playground, and Mum worried because I was always there. Ashley lived near the estate, like I did, her parents always saving to move away, but she loved being in the thick of it all. I too was drawn to it like a moth to a flame. I just didn't realise then that I would get burnt.

By the time I returned to the bedsit, my clothes were damp from the January drizzle and I hung them over the chair to dry, although I knew they wouldn't. The atmosphere was dank, a musty smell in the air. I snuggled down in my cold duvet and read *The Faraway Tree* by Enid Blyton. It had been one of my favourites as a kid and Helen had packed it for me. Twenty-two years of life shoved into a tiny red suitcase, the kind advertised as perfect for hand luggage when you were nipping abroad for the weekend and didn't want to check a bag. I'd never even been on a plane.

* * *

I went back to work the following day, after all, what choice did I have? Nothing was said and the next three days were uneventful. I kept my head down. Terry didn't call on me, in fact I only saw him once, and when I did, he awarded me a wink which made my knees turn to jelly. Karla was sullen and not particularly talkative, so when we were teamed together again, we worked quietly, loading and unloading. Going through the sheets, to see what we could clean and what had to be incinerated. I didn't mind, I liked not talking. What did I have to talk about anyway? I worked, I went home, I read.

Sometimes I found solace in the library in their last opening hour of the day when my landlord, Stuart, had his family round. If he could, he'd pre-warn me they were coming, as the noise would be unbearable. His young nephews were little tearaways who loved to scream the place down and it would echo around the bedsit. We spoke most days, arriving home at similar times. He loved a chat and would find a way to slot Helen into the conversation. So much so, I was sure he had a bit of a crush on her.

Dinner consisted of Pot Noodles and pasta sachets that just required hot water. The only appliance I had was a kettle and a small fridge, although Stuart had promised me a microwave at some point. Most of my money went on the launderette. I didn't have enough clothes to wear for the week and once worn for a day at Bright's, there was no way you could wear them again before washing. At the weekend, I promised myself a trip to the charity shop to see what I could scavenge.

On Friday afternoon, Barry, our rehabilitation officer, came in for a visit. He came around to each of his probationers, six in total, seeing us in action before individual meetings. His role was to help us transition back into mainstream life, smoothing any bumps along the way. I got the impression he thought he was saving us from ourselves where we'd be destined for a life of crime.

Karla went in to see him just before I did. She came out, nostrils flared, and fists clenched, storming past me out of the warehouse.

'Got a minute, Jess,' Barry called as my head whipped around. He'd seconded Terry's office for the afternoon.

I sat down on the chair; warmth Karla had left behind seeping into my jeans.

'Watch out for her, she's a wild one, that girl. Hard to keep on the straight and narrow. Some toe the line better than others, but I admire her spirit. I might actually miss her.' He chuckled to himself, rubbing the ginger stubble protruding from his chin. 'So,' he said, flipping open a beige folder with my name on it, containing the forms we completed and my rehabilitation plan from the last time we met. He fingered the pages, scanning my information.

I clasped my hands in my lap. Something about Barry's demeanour made me nervous. It was too formal compared to our time together before.

'Tel's told me some money has gone missing from his office.'

My jaw slackened. 'I haven't taken anything.' I laid my palms flat on the desk, already feeling the flutters of panic.

'Well, there's no proof anyone has taken anything currently. However, when it disappeared there were only a few of you left in the building. I just wanted to reiterate that any illegal activity could result in you serving the rest of your sentence banged up. You'd be whipped back inside quicker than you can blink.'

I ignored my impending tears, refusing to cry. I couldn't go back to prison.

Barry's face softened and he reached over to pat my hand. 'Just do whatever Tel asks of you, yeah, and you'll be all right.'

I stiffened, pulling my hand away. Glaring at Barry as the penny dropped. I'd been such an idiot. It had been too easy, coming out of prison, being assigned a lovely case worker. One who had found more a job quickly. Everything was going too well.

'What happens if I quit?' I asked, keeping my voice even. The alternative was too hideous to contemplate.

'Well, you can of course, but it'll be difficult to find employment with your kind of record. I don't have that many places up my sleeve I can refer you to. It's okay here though, isn't it? Tel treats you all right, doesn't he?' Barry frowned, his eyes warm and compassionate. Had I got it wrong or was Barry not the person I thought he was?

'Y-Yes,' I stuttered, mainly because I didn't know what else to say.

'Okay, just have a think about what I said. Keep your head down. Well done for your timekeeping and hard work.'

I left the meeting and went back to my machine, mind whirling, and a sour taste in my mouth.

3

Karla was wrenching the wet sheets out of the washing machine, swearing under her breath and grunting with exertion. Throwing the sheets into her trolley with such force it rocked on its wheels, I caught it just before it tipped over.

'What's up?' I asked.

'He's such a bastard,' she spat.

I stared at the ground, perhaps I hadn't been wrong after all? What had Barry said to upset Karla so much?

'Got us all by the short and curlies here, no-fuck-ing-where to turn.' She sighed and rested her palms flat on the folding table, head bowed low.

I had no idea what to say, how could I console her? I reached across the table and placed my hand on top of hers. Mine ice white compared to her darker skin.

Her head snapped up, watery eyes screaming with silent contempt.

'You'll be out of here soon, you said so yourself,' I muttered, taken aback. She looked vicious, like a rabid dog. I slowly withdrew my hand.

'Not soon enough.' She stalked off, pulling her cigarettes from her pocket as she went. I didn't follow.

A few minutes later, Barry left, giving me a wink on the way out, my insides squirmed like eels in a bowl.

For the rest of the day, I helped Agnieszka, a Polish lady with delicate features and the smallest feet I'd ever seen. She told me to call her Agnes, and we worked together to remove some hotel bedding from the pressing machines to fold and repackage. She talked continuously, about her mother coming over to England for the weekend and how she was going to cook *pierogi*, traditional Polish dumplings. I guessed she was around late twenties, dark hair and eyes, and she looked like she'd blow over if she got caught up in a gale. I got the feeling she wasn't one of us. Most of Terry's girls were ex-offenders Barry had told me, but not all.

I zoned out of the constant chatter in the end, thankful when five o'clock came around.

It poured with rain as I left and I jumped on the bus home, looking forward to the weekend ahead. Two whole days stretched out in front of me where I could do what I pleased. I'd rung Helen again, to see if she was free to meet. It went to voicemail and I'd left a message but she hadn't come back to me. Was she freezing me out too? Just like Mum?

I tried not to dwell, not to let it ruin my mood. I'd intended to get a Subway on the way home for dinner, but the weather was so awful I settled for a Pot Noodle and a KitKat. Where was Karla now? She was the closest thing I'd made to a friend on the outside, if you could call her that. She would likely disagree.

Tomorrow morning, I planned to head to the library and see if I could get some more books and maybe use the computer to find some faces from the past. My phone was so old it had no apps, no social media for me to search. I'd have to remedy that once

I'd saved enough wages. A smartphone was a necessity nowadays.

When I snuggled into bed, the rain hammering against the window, I was still unsettled about Barry and Terry. What were they up to? Why had Karla lost it? I hoped I hadn't made a mistake joining Bright's. I knew I could be too trusting, but it wasn't like I had many options. There were a few places that took ex-offenders; Timpson Shoe Repairs was one, but there was no way I was going to be working with people's manky shoes all day. It was bad enough working with soiled sheets, but I had a thing about feet.

I tossed and turned all night, dreaming I was back in my cell in Bronzefield. Darcy was threatening to set my hair alight if I didn't give her the chocolate digestives I'd bought. She wanted to swap them for a hit of Spice, a drug some of the girls smoked. Drones would regularly be flown over the wall with packets that looked like cannabis to me. They'd be mixed with their usual tobacco, but you could smell it straight away. Occasionally, letters would get through the post soaked in Spice and tiny strips would be sold at extortionate prices for smoking. Everyone was looking for some kind of escape from prison life, but I was always too scared to try. The ones I'd seen on it looked like zombies, completely out of it.

If Darcy had her way, she'd be zoned out all the time, so she was always looking for her next hit. I'd negotiated her down to half the pack of biscuits and offered to pick up some books for her from the prison library. She'd agreed, but I'd still curled up on my bunk, too terrified to go to sleep. When I finally did, I'd dreamt my hair was crackling, the scent of burnt flesh forced me awake. I'd woke in a puddle of sweat, my hair still intact and Darcy snoring above me.

Nightmares were part and parcel of life on the outside, a constant reminder I was never truly free. Not when I had to report into Barry and answer to the Community Rehabilitation Company. My life wasn't my own. It could be snatched away at any time and we were never allowed to forget it. Karla was right – they did have us by the short and curlies. Mentally, it was almost as much of a prison on the outside. Terrified to put a foot wrong in case I was sent back to Bronzefield.

* * *

Early the next day, I had a change of heart about my plans. I ran through the shower and put on the nicest clothes I owned, nothing fancy – a pair of boyfriend jeans, some scuffed biker boots and a midriff-skimming long-sleeved polo neck. All circa 2016. I had no idea what fashion was like in 2020, having not been around to find out. I didn't waste what little money I had on magazines and I had no television in my bedsit either. The outside world passed me by. Whether it was fashionable or not, it would have to do, although I had to wrench in the belt and the top was baggier than it used to be.

Thankfully, the rain had stopped overnight, and I jumped on the 151 bus outside the train station, which took me up to Rose Hill, near St Helier Hospital. My mum and sister lived in a terrace house in Thornton Road. The house I'd grown up in, although, much to Mum's disgust, I was always over on the St Helier Estate, knocking around with the wild kids as she used to call them. I know she was trying to shelter us, but we were no better off than them, living in a council house, scrimping month to month. My paper-round money and most of Helen's wages at

Topshop from her Saturday job, all went on keeping the lights on.

My mother was a resilient woman who fiercely protected us growing up. She'd be down the school to sort out the bullies, pulling them to one side and whispering in their ears, ensuring I was left alone. After Dad died of a brain tumour when we were still in primary school, she became two parents in one. The soft, loving mother always ready with a cuddle, but she was also a lioness shielding her cubs whenever we were threatened. I don't really remember Dad, but I never felt as though I missed out. Mum was enough.

All my friends thought she was stuck-up, thinking she was better than the families on the estate, but now I see she was just trying to keep me safe. Trying to steer me in the right direction, away from the crowd I was hanging around with. I wrote to her every week when I was in prison, but she only replied once.

I knew as soon as the verdict was announced, the moment I was pronounced guilty, my relationship with my family was broken. Helen visited a couple of times in the beginning but slowly withdrew as time passed. The visits stopped and the phone calls diminished. I was left to serve my four-year sentence alone.

With lead in my feet, I approached the all-so-familiar pebble-dashed house. The orange streak from the leaking overflow pipe to the left of the door had widened since I'd last been there. The front garden was a mess: crisp packets and bottles had been stuck into the hedge by passers-by. Red paint flaked from the wooden door and the house looked tired.

My hands trembled by my sides. I was a different person the last time I stood in front of the door, I was happy, loved and had my mother's comfort back then. Memories of her stroking my hair and putting plasters on my grazed knees as a child flashed into my mind. It seemed light years ago.

I bit my lip and, steeling myself, tapped on the door.

The wait was excruciating. At first, I thought no one was home, but a shadow appeared behind the glass. A flash of blonde hair – it must be Helen.

I formed my mouth into a smile, the exact opposite of hers when the door swung open.

'What are you doing here?' Helen hissed through her teeth and stole a glance over her shoulder.

I had expected our reunion to be awkward, strained maybe, but I hadn't expected such hostility.

'I came to see you and Mum,' I said, frowning. Wasn't that obvious?

Helen tutted and, after a second debating with herself, pulled open the door.

A musty smell hit me straight away, as though no fresh air had been allowed in for months. A faint aroma of urine followed, hitting the back of my throat. Helen turned and whisked into the kitchen. I followed, hoping she'd put the kettle on, but instead she turned to face me, leaning back against the counter and folding her arms.

'You can't be here. Mum is sick and she'll get upset if she sees you.'

'What do you mean sick?' The panic was rising in my voice.

Helen shushed me; her eyes narrowed. 'Mum had a stroke two years ago. Occasionally she gets confused, has accidents, gets upset. I'm trying to take care of her, but if she sees you, she'll lose it.'

My stomach sank to the floor. Why hadn't Helen

told me?

I looked around the crisp white kitchen, in stark contrast to the outside, inside was spotless. Everything was tidy, the worktops clear of clutter. The scent of bleach in the air.

'Where is she?' I said, turning to leave the kitchen, but Helen grabbed my arm, digging her fingers in.

'She's sleeping, and even if she wasn't, she doesn't want to see you.'

I brushed her off.

'Look, is this what you came for?' Helen grabbed her purse off the side and pulled out a twenty-pound note, thrusting it in my direction.

'Oh, fuck off, Helen,' I spat, storming into the hallway and yanking open the front door.

'What did you expect?' She rushed after me as I crossed the threshold onto the garden path.

'I just wanted to see you and Mum.'

'You fucking killed someone, Jess! It ruined all our lives,' Helen said, as though she was guilty by association.

'Who is it, Hel?' I heard a frail voice call out before the front door was shut in my face.

4

Blinking back tears, I stared at the red paint, the flaky door that stood between me and Mum, contemplating beating on it with my fists until Helen opened it. She was lying, Mum was awake, and I wanted to see her. Even if it was only for her to tell me never to return.

I couldn't believe she'd had a stroke. Was it all my fault? Had I caused it? A culmination of the pain and stress? I wanted to face her, let her tell me she didn't want to see me.

I banged on the door, refusing to leave it like this. I kept pounding until my fist was sore. Eventually, Helen opened it and pushed me down the small step, forcing herself out of the house and shutting the door behind her.

'It's half past nine in the fucking morning, Jess!' she hissed; her fingers wrapped tightly around a bunch of keys.

'I want to see Mum.'

'Not now, she's just woken up!'

'I've been calling, Helen. I want to see her; I want to see you. You're the only family I have, you're all I've got.'

She sighed, seemingly unmoved by my plight.

I clenched my teeth tightly together. We'd never been close, but the animosity came off her in waves.

'It's not all about you! She's not well, I don't want to cause her any stress and you hammering on the door isn't helping.'

'Well let me help. I want to help.'

'I think you've done enough.' Her words cut like a knife.

'Doesn't she want to see me?' I asked, not quite believing the mother I knew would abandon me.

'I'll talk to her okay. I'll be in touch.' Helen turned and let herself back into the house, swiftly closing the door. There was little point fighting when she was in this mood. She was like a dog with a bone. A pit bull guarding the gate.

Helen was my older sister, by three years. Always had her sharp little nose in the air, far more superior than the rest of us. Although she couldn't hide her bitterness, because even though I was the tearaway, the one who buggered up her exams, played truant at school, the no-hoper, I was Mum's favourite. Helen had always been jealous.

I knew it was because I reminded her of Dad whom she missed terribly. Helen and I looked similar, long blonde hair and deep-set greenish-grey eyes, but our personalities couldn't have been more different. Cut from the same cloth, yet she was silk, and I was polyester. We'd never really seen eye to eye. She seemed to think we were always in competition.

My molars crunched together, grinding as I walked past the bus stop and down the road. Inwardly I raged. Feeling stupid for not asking more questions. Was Mum bed-bound? Could she walk?

Helen had no right to keep me away. I'd have to come back when she was working. I still had a key, unless they'd changed the locks. I had a vague memory of them being handed back to me in a clear plastic bag as I left HMP Bronzefield, along with everything else taken away the night I was arrested. I hadn't thought to dig them out before I left. Now I wished I had.

Hearing my mother sound so frail made my heart ache. Had I done this to her? Had my crime torn the family to pieces as Helen said? I never meant for it to happen. It was an accident; I hadn't meant to hurt anyone. My sister was right though, someone had died.

I sniffed, fumbling for a tissue in the pocket of my bomber jacket, and hurried back towards home, making a detour to the high street where I knew there were three charity shops in close proximity.

My anger had subsided by the time I perused the racks. Oxfam didn't have anything other than old-lady clothes, but Cancer Research was a treasure trove. I spent just over ten pounds but walked away with two French Connection T-shirts, two pairs of Next jeans and a jumper. They all had that charity-shop smell I'd have to wash out, but in the meantime a bit of body spray would do the trick. I found a fluffy hot-water bottle too by the counter for a pound that I bought without hesitation.

I couldn't help but glance at the row of books for sale before I left. Having to return to the till again. Fifty pence bought me a teenage fiction book and I practically squealed when I found *The Enchanted Wood*, the first book in the Magic Faraway Tree series for another twenty-five.

'Don't I know you?' came a voice to my right as I sat on the bench outside, trying to roll a cigarette. The tobacco pouch balanced precariously in my lap.

I lifted my head, licking the paper to seal the roll as I did. A pockmarked man's face loomed down at me, pale skin with breath which stank of lager, even though it wasn't even lunchtime yet.

'No,' I said flatly, although he looked familiar.

He sat down next to me, buffing up until our thighs touched. He appeared to be in his mid-twenties, a cap covering greasy hair and a hoodie pulled up over the top for extra warmth.

I shuddered. Damn it, I knew I should have remembered to look for a new coat.

'I'm sure I know you, darlin', you look familiar.

You used to live up by the hospital, didn't ya? St Helier, right?'

I looked at him more closely, wrinkling my nose
at the proximity, throat suddenly dry. His name was
Gilby, one of the lads from the estate who we used to
knock around with. The years had been less kind to
him than they had to me and that was saying
something.

'Roll us up one would ya, love?' He nudged my
shoulder.

'I've got to go,' I said, jumping up and hurrying
across the road.

'Jess, that's it, innit? I remember your pretty face.
You killed my mate, Eddie,' he shouted, pulling himself to his feet. He followed up by hollering, 'Fucking
bitch,' but I didn't look back.

Shaken, I darted into one side street and then another, up towards the library, thinking I could get the
127 or 151 bus home. Perhaps it had been stupid to
come home? I hadn't changed my appearance and
Eddie used to run in some nasty circles. In the four
years that had gone by, I hoped the past might have
been forgotten, maybe a lot of the old crowd would
have left the area as we all morphed from teenagers

to fully-fledged adults? I was wrong. Should I be afraid? Would anyone come looking for me once word got around that I was out?

As the cold seeped in, I wrapped my arms around myself and hurried on, legs aching as it dawned on me I'd walked over four miles since I left the bedsit.

Warmth from the library escaped from the automatic doors as they opened, and I stepped inside, allowing myself to be enveloped. I had just over an hour before they closed for the day. Shrugging off my coat as I heard my mother's voice ringing in my ears about 'not feeling the benefit', I headed straight for the computers.

I tried to log on to my old Yahoo email account I hadn't touched for four years, but my username was no longer recognised. Perhaps I couldn't remember it. I spent a couple of minutes creating a new one, trying to think of a suitable password I'd remember. Glancing around, waiting for a word to pop into my head, the three computers to my right were taken by students. All were plugged into their phones, wearing oversized headphones and writing on large A4 notepads.

Could Ashley have sat there over the past four

years? Working on her degree? No, she would have stayed near campus, studied from there. Like me, she couldn't wait to get out of here and the chance to move away would have felt like a golden ticket.

When the accident happened, we were both doing our A-Levels at sixth form, although Ashley was a year ahead of me. She got her results while I was on trial and immediately applied for a degree in Science at Portsmouth University, a five-year course with an optional work placement. It wasn't an option to carry on my A-Levels inside. I could have picked up my course again on my release, but I needed money for a roof over my head. Education was a luxury I couldn't afford.

I finally selected a password and moved on to open a Facebook account under the name Emma Evans. Emma was the name I always wished I'd been given, what I called my dolls when I was small. It seemed so much nicer than Jessica. And Evans was the last name of the actor who played Captain America. The hottest guy on the planet as far as I was concerned. I immediately searched for Ashley Parsons and she popped up, the sixth in the list. Her profile picture was her in a tight-fitting dress, dark waves cascading over her shoulders, smiling at the camera with a glass of bubbly in her hand.

I sighed, eyes prickling from seeing my best friend's face again. One I hadn't seen in a long time. She looked happy, older and polished, a far cry from us in our jeans and hoodies back then. I wiped the moisture from my lashes. Perhaps one day our paths would cross. She could tell me all about university and how her life had changed. I couldn't help but be envious. Our lives had gone in opposite directions.

I flicked through her photos, grateful her account didn't seem to have any privacy settings. Clicking through, every single picture showed Ashley smiling, and I burned when I saw her arm slung around another girl. The same one in many of her photos. She was my replacement. Ashley had moved on whilst I was still stuck in 2016. I kept scrolling, as far back as I could, to see if there were any photos of me, but my breath caught in my throat.

The pointer rested upon a photo of *him*, a large pink heart framed a black and white close-up shot of his face with the words *Taken Too Soon* underneath. The photo had over four hundred likes and loads of RIP comments. His steely eyes seemed to lock onto mine and I squeezed them shut, swallowing hard, forcing the lump in my throat down and the guilt along with it. Voices from that night echoing around my head, the noise, the sound of knuckles against flesh and screams were as fresh as the memory.

I opened my eyes, clicking on the photo to enlarge it, and forced myself to take it in. The image on the screen was of Eddie Watts. Ashley's boyfriend back in 2016. The one I'd gone to prison for. The one I'd killed.

5

After a minute, I clicked back and Eddie's face disappeared. Once he'd gone, I was able to breathe again. I hadn't seen his face for such a long time, not since his picture was printed in the newspapers before my sentencing. Painted as the innocent victim, a shot of him with his mum, gazing at the camera through his dark eyelashes. I was painted the villain of the piece, although I knew better and so did Ashley.

It didn't stop me from feeling remorse though. Taking a human life was something I'd never get over or stop trying to make amends for. When I first arrived at Bronzefield, spending hours in my cell with nothing but my thoughts to keep me company, the guilt had driven me mad. I wrote to Eddie's family, pouring my heart out in pages of attrition for what I'd done, but I never received a response. I was sure it was because I'd pled not guilty at the trial, swept up in the advice from my solicitor, who turned out to be severely lacking. It was another reason my sentence was quite harsh for a first offence.

During the first year, I cried myself to sleep, even praying at times, hoping my repentance would bring me back from the edge. The listening service helped a lot. Prisoners trained in counselling would be available to talk to and I was there once a week. Getting the job at the prison library brought me back, it kept me busy but the guilt never went away.

My fingers lingered over the keys and I typed in various names of people I hung around with then: Andy, Ben, Nicola, Jo – some I found, some I didn't. I didn't friend request anyone or like any posts or photos. No one would have any idea who Emma Evans was, and I didn't want to draw attention to the fact I was back in town. As earlier proved, not everyone would be pleased to see me.

Helen had a profile on Facebook but hers was set to private so I could only see her main photo. It was recent, last summer maybe, in a pub beer garden. Wearing sunglasses with a bottle of Corona in her hand.

Just as I was about to log off, I had an idea and typed Karla's name into the search box. Hundreds of Karlas came up; I don't think I'd ever heard her surname mentioned. Sighing, I closed the internet down, aware my stomach was rumbling loudly. Lunchtime had arrived and I hadn't eaten yet today.

I couldn't hang around the library, although I was tempted for the warmth. There was no point, it closed soon, and I couldn't get a new library card as I had no way to prove my address. No bills in my name. I was anonymous. A nobody.

I popped into the bakers for a sausage roll and ate it outside whilst I waited for the bus to take me home. My eyes darted around the busy high street, sizing up the faces passing by to see if there was anyone I knew, or who might recognise me, but there wasn't. I stayed in the alcove of the boarded-up sportswear shop to keep out of sight until the double-decker bus rumbled into view.

The bus dropped me practically outside my new home and I let myself in, annoyed I'd forgotten to buy teabags. At least it gave me something to do tomorrow. Visiting Mum would have to wait until I knew Helen wouldn't be there.

'Jess.' A knock at the door followed Stuart's voice. He must have heard me come back.

I sighed and turned off the almost boiling kettle.

'Hey,' I said, swinging open the door. I could see Stuart look over my shoulder and I opened the door wider so he could see I hadn't wrecked the place. I didn't mind. It was his rental and he'd let me stay, not knowing me from Adam, with only the word of my sister to vouch for me.

'Hi, you all right?' He shoved his hand in his pockets and I tried not to smile. He was reserved, and I was sure he felt awkward around me. The convicted offender.

'Yeah fine, you?' I asked.

'Yes thanks. Just wanted to let you know in case I don't catch you tomorrow, I'm away Monday and Tuesday, so if you can keep an eye on the house, I'd appreciate it. You've got my number if you need it.'

I nodded, I had it written down somewhere, although I hadn't put it in my phone yet.

'Sure, no worries,' I said, and we exchanged smiles.

'Oh, and this is for you.' He stepped to the side, back up to his front door and returned with a small silver microwave.

'Thanks, Stuart, that's amazing.' I grinned, rolling onto the balls of my feet, excited at no longer having to eat pasta pots.

I backed up, letting him pass and he carried it into my room, placing it on the worktop of the kitchenette.

'No bother,' he said, before going back outside.

He stood staring for a moment longer than necessary, the silence stretching out until I was compelled to fill it. Social interactions with him were excruciating, he was painfully shy. Helen told me on the drive from Bronzefield that Stuart's mum had passed away and his dad had just gone into a home as he had stage five Alzheimer's disease. The house belonged to his parents and Stuart was slowly modernising it. The garage had been his first big project. Judging from the workmanship, he still had a lot to learn.

'Where are you going? Anywhere nice?' I asked,

my voice a higher pitch than normal.

'Bloody team building at work. Down to Lewes. I'm dreading it.' He grimaced. My ears pricked up.

'Oh no. Has Helen got to go too?'

He blushed at the mention of her name. 'Yeah, she's organised it. Poor cow, it'll be like herding cats.'

I clenched my jaw to stop the smile threatening to escape.

'Well, try and enjoy it if you can. I'll look after things here,' I said as Stuart turned to go back in the main house, giving me a wave over his shoulder. 'Thanks again for the microwave,' I called to his retreating back.

Once the door was shut, I leaned against it, closing my eyes, unable to stop the smile spreading across my face. On Monday, after work, I'd see Mum.

* * *

I spent Sunday sorting out my clothes and bagging up what needed to go to the launderette. The bag was heavy, but the launderette was only ten minutes away. I managed to get the washing machine going and popped to the Co-Op to get some milk, teabags and stock up on microwave meals. I just had enough time to dash home to drop it off and rush back before the cycle finished. I wouldn't have been able to manage the washing and the shopping on my own.

The bedsit was Baltic, even with the halogen heater cranked up. January's freeze was upon us and I wrapped up in my duvet, snuggling the hot-water bottle to read *The Enchanted Wood*. I read a lot of children's books inside. Their library was well stocked with books for all age ranges and abilities, but I leaned towards books from my childhood for comfort. On the outside, I had devoured crime and thrillers, but after my sentencing I couldn't face them. I considered carrying on with my A-Level English Literature text, *Wuthering Heights*, but it felt too painful. A reminder of the life I'd left behind.

Some prisoners couldn't read at all and many were at primary or junior school level. I found I was quite good at teaching, picking texts for some of the girls to read. Helping them with the language and trying to excite them with books. I got a bit of a name for myself and every day I would be visited by someone wanting help with a letter or another book that would stretch them; Darcy came every chance she got. It kept me going and no one hassled me after that. In fact, they teased me for the children's books, knowing I could read just fine, but I wanted to be transported back to happier times.

I remember Mum reading *The Gruffalo* whilst we snuggled up on the sofa under a blanket. Helen playing with her Barbies and pretending not to listen but getting drawn in towards the end of the story, when the mouse triumphed. I still knew the words off by heart. It was a lifetime ago now, memories tarnished by my later teenage years.

I'd grown up a lot inside, spent my twenty-first birthday in my cell on lockdown as there was a riot on C wing over the post not being delivered. I'd had no cards or presents; the best part of the day was Big Brenda from the tuck shop sneaking me a packet of Jaffa Cakes before lights out.

Things would change now I was out. I'd paid my debt to society. I just had to cling on for a few more months, six to be precise. Six months of keeping my nose clean and out of trouble. Barry would sign me off and I could leave, maybe follow Karla down to the coast. Start again as someone new. Someone who didn't have blood on her hands.

6

After the weekend shutdown, the temperature plummeted further, and the warehouse was cold initially until all the machines were working. The mood was strangely sombre, although perhaps it was just me. I'd pushed the thought of the missing money Barry mentioned out of my mind over the weekend. Now back at Bright's, I was skittish and couldn't wait to get out of there. Karla noticed I wasn't on the ball and threw a towel she was folding across the table at me.

'Catch,' she said, laughing as it hit me square in the face.

I scowled and threw it back.

'What you got your knickers in a twist about?'

'Nothing,' I snapped and watched Karla's mouth twitch, trying to suppress a laugh.

'Is it Barry? That prick gets under everyone's skin here, he's a fucking snake doing Terry's bidding. You'll get used to him.' She'd had a different story on Friday when she was annihilating his character.

'Some money has gone missing?' I said quietly and Karla threw her head back laughing, her tight curls bouncing on her shoulders. Her mass of hair made her head look too big for her body.

'That old chestnut. We've all heard it. Don't believe everything he says, Jess. He'll tell you anything to get you to do what Terry wants.'

The slapping of shoes on concrete saw Karla jerk her head down and she resumed folding. I followed suit just as Terry rounded the corner.

'Hanna, you got a minute?' he called from behind me.

Hanna, a slight Slovakian girl unloading the dryer, froze, staring straight ahead, unblinking. Terry didn't wait for her to respond but turned and left.

I clocked Hanna and Karla lock eyes, the fear in Hanna's obvious to see. An icy grip took hold and my feet became lead, watching the silent exchange between the girls. The atmosphere in the room became palpable.

A second later, Hanna dropped her gaze to the floor and shuffled out of the warehouse after Terry.

Karla sighed and carried on folding; her movements robotic. She wasn't laughing any more.

'What was all that about?' I asked.

'It's her turn is all. I'm going to the loo,' she said, leaving her station before I could ask more. Her turn for what?

All day, I carried tension in my shoulders, gripped by an invisible force. Hanna and Karla spent some time outside smoking at lunchtime, huddled together. I wanted to join them, but I didn't want to intrude. Hanna was clearly upset, and Karla's expression was fierce, hands gesticulating wildly. Instead, I nibbled at my lunch next to Agnes: crackers for me, while she had soup.

'Do you know what's going on with Hanna? Why Terry wanted to see her?' I asked, but Agnes shook her head vehemently like I'd just suggested playing chicken on the Purley Way. She quickly changed the subject to her mum's visit at the weekend and the gifts she'd brought from Poland.

Before I left for the evening, Karla and I were removing our tabards and shrugging on our coats, preparing for the cold outside when Terry came out of his office carrying his briefcase.

'See you tomorrow, girls,' he said, a glint in his eye.

I smiled tightly and Karla muttered something unintelligible.

He strolled out, shoulders swaying, without a care in the world.

'Who's going to lock up?' I asked, knowing there was a key code system at the front, but it had to be double-locked at night, surely?

'Dunno, maybe he'll be back. He's always in that shitty casino down the road,' Karla replied, stuffing her tabard into her locker. She seemed to know a lot about Terry. 'Fancy a beer?' she asked, her jovial mood returned now work was over for the day.

'I can't, got to visit my mum. Another time?'

Karla stared at me and grinned. 'Yeah sure, no worries. Catch you tomorrow then.'

Outside, I waited for the 407 bus, it would take me halfway and then I'd have to walk the rest unless I waited for another bus. I was a ball of nervous energy and was looking forward to the exercise so I could figure out what I was going to say to Mum.

I checked my rucksack for the old set of keys I'd put in there this morning. Thankfully, they were still in the zip compartment and I had to hope Helen hadn't changed the locks.

The 407 came and it was rammed with workers on their way home. I squeezed into the space by the door and clung on to the handrail, keeping my head down. Not making eye contact with anyone. Bumping into Gilby had made me wary of being recognised.

Bright headlights peppered the darkness outside through the steamed-up windows and every time the bus went around a corner a shot of cold air found its way through the gap in the door. I shuddered, pulling my coat in tighter and tucking my chin inside the collar. I risked glancing over my shoulder, but no one was looking at me. Most were glued to their phones or staring out of the window, but still I turned away, leaning against the glass partition as we neared my stop.

When the bus eased to a halt, I jumped off and walked as quickly as I could up the hill towards

Thornton Road. At just gone six, the streets were still busy, which made me feel better about walking in the dark and at least it was dry. I stopped off at the fish and chip shop, Plaices, just before my old road. It was a monthly treat to get fish and chips when we were young. Would Mum be hungry? Helen would have left her something, I was sure, but the smell of batter made my stomach growl appreciatively and I bought a small cod and chips Mum and I could share.

Mouth salivating at the smell of vinegar, I clung on to the packet, grateful for the extra warmth. Two minutes later, I stood outside the door, all the blinds were down, but I could see light inside. I debated on ringing the bell. The last thing I wanted to do was scare Mum, but I didn't want her trying to get to the door to answer it and potentially falling. I had no idea how mobile she was. Slipping the key out of my pocket, I put it in the lock, my heart speeding up as it turned with ease.

'Mum,' I called as I pushed it open, sighing with relief that the key worked. 'It's me, Jessica.'

I heard a mumble, followed by thudding foot-steps. Convinced I was about to be confronted by an angry Helen, I closed the door behind me and stayed where I was.

A rotund woman appeared at the top of the stairs, the familiar creak on the third step as she descended. 'Who are you?' she asked in a brusque Nigerian accent.

'I'm Jess. I'm Alice's daughter. Who are you?' Although the question was pointless as she came closer towards me into the light from the hallway and I could see she was wearing a navy tunic with white piping and a badge that read Grace.

'Her daughter is away tonight. She called an extra carer in. Have I got the dates wrong?' she tutted and pulled her phone out of her pocket.

'No, no. That's Helen, my sister. I'm Jess. I've been away for, well, a while and she doesn't know I'm here.'

'Okay, well, I've changed her sheets and she's had a bath, she's upstairs now. I was just coming down to prepare her dinner.' Grace seemed put out I'd turned up out of the blue and ruined the flow of her routine. I'd caught her off guard.

'You know, why don't you go. I'll feed Mum and

put her to bed,' I said with a weak smile and held up the now lukewarm chip wrapper.

She rolled her eyes and sucked her teeth loudly. 'Okay, okay,' she said, grabbing her coat and muttering to herself under her breath as she pulled open the front door.

'I'm sorry to mess you around, but I'll make sure you'll get paid fully,' I said, trying to appease her.

'Thank you.' She smiled, but it didn't reach her eyes and it was already fading as she pulled the door shut behind her.

Checking it was locked, I headed into the kitchen and put the fish and chips on a plate. The house was warm and well lit. Even with the dated décor, it was soothing. Tucking a knife and fork under my arm, I climbed the stairs, hairs on the back of my neck standing to attention. I hadn't seen Mum in four years, and I didn't know if she wanted to see me now. According to Helen, she'd turned her back on me, but I ached desperately for the kind, funny and no-nonsense mum I remembered.

I turned the corner at the top of the stairs and pushed Mum's bedroom door open. A frail woman I didn't immediately recognise sat in a pink armchair.

She was looking out of the window into the darkness, watching the light of the cars go up and down the road. As the door creaked, she turned to look at me, her mouth dropping open and a tiny amount of spit cascaded onto her chin. Eyes filling, I plastered a smile onto my face.

'Helen? Is that you?'

7

'No, Mum, it's Jess,' I said, rounding the bed and sitting opposite her.

Mum had changed so dramatically I couldn't comprehend it at first. Her face looked drawn, the lines around her mouth had multiplied and deepened. Her bottom lip drooped slightly to the right, but the most upsetting was the lack of spark in her eyes. It had gone.

Mum was fiery, a force to be reckoned with, partly because she had to be. Raising two daughters single-handedly, one of whom had been more difficult than the other. Shame draped over me like a blanket as I grasped her leathery hand. Helen had been right to want me to keep away.

'Jess?' Mum's eyes dampened and she squeezed my fingers.

'I've missed you,' I said, unable to stop the tears from falling.

She stroked my hair as I sank to my knees, laying my head in the folds of her dressing gown to sob.

'I'm so sorry,' I said eventually when I was able to speak again.

'You're too skinny.'

I laughed at her observation.

'You can talk!' I pulled myself up and glanced at our dinner, wrapped up. 'I bought us fish and chips, I'll go and warm it up in the microwave.' Mum smiled at me, her mouth slightly lopsided.

When I came back, I watched Mum eat half of the meal, just enough dexterity to stab at the food with a fork and feed herself. My heart shrank in my chest to see the enormous change.

'Why didn't you want me to visit Bronzefield?' she asked gently when she'd finished eating and laid her fork down.

'I did!'

Mum's nostrils flared; confusion etched on her face.

'Is that what *she* told you?' All at once, the pieces fit together. 'Did you not get any of my letters?' I continued, balling my hands into fists so hard my nails dug into my palms. Mum didn't stay away out of choice; Helen orchestrated it. The vicious bitch! How dare she.

Mum shook her head and sighed, spitting the words out like they tasted bad. 'I thought it was some misguided attempt to protect us.'

'Helen must have taken the letters I posted. Did she not give them to you?'

Mum shook her head. 'I'm sorry I never came.' She stared down at her cream fluffy slippers.

'It's okay, it doesn't matter now. I'm back. Did you know I was being released?'

'Yes, Helen told me. I made her promise that she'd get you set up. I told her you were welcome to stay here, but she wouldn't hear of it.'

I gritted my teeth, what had I expected? As far as Helen was concerned, I was no longer welcome here. I stood, gathering the wrappings, aware of Mum's woeful gaze. I could see she felt guilty but I didn't know what else I could say to soothe her.

I took the plate downstairs and made us both a cup of tea. My blood turning to molten lava as it streamed through my veins. All the nights I'd laid in my bunk, praying Mum would visit and the crushing disappointment when she didn't materialise the following day. The nights I'd wait until lights out to cry silently into my pillow at being disowned. Thrown away and forgotten about for one stupid mistake.

A phone rang while I was downstairs, it sounded like a mobile and I assumed it was Helen checking Mum was okay. I didn't ask, not caring if Helen knew I was here.

When I returned with two steaming mugs, Mum and I talked for a couple of hours about the years I'd missed. She told me about the stroke, how before that she wanted to move out of the area because things weren't the same round here any more. Had she been shunned because of the accident? Ostracised from the community? It weighed heavily on me and I could see there were things she didn't want to share although I pushed for more. I had to know the truth. Like a raggedy nail you can't stop picking at. Eventually Mum relented and it came out in a rush of words, each one stinging.

'No one spoke to us, we were ignored, no longer welcome. I had to give up the day job, they didn't want me as a teaching assistant any more. I was asked to leave when the parents stopped bringing their kids to school. There was a kind of protest.'

I winced, seeing the pain in Mum's eyes.

'No one wanted me as a cleaner either, so the evening work dried up too. I had to rely on Helen. Times were tough, Jess, not just for you. The court case was a huge spotlight being shone on our lives, everyone judging us. We were hounded, someone even put dogshit through our door!'

My eyes brimmed and I squeezed Mum's hand tight. I hadn't realised I'd caused so much trouble. Naively I'd assumed it would be forgotten about once I'd been sent down.

Mum sighed and shook her head. 'It doesn't matter now. You're back.' She gave me a slightly lop-sided smile. Mum still seemed together mentally, although the stroke had left her body in bad shape. She'd lost some movement in her left arm and could no longer walk unaided as her left leg was also weak.

She had a cane and a Zimmer frame, which she point-blank refused to use. Helen had carers come in three times a week, but otherwise she did everything for Mum. I offered to take her downstairs to watch television, but she was too tired. It was gone nine, so I helped her to the bathroom so she could use the toilet and clean her teeth.

When she shuffled into bed, I asked if I could stay so she wouldn't be alone. Mum said she'd love me to, and I slipped in beside her, snuggling into the warm duvet and wrapping my arm around her tiny waist. She fell asleep in minutes, her mouth slightly open, snoring quietly. I lay staring into the darkness, soaking up the scent I'd been dreaming about for four years. The smell of my mum's ancient floral perfume mixed with cherry blossom shampoo. I thought my heart would burst; we were finally together again, marred only by my anger of Helen for keeping us apart.

She'd lied to minimise Mum's stress, I understood that. Helen would have been struggling to cope, overwhelmed by the unexpected financial burden and Mum's ill health, while all the time juggling a full-time job. If I'd known, I could have sent money home, tried to earn more, at least been there to lean on. Instead, she'd shut me out, pretended I didn't exist. The family's dirty little secret. I wasn't sure I'd be able to forgive her.

Watching the shadows dance on the curtains as people passed under the street lamp on the road below soothed me. My mind drifted, as I tried not to think about Mum being a prisoner in her own home whilst I served my sentence. A minute later, I noticed the movement had stopped, the light outside appeared weaker. Sliding out from beneath the covers, I went to the window, pulling the edge of the dusky pink curtain to one side, enabling me to peek out.

A solitary figure stood under the lamp post staring at the house, their head rising until it looked as though they were staring straight at me. My heart leapt and I ducked out of view, stumbling backwards but quickly regaining my balance.

Mum was still snoring as I edged forwards, returning to the window. The figure was still there, but I was unable to see who it was at this distance and from the angle of the light – they were part shadow.

I could make out the peak of a cap pulled down disguising their face and the shape of a puffy jacket.

The red glow of a cigarette end moved in the darkness and the light of a mobile phone screen caught my eye. The figure lifted the handset to their ear before turning and walking away.

Could they have been watching me? Knowing I was inside? I'm sure they saw me looking out. Had word got back to Eddie's friends I'd been released? My mind turned to Gilby, him shouting after me as I fled. A chill crept down my back and I tiptoed downstairs to check all the doors were locked. Once satisfied, I returned to bed, but sleep evaded me. Whoever was watching me knew where I was. What did they want? If it was to scare me, then it was working. Had I done the right thing returning home? I hoped I hadn't put Mum at risk.

* * *

I woke in a panic, disorientated, and sat bolt upright in bed. Blinded by the light streaming through a gap in the curtains, I felt as though I'd blinked, finally dozing off around half past five. Next to me, Mum had pulled herself up and was leaning against the headboard.

'You snore.' She chuckled, turning the page of a battered copy of Virginia Andrews' *If There Be Thorns* in her lap.

I rolled over to check my phone, it was almost eight and I had to be at work in an hour. Jumping out of bed, I cursed. 'Shit, I'm late.'

'Helen said you've got a job at a laundry?'

I nodded; surprised Helen had given Mum any information about me at all. I shifted from foot to foot, anxious to get ready.

'Go, I've got a carer coming in later. I'll be fine.'

'No, no, I'll get you sorted first, Mum.'

I ignored her protests and dashed downstairs to make us both a cup of tea and toast, delivering it back to her bed.

'Can I use the shower real quick?'

Mum nodded and waved me out, her mouth full of buttered toast.

The shower was hot and more powerful than the one at the bedsit. I wished I could have spent longer in it. Roughly drying myself, I pushed Helen's door open and saw the bedroom we used to share almost exactly as I remembered it. She was always the untidy one of us, clothes strewn over the bed, hairspray and make-up littered her vanity table.

Our single beds had been replaced by a double and there was nothing left in the room of mine any more. I pulled open a drawer, then another, before finding some clean underwear. A T-shirt on her bed with a band I'd never heard of caught my eye and I wrenched it on after a quick spray of her deodorant.

'Mum, can I take you to the toilet before I go?'

'Would you, love, thank you.'

I waited outside, offering my help as I pulled my hair into a scraggly bun.

'I'm not at the stage where I can't wipe my own backside just yet,' she yelled through the door and I laughed. It was half-past eight and I knew it would be a miracle if I got to work on time.

Mum shuffled out and I wrapped my arm around her to walk back to the bed.

'Are you sure there's nothing more you need?'

'Go, you'll be late. Thank you for coming.' She beamed at me.

'Love you. I'll be back,' I called as I took the stairs two at a time and jogged down the road to the bus stop.

I paced along the pavement, waiting for the bus to come around the corner as the minutes ticked past. If only I had a car, but it was an expense I couldn't afford. I considered texting Helen, telling her what a bitch she was, but it could wait. I wanted to look her in the eye, I wanted her to feel the full pelt of my contempt.

Finally, the bus came at 8.51 a.m. but it didn't stop outside Bright's until 9.15. I rushed inside the building, clocking in and trying to keep my head low until I passed Terry's office.

Thinking I'd made it all the way to the warehouse without being seen, I slipped off my coat before Terry's voice boomed.

'Afternoon, Jess. Got a minute?'

8

My heart sank and I locked eyes with Karla, who frowned at me from across the warehouse. Putting my things in my locker, I returned to the office and saw Barry was there too.

'Come in, Jess,' Terry said.

I inched past him as he held open the door and sat in front of his desk next to Barry. It was a tight squeeze inside, three of us in such a small space. I felt the itch of claustrophobia start.

Terry closed the door and returned to his seat.

'Everything okay?' he asked.

I nodded, as my pulse quickened.

'Good, good. Listen, Jess, we need you to be on

time. Most girls would kill for this job. You're lucky, you know. Well paid, well looked after. There's not an abundance of opportunities for ex-offenders, Barry here will tell you.'

Barry nodded on cue.

'I'm sorry. It won't happen again.' I lowered my gaze to the floor, aware both Barry's and Terry's were staring at me.

'Is that money still missing, Tel?' Barry asked, his brow furrowed.

'It's not turned up yet. Know anything about it, Jess?' Terry rubbed his stubbled cheek.

'I haven't seen any money.'

'Okay,' Terry said, and we sat for a minute in silence. Out of the corner of my eye, I could see Barry and Terry exchanging a look, a wordless conversation between them.

'I'll see you here at five o'clock to make up the time,' Terry said flatly and leaned back in his chair.

I nodded and, with legs like lead, got up and left the office. Sure I'd heard Barry sniggering as the door closed behind me. *Tossers*.

'What was all that about?' Karla asked when I

ventured into the warehouse and began loading the dryer with freshly washed linen.

'I was late, he wants me to make up the time after work.' I shook my head, incredulous, it was fifteen bloody minutes.

'Oh,' Karla said, unable to meet my eye.

It didn't matter, I wouldn't let it ruin my day. I got to see Mum and that was the main thing. Things would be different from here on. Helen wouldn't be able to stop me visiting, now I knew Mum wanted to see me. Who the hell did she think she was anyway? She'd get a surprise when she came home later, when Mum told her I'd stayed over, that's for sure. Perhaps she'd come grovelling, but I knew she wouldn't, she'd take the moral high ground as always.

* * *

The day dragged and the knowledge I'd have to spend an extra fifteen minutes alone in the warehouse with Terry made my skin crawl. I couldn't bear to be anywhere near him, but he paid the wages and

I needed a job. Had Karla been right? Was the money going missing a load of rubbish?

At five, the girls clocked out one by one, but I kept my tabard on as I headed for Terry's office. He sat behind his desk, glaring at his monitor, his forehead shiny and hair slick.

'Want me to carry on folding?' I asked, interrupting him.

'No, no. Come in,' he said, waving me in. A sheet of paper stuck to his forearm as he lifted it from the desk, and he peeled it off his skin.

I swallowed, a lump forming in my throat. He stood beckoning me inside, nodding goodbye over my shoulder to Agnes and Hanna as they clocked out.

'Take a seat, let's have a little chat.'

I lowered myself into the same chair I'd sat in hours earlier.

'The last time we had a little talk, I got the impression you didn't really grasp how we do things around here.' He leant back in his chair; fingers interlocked behind his head, round yellowy patches beneath his armpits on display. 'So, here it is, Jess. I own this place and everything in it. While you're here, I own you girls too. If you're good to me, then I'll be good to you. When I ask for something, you do it. Understand?'

I tried to ignore the prickling sensation behind my eyes.

'All the girls who work here do me little favours and I do the same for them. That's how it works.'

I wanted to ask what sort of favours, but I already knew the answer. The dread climbing up from the pit of my stomach told me all I needed to know.

'You weren't very nice to me in our last chat, but you'll only get away with that once. There are a hundred other girls I can replace you with. They'll be only too happy to work here.'

I bit my lip and willed my heart to remain steady, unable to speak.

'So, I think we're clear. If you wouldn't mind closing the blinds and locking the door. We don't want any unexpected visitors now, do we?' He slid the leather strap of his belt out of the loop and un-buckled as I turned away.

I gave an involuntarily silent heave.

'I'll tell Barry.' My bravado was weak.

He threw his head back and laughed, his round

belly jiggling. 'Be my guest. I'm not sure how much good it'll do you. Listen, Jess, do you really want to find another job? It's payday next week and everything you've earned so far can disappear like that.' He clicked his fingers. 'Kiss goodbye to your rent. Before you know it, you'll be turning tricks on the street to eat.'

A single tear escaped, and I swiped it away. I needed a job; I couldn't pay my rent any other way. There was no room for me at Mum's and I had no idea how they were clinging on with only Helen's wage. I couldn't be a burden. I stared at the Kelly Brook calendar on the wall behind Terry's desk. Her January photo, stunning in a pink bikini and white denim jacket. I tried to zone out, remove myself from the situation.

'You also seem to have forgotten, any kind of misdemeanour whilst on probation could mean your immediate return to prison. Who knows what a snap inspection could find in your locker?' He grinned and I bit down until my jaw ached, utterly defeated.

Now I knew what Karla meant when she said Barry had us by the short and curlies. They both did. I stood and locked the door before twisting the handle of the blinds. Behind me, I heard a zipper lower.

'Now there's a good girl,' Terry said as I lowered to my knees.

* * *

I didn't see Karla waiting outside for me as I rushed past, tears erupting like a volcano. I was still wearing my tabard, my coat and backpack in my hand, desperate to leave the building. I spun around ready to strike as she grabbed my arm, thinking it was Terry behind me.

'Whoa,' she said, holding her palms up.

I carried on walking, unable to speak. Karla kept pace with me.

'Wait, come on, Jess, wait. Stop!'

I stopped once Bright's was out of sight, leaning over to vomit by a wall before sinking down to the ground.

'Here.' Karla handed me a bottle of water, which I used to swill around in my mouth, spitting it on the pavement to my left. Next, she handed me a lit cigarette and I sucked in deeply.

'He's a fucking arsehole,' I hissed through gritted teeth.

'I know, I told you he was,' Karla said softly.

I turned to look at her as she crossed her legs and folded down beside me in one swift movement. Both of us now sitting on the dirty pavement.

Her eyes carried a sadness I'd not seen in them before. I didn't need to ask why. Terry said *all* the girls, and I guessed everyone had to take their turn.

'He likes some more than others,' Karla said, as if reading my mind.

'We should tell someone?'

'Who?' Karla laughed bitterly. 'No one is coming to our rescue, Jess. Barry's in on it, the police and social workers don't give a shit.' She sighed and I flicked my ash on the ground.

A passer-by tutted at us down on the floor, an elderly man in a trench coat and hat.

'What of it, Granddad?' Karla shouted after him as I cringed.

I pulled myself up. It wasn't fair, the system sucked. A man like Terry abusing his position to take advantage of vulnerable women and we could do nothing about it?

'What if we recorded it or something? Got proof?'

Karla scoffed at my suggestion. 'Why do you think our phones are supposed to stay in our lockers. You gonna wear a wire? You been watching too much TV, girl!'

I didn't want to be around Karla any more, I knew she was right but I couldn't entertain there being no way out of Terry's clutches. I started to walk home, stopping momentarily to pull on my coat. It was freezing, but my adrenaline had kept me warm. She didn't follow this time, instead calling, 'See you tomorrow,' as I walked away.

What had my life become? I was stuck in a vicious cycle with little hope of any real freedom. I had to do as I was told because no job meant no money. Without that, I'd be living on the streets and I wasn't strong enough to survive out there. Terry had us exactly where he wanted us. Desperate, out of options and easy to control.

9

By the time I got home, I was frozen, my bomber jacket offered nowhere near enough insulation for the temperature outside. January was bitter and even though February was around the corner, there was no let-up to the chill in the air. I showered, scrubbing my skin until it was raw, before climbing into bed. Wrapped in the duvet, I sobbed. An overwhelming swarm of disgust clung to my bones. My old friend was back.

Being on the outside was no different. I was still a pawn, moved around and used at will. Trading my body, but for what this time? A shitty job with low pay and a corrupt boss who took advantage of his staff. No, it was the threat of going back inside that made me get on my knees. I wasn't cut out for prison and I did what I had to, to get through my sentence. I was too soft, too meek, too pliable and not much had changed. I screwed my eyes shut, willing the taste to leave my mouth.

I wanted Mum more than anything. A hug from her would make it all right, but I wouldn't bring that to her door. I'd done enough already.

My knees against my chest, I rocked, trying to muster the comfort I craved. Eventually I got up and made a gallon of hot tea, scalding my throat like it was disinfectant. I couldn't bring myself to eat, nor could I focus on the words of *The Enchanted Wood* that seemed to fly around the page unwilling to land. Tomorrow was another day. I just had to hope he wouldn't pick me again tomorrow, that I hadn't become one of his favourites.

* * *

Wednesday was hump day, only three more days until the weekend was my mantra on the way to work. I was dreading seeing Terry, already imagining the sickening smile I'd receive when he saw me. His eyes lighting up at his new prize. My stomach burned with it as I fought to push the thoughts away.

I checked my phone, surprised I hadn't heard from Helen, but I knew it wouldn't be long before she got in touch. I was biding my time, waiting for her explanation now Mum had told me everything. Surely, she'd be remorseful for the lies she'd told.

Karla was smoking outside the entrance just before nine as I approached.

'Thought you might not show,' she said, pulling her coat in tighter, wisps of frozen breath floating away. She threw her butt on the ground and trod it into the concrete.

'Don't have much choice,' I replied, and we entered Bright's together, clocking in.

I tried not to look in the office as we passed, but I couldn't help it. Terry was shovelling in a bacon sandwich, his fingers covered in brown sauce.

'Ladies,' he greeted, mid-chew, with a wink.

Karla gave him the finger, but I couldn't bring myself to react.

At the wall of lockers, we put on our tabards, both crumpled from being stuffed in our bags overnight and not hung up like they were supposed to be.

'Give me your number,' Karla said, and I pulled out my phone to look it up, the number so new I was unable to remember it off the top of my head. I hesitated before I read it aloud. Did I want Karla to be able to contact me outside of work? She was abrasive, even hostile at times but I had to start making new friends at some point. 'God your phone is a relic!' She snorted at my flip-style Motorola, as she typed the number in. I wrinkled my nose as I looked at the silver chunky handset. I believed it was Helen's old phone from years ago. My old phone had been smashed then seized in the accident.

'Yeah well I'm skint. How did you afford that?' I asked Karla as she tucked her iPhone in her locker.

'None of your business,' she said playfully as I put mine away and snapped the padlock shut. We strolled into the warehouse, keen to look at the rota to see what the day would bring.

Terry had split us up and I was teamed with Agnes again, who chatted about her love of period dramas and how she was watching the *Downton Abbey* series again from the start. Karla was paired with Lisa, a small girl with pixie-short hair and a button nose with a ring through it.

We were working on the pressing machines, feeding white and red tablecloths through from a trolley into the press where they were caught on a roll on the other side. It was one of the hardest jobs as you had to constantly feed the fabric through, and my shoulders ached from the repetitive lifting. The machine was noisy but not loud enough to drown out Agnes.

All day I was on tenterhooks, waiting for Terry to call me in. It reminded me of being sent to the head-teacher's office, which had been often. He moved around the warehouse, doing spot checks on our work, seemingly happy with our quota. It was then I noticed how all the girls physically shrank away from him, small movements I hadn't spotted before. Their body language changed whenever he was around. How many of us was he taking advantage of?

Surely only the threat of going back to prison would be a motivator. But then there was Agnes, who had children to feed, as well as her mum, yet to return to Poland. I hadn't heard her speak of a man at home. I was sure she'd not been to prison; she wasn't one of the girls Barry saw. Perhaps the threat of losing her job, the only income, was enough to give in to Terry's demands?

When five o'clock came, I waved goodbye to Karla and headed straight home without looking back. I didn't wait to see who was Terry's chosen one today. On the way I picked up some tobacco and microwave meals from the local shop. Turning up the halogen heater I sat on my bed with a plate of steaming lasagne and the rest of *The Enchanted Wood*. Bereft when I finished the final page. I'd have to look out for *The Folk of the Faraway Tree* next, but I had the teenage fiction book I'd picked up from the charity shop to start on.

Just as I finished washing up my plate, a thud came from the door, followed by a knock. I pulled it open expecting to see Stuart, but Helen stood outside, scowling.

'Can I come in?' she huffed.

I took a deep breath and pulled the door back, allowing her inside.

She moved around the small space, taking in the bed that doubled as a sofa, although I left it out all the time, and the peeling wallpaper where damp had started to creep in. Wrinkling her nose at the bedsit I now called home.

'I bought you some things,' she said, handing me a carrier bag like a peace offering.

I put it on the worktop without glancing inside.

'Why, Helen? Why did you do it? I don't get it. Do you have any idea what it was like for me inside? With no contact, no letters, nothing to look forward to. Thinking your family has disowned you?' My temperature shot skyward, underarms dampening as I tried to keep a lid on my fury.

'Did *you* think about what it was like for *us*? How Mum had a brick put through her window... twice!' Helen sniped back, her hands on her hips.

'Fuck's sake, I've apologised a thousand times, I can't do any more. I've done my time, paid my debt to society. You can't stop me from seeing Mum. She wants to see me, and I want to help, Helen,' I said, exasperated.

She sighed and sank down onto my bed. Eyes wide, she stared up at me. 'I was trying to protect her. You didn't see how hurt she was. We were victimised, hounded in the street. The stroke was the final straw.'

Helen sniffed, a single tear escaping before she swiped it away.

'When were you going to tell me about it?'

'I don't know, when you got out, I guess, but I wasn't sure how. Maybe I made the wrong decisions, but I was only trying to protect Mum.'

I flopped down beside her, hung my head and sobbed into my palms.

Helen rested her hand on my shoulder, rubbing gently. I had no idea how we could move on. Was our relationship broken?

After an age Helen spoke, her voice quiet and unassuming. 'Mum was happy to see you. She hasn't stopped going on about it. She wants you to come for dinner on Friday.'

'Okay,' I replied, turning my head away from Helen and wiping my face. She got the hint and stood to leave.

'Be round for half six, okay?'

I nodded.

'I'm sorry.' She sounded genuine.

'Me too,' I whispered as the door closed behind her.

A fitful night's sleep followed where I dreamt of

Mum in hospital, a constant stream of drool from her lips. Helen was wearing a nurse's outfit and kept wheeling her trolley in and topping up her meds. I was in the room, but no one could hear me shouting as I attempted to prevent Helen sedating our mother.

I woke in a sweat at around four in the morning, the birds already awake outside. All attempts to go back to sleep were futile, so I got ready for another day at Bright's. The rock in my stomach seeming to have doubled overnight.

10

Thursday morning was a laugh. Terry was out until after lunch, visiting clients, and Laura, one of the newer girls, snuck a radio in. We had three blissful hours of Kiss FM and were all dancing at our stations as we loaded, folded and pressed. I had no idea who sang most of the songs, massively out of touch, but it didn't matter. Lisa had a TikTok account and filmed us all dancing like loons. I'd never heard of the app, but she was addicted, constantly posting videos and showing us the latest dance crazes.

All afternoon the mood was buoyant, even with Terry back – we hummed to ourselves and shuffled to music only we could hear. Karla and I were a load behind as she'd forgotten to put any powder in our first wash and stains were still visible when we pulled them out.

'What the fuck is that?' Terry swore as he passed by and saw the stain on the tablecloth we'd dried and folded. He held it to the light, examining what looked like a curry stain. 'Wash it all again,' he snapped, throwing the cloth back at Karla, wincing as he thumped his chest with his fist.

'What's up with him?' I whispered when he'd gone.

'Fat fucker suffers with indigestion, probably because he's always fucking eating!'

I sniggered.

When five o'clock came around, we were still waiting for the dryer to finish so we could press the load we had to do again.

'Go on, you go, I'll do it. I forgot to put the stuff in.' Karla sighed, knowing everyone had to finish their jobs before they went home.

'It's all right, haven't got anywhere else to be,' I confessed.

'Karla,' Terry called before striding into view. He

beckoned her over and whispered in her ear just as the machine stopped.

'I'll be back in a minute,' Karla said, turning to me, her voice strained. My muscles twitched.

'Okay, I'll get this pressed,' I called after her.

After the door to the dryer unlocked, I pulled the tablecloths out and rolled the trolley to the press machine. All the time chewing the inside of my cheek and trying not to think about what Karla was being forced to do in the office.

I got the load pressed pretty quickly, as tablecloths, unlike the sheets, only had to go through once. They were folded and bagged up by twenty past and I headed to the locker to get my things.

Terry's office door was closed and the blinds down which only meant one thing. The closer I got, I could hear grunts coming from inside and my body clenched. I tiptoed closer and saw one of the metal slats of the blind had got twisted, allowing me to see into the office. The sight made me gag.

Karla was bent over Terry's desk, her jeans around her ankles. Hair bobbing as he held her down with the palm of his hand. Thrusting rhythmically from behind, making the desk squeak on its hinges.

I looked away, closing my eyes as though I could erase what I'd just seen.

I heard a low guttural noise as Terry climaxed, followed by a thud, and I scurried away, my heart hammering. I loitered by the exit, wanting to make sure Karla was going to walk out of that room. She clocked me as soon as the door opened and practically ran to the lockers to get her things and out of the building. Just as I had earlier in the week.

'I need a drink,' she said, visibly shaken, and we headed into the nearest pub, The Plough.

I sat Karla in a quiet corner and bought two gin and tonics after getting option paralysis at the bar, then returned to the table. We sat in silence as I didn't know what to say. Should I admit I'd seen everything?

'He's a monster,' Karla said, her eyes threatening but refusing to waste any tears. She was incredibly resilient, and I admired her strength. What had made her so tough? What had she done to warrant being sent to prison? I wanted to ask, but I couldn't just blurt it out. None of the girls at Bright's talked much about prison, I hadn't heard them mention what Karla had been inside for and I didn't want her to catch me asking questions.

'Has he done that before?' I asked.

'No,' she sniffed, 'it's because I've only got a month left and I'll be free.' Karla knocked her drink back.

'We have to stop him,' I said, finishing my glass.

Karla got up to get us another, pulling her provisional driver's licence out of her purse to show the barman. I glimpsed the date of birth, practically all I could see by the way she held it. Karla was a year older than me. 'They always ID me in here,' she explained.

I nodded, the heat from the alcohol warming my chest as I waited for her to return. I had no idea how we were going to get Terry to leave us alone. Perhaps we could try Barry, surely, he couldn't know the extent of Terry's abuse?

'What about Barry?' I asked when Karla sat down.

'Everyone has spoken to Barry at some point. He fobs us off, says he'll talk to Terry, take it further, but don't you get it? Barry's on the payroll. Isn't it a bit of a coincidence us girls are all so similar, small, light, skinny...? That's Terry's type. Barry gets a cut, favours or whatever from Terry for delivering him girls like us. Fresh out of prison, stuck in the system and easy to manipulate. He can do whatever he likes and if we misbehave, Barry has the power to put us back inside. Our suspended sentences gone in a flash.'

'But if we all had the same story, we could expose them both.'

'To who? No one gives a fuck, Jess.' Karla sighed, rubbing her temples.

We finished our drinks and left.

'Will you be okay?' I asked, as we prepared to go in separate directions home.

'Yeah, I'm going to meet with some friends, get smashed.'

My side twinged; I hadn't been invited, but we were friends by proxy not by design.

We said goodbye and I waited for the bus, watching Karla head up the road. I still didn't know where she lived, only that she was crashing on some-one's sofa.

Back at home, I found a bottle of vodka outside

the door with a bow stuck on the front and a note from Stuart.

Forgot to give this to you last week, won it in a
raffle on the team building.
Hope you like it. Thanks for watching the house.
Stuart

The timing couldn't have been better. I drank mainly cider before I went to prison, that's what all the teenagers drank then, but any alcohol would do to numb my brain. I treated myself to a tiny shot, which almost made me gag, before I sat down on my bed to go through the bag for life Helen had brought yesterday. On top I could see some clothes – a T-shirt, a sweatshirt and some leggings – beneath those were two more books, a towel, some dried pasta sachets, teabags, UHT milk, forty Silk Cut and a massive bar of Galaxy chocolate. She must have been feeling guilty.

I beamed from ear to ear, tearing open the chocolate. Snapping off a line, I nibbled at it, the taste popping on my tongue as I turned the books over. They were called *We Were Liars* and *The Host*, more teenage fiction, which I loved. Tucked inside *The Host* was an unopened envelope, still with its stamp, addressed to me at Thornton Road. On the back written in block capitals was FOR RELEASE DAY. I vaguely recognised the swirly writing and tore open the flap, pulling out the folded paper. It was signed from Ashley.

I remembered the sophisticated profile photo on Facebook, how changed she was, but the letter was dated 2016, just two months after my sentencing. After I'd asked her not to write to me at Bronzefield any more.

Jess,

I can never apologise enough for that night; I still don't understand how they thought you were to blame. I know you don't want to see me because you want me to escape from this place. You're right, I do want to leave, but I never wanted to escape from you or what I did.

Hopefully your sister will save this and give it to you when you're released. Please find me. You know where I'll be.

Your bestie,

Ash x

I opened the front door and lit a cigarette, leaning on the uPVC frame. A warm glow spread through me, trying to fight its way through the bitterness which coursed in my veins. It wasn't her fault, not really. Just circumstance. I'd never had a best friend like Ashley and I probably wouldn't again.

What would she think of me now? In my hand-me-down clothes, a bag of bones with no spark in my eyes. Scrolling through her Facebook photos back in the library, Ashley had moved on, new friends, new town. I was sure the last thing she'd want was a blast from the past.

11

There was no point in dwelling. Karla was right, I just had to keep my head down and get through my probation. Next week would be my fourth week, payday was looming, and I'd be one month closer to freedom. I texted Helen to say thanks for the stuff she brought over and I was looking forward to dinner. I couldn't deny I was still angry, but perhaps it was time to accept her peace offering and try to build bridges.

Elated the weekend was within reach, I walked to work, a bounce in my step. However, my mood deteriorated as soon as I saw Terry walking around the warehouse with Barry. He was in again, visiting, and throughout the morning, he called the probationers in one by one.

When it was my turn, I glared at him across the desk. The skin around Barry's eyes crinkled.

'What's up with you? You look like you've got a right cob on.'

'Nothing,' I replied, sullenly. There was no point saying anything, Karla was adamant he was part of it all.

Barry narrowed his eyes, taking me in and then the penny dropped. 'I know Terry is a bit... friendly,' he said, his words measured, 'but he's a good employer. You could do much worse.'

I scoffed, unable to believe what I was hearing. Had Terry told Barry what he'd made me do? Had I been scored out of ten, compared to the others? The idea sickened me.

I looked away, eyes stinging, and he started going through the checklist. When the meeting was almost over, he lingered over the comments box on the form.

'Anything you'd like to add, to put on the record?' Barry asked, his pen poised.

'No point is there.'

'Look, Jess, just keep your head down. I'm trying to keep you out of prison here.'

'So you keep saying.' I got up to leave, heat flushing through my body, powerless to do anything with the anger that bubbled below.

I was the last one to meet with Barry, he left shortly after a chat with Terry. I saw them in his office, Terry swigging from the Gaviscon again as Barry gesticulated wildly. I chewed my thumb when I saw them together, nibbling until the skin was sore. Was he reporting back about our meeting; telling Terry I wasn't playing ball? What if I'd just given him the excuse to get rid of me, to set me up with the stolen money? I was sure anyone seen to be making trouble would be quickly dispatched. My insides squirmed but I tried to push it from my mind.

I joined Hanna, who was without a partner, and we went through a dirty load which had just been delivered from the hospital. The lorry bleeped as it backed up to the warehouse doors and we stood ready to receive the laundry. Hospital sheets were my least favourite job, sorting out what we could clean and what would have to be incinerated. The hospital was pretty good at sorting them, but sometimes things slipped through the net.

We wore gloves and masks to go through the bags and it was difficult to talk through them. Once sorted we took a trolley round to the incinerator and left it there to be burned later. The rest we loaded on the hottest wash there was.

The temperature outside had warmed a little and, as a result, inside felt muggier than usual. Hanna and I took a quick break outside. I plucked a cigarette from the pack Helen had bought me.

'It's hot as balls in there today,' Hanna said, lifting her T-shirt to wipe her face.

'I can't imagine what it's like in summer,' I replied, thinking it must be torture. I had no doubt there was a high turnover of staff at Bright's. As soon as probations were up, the girls would move on. I was sure now many considered it an extension of their sentence. I knew as soon as I was able to, I'd leave, whether I had another job to go to or not. I'd take my chances.

When we went back inside, Karla gestured going for a drink and I nodded, mouthing 'quick one' at her. I'd have time if I didn't have to be at Mum's until half six. I was looking forward to seeing her again, although I knew it would be strained with Helen there. We could at least be civil, for Mum's sake.

At five to five, Terry's voice boomed through the warehouse, calling me. I froze, the hairs on my arms standing to attention. Any warmth in my skin evaporated as ice flowed through my veins. Turning around, I looked for Karla, but I couldn't see her, so disappeared to the toilet, resting my head against the tiles. It was my turn again?

Salty tears stung my eyes, but I held them at bay. The image of my cellmate Darcy flashed into my mind. Off her nut on something when they first brought her in, screaming obscenities into the air as I cowered on my bed. It was the same terror, knowing I couldn't escape. There was no way out now either, not unless I ran, or made a complaint, but Karla was right. No one gave a shit about us; we were scum in the eyes of the authorities.

Terry's voice rang out again, like a death knell and I forced myself to leave the bathroom.

Hanna, Laura and Agnes grimaced at me as they passed, on their way to clock out. They knew full well what I was going in to. All was quiet, the machines in the warehouse no longer whirring.

Terry's office already had the blinds closed, but his door was open.

'You wanted me?' I bristled.

'Yes I do.' He licked his lips like a bad porno.

My ears pounded with the beat of my heart. I closed the door, ready to tell him if he touched me again it'd be the last thing he ever did. Then I heard the belt buckle get released, the chime of metal on metal, the prerequisite to my surrender.

Gritting my teeth, overwhelmed by the unfairness of it all, I spun around. Terry's shirt was part unbuttoned and he already had his dick in his hand, his palm sliding up and down the shaft as a smile played on his lips. His bulbous stomach creased with imprints of his shirt. My throat closed and I looked away, dragging out the seconds.

'Don't keep me waiting.' The playful tone gone, his voice had an edge of menace to it.

I sank to the floor in front of him. The scent of him making me gag as I drew nearer.

'Why me?'

'Because you're my shiny new toy, Jess, my new

favourite bad girl. We're just getting started.' He chuckled and threw his head back in pleasure as I closed my mouth around him, trying to send my mind elsewhere.

Terry entwined his fingers through my hair, forcing me down. I was sick of being someone's play-thing, used and passed around. Would Barry be next? When would it stop?

When I was sentenced, just after my eighteenth birthday, I'd barely any experience with boys, they always wanted Ashley, not me. I was still a virgin and if Terry thought he'd be the one to take that from me, he had another thing coming. Consumed in a gulf of rage, the only sound the thud of my heart in my ears, my mind suddenly cleared. Without hesita-tion, I bit down.

12

An inhuman howl echoed above me and a palm belted the side of my head, casting me to the ground. Dazed, I tried to work out who the figure was looming over me, until my focus sharpened and I saw Terry holding his now limp penis, examining the damage. My lips tasted metal and I wiped my forearm across my mouth. I'd barely broke the skin, but it was enough. He wouldn't be sticking it anywhere near my face again.

Pushing myself up on one arm, Terry glared at me, face contorted. Fastening his trousers, I prepared myself for the kick which was sure to follow, but he took a step towards me and stopped abruptly, clutching his left arm. His mouth gaped and he rubbed his limb furiously. Eyes tightly shut, I scrabbled backwards.

A mobile phone rang, lighting up his pocket, the faint sound of the Imperial March from *Star Wars* filling the room.

I clambered to my feet and threw open the door to make my escape.

Terry took one more step, deathly pale, eyes now wide like saucers. His mouth hung open like a fish, sucking for air. One hand fumbled for the phone, one reached out towards me like a zombie. I backed away, legs like jelly but unable to avert my stare as he took his third and final step, before crashing into the door frame. The walls of the office shook, and his head walloped the metal edging on the way down, landing with a thud, half in, half out of the door.

My jaw dropped and I froze, knowing I should call for help. I should try and revive him, but he blinked, then his eyes turned to glass. Staring into the distance but not seeing anything.

I heaved and dashed into the toilet, throwing up lunch, my entire body shaking. *Get it together, Jess.*

Terrified to go back out there but terrified not to,

I returned to the scene, dropping to the floor beside Terry. His hair was matted with blood, a gaping wound on the side of his head. I tried to stem the bleeding with my hand, but it was already clotting. He had fallen face down, his tongue lolling to the side of his open mouth, body laying awkwardly. It was grotesque but a part of me felt relieved he'd never touch me again.

'What the fuck happened?' a voice hissed and I jumped, looking up to see Karla's goggle-eyes.

'I don't know, he just collapsed.'

'Did you hit him? He's bleeding!' She glared at me, incredulous.

I shook my head vehemently, opening my mouth to speak, but nothing came out.

'Well, he's fucking dead!' Karla continued, shaking her head in disbelief.

I clapped both hands over my mouth, trying to stifle the scream I could sense rising from the deep. You could hear a pin drop it was so quiet, but my thoughts were all jumbled.

'You have to help me,' I pleaded, staring at Karla.

She blinked rapidly, her brain working a hundred miles an hour. 'I... I've almost finished my probation,' she whispered, more to herself than to me.

'Please, I don't know what to do.'

'You killed him, Jess, it's fucking murder!' She stared at Terry in a heap on the floor.

'I didn't, he just dropped dead.' I clambered up on wobbly legs.

'Well, that's what it looks like,' she snapped.

Knees weak, I staggered backwards, trying to keep upright. In my mind, I saw Eddie's bruised and puffy face, his body sprawled awkwardly on the grass, those vacant eyes. The image coming back to haunt me. My jerky movements seemed to jolt Karla into action, and she spoke quickly. Her focus returned.

'Wash your hands with bleach. There's some under the sink in the toilets. I'm going to lock the doors.' She swept past me so fast, the air swirled, and I went to the toilet to start scrubbing.

* * *

We stared at the flames through the tiny viewing window. My throat thick, a tear escaped, dripping down my cheek.

'Don't shed any tears for that bastard,' Karla snapped, flexing her fingers through the latex gloves.

'We could have called the police, we should have.'

'You think they wouldn't throw away the key? Wake up, Jess, your DNA was all over him. He's got a head wound. It looked like a crime scene!'

'They could have done an autopsy?'

'We don't even know what he died from, anyway, do you want to take that chance?' I could tell she was exasperated with me. I'd happily let her take control; followed her lead, trusting her instruction would keep me out of prison and now I was whining.

I glanced at my watch; it was quarter to seven. Mum and Helen would be waiting for me to arrive. I'd never make it there now, my chance to make amends would be ruined. My heart raced.

'I need to text my sister,' I said, turning towards the lockers.

Karla's bony fingers gripped my upper arm and I wrenched out of her grasp.

'Are you fucking serious? We've just disposed of a body; we've got to get rid of any evidence. No phones. Keep them switched off until you're far away from here.'

I shook my head, trying to clear it. *Stupid!*

I imagined a steaming plate of cottage pie waiting for me, not that I would have been able to eat it. Not now. Mum would be disappointed though, and Helen angry. She'd use it as ammunition, another reason to keep me away, to stop me upsetting Mum.

Karla scowled at me and headed to the back of the warehouse, where the storage rooms were kept. She scanned the shelves, grinning when she found the floor tiles. 'We've got to replace the tiles we burnt.'

Pulling two from the pile, I followed her back to Terry's office.

'He's got some superglue round here some-where,' she said, rummaging through his drawers before announcing, 'Found it,' with a triumphant wave.

We glued the tiles on the floor, each standing on one to flatten it down.

'Right, now we clean. Bleach the chair legs and

arms, the door frame, the desk, anywhere there might be blood splatters.'

'How are we going to get out of here?' I asked, remembering the cameras at the back of the warehouse. It's the way Terry would come in and out each day as he parked his pride and joy – a 2017 black Audi Q5.

'I think I've got an idea. Let's clean first. I'll wipe down the incinerator and the toilets. Thank God it's Friday, the cleaners will be in at the weekend and they'll get anything we've missed hopefully. We'll have to get the ash out, and whatever else is left on Monday though, as he'll be burning for a few hours yet. I think each cycle runs for about eight hours with the warm-up. I just hope it's enough.'

I pursed my lips, not wanting to think about the flesh currently melting off Terry's bones.

We spent another twenty minutes cleaning, then changed our gloves for a fresh pair, pocketing the ones we'd been wearing to dispose of later.

Terry's office looked normal, as I cast my eye over it, the usual mess remained, but there was no evidence of a struggle. I spied a yellow jiffy bag on top of the in tray, the flap gaping. Was that cash? My chest fluttered as I picked it up and peeked a wodge of twenty-pound notes, there must have been a few grand inside.

Karla came through the door, seeing my eyes on stalks.

'What you got there?' She took the packet from me and slid the notes partly out, flicking through them with her thumb. 'Jesus!' She whistled, a wide grin spreading across her face as she folded up the packet and stuck it in the waistband of her jeans. I stared at her open-mouthed, I wasn't a thief but she gave me a pointed look that said it wasn't up for discussion.

Terry's phone, still on the floor, rang again making us both jump. I had a headache from the amount of adrenaline pumping around my system. There'd been no time to process what had happened and I was exhausted, but I had to keep going. We only had one chance to get it right otherwise we'd be back in a cell before we knew it.

'Right. You're going to put on Terry's coat and flat cap, and get in his car, reverse it right up to the doors, so close you'll be in a blind spot. I'll pull the shutters down, lock up and get in the boot. Grab his phone and wallet too.'

My eyebrows shot skyward. I couldn't possibly drive Terry's car. I hadn't been behind the wheel for years. My knees began to shake involuntarily. Couldn't Karla do it? How did she know I could even drive? 'Me, pretend I'm Terry? That'll never work. He's twice the size of me and easily six inches taller,' I said, my voice shrill.

'We have no choice, we can't risk doing anything to the cameras on the night he goes missing, it looks suspicious. It'll be fine, they are so high up; the picture quality isn't great. More of a deterrent, I think. Just try and make yourself look as big as you can. Look, he's got some steel toecap boots in here,' Karla said, rummaging through a cupboard. She handed them to me, and I put them on. They were so big, I could get my feet inside even with trainers on.

I had to go with it, though, I didn't have a choice; Karla was going to get us out of this. She was the only one of us thinking clearly and I had to trust her. After all, by helping me, she now had just as much to lose.

'Okay,' I said, tying the boots and pulling on his

long camel coat and flat cap. Terry thought he looked all gangster, I was sure, but he was more like Del Boy from the *Only Fools and Horses* reruns my mum loved so much.

'I'll get the stuff from our lockers – what's your code?'

'2148,' I said without hesitation.

Karla returned a minute later with our bags and coats. Holding Terry's keys, we had a last look around the office and pulled the door shut, locking it, just like he did every night.

'Let's get the fuck out of here.'

13

The shutters hummed as they rolled up automatically. I half expected there to be a gang of armed police outside in the yard pointing their guns at us; my imagination always got the better of me. However, the gravelled area was empty, only Terry's car remained on site. I was grateful we were under the cover of darkness, with the sun having gone down a couple of hours earlier. I ducked under the shutters, opening the Audi with the key fob and watching the indicators flash orange.

Knowing I was still out of view of the camera, I checked all my hair was tucked inside the flat cap, coat collar raised, and drew myself up as tall as I could manage. Widening my shoulders in a gorilla like stance, I walked to the car, moving in as manly a stride as I could in the heavy ill-fitting boots, and climbed inside. If this worked, it would be a miracle.

Thankfully, Terry's Audi had tinted windows, so I didn't have to worry about being seen slipping off the boots so I could drive in my trainers. In the rear-view mirror, I saw the shutters lower and heard a tap on the boot. I pressed the key fob to open it and watched the door to the boot lift slightly, closing again ten seconds later.

'I'm in,' Karla whispered.

'Where am I going?' I said, starting the engine. Anxiety about driving again rushed over me like a tidal wave. I hadn't driven for four years and the last time I had, I'd killed someone. Sweat beaded on my forehead and I lifted my T-shirt to wipe it away. I had to try and leave as little evidence I'd been in the car as possible, conscious of every hair strand, skin flake or droplet of sweat which could identify me.

'Head towards the town centre, I've got an idea,' Karla said, popping up from behind the back seats.

Still wearing the coat, the cap and the gloves, I

slowly drove out of the yard onto the industrial estate. The Audi was like a tank compared to the Vauxhall Corsa I'd had before.

'Stop over-revving it!' Karla sounded panicked for the first time that evening.

'I'm trying, I haven't driven for four years!' I snapped back, sweat pooling under my arms beneath the heavy material. At a set of traffic lights, I turned the air conditioner on and directed the vent towards me. Cool air blew into my face and my shoulders gradually eased down.

Karla's eyes were darting around the car and out of the windows, her cool composure slipping.

'How do you know so much about Bright's?' I asked to distract her.

'What do you mean?' Karla squinted at me in the rear-view mirror; her face screwed up.

'I don't know; like the shutters and where Terry keeps his stuff?' I asked.

'I've been here for five months. I see things. I'm always watching; where things are, how things work. I don't miss anything.'

I snorted, she sounded like Liam Neeson's character in the film *Taken*.

'Don't believe me? Okay. You – on your first day, this is something you do a lot.' She pulled down on her earlobe dramatically and I raised my eyebrows. 'You do it when you're nervous. You did it a lot that day, less the next day. You've done it loads this afternoon. It's a habit, a tick. These are the sorts of things I notice.'

I shrugged, turning my concentration back to the road.

Ten minutes later, Karla directed me to pull into a side street.

'I think this is the one.' She strained her neck, looking around.

We'd made it to the town centre, a narrow dead-end road behind the pedestrianised area, parked on a single yellow line behind a row of three cars. The two-storey buildings around us looked to be the rear of shops. A cage on wheels containing empty cardboard boxes was positioned outside a tall gate. Another had a large green industrial bin, despite the rubbish strewn around it.

'Got a space as it's still early for the pub-goers. Here is perfect.'

'How do you know about this road?' I asked.

'I used to be a Saturday girl at New Look years ago, we used to park here for free if we could. Around the corner is one of Terry's haunts. Admiral Casino.'

'There's a casino, here in Croydon?'

'Well not really, it's more slots, but I think Terry plays poker there, hence the wodge of cash. He might have been coming tonight. So, we'll leave his car here, bin his phone somewhere, take the wallet and scarper.'

'What about his coat and boots?'

'Pass me the boots,' she said, stuffing them in a carrier bag. 'When you get out of the car, quickly slip out of the coat and stuff it in here. We'll take them home with us.'

I nodded, my heart racing every time a car went down the main road behind us. I imagined blue flashing lights were only minutes away.

Once we'd given the car a quick wipe-down, in an attempt to remove any DNA we might have left, we waited for a break in the traffic and jumped out, hurrying away. As I removed Terry's coat and hat, I dropped the keys down a drain, pausing to hear the plop of the water. Karla took the opportunity to get rid of Terry's phone in there too.

We kept our heads lowered, peeling off our latex gloves as we walked. I followed Karla, who led us down one side street, then another, seeming to know her way around with ease.

'Are there any cameras in the road where we left the car?'

'No, I don't think so, I'm pretty sure anyway. There's loads in the town centre, they'll pick up the car on the route we've taken, but that doesn't matter. We want them to think Terry's driving,' Karla said, her voice muffled from the wind.

A stitch formed in my side as we were walking so fast. I was carrying my backpack and the bag with Terry's coat and heavy boots. Despite the chill, my skin was damp.

'Can you slow down? Where are we going?' I called out.

Karla was ahead of me and stopped abruptly. 'I'm trying to get us away from the town centre, away from cameras, that's why we're sticking to the side streets. In a minute, we're going to cross a big park and we'll have a rest.' Her eyes flashed and I could tell she was getting exasperated with me.

I couldn't help it, I was jittery, panic mounting at the situation we'd found ourselves in. Karla, although stressed, was still level-headed, just the sort of person you needed in an emergency.

I kept thinking of my phone, switched off in my backpack. How many voicemails would I have from Helen? I'd fucked it all up. Now I'd be going back to prison for murder because that's what it would look like. I had nothing to prove otherwise. We'd covered up Terry's death and with that implicated ourselves in a crime that never happened. We'd broken the law and I'd dragged Karla into it. What had I done? There was no time to dwell on the choices I'd made, how I'd got us into this mess, we had to keep going.

The noise from the traffic dulled as we moved further into the park, towards a copse of trees. Karla sat down on one that had been felled at the edge of the clearing and pulled out her cigarettes, offering me one and lighting it. It was so dark, I could barely see her face, only when she sucked on her cigarette and was illuminated for a second.

'So what happened?' she asked.

'When?'

'With Terry!' Karla sighed.

'He wanted...' I paused, finding it hard to get the words out, '...oral sex, and I bit him.'

'You did what?' Karla laughed out loud, the outline of her curls bouncing in the dark.

'I was so fucking angry, I just lost it, but then he grabbed his arm and hit the deck.'

'He deserved it, fucking scum of the earth. Couldn't have happened to a nicer bloke,' Karla sneered.

'What do you think caused it?' I asked.

'Heart attack maybe, or brain aneurism.'

I nodded in agreement, flicking the ash between my feet.

'I didn't kill him,' I said, just to make sure Karla knew, for the record.

'Of course you didn't, but your DNA was all over his dick. We did the right thing, with your record and that gash on his head, the police would have arrested you.'

'And what about now?' I asked.

'Well now, he's on the CCTV leaving the warehouse, his car will be seen on traffic cameras driving to the casino. The car is dumped there, no other prints and we've lucked out finding the money.' Karla patted her bag.

'Yeah and...' I faltered.

'And they'll assume he's gone to the casino, played poker, probably got fucked up by someone he owes money to. Plus, there's no body, so no crime. He'll be missing.' Karla had it all tied up.

'What about Bright's?'

'What about it? There's no evidence of a struggle, he's been seen leaving after locking up. We just need to dispose of his ashes out of the bloody incinerator on Monday.' Karla squashed the cigarette into the ground, and I followed suit.

I watched her go through Terry's wallet, pulling out the cash and pocketing it before looking through the cards. When finished, she began digging in the damp soil with a broken branch at the bottom of the closest tree and buried it along with our latex gloves.

I remained quiet, consumed by my thoughts. Something was bugging me, the incinerator. We'd left it on, burning Terry's remains. What if it stopped, malfunctioned in some way? Maybe Karla hadn't set it right? It could cause a fire and burn the place down. We had no idea how it worked. What if on Monday morning, you could see the remnants of a body through the viewing hatch or his wife went in over the weekend to look for him and found his roasted carcass?

14

We stayed on the stumps, resting whilst chain-smoking. Both of our bodies shattered from the exertion of the past couple of hours.

'I need a drink,' Karla said.

'I need a shower,' I replied, sniffing my T-shirt, which smelt anything but fresh. I wanted to go home, get clean and brush my teeth. Remove every trace of Terry from me.

Karla stood and picked up her bag and, as she did, it dawned on me I didn't want to be alone tonight. There would be too many monsters waiting in my nightmares.

'Do you want to crash at mine tonight? I mean, I

don't have a sofa, so we'll have to share a bed, but you're welcome. It's been a bit of a weird situation to say the least.'

Karla grimaced. 'You can say that again. You got any alcohol at yours?'

'Vodka?'

'Sold.' Karla took off in the direction of the path through the park.

When we reached the other side, we came out on a busy road and it took a while to get my bearings. It looked familiar.

'Quick, there's a bus,' Karla said, running towards the bus stop and leaving me behind. I chased after her as best I could, still lugging the extra bag of coat and boats.

We jumped on as I recognised we were on the main road out of Croydon, the bus would take us straight home. I sank into the spongy seat, muscles relaxing to liquid for the first time in hours. Everything ached. Karla sat across the aisle, staring out of the window and I did the same, watching the headlights stream past. No idea where to start processing the night's events.

Ten minutes later, I unlocked my door, curious to

what Karla would think of the bedsit.

'It's tiny,' I pre-empted, switching on the light and turning to face Karla, who was taking everything in. Just like Helen had, but without the distaste.

'It's all right, isn't it, your own space. What more do you need?' Karla flopped onto my bed, kicking off her trainers and rolling onto her back. 'Don't know about you, but I'm shagged!'

I laughed at her way with words. 'Me too.'

I got two mugs out of the cupboard and poured a large shot of vodka in each, handing one to Karla.

'I can't believe it.' I sank down onto the bed, nursing my mug.

'It'll be okay,' Karla said softly.

'He's dead and we burned him. How is it ever going to be okay?'

'He was a lecherous prick, Jess. We did the world a favour. We did everyone at Bright's a favour. Don't forget that.'

I sighed, lowering my head to rub the back of my neck. 'What are we going to do with those?' I gestured towards Terry's coat and boots.

'Burn or bury them, I guess. We'll need to do the

same with our clothes too.' Karla knocked back her drink and handed me her mug, wincing.

I swallowed my own, anticipating the scorch of the liquid as it went down, and refilled our mugs again. I opened the front door to let some fresh air in as we smoked, unable to believe it was almost nine. The last few hours had sped by.

'I need a shower,' I announced once we'd finished and I'd locked up.

I showered at breakneck speed, aware a stranger was in my home, and although I had nothing worth stealing, it was unnerving. Karla was the closest thing I had to a friend, but we knew nothing about each other really.

It felt so good to let the hot water wash away the sweat, grime and dust stuck to my skin. The memory of Terry erased in part as I gargled water, launching it into the air. I washed my hair and when I returned, wrapped in a towel, Karla was where I'd left her. Laying on the bed, scrolling through her phone. Mine still hadn't been switched on. I was putting it off, knowing an influx of angry messages were waiting for me.

'Here you go,' I said, passing her a clean towel.

'Cheers,' she replied and stepped past me into the bathroom, closing the door behind her.

I got dressed in jogging bottoms and a T-shirt before towel-drying and plaiting my hair. I found spare clothes for Karla too – we were about the same size and she'd need something comfortable to sleep in.

She took ages in the bathroom, so I made up two sachets of pasta in sauce using the microwave, while my stomach cramped from lack of food. Especially now the alcohol had hit my bloodstream.

Karla emerged practically dry and I gave her the clothes to put on. She dropped her towel without hesitation, and I turned away, my cheeks blazing. Karla was so different, unfazed by anything. It frightened me almost as much as I admired it.

'Wicked, thanks. I'm starving,' she said when I handed her the bowl of pasta.

We sat down on the bed to eat. Both of us shovelling spoonfuls in. It was a habit from being inside, fearful it was going to be taken away at any second.

'Why were you sent down?' Karla asked out of the blue.

'I killed someone. Death by dangerous driving,' I

said quietly, the words sticking in my throat. It never got any easier to say.

'What happened?' Karla's eyes narrowed, her forehead creasing in waves.

'I got... distracted,' I admitted, not wanted to delve deeper into the memory I kept locked away. I didn't want to go back to that night, replay what happened and what I could have done differently.

Karla gave a solitary nod, as though she understood.

'You?'

'Possession, with intent to supply. Got three years.'

'Were you using?'

'Occasionally. Don't touch it now though. Trying to keep my nose clean, until tonight it seems.' She rolled her eyes.

How did Karla get mixed up in selling drugs? Who had led her down that path? I didn't want to pry. She'd tell me more when she felt comfortable.

We finished our pasta, had one more cigarette and a last shot of vodka before getting into bed. Laying side by side, our elbows touching, we stared up at the ceiling. It felt awkward being so close, sharing the duvet, but it wasn't long before Karla drifted off. I closed my eyes and tried to sleep but my thoughts were consumed by images of Terry staggering towards me, his arm outstretched.

* * *

I woke early, before seven, to the sounds of pigeons scuttering on the felt roof. Sleep had been hard to come by. I'd tossed and turned all night, worrying about the incinerator and all the things that could expose us. Fearing a knock on the door any second, as though the police would know exactly what had happened to Terry and turn up here.

Karla was stirring, and I switched on my mobile for the first time since yesterday morning, turning it quickly to silent before the tirade of messages came through.

Where are you?

We're waiting to eat?

Really? You're just not going to show up?

Fuck you Jess

There were two voicemails, but I deleted them, I knew it would just be more of Helen ranting. I sent a text.

* * *

I'm sorry Helen, I got stuck at work. We're not allowed phones and a big order came in late and we had to stay behind. I'll be over today.

'Fucking hell, who's up there, Michael Flatley?' Karla groaned, rolling onto her back.

I sniggered. I had no idea who Michael Flatley was.

'Pigeons. Want a tea?'

Karla mumbled in agreement and I got up and stuck the kettle on.

'It's freezing in here,' she said, pulling the duvet up to her chin. I'd got used to the cold, but I switched the oil-filled radiator on anyway.

I offered breakfast, but, like me, Karla didn't have much of an appetite first thing in the morning; my stomach was still bloated from last night's pasta.

'What you are doing today?' Karla asked, sitting up as I handed her a cup of tea.

'Visiting my mum. I've also got to go to the launderette and get some shopping. You?'

'A few errands.' Karla was always so vague, she never seemed to give anything away. I still knew nothing about her family, where she grew up, friends, even where she was living. 'Want me to take that?' She gestured to the untouched bag of Terry's coat, hat and boots.

'No, it's fine, I'll sort it,' I replied, although I had no idea how, but Karla had done more than enough to dig me out of the hole I'd landed in.

'Don't forget your clothes from last night too. Also, we need to be each other's alibi.'

'Alibi?'

'Yes. After work last night. You had a quick chat with Terry – make up a reason why – I waited for you outside, then we walked back here. Don't say we got a bus, there's cameras on most of them. We just have to hope they don't check.' I felt the blood drain from my face. It was all too real. If caught, we were going back to prison without a doubt.

'Are you sure there's no cameras at the front of Bright's?' I asked.

'Positive. He only has one covering the yard.'

'Okay. Do you think we should go back? Check the incinerator?'

'No, we have to stay away until Monday, we've got to stick to our usual routine. If we went to work at the weekend and were seen, it would be suspicious. All you've got to do is hold your nerve, Jess.'

My eyes prickled with the onset of tears. 'I just... I can't go back to prison.'

15

Karla was gone before eight, counting me out half of the money before she left. There was a total of five grand in the jiffy bag – it was more money than I'd ever seen before. The only rule was no big purchases. Giddy with all the things I could get for the bedsit and new clothes instead of second-hand ones, I momentarily forgot the money was stolen. It was blood money and I'd never stolen as much as a chocolate bar before, but it was of no use to Terry now.

We'd arranged to meet outside work half an hour early on Monday, and if we were the only ones in, we'd empty the ash from the incinerator and bag it up. Karla didn't offer to get together over the weekend, and I didn't ask. We weren't there yet. Making friends with Karla was slow progress and I could tell she didn't let people in easily. Her brusque manner would likely put most off, but I didn't have an abundance of options for social interaction.

I got to Mum's at ten, holding a bag of washing for the launderette in one hand and a bunch of flowers from the petrol station in another. I stopped as I got to the gate, my mouth hanging open. The word bitch had been spray painted across Mum's front door.

'Finally decided to show up then?' Helen said as she pulled open the door to see me standing at the gate.

'What happened to the door?'

'You're what happened to the door!' Helen snapped.

I cringed. Was Mum victimised like this when I went away? Had I brought it all back upon them now I was out? 'I'm sorry, Helen, I'll paint it today.'

She shrugged. 'And what happened yesterday?'

'I got stuck at work,' I said stiffly.

'Yeah I'm sure. You've always been such a fucking let-down,' she taunted.

'Do we have to? I really can't be arsed.' I sighed, pushing past her into the house and calling Mum's name.

Her small voice came from the sitting room.

'She doesn't know about the door yet, think it happened last night. Get it sorted before you go home,' Helen whispered.

I hadn't been in the sitting room for years, but nothing had changed except for the addition of a high-backed green armchair Mum was tucked into. The striped pink and green wallpaper remained, as well as the ancient gas fire with stone surround.

'Hello, love, how are you doing?'

I leaned down to give her a kiss on the cheek. She looked good, not so pale. This time she was dressed with her hair pinned up and a bit of make-up on.

'I'm good thanks. Sorry about yesterday, Mum, I got stuck at work.'

I heard Helen tut from the kitchen before the kettle began to boil.

'I bought you these, I'll put them in a vase,' I said, lowering the bunch so Mum could look at them.

'Ah they're lovely, thank you.' She reached out and stroked the petal of a yellow rose.

'Your favourites.'

A clatter came from the kitchen.

'You didn't get in trouble, did you?' Mum said, and the colour drained from my face as she stared at me.

'Trouble?'

'At work,' she clarified.

'No, Mum.' My hands trembled and my eye began to twitch. I used the excuse of the flowers to leave the room and get myself together, heading into the kitchen to find a vase.

Helen brought in tea on a tray and a slice of Battenberg, which I wolfed down as she rolled her eyes at me. We made polite conversation, some of it strained in Helen's company. She felt the need to swipe at me whenever the opportunity arose. I tried to ignore it, thanking her for the bag of bits she'd brought round.

'Mum said you might need some stuff.'

'I always need clothes, there's no washing machine at the bedsit.'

'Did you bring your things? Go and put them on, love, there's an hour wash-and-dry setting if you need them done quickly.'

'I was going to take them to the launderette.'

'Don't be daft!' she berated.

I nodded gratefully and got up to use the machine. The washing powder and fabric softener still under the sink where they'd always been. I smelt the silky pink liquid, it reminded me of Mum's dressing gown.

'What are you doing?' Helen said, frowning at me as my nose was hovering above the open bottle.

'Nothing,' I replied, hastily putting the lid on and returning to the sitting room.

'There's lots of your things in my wardrobe for you to take whenever you want,' Mum said, trying to control a tremor in her left hand. I leant over and held it, interlocking our fingers.

'Is there anything you need, Mum?' I asked.

'No, we're fine thank you. I provide everything she needs,' Helen butted in.

I rummaged in my pocket and pulled out the

hundred pounds in five twenty-pound notes I'd rolled up earlier, handing it to Mum.

'This is for you, both of you, I'll bring some more. Even if you don't need anything, treat yourselves to something. Get your hair done, or a takeaway, anything.'

'Where's that from? You been up Kings Cross?'

'Helen!' Mum interjected.

'No, it's my wages.' I gritted my teeth, struggling to contain my temper.

'For goodness' sake, you two, always at each other's throats. Why can't you just get along. You weren't always like this!' Mum sighed and Helen lowered her eyes, abashed.

Mum was right, we hadn't always fought. I knew I was a difficult teenager and Helen, as the oldest, had to clean up my messes. She hated that I was wild and uncontrollable when she was studious and relied upon by Mum. It turned to resentment in the end and me going to prison would always be the stick she'd beat me with.

'I'm going for a fag,' I announced.

Helen came to join me in the back garden after some raised voices from the sitting room, where I guessed Mum was giving her what for. She took one of the cigarettes when I offered her the packet and we sat on the wall facing the house.

'She been in touch with you? That Ashley?' Helen asked.

I shook my head, not since the letter anyway.

'At the start, she was round here every bloody day, doing the shopping, helping out, like it was her penance. Convinced the whole thing was her fault. So much so, I thought she might have been driving the car?' Helen raised an eyebrow at me, and I gave a little shake of the head.

'No, I was driving.'

'You never did tell us what really happened.' Helen narrowed her eyes, I could tell she was suspicious.

I sighed and gave her the abridged version of events, the one I'd told so many times I'd almost convinced myself there was nothing more to add. 'They were arguing in the back, Ashley and Eddie, and I took my eye off the road.'

'Hmmm.' Helen sucked on her cigarette.

We smoked in silence until the sound of the washing machine going into full spin mode echoed.

It wasn't until we stood to go back into the house that Helen spoke again.

'Why were they both in the back?'

'My passenger seat didn't work properly, don't you remember, the adjusters, they wouldn't lock into place and kept sliding backwards and forwards. I was going to get it fixed before the next MOT.'

'Yes, I remember,' Helen said thoughtfully before continuing. 'What I don't understand is neither of them were wearing seat belts, were they?'

'No.'

'Then why was only Eddie thrown through the windscreen?' It was a rhetorical question which didn't require an answer, so I stayed quiet.

'Just going to grab my stuff from your wardrobe, Mum,' I called when we came back inside before disappearing up the stairs.

Mum's room was tidy, her bed made and hoover marks still apparent on the grey carpet. In her wardrobe was a large plastic box of things from the room I shared with Helen. As though I'd been packed up and put out of sight. Every inch of me removed. As well as clothes, there were trinkets, jewellery, photos, old make-up and a few books.

Sitting on the floor, I went through the box, taking items out in turn and examining them before spreading them out on the carpet around me. There were four books I wanted to take but hardly any of the clothes. They all looked like they were from the wrong era. If I turned up at work looking like a Belieber I'd be laughed out of the place.

I found a pair of Ashley's sunglasses, the enormous ones she'd bought from Primark which looked ridiculous on her tiny face. Next, I lifted a printed scarf out of the box and a load of photos slipped out from the fabric. Most of them were from my schooldays, and some of me and Helen as children. I took a few, sliding them into the pages of *Harry Potter*. A strip of Ashley and I from a photo booth was stuck down the side of the box. We looked so young, crazy smiles; ridiculous fake eyelashes bought from the local chemist. God knows where we were going. To a party probably. We were always partying; life was too short, that was our motto. Until it turned out, it actually was.

I slid the photo in between the pages of the book, my chest caving in. I so desperately wanted that again, to have Ashley back, my life back. Those years I'd missed.

Everything had changed and now I'd gone and done something stupid again. Like I'd never learnt the first time. I crunched down on my molars, jaw aching. Karla's voice ringing in my ears 'hold your nerve, Jess'.

16

I left Mum's after I'd painted the door. I found a half-used tin of red paint in the shed, the lid crusted. Probably from the last time the door was painted. It should have been thrown away, but it would do for the cover-up job. I spent ten minutes sanding down the flakes and the words before wiping it clean and applying a coat, trying to avoid covering myself in crimson.

The washing had finished, and I made myself a quick sandwich before making my excuses. The atmosphere in the house was oppressive and Helen's beady eyes watching my every move put me on edge. I should have been buoyant, with the money hidden at the bedsit. Initially there'd been the idea of shopping for new clothes and getting a haircut from someone not wearing standard-issue prison joggers. Instead, after leaving Mum's, I went home via the local shop and picked up some supplies, a couple of meals, chocolate, milk and cigarettes. The graffiti had been the icing on the cake.

Back in the bedsit, I listened to the rain as it pelted onto the roof, and once I'd hung up the clean clothes, I changed into my pyjamas, deciding I was in for the day. Whatever I did, however long I cleaned or pottered, I couldn't shake the feeling I'd forgotten something at Bright's. I'd left something of Karla's or mine behind and any moment now there would be the telling thud of police at my door.

Karla was right. Terry was a pig, a monster who took advantage of the vulnerable. Exploited us just because he could, but he had a wife and a child he'd never see grow up. She would be at home worrying about him, no idea she'd never see him again. I had stolen her right to bury him, to mourn him, instead all I'd done was leave his family with questions they would never know the answers to. He'd be a missing person forever. It was a life sentence I'd delivered and it weighed heavily on me.

The shadow of remorse hung over me all weekend. I found myself skittish, every noise outside sent me loopy and I was exhausted from being on high alert. The only thing that helped was the vodka, which I was now running low on. I was drinking to block out Terry and to pass the time.

As much as I didn't want Monday to come around, I had to know if the incinerator had done its job. Whether Bright's would be crawling with police. I knew it was my imagination overreacting and I wished I could talk to Ashley. She would always be the one to talk me down off the ledge when I got worked up about something.

I texted Karla late Sunday.

See you tomorrow

She responded with *Sure, 8:20* but nothing more.

* * *

I slept fitfully again. My dreams sent me back to Bronzefield, queuing for breakfast and watching a prisoner spit in my porridge before dumping it in my bowl. I woke in a cold sweat, hearing footsteps, only to realise it was those bloody pigeons. I'd have to ask Stuart if he could put some rat poison on the roof as their tap dancing was starting to annoy me.

I couldn't stop thinking about Terry, my stomach hollowed out with guilt. We should have gone to the police. I should have taken my chances, told the truth and let the scales of justice decide. Instead I'd roped in Karla and then followed her blindly. She'd come up with everything – the incinerator, dumping the car, even the alibi. She was the smartest of us and I'd let her take control, begged her to help me, but now I wasn't so sure we'd done the right thing. I'd risked both our freedom.

At eight-fifteen, I loitered outside Bright's, smoking my fifth cigarette of the day, before wrapping my arms around myself. It was freezing and I couldn't control the tremor in my hand or my stomach churning like I was on the Big Dipper.

Karla came into view after I'd been waiting a minute or so, her mass of hair taken in the wind. She didn't smile, just nodded a greeting as she approached, cheeks pink from the cold. 'Seen anyone?'

'No,' I replied.

'Right, let's go in.'

Bright's access was via key code, a six-digit number Terry gave to a couple of the girls, the long-standing ones like Karla. He kept nothing much of value on site overnight. The most expensive things were the machines and they'd need an army in a lorry with a forklift to get those out.

No one was due in until nine, but still we crept in quietly, checking the office, toilets and warehouse were empty.

It was strange seeing Terry's office; I couldn't help but examine the closed door for any missed blood, before meeting Karla back at the incinerator.

'We don't have long,' she said, lifting the viewing hatch and peering inside. She gasped, stepping aside to let me look. There were bone fragments still inside the chamber, more than I would have anticipated.

I shuddered, feeling sick.

Karla pulled a brand-new dustpan and brush out of her bag. 'Bought it yesterday, but I think we'll have to get our hands dirty. Let me just go and get the medical bags and some gloves.'

Her footsteps echoed on the concrete and it felt eerie standing so close to Terry's remains. My breathing quickened and I felt the hairs on my arms stand to attention.

'I think the ash is collected here,' Karla said, already back and lifting the metal lid of a compartment at the side of the machine with her gloved hand.

'How do we get it out?' I asked.

Karla pulled a yellow waste bag from the pocket of her hoodie and motioned for me to hold it open underneath the compartment. I slipped on my gloves and got into position.

'There must be a lever or something,' she said, scanning the machine.

Seconds later, there was a whoosh and a cloud of ash flew into the air, causing us both to gasp. It thudded into the bag, weighing a ton. Particles swirled around before settling upon us. I wanted to shake, to brush Terry off me, but my hands were holding the bag upright. The incinerator was covered in a film of it, but thankfully most had been collected. I always imagined ash would be light, how wrong I was.

'Shit!' Karla said, opening the bag for me to see some more bone on the top of the pile.

I trembled, holding my breath, conscious I didn't want to inhale him.

'I need to sweep the chamber,' I said, even though it was the last thing I wanted to do, grateful to pass the bag to Karla and occupy my shaking hands.

Climbing up, I lifted the heavy door, reaching inside to pick out some more fragments.

'I think we might need another bag,' I said, saliva filling my mouth.

Hold it together, Jess, don't lose it now.

Karla tied her bag and held open another; the bones clattered to the bottom and I brushed the smaller ones towards me. I wouldn't have been able to tell they were human if I hadn't known.

Filling up the dustpan twice, I found Terry's belt buckle in amongst leftover metal scraps. I emptied the remnants into the second bag, catching sight of a small blackened gold crown from one of Terry's molars as the contents slid out of the pan. I baulked, climbing down and lowering the lid.

'Right, let's go.' Karla threw in our gloves, tied the bag and dragged both to the store cupboard, where between us we put them inside a thick black sack. Then we heaved it over by the warehouse shutters with some other rubbish.

'We can't leave it there!' I said.

'We have to. I can sling it in the bin outside the yard gates, you know the big industrial ones, but I can't do that until the shutters are opened. The dustmen are coming today. It's the easiest way to get rid of him.' She was right. Karla was always right.

'We've got to clean up,' I said, staring at the film of Terry's remains lingering on my skin, head swimming at the thought. I was spooked to say the least, but Karla was methodical.

'Grab those cloths on the bottom shelf,' she ordered, pointing back towards the store cupboard, 'and a cleaning spray. We need new tabards too.'

I did as she asked; rushing back to put the fresh tabards in my locker. It was already ten to nine and some of the girls would start arriving any minute for their shift.

Tiny palpitations flittered through my veins, as we first brushed each other down and then cleaned the machine as fast as we could, trying to get rid of the dust. The shiny red metal was cool to the touch. I kept having to run to the toilets to rinse my cloth out as it blackened so easily, watching the grey particles swill down the drain trying not to think they were the remnants of Terry.

Karla was sweeping the ash which had settled onto the floor under the nearest washing machine when we heard footstep approaching.

We stared at each other; eyes wide. A silent scream stuck in my throat as Karla ditched the broom and grabbed me by the hand. She pulled me over to one of the trolleys and lifted out a clean folded sheet and began to refold it. Nodding at me to do the same. I copied her immediately, but I was all fingers and thumbs. Karla tutted at my lack of composure.

'You didn't clock in,' Agnes called across the warehouse.

My shoulders eased down.

'Shit, we forgot. Too busy gassing.' Karla giggled.

It was the first time I'd seen her smile; she was a natural actress.

'And you forgot your tabards!' Agnes chided as we walked back to the lockers to put them on. 'Have you seen Terry?' she asked when we returned, now clocked in and wearing our uniform.

I froze on the spot and Karla walked into the back of me, propelling me forward. The mention of his name sent ice shooting through my veins. I was going to fold under the pressure.

Karla sent daggers at me before turning back to Agnes. 'No, not yet. Perhaps he's late?' she replied.

'He's always here before us.'

I shrugged, not trusting my voice to remain steady.

When Agnes went to check the rota, Karla whispered to me, 'Get your shit together. I ain't going down for you, got it?'

I nodded, taking slow breaths to calm my nerves.

'There's not a new one out, it's Friday's rota.' Agnes came around the corner with Hanna, who had just arrived. More of the girls started filing in.

We all stood around in the warehouse, wondering what to do. Terry had a rota which he'd leave out, who was on what machine and teamed with who. The shutters hadn't been opened and no deliveries received into Bright's for us to get on with. The girls were perplexed.

'Should we call someone?' Laura asked above the chatter.

'Call who?' came a deep voice, and we all spun around.

17

Barry turned the corner into the warehouse, the collar of his brown leather jacket pulled up to protect him from the elements. He frowned at us all standing around.

'Terry's not shown up,' Karla said quickly, her hands on her hips.

'Oh, that's unusual. Perhaps he's ill. Let me give him a ring.' Barry pulled his phone out of his pocket and walked away from us, towards the shutters.

The voices quietened down as we listened to Barry leave a message on Terry's voicemail. Inwardly, my heart was close to leaping out of my chest.

Karla eyed me carefully as I folded my arms and

glanced around at the others. Concentrating on looking like I had no idea where Terry was either.

'Voicemail,' Barry said, eyebrows raised. He looked around at us, momentarily at a loss as what to do. 'Isn't there anything you can be getting on with?'

Some of the girls scattered, finding trolleys where linen needed folding and packaging, but there wasn't much to keep us busy. Laura picked up Karla's discarded broom and began sweeping. It was almost comical.

'I don't think there's been any deliveries. We can't open the shutters or Terry's office. We've only got what was left over on Friday and, as you can see,' Karla waved her hand around the barren warehouse, 'there's not a lot.'

Barry nodded, stroking his chin.

Voices came from the entrance and I peeked around the corner to see a man and a woman looking through the glass into Terry's office before unlocking the door.

'Barry, someone's here?'

Karla and I lingered from a distance as Barry puffed out his chest and approached them.

The petite woman with long blonde hair and a

chunky fringe was talking animatedly, the man patting her arm as though to appease her.

'Who the fuck are they?' Karla whispered.

I made a face. 'Pass,' I replied, although the woman looked familiar. I watched the three of them enter Terry's office and continue their conversation.

After a minute, we separated, moving around into the main part of the warehouse to try and find ourselves something to do. I could see Karla's eyes kept wandering to the incinerator, but there was nothing to show it had been used recently. She took charge, making sure all the orders were packed up, ready to be collected and soon we were gathered by the trolleys again. Everyone putting their pennyworth in about where Terry had disappeared to. I craved nicotine, struggling to listen to their outlandish theories.

Outside the front of Bright's, the weight of what we'd done sat on me like a tonne of bricks. How did we ever think we'd get away with it? Had Terry's car been found yet? What if the man was looking at the CCTV from the yard now? He could be from the police station. Watching me in Terry's coat and cap. How did we think that would work? At least it was the only CCTV at Bright's, there was nothing at the entrance, so he couldn't prove what time we left.

I was so wrapped up in my thoughts I didn't realise the visitor was standing beside me, looking up at the entrance. It was as if he was searching for cameras, but there were none at the front.

He was average height, slim build with short dark curly hair. We stood awkwardly next to each other for a second as I considered chucking what was left of my cigarette and going back inside.

'I'm Dan, Terry's brother,' he volunteered, holding out his hand for me to shake.

'Oh,' was all I could manage as I shook it.

The resemblance to Terry was non-existent. Dan's eyes weren't squinty, and he didn't have the double chin or receding hairline either.

'Sorry, it's just, you look nothing like him,' I said, realising my mouth was gaping.

He chuckled and my face flushed pink. 'Thank God for that. He's got a few pounds on me, and a few years.' Dan looked to be in his early thirties.

'I'm Jess,' I said before quickly adding, 'where's Terry?'

'We don't know. Kim, his wife, is going out of her

mind. He didn't come home on Friday and no one can reach him. Did he seem all right to you the last time you saw him?'

No not really, he was engulfed in a fireball.

'Yeah, I guess.'

The woman inside must be Kim, I realised I'd recognised her from the photo on Terry's desk. Had she been in Bright's at the weekend?

'I'm Terry's silent partner, I've been working in Aberdeen for the past six months until Kim called me on Saturday. I'm the only one with spare keys,' he said, swinging them around on his finger. He obviously didn't know the key code, which meant Kim didn't know it either.

'Where do you think he's gone?' I asked.

'No idea, but Kim's doing her crust and I've got a laundry full of ladies to sort out.'

I flicked my cigarette into the road, and we made our way back inside, Dan holding the door open for me to slip past.

Inside, Terry's office door had been unlocked and Kim was rummaging through the drawers and cabinets. Long glossy red fingernails catching the light. She looked well kept, perfect make-up in skinny jeans and tan UGG boots. Terry's trophy wife. God knows how he'd kept her.

'He never goes anywhere without his bloody Gaviscon, swigging from it all day long he is! Gets such bad indigestion,' she cried, brandishing the bottle at Dan.

Barry had left, deciding to come back another day to see his probationers, and I found Karla in the warehouse, bringing in a delivery that had been left outside. The shutters had been raised, letting the cold air in as we moved the hospital sheets from the pallet to the machines.

'He's Terry's brother,' I hissed at Karla as we heaved the packets of fabric onto the tables for sorting. Her screwed-up face said it all. They didn't look like they belonged to the same gene pool. Dan was well turned out, good-looking even, the opposite of Terry in every way.

'Ladies, can I have your attention please?' Dan's voice boomed and we all stopped what we were doing and gathered around. Kim stood next to him, bags under her eyes like she hadn't slept, chewing her nails. 'As you may have heard, Terry has gone AWOL. Has anyone seen him since Friday?'

Everyone shook their heads and looked around at each other.

'Okay, let me know if you remember anything strange about that day, anything at all. We're just going to head to the police station to make a formal report.'

My eyes bulged, but Karla, in my peripheral vision, remained stoic.

'If you can carry on as best you can, keep doing what you're doing. I'll be back in an hour or so.'

Every muscle tensed of its own accord and I stood rigid. Karla met my eye and gave the slightest shake of the head. I got the message.

'Jess.'

I turned around and Dan was behind me.

'Won't be long, any problems, give me a ring.' He slipped a business card into my hand, his fingers grazing my icy palms.

I swallowed.

'Sure.' I stared at the card, the writing in black modern print: Daniel Bright, Director at Bright's Industrial Services, his mobile number beneath. I ran my thumb across the smooth surface as he left, listening to the girls' giggle about how hot Dan was and how he couldn't possibly be related to Shrek-like Terry.

'Don't get any ideas,' Karla said, throwing me a clear packet of what looked like dirty pillowcases to open.

'What do you mean?' I huffed.

'You're pulling on your ear again and you've gone all pink.' She smirked.

18

By the end of the day, we'd worked through the order that had been delivered and packaged up what was ready for collection. The atmosphere without Terry around had been relaxed, there was an abundance of chatter and laughter in the warehouse.

Although Karla and I didn't participate much. Laura put her radio on again and because all the machines weren't working at once the temperature was comfortable.

Dan came back with Kim and they sat in Terry's office with a takeaway coffee from the café a few doors down. I tried to earwig, but their voices wouldn't carry. He waved as we clocked out. Would he be back tomorrow? I hoped so. I couldn't deny he was easy on the eye.

'Fancy a coffee?' Karla said.

'How about a burger, I'm starving,' I replied. There was a local Wimpy down the road and we walked quickly to get out of the cold. We both ordered a cheeseburger and chips with a milkshake and sat in the front by the window, watching people scurry past.

'He's a bit of all right, isn't he?' Karla said.

'I guess so.'

'Looks like no one went in at the weekend.'

'No, but who knows what the police are going to dig up, now they are looking for him.' I scooped a load of tomato sauce onto a chip and popped it into my mouth.

'Like what?'

I leaned forward in my seat. 'I'm worried they are going to look at the CCTV and see a girl dressed as a bloke getting in Terry's car and driving it away,' I said, my voice low.

'It'll be fine, you worry too much.' Karla took a bite of her burger, ketchup dripping onto the paper wrapping.

'I can't help it; we should have just called the police.'

Karla sat bolt upright in her chair. 'I saved your arse, and don't you forget it. They would have charged you with manslaughter or something and you wouldn't have had a leg to stand on,' she seethed, eyes flashing.

I lowered my gaze back to my burger. She was right and even if she weren't, there was nothing I could do about it now. We'd started a chain of events that couldn't be stopped.

'We've just got to sit tight. It'll be fine, I promise.' Her voice was softer now.

'What did you get up to at the weekend?' I asked, changing the subject.

'Not a lot. You?'

'Same.'

'You not got any friends to knock about with?'

Cheeks blazing at Karla's incredulous tone, I looked away. 'No, not really, they've all... moved on. My best friend, Ashley, I haven't seen since before. She's at university now,' I said proudly as though I was her parent.

'So, who did you kill?' Karla said, taking another large bite of her burger.

My mouth dropped at the casualness of her words. She didn't even bother to lower her tone.

'Her boyfriend,' I whispered.

'Whose, Ashley's?'

I nodded.

'Holy shit, no wonder she ain't your friend any more.' Karla's words stung like a slap in the face. Why was I bothering? The problem was Karla and I were connected forever now, a secret that bound us together.

I pushed my half-eaten burger to the side and stood, shrugging on my coat. Karla frowned up at me.

'I gotta go.'

I didn't wait for a response, just grabbed my milkshake and left, walking past the bus stop outside to the next one further down the road. Thankfully, I didn't have to wait long and when I got to the bedsit, Stuart was just returning from work.

'Hey, how's it going?' he asked cheerfully, always disconcerting for a Monday.

'Okay thanks, you?'

'Yeah good, I'm taking your sister out this week.'

I raised my eyebrows. Helen and Stuart? It wasn't a match I could see working, she was far too highly strung, but he looked excited at the prospect.

'Oh, great. Hope it goes well. Thanks for the vodka by the way, it was kind of you.'

He waved me away. 'No biggie, I can't stand the stuff. I'm a bourbon drinker myself. Everything all right in there?' he asked, nodding towards the bedsit.

'Yeah fine, although the pigeons are driving me mad – any chance you could put something on the roof, poison or something to scare them away?'

'I'll see what I can do.'

'Also, do you think I could get a TV? I mean would I need an aerial if I bought one?'

Stuart rubbed his chin thoughtfully. 'Yes, I think you would. Leave it with me and I'll see if I can get a connection run off mine.'

'Thanks, Stuart.' I smiled.

He chuckled, before giving me an odd little salute and heading inside.

If Helen had a date, I'd go and spend the evening with Mum. I rang her inside, but it went to voicemail, so I left a message asking if everything was all right and could I come over one night this week? I didn't mention Helen's date but hoped Mum would get the message.

I'd never been on a date, not a proper one. I'd never been taken for dinner, wined and dined or even treated like a lady. I'd often dreamt about the perfect date, a nice Italian restaurant, all dressed up. I imagined myself sitting across from Dan, him smiling as he poured wine into my glass.

Fat chance. I bet he went out with classy girls, perhaps he was even married, like Terry. I hadn't seen a ring on his finger though. Maybe he had a girlfriend in Aberdeen, a Scottish lass with fiery red hair and temper to match. I pushed the thought from my mind, having anything to do with Terry's brother would be asking for trouble considering what I'd done.

I snuggled into bed, picked up a book and tried to concentrate, but the words bounced around on the page and I couldn't catch them. I kept thinking about Kim, going out of her mind with worry. Did she think Terry had just left her, disappeared off the face of the earth? What about the child from his photo? Had I robbed a child of knowing what had happened to its father? Now the police were involved, how hard would they look if they suspected foul play? My stomach churned in anticipation of tomorrow.

Somewhere underneath the covers my phone buzzed and I reached for it.

Sorry about earlier. I shouldn't have made a joke. It's not funny.

No, Karla, it wasn't funny. I'd killed Eddie and now, every night in my dreams, I could add Terry to the list of faces who haunted me.

* * *

In the morning, the dark circles under my eyes were almost purple. I rummaged in the bathroom drawer where I'd discarded the make-up I'd bought back from Mum's. Luckily the concealer still had some life left in it and with a bit of help I began to look more human. I carried on with mascara and a brown eye-liner, the face staring back at me from the mirror looked like a stranger. I piled my hair into a messy topknot and got dressed, ready to face the day, whatever it would bring.

The bus never arrived to pick me up, so I started walking. When one finally went past, I was nowhere near the next stop. Shit. I'd definitely be late. There was no way I could make the walk in half an hour, but I sped up.

When Bright's came into view, the first thing I noticed was the police car parked outside the entrance.

Fluttering in my chest, tiny palpitations rippled through me as I neared the doors. I checked my phone; it was ten past nine. Rushing inside, I pulled off my coat as I clocked in, spying the uniformed officer in Terry's office, looking at something over Dan's shoulder. I moved quickly past, my bag at my side, ready to put in my locker.

'Ah, Jess, brilliant. We've be waiting for you.'

I turned around and Dan was leaning against the door frame, his leg touching the spot where Terry's head had struck the metal.

'Me?' I muttered.

Dan nodded and beckoned me inside.

19

My legs wouldn't work, it was like they didn't belong to me any more. I saw Dan looking, his smile turning to an expression of confusion.

Move damn it! I propelled myself forward and entered the office.

'Take a seat, this won't take long.'

'I'm sorry I'm late, I missed the bus. It won't happen again,' I blurted out.

Dan chuckled. 'Don't worry, it's not important. Officer Stokes here just wants to ask you a couple of questions.'

The policeman stood straight, picking up his notebook from Terry's desk. He was in his early thirties, pale blond hair like mine. We had similar colouring. Mum always said Helen and I looked like we were Swedish. His radio burst to life and made me jump with a screech.

'Sorry about that, take a seat, Jess...?'

'Strickland,' I answered and watched him write it down. I hadn't failed to notice our personnel files on the desk, mine buried under Karla's. I could just make out her surname Grant on the front as I lowered into the chair.

'I've had a quick chat with most of the girls. Some said when they left on Friday you were in here having a chat with Terry. Can you tell me what that was about?'

I tried to keep my voice steady as I answered, although I was sure the vein in my forehead was pulsating. 'I was reporting an issue with the washing machine I'd been using that day. It appeared to be leaking mid-cycle.' It wasn't the best lie, but it was all I could come up with on the spot.

Officer Stokes nodded as he took it down. 'How did Terry seem?'

'Fine. Normal. I wasn't here long.'

'And he was still here when you left the premises?'

I nodded.

Dan pointed towards the screen and I was desperate to crane my neck round to see what was on the monitor, but I remained still.

Were they looking at me, wearing Terry's coat and boots, climbing into his car? Had they spotted Karla pulling down the shutters before climbing into the boot of the Audi? Was the game up?

'We have him leaving at about seven. What time did you leave again?' Dan asked, rubbing his hands together. He looked more casual today, the shirt had been replaced with a jumper, black boots instead of the smart shoes he wore yesterday. The aroma of his aftershave filled the small office, which was tight with three of us inside. It made me heady.

'Umm, it was about quarter past five, I think.'

Officer Stokes nodded. 'Okay thanks, Ms Strickland. I think that's all for now.'

I stood, ready to go, wanting to ask so many questions but not daring to. I had my alibi ready, but no one asked where I went when I left Bright's.

'Thanks, Jess.' Dan flashed a genuine smile at

me, displaying perfectly straight teeth, and it was like being branded with a hot poker.

When I got back to the warehouse, via the lockers, Karla was ready to pounce.

'What did they say?'

'Nothing really, just asking about the last time I saw him. Didn't even ask where I went after work.'

Karla looked me up and down, her brows knitted, before nodding an acceptance and allowing me to pass.

Only Lisa didn't have a partner, so I teamed with her, feeding the flat sheets through the press. These were larger and trickier than the tablecloths, having to go through multiple times. I was amazed she'd been doing them by herself.

We chatted about Terry, it was all anyone wanted to talk about, his mysterious disappearance. Kim hadn't shown up yet today, but the police were speaking to all the girls individually. I was sure they had been looking at the CCTV earlier.

'Earth to Jess.' Lisa was staring right at me, her hands on her hips.

'Sorry I was miles away, didn't sleep well,' I

replied, rubbing my eye for effect and smudging my mascara.

'I was saying, Terry, I reckon he fucked with the wrong girl and her pimp took him down.' Lisa sniffed, rubbing her nose ring.

'It's all a bit gangster, isn't it? Plus, Terry never went for working girls, he liked the non-working variety, remember?' I raised my eyebrows and looked pointedly at her.

'Yeah. Let's hope some bastards murdered him though, eh,' she said cheerfully.

I shuddered at the words, reminding myself for the thousandth time, I hadn't killed Terry, just disposed of his body.

I glanced over at Karla, working with Agnes whose mouth was moving, it was always moving. What would Agnes's topic of conversation be today? Whatever it was, Karla wasn't listening; she wouldn't take her eyes off me. I turned away, still able to feel them burning a hole in my back. What was her problem? Did she think I'd sold her out?

At lunchtime, I went to the café to get a roll and some crisps, the lettuce was limp in my BLT, but I didn't care. I wanted out of Bright's today, the atmosphere was claustrophobic with the police hanging around. Officer Stokes had been joined by a lady, tall and imposing in her uniform. Her eyes were distrustful, and put me on edge as they wandered around, taking notes, searching the warehouse.

When they looked over the incinerator, I stiffened, trying not to watch as Dan showed them the machine. My heart leapt into my throat when he pulled open the ash collection compartment. I had no idea why; it wasn't as though Terry was still in there. I hadn't seen it used yesterday for the stained hospital sheets, because Terry was normally the only one that ever operated it. Perhaps some of him was still in there?

I gagged on my sandwich, putting it back in the wrapper.

'You're acting weird today?' Karla came up behind me as I stood in the yard.

'No, I'm not. Listen, we need to get those sheets incinerated, get something burning so that *he* wasn't the last thing in there.'

She nodded and joined me for a cigarette, but I didn't bother with general chit-chat. I couldn't wait to finish mine and get inside.

When I did, Dan invited me to the office, sliding into Terry's seat as if it had always been his own. The police had gone.

'Can you help me with something? I've found the personnel files, but I'm struggling to access the payroll system.' He worked the mouse and I stood beside him, watching it zoom around the screen, from programme to programme.

'I'm sorry, I have no idea how to get into it. This is only my first month. I've not even had my first wage slip yet.' I smiled awkwardly, disappointed I was of no use.

'Okay, no worries. I tell you, this is a nightmare. Terry's so unorganised, nothing is where it should be. I set all this up for him when we started Bright's, he's no IT whizz. Looks like he's changed the password to the payroll system. I'll have to ring them up,' he vented, shaking his head.

I shifted position and our arms brushed accidentally. I moved back to the other side of the desk, tripping over a pile of ring binders discarded on the floor.

'See what I mean! You okay?' Dan stood up to help, but I waved him away.

'I'm fine.' Why couldn't I be cool and aloof? Why was I such an idiot? 'No news about Terry?' I asked.

'Nope, it's like he's just upped and disappeared. Kim got a fine through the post from Croydon council, his car was towed from the town centre. She's hoping they'll let her pick it up today if she takes the police with her.' Dan sighed. 'There's money missing, the accounts are all over the place. Fuck knows what he's got himself into.' He rubbed his forehead and I could see the stress etched on his face.

'I'm sure he'll turn up,' I managed.

'He better. I've got a life to get back to, without clearing up his shit. Sorry, sorry, it's not for me to moan at you.' He beamed at me and a strange sensation darted the length of my spine. I was attracted to him; I couldn't help it, but falling for Terry's brother was the last thing I needed.

20

Helen called on the way home. She was cagey about her date with Stuart but asked if I could come and sit with Mum tomorrow, offering to leave dinner out for both of us.

'How about I bring fish and chips, then you don't have to cook if he's taking you for dinner.'

'God knows if it's dinner, I haven't had a date in so long I have no idea what the plan is.' Helen sighed; she didn't seem overly excited about her upcoming night out. If it was me, I'd have been unable to keep still.

'At least you have a date! I haven't had any interest since, well, ever!'

Helen sniggered and I could imagine her tossing her hair back, happy to have one up on me. I rolled my eyes.

'Well, I better go. Shall I tell Mum you'll come straight from work?'

'Yep.'

'And you will show this time, won't you?' I could hear Helen's reproachful tone.

'Yes,' I replied sharply.

'Good, oh, and a letter came for you today. I think it might be from Ashley.'

I stopped on the pavement at the mention of her name, causing someone to bump into me from behind. I apologised and moved to the kerb.

'Okay, I'll get it tomorrow.'

We said a brief goodbye and Helen hung up.

Why was Ashley writing now? Had she heard I'd got out? I bit my lip, excitement bubbling beneath the surface, although I wasn't sure why. Things would never be the same between us again. They couldn't be. Too much time had passed, too much had changed.

When I reached home, I heard pop music blaring from Stuart's lounge and voices carried along the breeze. He must have his family round to visit. My shoulders sagged and I turned and walked back down the path. They'd be noisy for hours; his nephews clattered around and screamed the whole time they were there. I think Stuart played the music to drown them out, but it only added to the problem.

I wandered around, contemplating the library at first, but it would soon be closing. I passed a near-empty coffee shop and sat in there for an hour, my fingers wrapped around a mug of hot chocolate. I had to do something; this was no life for someone of my age. Spending your evening hiding in a coffee shop, not wanting to go back to the one room you called home. I needed to make friends, get out, go for a drink down the pub, go shopping, do normal things, but I was acutely aware I was not a normal twenty-two-year-old.

I'd missed out on so much, everyone I knew had become an adult in that time, learnt how to act, what to say and how to dress whilst I'd been gone. Now I was thrown in the midst of it all and felt totally clue-less. I had a second-hand iPhone 5s, at seventeen, be-fore the accident and was an avid user of Facebook, Instagram and Snapchat back then. So much so my mum said it was permanently glued to my hand, but it all seemed pointless now. You needed friends for social media, or at the very least an interesting life to post about and I lacked both.

Karla was not going to be the sort of friend I needed, one who could help me learn to live again. She was more shut down than me. I wasn't even sure she liked me! We'd done something terrible together, committed a crime, and it would always be the basis of our relationship.

If money were no object I'd go back to school, finish my A-Level English and see if I could get into teaching. That was the dream, something to focus on, although I had no idea how to make it happen. Right now, it seemed insurmountable. I needed to take small steps, build relationships, work hard and climb the ladder. Not at Bright's, somewhere else, although I knew it would be difficult to get a job with a criminal record.

At around seven when I returned home, Stuart's nephews were still there, but the music had been replaced by cartoons on the television. I ignored the sound carrying through the wall and laid down on my bed. This weekend I might buy a small television with the money we'd taken from Terry. That was if Stuart could get me connected to his aerial. I'd get some new clothes too and maybe a haircut, make more of an effort. After all, I didn't know how long Dan was going to be around for.

* * *

My alarm went off at seven and I came to. I'd fallen asleep in my clothes, my book discarded further down the bed. I'd stayed up reading with the light on, trying to chase the demons away until I couldn't keep my eyes open any longer.

The morning air was cold, and I turned the heater on. Knowing I was going to see Mum later immediately put me in a good mood despite my bad night and I hummed as I made a cup of tea, stomach growling from the lack of food the night before.

It wasn't until I was out of the shower and looking around for something to wear, that I spotted the brown envelope, folded in half and shoved through the letterbox. That was why the bedsit was so bloody cold, with the flap up, icy air streamed in. Tutting, I pulled the envelope out and moved back towards the heater. The envelope had no name or address. I turned it over in my hands, easing my finger underneath the lip and prising it away. Inside was an A4 piece of paper, a black and white photo. Because of the strange angle, it took a moment to work out what it was.

The photo was of Terry in his office, looking down from the top right-hand corner. He had a hidden camera somewhere, in the roof maybe. There was a filing cabinet behind Terry's desk, perhaps it was tucked in there? In the image, I was kneeling in front of Terry, my head bowed. It wasn't clear it was me on the ground, but I recognised my T-shirt and the top of my head. I wavered on my feet, head swimming, the notion of being aboard a boat in choppy water. It transported me back there, back to last Friday.

The image was taken less than a minute before Terry forced himself on me, before I lost control and bit down until he screamed. I threw the photo onto the bed and turned away, tears streaming down my face. He had fucking cameras in his office! Everything he'd done to us had been recorded. How had Dan not seen the video? The police had been in, looking at the CCTV, how had it been missed? And who had posted this to me? Had I been followed?

I sank down to the bed, dropping my head in my hands. Until I realised there would be proof to expose him for the monster he was, footage of his assault on Karla. No, I could hear Karla's voice now. It would give us motive.

I rushed to get dressed, folding the paper into a small square and putting it in my bag. My hair was still wet, but I didn't wait to dry it, I plaited it quickly and let the end drip. It would only be my coat that got damp. Mum's voice echoed in my ears about going out with wet hair. I couldn't wait to fold myself into her arms tonight. How I wished she could protect me.

I stared at everyone I passed as I hurried to work, eyes connecting. *Was it you? Did you post a photo through my door?* My skin crawled as though I was covered in ants. Why that photo, it could have been anyone in front of Terry? How had they known it was me and how did they know where I lived? My mind spun with questions until I was dizzy. I texted Karla as I walked.

We need to talk, meet me asap

She would know what to do.

I marched along, not bothering to wait for the bus, my calves aching.

An older-style black BMW pulled up beside me, crawling along the kerb. I ignored it, feeling my heart start to race. I picked up my stride, staring straight ahead until the window wound down and Barry called out from behind the wheel.

'Get in.'

21

I didn't have a choice, I told myself as I strapped into the passenger seat, willing my heart to return to a normal rhythm.

Barry flicked a switch on the dashboard. 'Heated seats. You must be bloody freezing.' He pulled away into the traffic, driving further up the road until it came to a halt, queuing at the lights ahead.

'Nice car,' I indulged him, making conversation would speed up the journey.

'Yep, BMW 3 series Sport. She's my pride and joy, still gorgeous at ten years old. So, what's up, chick-adee?' Barry sounded cheerful and I narrowed my eyes. Did he suspect something? Had he put the photo through my letterbox? My skin began to itch.

'Nothing. Are you going to Bright's?'

'Yep, thought I'd give Terry a couple of days before I came back for my visit with you lovely ladies. He shown up yet?'

I shook my head.

Barry frowned and we jolted forward slightly in the car as though he'd had a lapse in concentration and his foot slipped off the pedal. 'Really?'

'He's not come back. Dan, his brother, has been looking after things.'

'Shit,' Barry said, his face crumpled like he was in pain.

'What is it?' I asked, innocently, my panic slowly subsiding. It wasn't him who'd posted the picture to me.

'Nothing, he owes me money, that's all.' He waved it away, like he regretted saying too much.

My mind flashed to the jiffy bag at home with two and a half grand inside, I'd barely touched it. I felt little guilt about taking it. It was what Terry owed Karla and I, for what he'd done to us. I just wished I could share it with the others.

'I think he owed a lot of people money,' I said without thinking.

Barry stared at me, a smile creeping onto his face. Gone was the easy manner, he looked shifty and I no longer wanted to be alone with him. 'I bet you see a lot of things, eh, Jess?'

I didn't answer, instead stared out of the window, soaking up the warmth of my seat, until we reached Bright's.

Barry liked to park around the back, even though he had no keys to open the shutters. As we walked around to the front, him talking about how he was looking at getting out of the probation gig, Karla met us on the pavement.

'Wow, you're an early bird too then. You girls are so keen,' he said, the sarcasm in his voice obvious.

Karla rolled her eyes and keyed in the code.

Dan was already inside, sat at Terry's desk, squinting at the monitor. For one awful second, my stomach sank. Was he looking at footage from the office? Me on my knees, meeting Terry's demands?

As we passed, he smiled and waved, but my eyes darted, searching the office, trying to find where the camera might have been positioned. The top of the filing cabinet in amongst the reams of paper was my best guess. I needed to get in and search. If the camera was still there, I had to destroy it before the police found it, if they hadn't already. Although whoever was sending me photos, I imagined, had a whole lot of images to choose from now.

Barry knocked on the door and popped in to have a chat with Dan.

I steered Karla straight towards the lockers by the elbow.

'What's with you? What's the emergency?'

I dug in my bag and drew out the paper, watching her unfold it, then reposition it, trying to work out which way up it should be.

'Is this you?'

'Yes. It was Friday.'

'Where did you get it?'

Before I could reply, Agnes joined us at the lockers, deep in conversation with Hanna. Karla folded the paper, the photo now out of view, but I beckoned her into the ladies', where we could talk in private, after checking all the stalls were empty.

'It was put through my door by someone. If

there's CCTV in there, why haven't the police or Terry's brother spoken to us?'

'It can't be connected to the CCTV. Maybe it's Terry's, you know what a sick fuck he was. Probably liked to make home movies.'

I gagged, my stomach empty. 'Someone has video or images of us; of me, of you, all of us. Him doing stuff to us.'

'It isn't what Terry did to us I'm concerned about, it's what we did to him!' Karla rubbed the back of her neck, eyes staring upwards towards the ceiling as though seeking divine intervention.

'Shit,' I said, only just realising someone must know what we'd done. Not only that, they may have proof.

I paced the floor, fingers interlocked behind my head. Panic stirring within me like a tornado.

'I knew we should have called the police.'

Karla groaned at my words.

'If we had, there would be evidence I didn't hurt him. Evidence that would have cleared me. Now, either way, we're fucked,' I snapped, close to losing it. Why had I listened to her?

Karla pulled open the door of the toilets and made to leave.

'Where are you going?'

'I can't be arsed listening to this. You needed my help, remember?'

She slammed the door in my face, and I deflated like a popped balloon. I wasn't being fair, but the idea of going back to prison terrified me.

When I emerged, I was collared by Barry as the first on his list. Dan was no longer in Terry's office and we sat there for our meeting. I found it hard to concentrate, my eyes wandering to the filing cabinet, but I couldn't see anything up there.

'So, everything okay this week? Been staying out of trouble?' Barry asked and I nodded. 'Seen any of your old friends? Are you getting out, socialising again?'

I shrugged. 'Not really, but I'm back in touch with my mum and sister.'

'Okay, well it's good to start afresh, but you need to have a good support network. It's hard to fit back into society without help.'

I almost sniggered at the sincerity in Barry's voice.

He'd sold us out to that monster, I was sure of it. How could he not have known what Terry was up to? Had Barry seen the tapes? Perhaps Karla was right, and they were for Terry's own private collection. He could have shared them with anybody. I bit down on my lip until it hurt, the thought was too awful to bear.

'Well, you've almost done your first month here. You'll be getting paid at the end of this week. Otherwise, you okay for money? Your sister got you a place, didn't she? Things still okay there?' Was he toying with me? Had he been the one to put the photo through my door? Or was there another reason he was nearby this morning?

'Yes. Everything's fine,' I said, just wanting the meeting to end.

'You don't give a lot away, do you, Jess? Not the most talkative of my girls.' His eyes twinkled and I wrinkled my nose. He talked about us like we were his harem. 'Righty-ho, you crack on then. I'm going to nip to the men's. Can you send Hanna in?' Barry looked down at my file and scribbled some notes on the sheet, satisfied with our catch-up, before heading out of the door.

I made to follow him, taking a few steps out of

the office and watched him go into the toilet. Dashing back, I reached up and felt along the top of the cabinet, fingers sliding over layers of grime, but nothing was stuck in between the files and paper. To be sure, I pulled over Terry's chair and climbed up on it. Dust swirled in the air and I sneezed. There was nothing in the corner or on top or on any of the shelves which looked remotely like a camera. Sighing, I climbed down. Whatever was there had gone. An empty feeling in the pit of my stomach reminded me that although the camera had been removed, someone had it, and on it was not only Terry's crimes, but mine as well.

22

'You're up,' I said to Hanna back in the warehouse, finding her midway through loading a washing machine.

She nodded and I replaced her, thrusting the stale towels into the drum. I watched Dan move around the warehouse, clipboard in hand. He looked to be taking stock of all the equipment on site. Overly smart in a white shirt with black suit trousers, he looked out of place, overdressed for Bright's.

Catching my eye, he smiled and made his way over, pulling his phone from his pocket. I tried my hardest not to blush, but when he got close, he smelt good enough to eat.

'Hey, how are you doing today? Got the bus all right?' he joked.

'I walked today, but I was on time.' I smiled tightly. Was that a dig or a joke?

'You're a local, aren't you?'

'Of sorts. What do you want to know?'

'Well, it looks as though I may be staying longer than anticipated. I've got a couple of places to look at and it's been so long since I've lived round here, I'm not sure where to avoid.'

'I thought you'd only been in Scotland for six months?' I asked, trying to hide my delight he wouldn't be leaving just yet.

'I was, but before that I was down the south coast and then the Midlands. Sometimes quite remote places.'

'Oh well, sure, where are you looking?'

He peered at his phone, swiping the screen. 'Um, there's places to rent in Wallington, Sutton or here in Croydon.'

'Wallington is nice, but it all depends where.'

He handed me his phone, too large for my small hand, and I was paranoid I'd drop it. The Wallington flat looked nice, but the Sutton one was a maisonette with access to a back garden. I recognised the road when I clicked on the map.

Dan moved to my side, our arms almost touching.

'This is in a nice area, lots of big houses around there. That must be what they've done, split it into two maisonettes maybe.'

Dan smiled at me and I squirmed, handing him the phone back. 'What are you up to after work? Are you busy because you could come with me? I could do with a second opinion.'

'I... I... can't. I'm sorry. I've got to look after my mum.' Automatically I took a step back, heart in my mouth.

'All right, sure, of course. No worries. Thanks for the location advice.' Dan turned and walked away as I gritted my teeth. I'd embarrassed him and myself.

'Another time?' I called after him, fearing I'd missed my chance but he didn't hear and carried on walking. Why was I such a moron?

* * *

Karla avoided me for the rest of the day. I knew I'd pissed her off and she didn't want to be around me. I couldn't blame her; I'd spoken without thinking. Without her help, I'd already be back in Bronzefield. As I sat on the bus on the way home, I sent her a text to let her know I'd found nothing in Terry's office. She replied with a solitary 'okay'.

I remembered the photo in my pocket and shifted in my seat. I hated being watched and it looked as though someone had all of us under surveillance. Whoever was behind it was letting us be abused and blackmailed. Watching us for their own perverse pleasure. It made my toes curl. What did they want? It was a message, I wanted to take comfort that, from the still image, you couldn't tell it was me, but whoever sent it knew it was. Not only that, they knew where I lived.

With my joints aching, I got off near home and waited for the second bus to take me to Mum's. I couldn't be arsed to walk. It stopped just outside Plaices and I queued up to get two small cod and chips. My stomach gurgled at the smell of the grease and vinegar ingrained in the walls.

The red front door was looking good when I arrived – I hadn't done a bad job. No one had been back to paint any slurs and I was relieved it seemed to be a one-off. I hated to think of my family as a target, especially when they'd done nothing wrong.

Helen was in the kitchen making tea when I entered the hall, freshly out of the shower and with a towel upon her head. I'd let myself in with my key, shouting hello as I crossed the threshold.

'I'm in here,' she called.

'Want some chips? There'll be loads,' I offered, pulling two plates out of the cupboard. It was just six o'clock, the cuckoo from the sitting room announced.

'No thanks, I've got to go and get ready.'

I nodded. 'No one's been back then, to do the door again?'

'No, but there's been phone calls, all hours, silent ones. We had them before. I've unplugged the bloody thing now. We've all got mobiles. It can stay like that for a few days until they get bored.'

I sighed. 'Helen, I'm so sorry, I didn't want to bring any of this to your door.'

'Well, it is what it is. They know you're out and they want to cause problems. It won't go on forever.'

Helen sounded unnaturally calm, but I didn't know exactly what they'd endured last time. I just didn't want it to escalate. 'Anyway, we're moving on aren't we, starting afresh?'

I raised my eyebrows at Helen's words.

'Sure,' I replied, knowing that it would be difficult to close the gap between us, but I'd be willing to give it a try if she would.

'Oh, here's your letter, think it's from Ashley, looks like her handwriting.' Helen passed me the envelope, which had been wedged behind the biscuit tin. It looked almost identical to the one I received inside.

'Cheers,' I replied, folding it in half and tucking it in my jean pocket.

I put a dollop of ketchup on each plate and grabbed some cutlery before taking the plates in to Mum. She was sat in her green armchair watching a game show on Channel Four.

'Dinner is served.' I put a plate on Mum's lap, a cushion beneath.

'Thanks, love. How's your week been?'

'Yeah okay, the boss's brother has been in and he's really nice.'

Mum raised her eyebrows at me, a smile playing on her lips. I didn't tell her Terry had gone missing, not wanting to open a field of questions.

'And how's your probation officer?'

'They don't call them that, Mum, it's community rehabilitation officer now, but his name is Barry and he's just about bearable.'

Mum's hand shook, and I took her fork and impaled a piece of cod on it for her.

'Well, as long as you stay out of trouble, you'll have nothing to worry about.'

I rolled my eyes, handing the fork back.

We chatted about her week, she'd managed to get up and about a bit, but it had left her drained. The stroke had a massive impact; before, she was fit and mobile, now she was weak, her body unstable. I had no idea what that had done to her mentally, having to rely on the help of others when she was fiercely independent before. Her physiotherapist wanted to work on muscle mass, but Mum had neither the patience nor inclination to be wading through a pool every week. She was a force to be reckoned with and didn't always know what was best for her.

Helen came down to leave at seven, wearing a figure-hugging dress with black tights. She was all glammed up, hair straightened and a full face of make-up. I'd never seen her so attractive.

'You look lovely,' Mum said as she came in to say goodbye.

'Gorgeous,' I added and she beamed at me. 'Have a great time.' Stuart wouldn't know what had hit him.

I'd already decided to wait until Helen came home before I left so Mum wouldn't be on her own at all. I washed up and made tea, then we sat and watched a game show, followed by an ITV drama. Come ten o'clock, Mum was yawning, so I helped her upstairs to use the bathroom and tuck her into bed.

'Love you, Mum. I'll be downstairs until Helen gets back, so shout if you need anything.'

I slipped away, heading out to the back garden to have a smoke and open Ashley's letter. It had been niggling away at me since Helen handed it over, but I wanted to read it alone.

Hey you,
I hear you're out. Can't find you on Facebook and

your old number doesn't work?
Can't wait to see you. Are you free this weekend?
I could come and visit?
Call me on 07787 547231.
Miss you,
Ash x

I read it four times, my heart swelling with each word. I really wanted to see her, but inside I was terrified. It had been over four years and we'd both changed and moved on. Our lives couldn't be more different. Seeing Ashley would reinforce all the things I'd missed out on. I knew it would, in part, be painful but I wanted to get back in touch as soon as I could muster the courage.

Helen crept back in around eleven. I woke to find her drawing a blanket over me on the sofa. I made to get up.

'No, no, it's late, stay. I'll get you up for work tomorrow,' she whispered.

Her eyes twinkled in the glow of the lamp. She must have had a good evening with Stuart as she hadn't been that nice to me for years. Yawning, I laid back, listening to the sound of Helen's footsteps padding up the stairs.

I lay awake thinking about the black and white photo and what it meant. Someone knew what had happened to Terry and I lived in constant fear the police would knock on the door. He'd never be able to hurt any of us again, but it didn't stop me seeing his clammy face every time I closed my eyes. I needed a distraction, something to take my mind off that monster and his abuse of power.

Life was for living and if I didn't put myself out there, nothing would change. I'd still be living in a bedsit with no friends and a dead-end job in a year's time. I couldn't let that happen. Perhaps tomorrow I'd be brave and ring Ashley and we'd make plans to meet. I'd apologise to Karla and see if Dan had any more viewings I could tag along to. I'd been away for four years, I couldn't live in the shadows any longer, no matter what I'd done.

23

Helen woke me in the morning around half seven. I had a crick in my neck from being wedged onto the two-seater sofa for the night. Sitting up, I rubbed the pain away, blinking sleep from my eyes.

'Bedhead!' Helen snorted as she helped Mum shuffle into her chair.

'Shut up,' I groaned, trying to flatten my double crown.

'Sleep well, love? It's nice to have you here this morning.'

I smiled at Mum, not wanting to tell her the sofa had been uncomfortable. It was nice Helen hadn't kicked me out when she got home.

'Did you have a good night with Stuart?' I asked as Helen returned with mugs of tea. There was a spring in her step, and it amazed me she would find him attractive. He did nothing for me.

'It was nice actually. I'm going around there for a curry on Friday.'

I raised my eyebrows, second date already. Perhaps she could move into the damp bedsit and I could have my old room back? I sniggered inwardly, imagining her face at the suggestion.

'Do you mind if I have a quick shower? Oh, and you don't have a pair of knickers and a T-shirt I can borrow, do you?' Wanting to capitalise on her good mood.

'Yes,' Helen rolled her eyes, 'although I already have a T-shirt missing. I can't imagine where that's gone?' She stared pointedly at me and I averted my eyes.

'Thanks,' I said before racing up the stairs. I didn't have long before I'd have to be outside to catch the bus. The last time I'd slept over, I'd been late, and I wanted to maintain the good impression I'd made with Dan.

Helen left me out some underwear and a faded

Rolling Stones T-shirt. I threw them on before heading downstairs.

'It doesn't fit me any more so you might as well keep it and bloody eat something, you're wasting away.'

'No time.' I gave Mum a kiss on the cheek and caught Helen as I went past, my lips brushing the top of her head before she pushed me away.

'Piss off,' she chuckled. Perhaps all Helen needed was a bit of romance to thaw her icy demeanour?

Drizzle descended as I headed outside and I was glad I'd pulled my hair into a bun, knowing it would frizz in the damp conditions. Hopping from one foot to the other, I waited at the bus stop, all the time trying to ignore the gaze of a man in his fifties. I could tell he was desperate to chat, but it was too early for me and I couldn't face it, especially not on an empty stomach. If I got to work early enough, I might have time to get a pastry from the café.

It seemed it was my lucky day as the 151 bus rumbled around the corner and into view. I smiled as I let the man have my seat, he appeared unsteady on his feet, and I moved further down the bus to avoid his stare. The clouds had cleared by the time I had to get off and walk the rest of the way, eventually reaching the café at quarter to nine.

'You caught me,' came a voice from behind. Hot breath hit my neck, sending a bolt down to my heels.

I spun around, Dan stood behind me in the queue, a boyish grin on his face. I stuttered a greeting, but the old bat behind the counter practically shouted, 'Next customer,' and I put my order of an almond croissant in.

'Make that two, and two cappuccinos to go please,' Dan said over my shoulder, pulling a twenty-pound note out of his pocket. He stood so close, his chest grazed my back as he leaned over to collect our breakfast.

'Thanks,' I said, and we stood out the front, eating our pastries, crumbs covering our clothes.

'These are nice!'

'You never had one before?' I asked.

'Nope, gotta watch out for the paunch,' he said, giving his non-existent stomach a tap. What was under his shirt? I imagined washboard abs and my face grew hot.

'I don't think you need to worry,' I said. 'Have you heard from Terry?' I continued, hating the false concern in my voice.

'No nothing, Kim's coming back in today, she wants to do a tour of the pubs and places she knows he goes to. I think she's got posters too. I keep ringing him, but it just goes to voicemail.'

'Has she not given the list of places to the police?'

'Yes, but she says they're dragging their heels, they think he'll turn up. He's not vulnerable according to them. I think she'll be banging on their door today too.'

I cringed inwardly. Kim clearly wasn't going to let Terry's disappearance lie.

'I've got another viewing tonight, the Sutton one you liked best. The other two were all right, liveable, but I reckon this one will be nicer.' I waited for him to ask, but he didn't. Instead we chewed in silence until I was finished, and I lit up a cigarette, prolonging our time together.

Sipping my coffee, throat as dry as sandpaper, I murmured, 'I'm free tonight, if you want me to come?' I barely heard it come out over the thud of my heart in my ears.

Dan nodded vigorously, flakes of pastry falling from his fingers as we walked slowly back to Bright's. 'Sure, that would be great. It's not until seven, but I can pick you up if you give me your address.'

'Where you two off to tonight?' Karla said, a hint of a sneer on her face as she approached, her time-card already in hand.

'Flat hunting,' Dan replied, scrunching up the paper bag and tossing it into the bin.

We all proceeded to go through the door to Bright's once Dan had punched the code in.

'You move fast, don't ya!' Karla whispered behind me as we followed Dan inside.

'Catch you later, ladies,' Dan said, heading straight into the office as we clocked in and moved round to the lockers.

'I can't deny, he's quite fit, but I like mine a bit taller,' Karla said as she watched him through the office window.

I chuckled, Karla was tiny, about five foot two, similar height to me. She'd look ridiculous with a six-foot bloke.

Karla seemed chirpy this morning and at least I wasn't getting the silent treatment any longer.

'I'm sorry about yesterday. I hate always looking over my shoulder and now I think I always will be. Paranoid the police are going to show up any minute and drag me away in handcuffs.'

Karla rolled her eyes. 'Dramatic.'

'Yeah well, *it* was "dramatic", wasn't it? To say the least and fuck knows what the photo is about.'

'Dunno, just gotta lay low. It'll blow over.' Karla shrugged, seemingly without a care in the world. I didn't know how, she had just as much to lose as me, with only one month left of parole. She must be able to smell the freedom.

We took our places, according to Dan's new rota, on washing machine number one. I loved and hated it in equal measure. It was loud and clunky but closest to the shutters where the draught came through. No doubt in the height of summer it would be a prime spot and I'd imagine that's why the rota was introduced in the first place. Until the machines got going, the warehouse was cold and I shivered in the T-shirt Helen had given me.

All morning, Karla tried to squeeze me for infor-mation on Dan, although there wasn't much to tell that she hadn't already heard from the other girls. I tried to hide the fact I liked him, but she called me out on my rosy cheeks every time he was mentioned.

Kim came in and her and Dan left for a few hours. She looked bedraggled, growing dark circles under her eyes and her bright blonde mane was tied up, her ponytail hanging limply down her back.

'Can't believe he's related to that pig,' Karla jeered as she watched them leave.

'I know. How was Barry with you yesterday?' I asked.

'Fine. He's clueless, but he's digging. Be careful with him,' she advised.

'I know. Terry owes him money,' I whispered just above the rattling of the drum on spin. Karla nodded, it seemed she already knew.

Before I left, I popped into the office to write down my address, Dan hadn't been back long. I told him I was the door to the left, 7A but the A kept falling off as Stuart had bought stupid stick-on door numbers. I wasn't too embarrassed being picked up there as Stuart's house was an attractive three-bed semi-detached which looked like it had been extended. Although I wasn't planning to invite him in.

'Great. See you around half past six, okay?'

I nodded, trying to force down the squeal threatening to burst from my chest.

24

I got the bus home, but this time was able to get a seat. My mind raced with what I'd wear, the need to have a shower and put make-up on, but also how I shouldn't look overdone. I didn't want to scare him off. My insides bubbled with excitement and I shifted in my seat, anxious to get home and get ready. Perhaps I was reading too much into it? We were only going to a viewing. Plus, Dan was at least ten years older than me, I doubted he'd be interested.

Thoughts spiralling, I almost missed my stop, having to jump off at the last minute before the doors closed as the driver tutted. I knew I wouldn't have time to call Ashley before I went out today, but I would tomorrow, and maybe by then, I'd have something interesting to share with her.

The second I saw the brown envelope on the doormat, my heart sank. I stepped over it and shut the door before reaching to scoop it up. Same as last time, same type of envelope. Blank with no address or postmark. When had it been delivered? It could have been any time in the past twenty-four hours, longer even. I hadn't been home since yesterday morning. Thoughts of Dan momentarily pushed aside, I flopped onto the bed and kicked off my trainers before ripping open the flap. Like ripping off a plaster, easier to do it quicker than drag it out.

Unsurprisingly, it was another photo and I was on my knees again. The difference was this time I was leaning over Terry's corpse. As my eyes registered the moment in the photo, I gasped for oxygen like a marooned fish.

It's just a panic attack, breathe, you can breathe. I put my head between my knees, hot tears splashing onto my hands. It wasn't until I started to feel light-headed that my body's reflexes kicked in and I sucked in a lungful of air.

This photo was different. This was proof, a

smoking gun so to speak. Another shot of the top of my head, nothing of my face, but you could see my T-shirt and its logo. I screwed the paper up into a ball and launched it across the room. I had to get ready. I didn't have time to be tormented by some faceless person, I had to get going if I was going to be ready for Dan. There was no way Terry was ruining the first glimpse of a normal life for me.

The shower was boiling, cleansing my thoughts, and I emerged, skin glowing pink but my head calmer. It must be someone fucking with me. No one had turned up at my door asking for money or trying to blackmail me. What was the point otherwise? If they wanted to scare me, then yeah, I was scared, but what could I do? Go to the police? Not an option. I had to take comfort that whoever it was who had the photos, or video, they hadn't gone to the police yet either. Was it because there must have been photos of us all? Was every girl that got called into Terry's office filmed in their depraved acts? I wanted to talk to Karla, but there was no time. I sent a quick text.

I've had another one delivered

It was difficult to steady my tremoring hands so I could apply make-up, not a lot, just a little to cover the dark circles and emphasise my eyes. Perusing the limited choice of clothes for something to wear, I sighed. Everything was so casual, but there was a white fluffy jumper which would look okay with jeans and biker boots. It would have to do. Even though the jiffy bag full of money was hidden under the mattress, I still hadn't got around to spending any of it. I brushed my hair, trying to control the white blonde static strands flying around.

Before I knew it, there was a knock at the door and Dan stood outside, his car keys in his hand. I was vaguely disappointed he was still in the same clothes he wore to work but reminded myself it wasn't a date; we were going to look at a maisonette. *Don't get carried away, Jess*, my inner voice chipped in. I pulled the door closed quickly behind me, thrusting on my bomber jacket and pocketing the keys.

'All right?' Dan asked. His eyes were bright, and he seemed in good spirits.

I couldn't help but smile. It was infectious. He was the exact opposite to Karla, whom I seemed to spend most of my time with. She hadn't text me back yet.

'Good thanks. Fingers crossed this is the one,' I replied as we approached the car.

Dan stepped ahead and opened the passenger door for me. Eyes to the ground, I stifled a girlish giggle.

'Hopefully. I need to get something sorted as the hotel is costing a fortune and so are all the take-aways.' His eyes twinkled as he started the car and we pulled away. He drove a silver Mazda 3; it was gorgeous and sleek. A car I'd love to own.

'Don't you have any family who can put you up?'

'Nah, my mum and dad have both passed away, cancer got them both, two years apart.'

'I'm sorry,' I said, watching Dan's eye twitch for a second. Couldn't Kim put him up? Perhaps he didn't know her very well?

'No bother, was years ago now. In fact, I'm glad they aren't here: Terry was Mum's favourite, she'd be going mad about now with him missing.'

The satnav instructed Dan to turn right and he stopped sharply and indicated.

'Sorry, wasn't concentrating.'

'That's okay. Did you get anywhere with Kim today?'

Dan shook his head as he made the turn, his large hands sliding the wheel in his palms. I was mesmerised. 'Not really, we took some flyers around she'd printed. Asked at the pubs where he was a regular. She did pick the car up though. Police have said they've found nothing on CCTV as to where he went once he left his car and there's been no transactions from his bank account. Fuck knows where he is.'

I looked away, out of the window at the enormous houses flying by as my shoulders relaxed.

They weren't looking too hard for him. Karla was right, no body, no crime. Thank God there had been no CCTV where we left the car.

'I'm going to keep the pressure on though. It all seems dodgy to me. He was happy with Kim as I understood it. They have Harriet, my niece, too. I thought things were fine between them.'

I swallowed hard, the lump in my throat growing as the satnav announced we were at our destination. Perhaps we weren't off the hook after all.

25

I didn't wait for Dan to open the door for me, he wasn't a chauffeur and it would have been weird, so I jumped out. He had parked behind the estate agent's tiny Smart car, the logo branded on the side. In a flash, the smartly dressed man who looked barely older than twelve was beside us.

'Hi, Dan, I'm Paul,' he said with a kilowatt smile, shaking Dan's hand and nodding a greeting at Jess. 'Shall we go in?'

From the pavement, the house loomed large, with external oak beams, whitewash walls and bay windows. One big house split into two maisonettes. The entrance to the upstairs maisonette that we were going to see was around the side. Dan cast his eye over the pristine front garden, striped lawn and raised flower beds filled with shrubs.

'The lady below you, she's green-fingered as I understand it. A widow in her seventies,' Paul whispered as he unlocked the dark blue front door.

Dan leaned back and like a ventriloquist's dummy whispered, 'I hope she's not deaf. I don't want to be listening to *Coronation Street* every night.'

I sniggered beneath my hand.

The maisonette had been painted white throughout; modern cube-style furniture filled the space. I could imagine Dan sitting at the breakfast bar on the tall stool, spooning cereal into his mouth.

'What are you smiling at?' Dan asked, grinning too.

'It's nice, I can imagine you here.'

'Through there is the bedroom.' Paul held his hand out for us to walk through. 'Plenty of storage for clothes, I know you girls always have a lot of clothes.' He winked and I chuckled.

'We're not—'

'No, I'm not—' I interrupted Dan. I bit my lip, stifling a laugh as our eyes met and Dan's neck mottled.

'Oh, sorry. Never assume,' Paul berated himself.

Dan stopped in the kitchen to have a chat to Paul about the rent and what furniture was included. I moved around from room to room, imagining living here. My *Magic Faraway Tree* book on the bedside table and toothbrush in the holder. It was a far cry from my bedsit and something I'd never be able to afford.

'You ready?' Dan said, popping his head into the room. My fantasy evaporated immediately.

'Sure.'

We climbed into the car and watched Paul drive away.

'Shall we celebrate?'

'Celebrate?'

'It's mine, just got to fill out the paperwork, supply references and a deposit, but I can move in at the weekend.'

'Fantastic!'

Dan started the engine and we drove back the way we came.

'There we go, I saw this on the way past, looks all right, doesn't it?' he asked, pulling up outside a pub called the Black Swan.

I fished around in my pockets. Shit. I'd left my purse at home. 'Ummm.'

Spotting my reluctance, Dan piped up, 'My treat to say thanks for coming, just one drink and I'll take you home.' He raised his eyebrows, trying to look cute. It wasn't as if I wasn't keen, although I assumed he believed otherwise. I just didn't want to look foolish with no money.

'Okay, yes. Thank you.'

Pushing open the double doors, the pub was full of people, but Dan quickly directed us to a small round table next to the open-hearth fire that had just been vacated. I clocked us getting daggers from a couple propping up the bar who obviously had been intending to claim the table, but I shrugged off my coat and tossed my hair back as though I believed I had every right to be there.

'What can I get you?' Dan asked, pulling his wallet from his jacket and placing it on the back of the chair.

'Vodka and Coke please.'

He disappeared to the bar and I looked around at the punters. Couples mainly and a group of suited men in their fifties who had popped in after work it looked like and were yet to go home. My stomach rumbled, reminding me I hadn't had any dinner. Perhaps I should ask Dan for a packet of crisps?

A second later, he was back with my vodka, sliding into his chair as I was already gulping it down, enjoying the familiar burn of the alcohol.

Dan's eyes widened momentarily as I realised I'd necked half my drink, but he was too polite to mention it. I placed it back on the table.

My hands fidgeted in my lap. This was like a proper date and I'd not been on one before. I wasn't sure how I was supposed to act.

'I'm pleased about the maisonette. It's a weight off my mind, now I can concentrate on what I'm doing with Bright's and finding that bloody brother of mine.'

'How long will you stay?' I asked.

'The contract on the maisonette is six months, then we'll see. I was due to come back anyway. Terry wanted to talk about expanding, but it looks like Bright's needs a good going-over – the accounts, the lease of the machines, not to mention the rent. The price of the yard is extortionate for example, it should be included in the overall cost, but it's charged as an extra.'

I nodded, soaking up the information.

'What did Barry want earlier?' I asked.

'He was just asking about Terry, if I had any idea where he was. I find him a bit abrasive actually, do you? He's your parole officer, isn't he?'

'Yeah, of sorts. He comes in to meet with us weekly.'

Dan nodded. 'I must admit I was surprised when Terry suggested we look at hiring ex-offenders. He said Bright's could be a way to re-enter society, giving local girls a second chance.'

I almost choked on my drink. Dan really had the wool pulled down over his eyes. Terry sounded like some kind of fucking philanthropist!

I smiled tightly and mumbled in agreement. Dan looked at me quizzically and I thought he was going to ask what I'd been in prison for. Everyone always did eventually, but instead he rose to his feet.

'One more?' he asked, the empty glass in his hand, moving towards the bar before I could answer. I drained my glass although I knew I was drinking too fast.

He returned with another vodka and I took it, nodding gratefully. He had a half pint glass. Would he be over the limit? I guessed he knew his tolerance.

'It's a shandy.' He grinned, watching me frown at his glass.

I blushed; he didn't miss a thing.

'Do you think you'll sell Bright's?' I asked.

'Terry will be a bit pissed off if I did. Not sure I could anyway without his signature. It's a real mess, and to be honest, it's not what I want to do, hence me being a silent partner. Terry will come back eventually; he's probably holed up somewhere with a bit on the side. I don't know.' There didn't seem to be much love lost between them. Dan had already mentioned Terry was the favourite of their parents and perhaps their inheritance had been poured into Bright's?

'Has he gone off before?'

Dan nodded and gave the slightest roll of the eyes as he took a mouthful of his drink. 'You'd think I was the older one out of the two of us.' Perhaps that's why the police hadn't seemed overly interested at first?

I pulled on my earlobe; it was my fault Dan's life had been turned upside down.

'What sort of boss was he?'

I opened my mouth to speak, but Dan's face looked so earnest and my chest tightened in anticipation of the words I was about to say. He didn't want to know the truth and I couldn't tell him. Instead I drank to buy myself some time.

'Oh, say no more,' he said, his voice low. I'd taken too long to answer. I blinked rapidly, trying to focus and ignore the alcohol swishing around my empty stomach.

'Did you two not get on?' I asked, filling the silence. Dan took a moment, rubbing the stubble on his cheek, as though he was choosing his words carefully.

'Yes and no. There was a bit of sibling rivalry, but that's common right?' I nodded, knowing only too well what that was like.

'Our parents gave us the money to start up Bright's, the condition was we had to work together. It was to be a family business. Hence the reason I opted to move around, source the machines, buying and selling was my part and Terry managed the operation,' he continued.

'Makes sense,' I replied.

'I left the running of things to him, it's only now I wished I'd got more involved.'

Dan checked the time, it was gone nine, the past couple of hours had flown by.

'Right, I better get you home in case you turn into a pumpkin.' He chuckled, downing what was left of his drink. I followed suit.

I slipped on my coat, stumbling slightly as I stood and hoping he hadn't noticed. Had those drinks been singles or doubles? I was a bit light-headed and it worsened when the cold air hit me outside.

We got into the Mazda and Dan chatted about music all the way home and what he liked to listen to. I nodded in the right places, trying to snap out of the wooziness. Had Dan slipped something into my drink? I blinked hard, trying to remember what I'd eaten today, not much by all accounts. That must be it.

'Thanks for coming with me. I appreciated a second pair of eyes,' Dan said as we pulled up outside the bedsit.

'No worries. Thanks for the drinks. See you tomorrow,' I said, climbing out of the car.

Dan was beside me in a second, walking me to

the front door. Nerve endings tingled with anticipation as I considered inviting him in. No, it was too forward. He was my boss and I had no idea if he was even interested, plus the place was a mess and I was tipsy.

As we reached the step, he leaned in to kiss me on the cheek. I don't know what possessed me, but I turned my face towards his so his lips grazed mine instead.

He stepped back; brow furrowed.

'Jess, I'm not sure...' he began, but I kissed him again, not waiting for him to finish.

Caught in the moment, I didn't care I was being forward, and after a second, he relented, wrapping his arms around me, reining me in until we couldn't get any closer. Everything seemed to spin, and I wasn't sure if it was the alcohol or the ecstasy of being kissed, it had been so long. Eventually we pulled apart and I held on to Dan's forearm to steady myself.

'Do you want to come in?'

26

We made it across the threshold just long enough for me to kick the scrunched-up photo left by the front door to the side before we were entangled again. Being kissed by Dan felt heavenly, my body responded to his touch without hesitation. Goosebumps peppered my skin, the new sensations made me breathless. We shuffled the short distance to my bed, where I hesitated.

'I've never done this before,' I panted.

'Wait, never done what?' Dan pulled away from me, the spell broken.

'This.' I looked away, unable to bear his incredulous expression.

'I'm sorry, I shouldn't have let it get this far.' He paused, looking abashed. 'It's been a while.'

I felt like an idiot. I'd made a pass at my new boss and now he was backtracking. For a stupid second, the telltale tickle in my nose started, announcing the onset of tears.

'It's my fault,' he said, backing away and picking his jacket up from the floor. I hadn't even remembered it coming off. Where was he going?

'You're leaving?'

'Yeah, I better go, Jess. I'll see you tomorrow. Thanks for coming with me tonight.'

After he left, I flung myself onto the bed and sighed loudly. I'd made a fool of myself. I should never have said anything.

I pushed off my shoes and checked my phone, still no response from Karla. Where was she? I wrapped the duvet around me, letting my head swim.

* * *

Nausea hit as soon as I woke, my stomach cramping, and it took a coffee and numerous slices of toast before

I could think about the shower. At least it was Friday. I'd ring Ashley today and see if she was free to come back from Portsmouth at the weekend. Perhaps Dan would invite me round once he'd moved into the maisonette? I squirmed as I imagined seeing him at work. The way he'd left was awkward. He probably thought I was weird. How could I explain it just hadn't happened for me before I got put away? The memory of his hands on my skin, pressure that remained long after he'd gone, I'd be lying if I said I didn't want it again.

I shuffled in to work, ears ringing and head cloudy like I'd been through a wind tunnel. All this from four vodkas? Assuming they'd been doubles?

'Hiya,' Agnes and Laura said almost in unison as they waited behind me to clock in.

'Morning. Thank God it's Friday,' I grumbled.

Dan was in the office, deep in conversation with Barry.

'What's he doing here again this week?' I asked.

Laura shrugged, twisting the stud in her nose. 'God knows, probably trying to find someone else to pimp us to.'

'Ain't that the truth.' Karla slipped in beside me as we walked around to the lockers.

'Your stud is pretty,' I said, turning to Laura.

'Thanks, my boyfriend gave it to me. Our three-month anniversary.' Laura smiled and practically skipped away; in my peripheral version, I saw Karla roll her eyes.

'Did you get my text? I got another photo?'

Karla shook her head and checked her phone like she'd not seen my message.

I tutted as I opened my locker, about to lift my bag inside but froze, dropping it to the floor.

'What is it?' Karla asked.

I opened my mouth to speak, but nothing came out. A gold wedding band sat on the base of the locker. I picked it up with my thumb and forefinger, peering at the inscription and clutching my middle like I'd been hit in the gut with a sledgehammer. My legs buckled and I flattened my palms on the locker doors to keep myself upright.

'What? What is it?' Karla's eyes were like slits.

I pushed the ring into her hand, trying to abstain from heaving.

Karla lurched backwards, fearing I was about to be sick all over her. Nothing came and I inhaled deeply, wiping my mouth with my forearm. She eyed the ring, holding it in front of her as though she was Frodo, as it glistened in the overhead fluorescent lights. 'Kim + Terry' engraved on the inside of the band.

Karla's mouth gaped, but as footsteps approached, she dropped the ring into the palm of her hand and closed her fist around it.

'Morning,' Hanna said brightly as she busied herself with her locker.

I slipped on my tabard and dumped my bag, closing the locker and striding out of the cramped area into the warehouse.

'You're on the press today, hon,' Agnes called as I slowed by the rota.

'Cheers.' My shoulders ached in protest as I knew what was to come. The press machine was tough, feeding the cloth in, arms up most of the time. I didn't have the energy today. 'Where the fuck did that come from?' I hissed to Karla as she fell in step behind me.

'Someone must know what we did?' She scanned the area, making sure no one was in earshot.

'You think? Two photos through my door and now this! Who?'

'I don't know.' Karla's voice had an edge to it I hadn't heard before. Fear?

Limbs jittery I walked to the presser. Who was tormenting me?

'Have you had anything?' I asked.

Karla shook her head and I chewed the inside of my cheek.

'Why me?'

'No fixed address, remember.' I wasn't sure how that could be true. Didn't Barry need to have a permanent address? Wasn't it part of parole conditions to stop us turning back to a life of crime? I frowned at Karla but she was distracted unloading a trolley, the discovery of the ring seemingly forgotten. I wish I had her ability to compartmentalise. Perhaps throwing myself into the task was the answer.

Thankfully, we had tablecloths instead of sheets to press, which made the job easier due to the amount of fabric involved. Karla and I got to it, barely speaking as we fed the linen over the rolls and watched it go in the machine, ready to catch it as it came out. My mind was working overtime, trying to figure out who had it in for us.

'Hey.' Dan stood behind me, his hands on his

hips.

'Hi,' I replied.

His eyes darted around the warehouse, like they couldn't settle on my face for too long. Was he nervous? Embarrassed?

I rubbed my ear and the machine halted. Karla had paused it, eyeing the awkward exchange between us as the silence stretched out.

'I'm going for a piss,' she exclaimed, striding off.

'How are you?' I ventured.

'Fine. You?' Dan asked.

I nodded weakly.

'I'm sorry about last night,' he said.

'What for?' I frowned.

'You know. I took advantage, and it went too far. You've been so nice, and I don't really know anyone here other than Kim.' He pushed his hands into his pockets, deep creases in his forehead.

'I wasn't the one who wanted to stop,' I said flatly.

He didn't respond.

'You ready?' Karla was back, her hand hovering over the green button to start the machine.

Dan cleared his throat. 'I wanted to make sure

you've been paid as normal. I've had issues with the payroll system, but the company tell me it's done.'

Karla pulled out her smartphone, logging on to her bank to check her account straight away.

I didn't move but carried on staring at Dan, watching him, watching her. I ached for him and blushed as soon as the revelation hit me, as though everyone might be able to read my mind.

'Yep. It's gone in,' Karla confirmed.

'Great.' Dan smiled. 'Catch you later,' Dan said to both of us, his gaze resting on me for a second longer than necessary, trying to convey a message I didn't comprehend. I watched him walk away.

'Jesus, what's gone on with you two?' Karla said as soon as he was gone.

'Nothing,' I said truthfully.

27

I hung back when Karla left, hoping Dan would corner me, steal a kiss or even take my number, but he was nowhere to be seen. Like a schoolgirl with a stupid crush, I slunk out of the warehouse last. It was only then I remembered Karla had kept Terry's ring. Perhaps it was for the best, I'd lose it or leave it somewhere for someone to find accidentally, with my fingerprints all over it. Fingerprints which were in the system. Fuck. I hadn't considered that. I hoped Karla would keep it safe. She was the smartest of us. It would be fair to say I wasn't a career criminal and if Karla hadn't been there to save my skin it's likely my kiss with Dan wouldn't have happened at all. I still had flashes of guilt for Terry, but whenever the image of us tipping his body into the incinerator entered my mind, it was quickly replaced by Karla's face as he pummelled her across his desk.

I got on the bus to go home; partially glad it was Friday but also aware I wouldn't see Dan until next week. My shoulders sagged at the thought. I'd have to keep busy, otherwise I'd be sulking around all weekend. Helen hadn't been in touch and I had no idea if her date with Stuart was still on. My mind had been on other things, but I was sure if she needed me to sit with Mum she would have asked. I called anyway, just in case, but as usual it went to voicemail. Helen rarely picked up the phone on the first attempt.

Unlocking my front door, I steeled myself for another brown envelope, but there was nothing on the carpet. I felt lighter as I stepped over the threshold. After the wedding ring in my locker this morning, I'd had about as much as I could take as far as surprises were concerned. Where had it even come from? Was Terry wearing it when he died?

That whole day was such a blur, I couldn't remember. Someone knew what had happened, but I had no idea what their game was? It was freaking me out though. I'd bitten my nails to the quick and the vodka was disappearing fast. Living on a knife-edge was not much fun. I just had to keep my nose clean for the next five months and the threat of being hauled back to prison for the slightest misdemeanour wouldn't hang over me. A noose tight around my throat, ready to yank at any time.

I had a quick shower, put on my joggers and microwaved a cottage pie before I settled on my bed. Lighting a cigarette, I read Ashley's letter laid in my lap, her swirly handwriting was so pretty.

My mouth filled up with saliva as I dialled the number she had written; the thud of my heartbeat sounding in my ears. She answered almost straight away, and I was momentarily tongue-tied.

'Hello?'

I opened my mouth, but no words escaped, a wave of sadness washed over me, and my eyes swam with tears.

'Hello? Jess?'

'Ash,' I croaked, wiping the dampness away. I hadn't expected to be overwhelmed, but her voice was a blast from the past.

'Oh, Jess, I'm so glad you called. How are you?' She sounded excited to hear from me, the background noise I initially heard quietened, like she'd stepped out of a busy bar into a corridor or a side street.

'I'm okay. I'm home, well not home exactly, but close. I'm near there. Working at an industrial laundry. How's Portsmouth? How's the degree?'

'It's great, hard work, but still good to be... away.' I forgot that even though I was the one who went to prison, Ashley had to put up with the stares and local gossip. The only one still around from that night, with a lot of unanswered questions after the accident.

'I'm pleased for you.' It sounded weak, but I meant it. If anyone deserved to get out it was her.

'Are you free tomorrow? I can get the train down, take you out for lunch, go shopping?'

'Sure, I'd love to see you. You've got my number now, text me and let me know when you're arriving, and I'll meet you at the station.'

'Okay great, I think there's a train that arrives around lunchtime. I'll text you.'

'Ash, come on Happy Hour is almost over and we

need to get some shots,' a screechy voice interrupted, and the line was muffled for a second.

'Sorry about that. Can't wait to see you, Jess. I mean it. It's been too long.'

We said our goodbyes and the line went dead. Just over four years, that was how long it had been. I'd served four years of my sentence, the judge had been specific, those years to be spent in prison, no early release allowed, followed by another six months of probation. Four years for a life. Even I wasn't sure it was enough.

I lit another cigarette and poured myself a vodka, hands shaking, Ash's voice echoing in my ears. Excited and apprehensive in equal measure to see her tomorrow. There were so many things left unsaid. How would we even begin to fill the crevice between us? Or did we accept that was then and move on with our lives? I guessed we could never go back; we couldn't change what had happened. I'd never reclaim the years I'd lost, but it wasn't her fault. We were both victims, I just happened to be the one behind the wheel.

* * *

I stood outside the train station, loitering on the pavement and chain-smoking, which didn't help the tension in my chest. I'd been having mild anxiety all morning, my stomach in knots, multiple trips to the bathroom. Even agonised over what to wear, like I was meeting Dan and not my oldest friend who likely wouldn't care if I turned up in a bin bag.

Ashley had texted me her arrival time of half past eleven; she'd boarded the train just after nine. Would she arrive in a hangover fog?

I paced back and forth, ignoring the pangs of hunger because I hadn't been able to make myself eat anything.

Suddenly there she was, walking out of the station archway, looking around for me. Her dark waves lifted by the breeze.

I stuck my hand out and waved, watching her face fall for a split second before she caught herself. I knew I looked different, thinner and drawn. An enormous flash of teeth illuminated her face and she threw open her arms, rushing towards me.

We collided together and I buried my face in her zebra-print fur coat, fearing I would cry, but when I pulled away, Ashley was the one who'd crumpled.

She sobbed so hard; her body heaved. I squeezed her tightly and it was just like before, me looking after her.

'Sorry,' she sniffed, dabbing her eyes with an old tissue pulled from her bag.

'It's okay. You look great.' Ashley wore dangly earrings and rolled-up jeans with Doc Martens. The epitome of cool to my scruffy attire. Was that what all university students wore? At least Ashley would be perfect to help me with a new wardrobe.

'So do you,' she said automatically, but I knew she was being polite.

'I look anything but great,' I replied with a snigger.

'Okay,' she conceded, 'you do look like you could do with a good meal, you're so skinny!' Ashley linked her arm through mine as we walked towards the high street and, for a second, the years between us melted away.

28

The next few hours were a whirlwind. I learnt Ashley's new passion was fashion and she took me under her wing, dragging me in every shop and providing me with clothes to try on. Her face lit up when something looked good; she was in her element and I was happy to go along with it. Although we were both aware of the elephant in the room. I kept catching Ashley stare at me when she thought I wasn't looking, like she wasn't sure I was real.

Shopping was a success and we were both shattered. I'd spent over two hundred pounds on skinny jeans, tops, trainers, a coat and a dress which made me look as though I had some curves. Maybe I'd make Dan's eyes pop with it someday. Laden with bags, we flopped into a booth in the nearest café, hoping for a cheese toastie and a cuppa, a very late lunch.

'I thought students were supposed to be skint?' I said, nodding towards the shopping underneath the table.

'I have two jobs, you know, nannying at the weekends, but thankfully they are away this week, hence why I was out last night.'

'And the other one?'

'Waitressing three evenings a week at the local Italian.'

'Where do you find the time to study?'

Ashley let out a long sigh as she perused the menu. 'When I'm supposed to be sleeping. I need a heavy-duty concealer!'

After deciding what to eat, I put our order in at the till, grateful Ashley hadn't questioned why I had over three hundred pounds in cash in my purse, until she'd helped me spend it.

It was lovely to be back together, but all the time we were shopping, it was there lingering between us, words left unsaid. I wanted to clear the air.

'Thanks for writing to me – inside, I mean. I'm sorry I didn't want you to visit,' I said. My words came out in a rush as I delivered the mugs of tea from the counter.

'It's okay, I understand. I couldn't wait to get out of here afterwards. The accident was all anyone talked about.' Ashley's mouth twitched, something I'd forgotten she did when she was uncomfortable. She looked down at her mug, eyes damp. The mere mention of such a painful time brought back strong emotions for us both. If I knew Ashley, she would have buried it deep inside, pretended it never happened. I bet she hated being the topic of speculation, knowing it would have gone on for months. No wonder Helen had felt harassed, Ashley would have been too. 'Everyone wanted to know what happened. I hated lying about it,' she whispered, her eyes darting around the café to see who was listening as she wiped them with her sleeve.

'Why did you lie?' I leaned forward. It was a question I'd never asked, assuming I knew the truth, that in some way her lying about the accident sold me out. I'd accepted it, the fact was I'd killed someone, no matter what went before it.

'Protecting Eddie's memory, I guess. Perhaps if I'd told the truth, things might have been different.' Ashley gazed down at her mug again, sniffing, and I placed my hand over hers, unsure what to say, because she might have been right, and I didn't want to think about that. 'I'm so sorry, Jess.'

'It doesn't matter now. I wanted you to get out of here and go to university with a clear conscience.'

Ashley coughed, swallowing a mouthful of tea. 'I never had that.'

'Sorry, that came out wrong. I meant, I didn't want you ruining your opportunity by staying behind. I didn't want to drag you down with me.'

Ashley weaved her fingers through mine and squeezed, ignoring the look from the waitress delivering our cheese toasties. She looked devastated and I remembered that she'd carried so much, would have felt so guilty that she'd been handed her own self-imposed sentence too. I knew Ashley; she was kind, it would have been a blow when I asked her not to write, but I didn't do it out of malice. I knew it would be easier for us both to move on. We couldn't change what happened, however much we wanted to.

I leaned back in my seat, and sighed, blinking back tears that were threatening to spill. I knew if I started crying, I probably wouldn't stop. I picked up my sandwich and took a bite, leaking hot cheese back onto the plate.

'How often do you go back to see your mum and dad?' I asked, knowing Ashley's relationship with her parents deteriorated after the accident. They blamed me, which was always going to happen. I was the wrong crowd, the dodgy friend. Ashley was practically middle class; everyone knew she hung out with us on the estate because she fancied a bit of rough. She certainly got it with Eddie Watts. He was more than she ever bargained for.

'They moved once I left, they're in Chichester now, so I see them around once a month or so. My nan and grandad are still around here.' Ashley took a bite of her sandwich, the cheese stretching out.

I was almost halfway through mine, my appetite from earlier rushing back.

'So any guy... or girl action I should know about?' Ashley winked and I almost choked on the bread as I swallowed.

'Guy, and no. Honestly, Ash, I'm still as clueless

as I was before.' Remembering hours spent moaning about my lack of experience when she stayed over. She had been more worldly back then, spilling the beans on how it all worked and what Eddie and she got up to. Boys gravitated to her vivacious personality and she was never short of offers, but I kept myself to myself, too shy to get involved.

'There's plenty of time, no need to rush into anything you'll regret.' Wise words as ever, combined with a stab of jealousy that I knew was going to raise its head eventually. I forced it away.

'There is a guy at work, the boss,' I confessed.

'At the launderette?' Ashley licked her fingers and wiped them on her serviette.

'It's an industrial laundry! It's massive, not a bloody launderette,' I said with a shake of my head.

'Sorry you did say. So is he older?'

'Yeah, in his thirties.' I slurped my tea, now lukewarm.

'Well, let him chase you, make him bloody work for it.' Ashley chuckled, her laugh infectious. We finished our sandwiches quickly, stomachs groaning in appreciation.

'I've missed you so much.' My bottom lip quivered, and I gritted my teeth, refusing to cry in public.

Ashley put down her mug and grabbed my other hand across the table, our arms stretched, hands clasped, mine icy cold as always. Her deep brown eyes bored into mine, desperate to convey every ounce of emotion. 'I'm so sorry for what happened.'

'It's okay, stop apologising, you've done it enough. It wasn't your fault either.' I leaned forward, squeezing her hands.

'I got you caught up in it.' Ashley's chin wobbled.

I couldn't defend her there, it was true. If she hadn't called me that night for a lift, it would never have happened.

'How bad was it?' Ashley whispered, shuddering as though someone had walked over her grave.

Before I could answer, the waitress came to collect our plates, chewing gum rhythmically and we released hands, sliding them back to our halves of the table.

'I've had better holidays.' I managed a smile.

Ashley grimaced.

'Let's not talk about it. Tell me all about university, I want to hear everything, so you're not allowed to leave anything out.'

Two lattes and a shared slice of Bakewell tart later and all talk of my incarceration was forgotten. My jaw ached from laughing at Ashley's outlandish stories of Freshers' week; being locked out of her room wearing next to nothing, to waking up last summer in the local park with no memory of how she got there. I was surprised her liver was still functioning.

We slipped back into our routine of banter, the easy way we were together, like nothing had changed, although in reality everything had.

At five o'clock, we left the café, the waitress giving us evils as she wiped the surrounding empty tables. Ashley's train was at half past five and I regretted not asking her to stay over. When I mentioned it, she said she had an early-morning lecture on Monday, and she was going to spend Sunday catching up on the studying she'd missed.

We looped arms to walk back up the high street towards the station, watching the shops start to shut up for the day.

'It was fun though, wasn't it, before Eddie, when

we'd knock around with that lot on the estate.' Ashley giggled as she spoke.

'Yeah it was, got into a few scrapes, didn't we?'

'Remember the time Whizzie and, God who was the other one, bad acne?'

'Gilby?' His face instantly in my mind.

'Yeah, Gilby, when they jumped out of the taxi on the way back from Brixton,' Ashley said, and I sniggered, recalling my heart leaping into my throat as I had a crush on Whizzie at the time.

'When it was still moving, yep I remember. Such idiots.' I winced inwardly remembering the last time I saw Gilby, shouting at me in the street a few weeks ago.

'Those were the days.' Ashley bumped my hip and our bags swung, colliding together.

We reached the station and Ashley pulled me into a hug.

'I've had a great day; it's been lovely to see you. I'll be back in a couple of weeks or you can come to me maybe?'

'I'd like that.' A change of scene would do me good.

I watched her disappear into the station before

retracing my steps to wait for the bus. I could walk home, but my arms were already aching from the weight of the bags. I felt emotionally drained but as though a weight had been lifted. Ashley was okay, she was doing fine, and I would be too.

I didn't have to wait long before the 151 came, taking me all the way home, past my mum's house. The bus was busy, but I got a space by the window, my bags on my lap. As we approached the looming white hospital and the estate I used to frequent as a kid, the bus came to a halt, waiting to turn left. Craning my neck, I saw the frizzy curls first, before recognising Karla, her petite frame in Adidas tracksuit bottoms leaning against the road sign for Blenheim Court. She was laughing, her head thrown back, talking to someone, with their hood up.

The bus jerked forward and turned. Karla didn't see me as we passed by, but when I saw the pockmarked face of her companion, I instantly recognised Gilby.

29

What was Karla doing with Gilby? I didn't think she lived over this way; she lived nearer Bright's. Had she told me that before? I couldn't remember and anyway how did she know Gilby? Thoughts jumbled, I had meant to jump off the bus and pop in at Mum's for a cup of tea but missed the stop.

When I got home, I pushed Karla from my mind and set about giving the bedsit a good clean, wiping all the surfaces, cleaning the fridge and changing the sheets. I borrowed Stuart's hoover – something else I'd have to get of my own. He was more than happy to lend it to me when I handed over an envelope containing the next two months' rent. I had to spend

Terry's money on something, and a roof over my head was vital.

Tomorrow I wanted to get a new phone, a smart-phone. I was going to get back out in the world, back onto social media. I'd decided while I was out shopping with Ashley. I'd served my time and had to start living again. Fed up of being on the sidelines, coasting until my sentence was up.

Once the bedsit was clean and tidy, I gathered up my washing, ready to take to Mum's, and looked at what food I had left. There wasn't much, the fridge now empty, apart from milk, and my bread had gone mouldy. Another chore to do tomorrow.

Filling the kettle with water, I found a pasta sachet at the back of the cupboard that would do for dinner and rang Helen while I waited for it to boil.

'All right?' I said when she answered it, amazed it hadn't gone to voicemail.

'Hiya.'

'How was your date, did you come over last night?'

'No, he cancelled. Have you seen Stuart?'

'Yeah, I just borrowed the hoover.'

'Did he mention me?'

'No, afraid not.' I poured the pasta into a bowl, the powdered sauce spilling over the side.

'Oh.' Things must have obviously stalled on the romance front.

'Did he say why he had to cancel?' I asked and listened to Helen mumble something about his sister which I didn't catch. It sounded like she was cooking, pans clattered in the background. 'I'm going to come over tomorrow, can you ask Mum if I can use the washing machine again?'

Helen shouted my request out to Mum, who called back it was fine.

'I've got to go, Mum needs feeding,' Helen said brusquely and hung up. Her award-winning personality had resumed. I knew it was too good to be true. Mum didn't need feeding, she wasn't a toddler, Helen just had to cook a meal – she was so dramatic.

My mind returned to Karla. I knew it was a small world, but it was funny she knew Gilby. Did she know Whizzie and Eddie too? It reminded me I still knew nothing about Karla. She kept her cards close to her chest, never giving anything away. Was she like that with everyone, or just me? Maybe I was being paranoid. The photos and Terry's wedding band had put my nerves on edge. I had no choice but to carry on, burying my head in the sand and hoping whoever it was went away.

* * *

On Sunday morning, I got over to Mum's early to put the washing on. I had to nip to Tesco and offered to get Helen some bits too. I managed to get a new phone in the supermarket, sick at handing over such a large amount in cash for the cheapest Samsung smartphone they sold. I checked my account at the cashpoint, seeing I'd been paid, although I used Terry's money to buy the phone. Squeezing it into my inside jacket pocket before I left the shop; certain I would get mugged before I made it home again. I'd never spent that amount of money on one item before.

I struggled back with the bags, keeping my eyes peeled for Karla, but she wasn't around. What relationship Karla and Gilby had was still niggling at me, I just couldn't work out what they were to each other? Old friends? Something more? It was no surprise there was no sign of either of them. Most people my age would be in bed with a hangover, not surfacing until Sunday afternoon. I had deep red indents on my palms from the handles when I finally reached Mum's, nerve endings firing in my arms even though my hands were numb.

Helen helped me unpack and I told her and Mum about my shopping day with Ashley. Mum was pleased that we'd met up again and said next time to bring her round, she'd love to see her. Mum always had a soft spot for Ashley, even after the accident. Helen was in a better mood as Stuart had called while I'd been out and arranged to take her for a Toby Carvery.

I offered to take Mum for lunch so she wouldn't feel left out, but she didn't fancy it, her leg ached, and she hadn't slept well the night before.

'Thanks, love, but I'd much rather eat here. I can stay in my nightie and *Carry on Camping* is on the TV this afternoon.'

'Are they even still showing those?' I sighed, remembering being forced to listen to Mum cackling every time a Carry On film was on.

'I love them, reminds me of being a kid,' she said wistfully.

I had no idea how to cook a roast, so I couldn't offer Mum the same service at home, but I did cook spaghetti bolognaise, out of a jar, with garlic bread. Mum needed a bit of help with some unruly spaghetti, but otherwise it was great and once the film got going, it was like putting on a comfy pair of slippers. We sat back, giggling at Sid James. Now I understood all the jokes I was able to appreciate how funny it was.

'They wouldn't get away with half the stuff now, you know,' Mum said.

After dinner, I set up the Samsung with the new SIM, getting my PAC code and sending it on to my new provider so I could keep my number. I spent ages downloading the apps I thought I'd need before transferring the handful of numbers across from the ancient flip phone.

'Mum, who cuts yours and Helen's hair?' I asked, as I looked at the phone on my lap, my hair across my shoulders, all my split ends apparent. I hadn't had a proper haircut for years.

'Donna still comes every month.'

'Really? That's great, would you mind if I came by next time she's here? I need at least two inches off; it's got so long. I was thinking of doing the ends a lilac colour.' Positive it would be a great contrast with the white blonde.

'It'll be on the calendar in the kitchen, love, end of the month, I think.'

I checked the calendar and on 12 February Donna's name was inscribed in the box. I flicked back to January and saw right at the beginning of the year, JESS HOME had been written in capitals, followed by lots of exclamation marks.

Stuart brought Helen home a little while later and stayed for a cup of tea while I washed up. Mum hadn't met Stuart yet, although she knew him as the 'nice young man who had let her delinquent daughter live at his house'.

Helen floated around, her voice an octave higher than usual, as though butter wouldn't melt. She had it bad for Stuart, but I just couldn't see why. He looked okay, I guessed, nice enough, tall, dark cropped hair, a scar through his eyebrow which made him look rugged, although I believed him to be as soft as a teddy bear. I'd seen him chasing his nephews around on all fours in his front room.

He was different to Dan, who was shorter, more

athletic, with harder features until he grinned and that's when he looked like a naughty schoolboy. I liked him best like that. I bit down on my lip; I'd be seeing him again tomorrow. Was it sad I was looking forward to going back to work? Valentine's Day was fast approaching. I'd forgotten until I heard Helen mention an Italian restaurant in town was taking bookings for a set menu. Dropping hints in front of Stuart, she was as subtle as a brick. Maybe I'd get Dan a card. No, that was too childish, plus I barely knew him and had already scared him off, it seemed. I was sure Stuart, who looked like a puppy dog making eyes at Helen, would be buying her more than a card. I swiftly decided it was time to leave.

Stuart kindly offered me a lift back home, which was great as I had my washing and food shopping to carry. The only price was having to endure him kiss Helen goodbye on the doorstep. The jar of bolognaise almost made an appearance.

He was chirpy, chatting the whole drive back about plans he had for the house. A new bathroom and kitchen eventually that he was going to do himself. I nodded in the right places, thanking him when he mentioned the rat poison he'd put on the roof to deter the pigeons. No wonder they hadn't woken me for a while.

I hurried inside once he pulled up, desperate to create my social media profiles. I washed and towel-dried my hair, then put on make-up, and after around twenty attempts, finally took the perfect profile picture for Facebook. Gone was Emma Evans, the fake profile I'd created at the library. Jess Strickland was back.

30

Slouched on the bed, stomach still bloated from too much pasta, I wiped away the make-up I'd put on for just twenty minutes, while searching for people I knew on Facebook. I found Helen first and sent her a friend request; she was friends with Stuart, so I sent one to him too. Ashley was next and my phone rang seconds after she'd accepted, with her shrieking down the phone, excited I'd 're-joined the world'. Her enthusiasm was infectious and before I knew it, under her influence, I'd created profiles on Twitter, Snapchat and Instagram whilst chain-smoking cig-arettes.

I found Karla on Facebook, remembering her last name was Grant from the personnel file on Terry's desk. Her profile wasn't private, and I was able to search through her friends, finding not only Gilby, but Whizzie and other names I recognised. Faces from the past, hardly having changed at all. A sinking feeling in my gut as I scrolled through them all. Had she grown up around the St Helier estate too? Had we mixed with the same crowd? I wracked my brain trying to remember but Karla's face and name was unfamiliar. If she'd known Gilby and Whizzie then she must have known Ashley. That would also mean she'd known Eddie. My body stiffened at the thought.

Without hesitating I sent a friend request to Karla, perhaps once she'd accepted, I could bring it up without looking like I'd been stalking her friends list. I friended Agnes and Laura too, as they popped up as people I may know. I scrolled through the suggestions, friends of friends, until my blood ran cold at the image in front of me.

I tapped on it and a photo of Terry and Kim, all dressed up and clinking glasses, filled my screen. He had his hand on her shoulder, his fat fingers touching her neck. It took me straight back to being in his office. Where I'd been weak, his clammy hand on my shoulder, as he *helped* me onto my knees. Vomit shot up the back of my throat and I clamped my lips shut, waiting for the acid to withdraw. I lit another cigarette and swigged vodka to get rid of the taste. Both photos, including the crumpled one of Terry dead on the floor of his office, had been hidden under the mattress, where the rest of the money was. Not the most original hiding place, but there wasn't an abundance of options in my tiny home and I wasn't ready to get rid of them just yet. Before I did, I wanted to be sure who'd sent them. Who'd been targeting me as the photos were bound to lead to something. Blackmail maybe? I just had to wait until whoever it was got in touch.

I checked the time, it was eleven o'clock, and I yawned, stretching my limbs before finally giving in and turning my phone off, eyes stinging. I feared I'd now become a zombie like the other smartphone users who couldn't tear their eyes away from the screen.

Sleep came quickly and so did the morning. One of those nights where you've blinked, and the alarm goes off. I resisted the urge to wear my new clothes to work, but I did put on another T-shirt I'd pinched from Helen. A black Hells Angels one that made me look a bit edgy. I had new trainers too, which were clean and not scruffy like the old ones. Applying a little make-up and with my hair in a messy topknot, I looked okay. Good enough to see Dan at least.

His number was on the business card he'd given me when we met, now stuck on my mirror, but I hadn't been brave enough to text him over the weekend. Ashley said I had to let him do the work, he had to chase me. But what if he didn't? Perhaps he didn't want to get involved as I was his employee? I wasn't worried about that, but maybe he felt he had a duty of care as our boss? Perhaps he was just busy, he was moving into a new place, so had a lot of things to fill his weekend.

I giggled at the ridiculousness of my stupid crush as I walked to work, soaking up the sunshine and the dewy morning air. Finally, I had a big fluffy coat fit for winter, the last few weeks of it at least.

I got to Bright's with ten minutes to spare, so stood outside the café to have a cigarette, hoping Dan might be inside getting his morning caffeine fix but no such luck.

Karla came along a few minutes later, rubbing her eyes.

'Morning,' I said brightly, figuring the best way to find out more about Karla was to be as friendly as possible.

'Is it?'

I rolled my eyes at her sarcasm. It wasn't going to be easy to get closer to her. 'Who peed on your corn-flakes?' I asked.

'No one. Had a banger last night, that's all, I'm suffering,' she grumbled, stifling a yawn.

She pushed in the code and swung open the door, as we queued to punch our cards before heading to the lockers.

Dan wasn't in the office and Karla sniggered at my look of longing as we passed.

'Christ, you not fucked him yet?'

I gasped at Karla's unfiltered choice of words. Was it so obvious?

'Ssshhhhh,' I hissed, quickly followed by, 'and no, I haven't.' I scowled at my locker, opening it slowly. Thankfully, there were no surprises inside today. 'Where are you living now, still sofa-surfing?' I ventured as Karla put on her tabard. I had to find out something, anything. I needed to build trust so I could learn her background and broach how we'd mixed in the same circles but never realised.

'Addington, my mate John has a spare room.' She hadn't mentioned John before, was he just a mate, or something more?

'Haven't you managed to get your own place yet?'

Karla narrowed her eyes. 'I'm saving to get out of here, aren't I? Two weeks left of probation. It'll be my last visit with Barry next week; another month or so and I'll be gone. Out of this dump.'

Karla turned and walked towards the warehouse. I hurried after her, still fixing my tabard.

'Doesn't anyone stay on after?'

'Would you? Knowing what went on? That's why there's such a high turnover of staff, as soon as their probation is up, they're off.'

'Where will you go?'

She shrugged but didn't answer. I shook my head; it was like getting blood out of a stone.

'Where did you grow up?' I asked, realising quickly I'd pushed too soon.

'What is this, twenty questions? I ain't in the mood,' she snapped, grabbing a large trolley of laundry and wheeling it towards one of the machines. I hadn't even checked the rota, but whoever was stuck with Karla was not going to have the best day.

'Morning, ladies, good weekends?' Our heads snapped around as Dan walked in from the yard, bowing his head under the open shutters.

'Yes, good thanks,' I replied for both of us.

'Big delivery today from St George's, needs a fast turnaround. That's priority one. I can see you've already started. Excellent, cheers, Karla.'

She managed a nod but didn't stop pulling the sheets out of the trolley.

Dan shoved his hands in his pockets. Dark denim jeans today with beige desert boots and a moss-green jumper. He looked gorgeous and I turned away to stop myself drooling. Since sex had come up as something I might possibly get to participate in, voluntarily, I hadn't thought of much else in Dan's company.

'Jess, can I borrow you a minute.' Our eyes locked, his twinkling mischievously.

Karla's hostility forgotten, I followed Dan into his office, my mouth suddenly dry.

'How's the new place?' I mumbled, filling the silence.

'Good, it's great thanks. I didn't have much to move in, so it's all done. You'll have to come over for dinner or something.' He blushed, edging closer.

'I'd like that,' I managed as the tiny hairs on the back of my neck stood to attention.

'We probably shouldn't, I mean, I don't want you to think I'm taking advantage, but I like spending time with you.'

I giggled, like a dumb schoolgirl.

'Taking advantage how?' I asked, genuinely perplexed. Did he mean the age difference?

'Well, me being your boss, I guess, and, well, obviously a few years older.' His ears were pink now and I could tell he found this excruciating.

'I won't tell anyone,' I offered.

Dan took another step closer, an arm's-length away. 'That may be a good idea.'

'Okay.'

'Tomorrow maybe?'

My eyebrows shot skyward.

Picking up on my surprise, he admitted, 'I meant to take your number on Friday, but I had an errand to run and when I got back, you were gone.'

I nodded, my stomach churning.

'Did you want me for anything else?' I asked, my tone light as I remembered the chase I was supposed to be inciting.

'No, no, sorry. I'll let you get back.' He gestured with his hand I was free to leave, so I did, hoping he was going to watch me go. I exaggerated the sway of my bony hips as I sauntered back to the warehouse, my head floating in the clouds.

According to the rota, I'd drawn the short straw and had been paired with Karla, who was already grunting with exertion, her brow glistening. The air temperature had shot up since the machines had gone on and my underarms dampened in protest. She threw the sheets around like they had upset her, and I stepped in when one got tangled in the trolley.

'Fucking thing.' She kicked the wheel, sending it flying as it was half empty.

'Let me do it,' I said, winding the fabric back on itself.

She huffed, disappearing outside for a cigarette. Once I'd loaded the machine and put it on, I joined her in the yard.

She was sat on the gravel, knees to her chest, flicking the ash of her cigarette into the air and watching it get carried away on the breeze.

'You had anything else delivered? More photos?' Karla asked.

'No, thank God. I'm hoping that's it. I was thinking, if they've got photos of that, they've got photos of everyone with him,' I said.

'Yep, that would be some horrific viewing.' Karla rubbed her eyes, the circles beneath darkening as the day went on.

'I got a new phone yesterday; I friended you on Facebook, did you see?'

Karla shook her head, not meeting my gaze, though I registered a flicker of surprise. 'Not yet, I had to do an Apple update yesterday and now the bastard thing won't switch on,' she huffed.

I wasn't sure she wasn't telling the truth, although Karla spoke convincingly. Maybe she wanted to keep work separate from her friends, but after what we'd done, we'd forever be connected.

I chewed the inside of my cheek as I considered what to say. There were things she wasn't telling me, I was positive. Something was bugging Karla, and it wasn't just a hangover.

31

'You having a smoke?' she asked, breaking the silence.

Realising I was standing there awkwardly, I nodded, pulling my cigarettes out of my pocket and lighting one.

Karla didn't wait, instead going back inside. Normally she would have had another one with me.

I pulled my phone out of my back pocket and opened Facebook. We weren't allowed them in the warehouse, but I hadn't wanted to leave the most expensive thing I now owned in a locker which had already been broken into once.

I found Karla quickly and scrolled down on her

page, through some of her photos and uploads. A second later, the app crashed, throwing me out and back to the home screen.

'Shit,' I muttered, taking a drag of my cigarette and clicking into Facebook again. This time, Karla's profile photo of her pouting was the only thing I could see. Access to her other photos and her wall had gone. Had she changed her privacy settings? Just now? But why?

I chucked my half-smoked cigarette to the ground and headed back inside, meeting Karla at our station as she came from the opposite direction. The direction of the toilets and the lockers. I frowned and took the empty trolley back to the holding pen, pulling a full one back again.

'What's up with you?' Karla said, taking in my face, her tone dripping with attitude.

'Nothing,' I replied, hauling the sheets into an empty machine.

We didn't speak much for the rest of the day, there was no light conversation and I stared over at Hanna, envious of her working with Laura, swaying to tunes blasting out from her radio. Everyone was happier with Terry gone. *Everyone except Kim and Dan*, the voice in my head piped up.

Before I left for the day, I wrote my number on a scrap of paper and left it on Dan's desk. He'd gone out to see a supplier and Karla and I were the last ones left in the building. The load we'd done from the hospital all pressed and packaged, ready for collection. We'd worked hard, my joints ached, and stomach rumbled, but I'd decided I wasn't going straight home.

Instead I loitered down the road from the entrance to Bright's, managing to get out while Karla was in the toilet. I'd shouted goodbye through the entrance to the ladies', saying I was rushing to my mum's and not waiting for a reply. Watching from behind a postbox, I saw Karla come out and head towards the bus stop where I'd normally catch the 407 to get home. I straightened up, my back aching, but I didn't have to worry she'd spot me; her head was bowed, staring at her phone. I wanted to see where she went after work, sure she was hiding something.

I'd intended to follow her on foot, keep my distance, but I hadn't anticipated she'd get the bus, especially not the one going in the same direction as me. Now I was stuck. Should I walk back to the bus stop? Say I'd forgotten something at Bright's? I couldn't even see the board with the bus arrival times from where I stood.

After ten minutes of deliberating, just when I'd decided to give up on the mission and walk home, a 407 arrived and Karla got on it. I moved around the postbox as it passed, shielding myself from view as I watched her head to the back of the bus.

Back at the bus stop, another one rumbled up. I raced to jump on it. At least I'd be able to see if she got off ahead of me, for part of the journey.

Wherever Karla was going, it wasn't home to John's spare room, she was heading in the wrong direction for Addington. I craned my neck to look ahead, my face pressed to the glass, to see if she got off at any of the stops. Where was she going? The 407 went towards the St Helier estate, not all the way there, but in that direction. Her bus moved through the traffic and the bell rang on mine for every stop, so someone could get off. Before long, hers was out of sight.

At the closest point to home, I jumped off and began walking. I could only guess as to where Karla was going, perhaps meeting a friend? I wasn't particularly good at playing detective. I could try again another day, but it was virtually impossible to follow someone without a car. There had to be another way to find out what was going on with her?

When I got in after a brisk ten-minute walk, the place was quiet. Stuart was likely still at work and I microwaved a curry I knew would stink the small room out, but I didn't care. I was starving. As I waited for the machine to beep, I thought about the ring left in my locker. Terry's wedding band. It was now in Karla's possession, but could it have been all along? The microwave sounded, signalling dinner was ready, but my thoughts were elsewhere.

Shoving the mattress aside, I pulled out the images of Terry and laid them on the bed, flattening the creases as best I could. In the second one, you could just make out Terry's left hand, limp, by his head. Squinting at the picture, I could see a ring on his third finger. Fuck. I stood and let it sink in for a second, the smell of tikka masala permeating the room even before I'd released it from its plastic carton. If Terry was wearing the ring when he died, then it should have been incinerated with the rest of him.

The only person who could have removed his ring other than me was Karla.

My brain was firing, I was skittish, adrenaline pumping around my body making my heart thump. Shit. Karla had planted the ring. Why though? To scare me. To make me think someone knew what we did. None of it made any sense, yet it was the only logical conclusion. If she planted the ring, then she must have sent the photos too. Perhaps I didn't know Karla at all. Which, of course, I didn't when I thought about it.

Head spinning, I wolfed down the curry without tasting it, too busy trying to sift through the scenarios that popped into my head, but nothing seemed to fit. I couldn't confront her; because letting on I'd found her out would get me no answers. Better to pretend I was clueless.

I stood outside with the door open to air the room as I smoked, almost jumping out of my skin when a text message came through. Still not used to the random tinkle I'd chosen as the message alert. Was it Karla?

Snatching the phone from the bed, I saw it was Dan and my chest fluttered.

Dinner at mine tomorrow? Do you eat sea bass?

I replied that was fine, although I'd never eaten sea bass before. It didn't matter, I'd eat anything if Dan was going to the effort of cooking for me. It would be my first real date and I needed something to take my mind off things. I had to pretend everything was fine. Just until I'd figured out what was going on and if Karla was my enemy.

32

Karla still seemed stand-offish the following day, but I avoided her. I managed to get in before nine and look at the rota. I'd been put with Agnes, and even with her constant chattering, it was a much better option than Karla's mood. Laura lucked out there and every time I looked over, Karla was scowling at her cheerful co-worker.

Around mid-morning, Dan confirmed arrangements for dinner, calling me into his office to help find something he wasn't looking for. He seemed nervous, struggling to get his words out as he offered to come and pick me up at around half six. I hoped the evening would end differently to the last time I saw him.

What might happen made my insides fizz, like tiny electric shocks pulsed beneath my skin. I wouldn't have a lot of time to get ready after work, but it was better than making my own way there. I'd be even more harassed if I got lost and arrived all sweaty and dishevelled.

I chewed my nails all day, worrying what to wear, whether to be presumptuous and sneakily pack a toothbrush and a clean pair of knickers? If we ended up in bed, would I be staying the night, or would he bring me home? Perhaps he'd call me a taxi? How would it all work?

My stomach churned with nervous energy and I couldn't concentrate on anything. Taking my eye off the ball, I burnt my hand on the pressing machine as I fed a sheet in.

'How you say... careful, careful,' Agnes berated me as I sucked on my thumb.

'Sorry, miles away,' I explained, trying to ignore the searing pain.

She tutted but fussed around me like a mother hen, ensuring I wasn't badly hurt.

'You have thing for boss?' Agnes tilted her head to the side and my eyes widened.

'Jesus, does everyone know?' I glared at Karla, who caught my eye and glared back, even though she was unable to hear what I was saying. What was with her?

'Ignore her, she's jealous,' Agnes said, glancing in Karla's direction.

I snorted. I was sure her mood couldn't be because we liked the same guy.

'It's way he looks at you,' Agnes continued, pulling a sheet from the machine, smoothing out the fabric and folding it neatly. I hid my smile beneath the sheet, surely Agnes hadn't seen Dan look at me in any kind of way. Although the notion made my insides flutter.

I went for a walk at lunchtime to stretch my legs, desperate to get away from listening ears as I rang Ashley, bursting to talk to someone. Just as the call was about to go to voicemail, she came on the line, sounding like she'd been for a run.

'Sorry, Jess, the phone was in my bag,' Ashley said by way of explanation.

'Are you busy?'

'No, I'm just about to head to a lecture, but I can walk and talk.'

I heard the jangle of keys and the slam of a heavy door.

'I'm hoping tonight's going to be *the* night,' I said, trying to sound cool and keep myself from squealing. It must be weird to Ashley that I was years behind, only experiencing things now she'd faced ages ago.

'Tell me everything!'

I described how Dan had invited me for dinner, which surely meant it would lead to more. 'He's cooking sea bass,' I gushed.

'Fancy!' she replied and we both laughed. I was grateful she was humouring me. I didn't have anyone else I could talk to. Not Helen and I wasn't sure Karla could be trusted. 'Be safe okay. Make sure he wears something. If it doesn't feel right make an excuse and leave. Call me or text an SOS if you need it, like if you need me to ring with some fake emergency.'

'I hope I won't need that. Oh, Ash, I'm bloody terrified,' I admitted.

'You'll be fine, have a glass of wine, relax, and if he's worth his salt, he'll take it slow. Does he know this is your first time?'

'Yep.' I squirmed, remembering the awkward exchange before he practically ran away.

'Well then, I'm sure he'll be the perfect gentleman.'

I changed the subject and asked if she remembered anyone called Karla Grant from the old days, but she said the name didn't ring any bells.

'Is something troubling you? You know you can tell me anything,' Ashley said.

My heart swelled, as the years apart seemed to shrink. Ashley always knew when something was bothering me. 'No, maybe, I don't know. I need to check some things out first,' I replied, not wanting to let on there was anything to worry about until I was certain.

We chatted for a few more minutes until she had to head off. I took a slow walk back to Bright's, going around the back to the yard, where Barry stood beside his BMW, a cigarette dangling from his lips as he scrolled on his phone.

'Watcha,' he said, his brown leather jacket collar tugged up around his ears.

'Hi,' I replied, moving to join him until I finished my cigarette. It would be impolite not to and unfortunately it was important to keep Barry onside.

Being around him now made me uneasy, I was convinced him and Terry had a ruse going. Was it any surprise Terry was only too pleased to take Barry's girls on when he could pay them minimum wage and exploit them for more than just financial gain? He had a hold on them as soon as they arrived. Since Barry had let slip Terry owed him money, it was clear Barry was doing all right out of the scheme. I could be barking up the wrong tree, but I doubted it.

'When's Karla's last visit?' I asked, remembering her mention she only had one left.

'Next week, she'll be signed off and someone else's problem.' Barry sighed.

'Is she difficult?' I asked.

'Too smart for her own good that one. Any news on Terry? Seems to have gone quiet here?'

I nodded, thinking the same thing. Perhaps I could ask Dan about it tonight?

I went to flick my ash and Barry wrapped his fingers around my wrist, tiny red hairs visible on his knuckles. I tried to snatch it away, but he held firm.

'You would tell me if you'd heard anything, wouldn't you, Jess? I need to find out where Terry is.'

'Get off me,' I spat, wrenching my arm away, but Barry's face darkened further.

He chuckled, taking a long drag of his cigarette, his eyes never leaving mine. 'Don't forget who I am to you.'

I stalked back inside, a chill running the length of my spine. It didn't take long for Barry to show his true colours. Why did people in power often abuse it? My blood seared, but I took comfort in one thing. Barry was obviously desperate to know where Terry was, likely because of the money he owed him. The money sitting under my mattress, and, if Barry was eager to find him, it meant he had no idea what had happened. I imagined he was really pissed off his little money-making scheme had folded.

I headed straight for the toilets to wash Barry off me and found Karla inside, eyes red-rimmed.

'You okay?' I asked.

She nodded but didn't speak, and still caught up in my rage at Barry, I didn't hold back.

'Seriously what's up with you? What have I done to piss you off?' I said, exasperated.

'Nothing.' Karla shrugged and I nearly blurted out I knew she'd put the ring in my locker. Instead I washed my hands, pushing the soap right up my forearms. 'Do you still have your half of the money?' she whispered.

'Yeah, why?' I frowned.

'I might need to borrow some.' Karla's face changed, an expression I'd never seen before. Fear reflected in her twitching eyes. She was terrified.

I softened instantly, rinsing my hands. 'Sure.' The money under the mattress made me nervous. I'd got a phone, some new clothes and paid a couple of months' rent, there was nothing else I needed. In fact, the sooner I got rid of it the better, it felt like a noose around my neck. Evidence tying me to a crime. If anyone found it, how would I explain away that amount of money, working in a laundry on minimum wage. Even if Karla never gave it back, I couldn't miss what I'd never had.

'Thanks. Can I come this evening?' Karla sounded meek, the bravado which normally came off her in waves had disappeared. She looked drawn, her cheeks hollower than usual.

'No, I won't be home. Tomorrow, okay?'

She nodded and turned back to the mirror; the colour having left her face. I wanted to ask what she'd got mixed up in, get everything out in the open and get her to tell me the truth about the ring and if she was behind the photos, but before I could, the toilet door swung open and Laura bounced in.

'There you are, Barry's waiting to see you,' she said, grimacing at Karla, who nodded and trudged out the door.

I joined Agnes back at the pressing machine, who proceeded to tell me about her mum's dodgy knee she was hoping to get sorted on the NHS before going back to Poland. I nodded in all the right places, but my mind was elsewhere. I wished I could be a fly on the wall in the office with Barry. I hoped he wasn't threatening her like he had me. Whatever it was, I had no doubt Karla would be able to handle him. I wasn't sure I had the same constitution.

33

Barry called out to me as he went past, heading towards the yard, swinging his car keys around his finger as though he was a cowboy with a gun.

'I'll be back tomorrow for you.' He winked and my throat tightened.

I hadn't noticed the time; it was almost four and Agnes and I still had one more load to do. They were only tablecloths from a local Indian restaurant so didn't take long between us. By five o'clock, we had everything packaged and ready for collection in the morning.

'See you tomorrow,' Agnes called as she gathered her things.

I hadn't seen Karla since Barry's meeting and despite everything I sent her a quick text to see if she was okay. In the short time I'd known Karla, I'd never seen her rattled. Not even when faced with Terry's body. I had to remind myself that she'd stuck her neck out for me, got involved in something that could see her sent back to prison. Perhaps whatever was going on with her had nothing to do with Terry, the photos or the ring. Maybe I'd made a mistake?

'See you in a while,' I said, popping my head into Dan's office on the way out.

'Pick you up around six thirty?' Dan checked and I nodded, trying to look cool even though my legs were like mush.

I punched out and waited at the bus stop, pleased when it arrived on time. I'd have around forty-five minutes to get showered, shaved and primed for the biggest night I'd had in years. Excitement mixed with dread swallowed me whole, emotions that were alien to me. My mouth kept filling with saliva, and when I got off the bus, I lit a cigarette, hands trembling. *Christ, Jess, get a grip on yourself.*

Taking a detour to the corner shop, I bought a bottle of wine and more cigarettes. I had no idea what wine you were supposed to drink with sea bass, or if the one I'd bought was any good.

Stuart tried to catch me in conversation as we arrived home at the same time, but I mentioned I had to dash as I was going out. Apparently, he was going to Mum's for dinner. Helen must think they were serious if she was inviting him for a meal with Mum. I was pleased for her, she seemed less highly strung with Stuart around. Perhaps that was what getting laid did for you?

I showered as quickly as I could, standing on one leg as I shaved, trying not to cut myself. Once done, I smothered myself in vanilla-scented body lotion, realising I didn't own a single bottle of perfume any more and I wasn't going to spray myself with Impulse for a night with Dan. I left my hair loose, white blonde tendrils hung down in front of my chest like a mermaid, long overdue a trim.

As the time ticked on, I became more nervous, even a cigarette and a shot of vodka couldn't slow my thumping heart. I feared when he came close enough to touch me again, I might have a heart attack.

At half past six on the dot, a tap came from the

door. I grabbed my things, deciding last minute to pack my toothbrush and a spare pair of knickers in my bag.

'Hey,' he said as I swung open the door. He must have come straight from work.

'Hi.' My face flushed as he took the carrier bag of wine from me.

'Let me carry that.'

I pulled the door shut and followed him to the car, sliding into the seat and strapping myself in.

Palms damp, I struggled for something to say, the tension in the car palpable.

Dan gripped the steering wheel tightly and I pressed my knees together.

'Are you hungry?' Dan asked and my stomach rumbled on cue.

'Yes. Always. Did you just finish?'

'Yeah, I had some paperwork to do. Trying to find anything in that place is like looking for a needle in a haystack. Terry wasn't exactly the most organised of people.' Dan's jaw clenched and I saw lines etched into his forehead. Running Bright's was taking its toll.

'Has there been any news on your brother?'

'Yes, actually.'

My stomach somersaulted, but I had to wait for Dan to navigate the roundabout before he continued. Had they found the hidden camera?

'There's been a sighting in Portsmouth of all places, the police seem to think it could be significant, so they are following up. I told you he'd be off, probably shacked up with some prostitute who's bleeding him – no, wait – us, dry.' Dan shook his head, gripping the steering wheel tighter. 'It's Kim I feel sorry for, she's beside herself. They're mortgaged up to the hilt and he's done a runner, selfish bastard. You would think he was the younger brother, not me. I'm here trying to hold everything together whilst he's off getting his nuts wet!' Dan sounded angry, he seemed convinced no harm had befallen Terry but that another woman was the cause of his disappearance.

I sank deeper into my seat, the slow spread of relief flooding my veins. With Dan believing Terry was hiding out somewhere I was able to push thoughts of him to the back of my mind. Turning my attention back to the moment my stomach swirled with nervous anticipation as we neared our destination.

We got to the maisonette with its picture-perfect garden and made our way down the side to Dan's front door.

'You okay?' he asked, sliding the key in, and although I felt like I was at the top of a roller coaster about to take its first drop, I tried not to let it show.

'Yeah, sure.' I flicked my hair over my shoulder, hoping my bravado would cover the jitters I felt.

The inside looked the same as when I'd last been there, with the addition of a few of Dan's things dotted around; his jacket draped over a chair, a plate on the draining board and some kettlebells in the corner of the lounge.

'I'll put your wine in to chill. This one has been in since yesterday, fancy a glass?' Dan put my bottle into the fridge and retrieved a Sauvignon Blanc.

'Sure,' I replied, grateful for something to calm the nerves.

Dan opened the bottle and poured two glasses. He tapped his phone and music filled the room, blasting out from speakers in the corners before he turned it down, Amy Winehouse providing us with some background noise.

'Do you mind if I just run through the shower?'

Dan asked, already undoing his collar as he turned the oven on to warm up.

'Sure,' I said again, my voice a higher pitch than necessary. My face burned. Why was I being so awkward? It was going to be fine.

He left the room and I heard the shower start up. I blinked away the image of Dan undressing that had popped into my head and took a gulp of wine. Could I smoke in here? I didn't want to assume. Instead I necked the rest of my glass and poured another, a half-measure, forcing myself away from the bottle to wander around the lounge. There were no photos or mementos, but I guessed it was a bit early. He'd only moved in a few days ago. Perhaps all his stuff was still in Scotland?

I stared out of the window, onto the pretty striped lawn. The street below was quiet, large brightly lit houses lined the pavement, all bay windows and glossy front doors. It was miles away from anywhere I'd ever lived. Far too upmarket for me.

'Want a top-up?' Dan's voice came from behind me. He was in the kitchen, rubbing his head with a towel, a grey T-shirt crinkled on his body where it had been put on damp skin.

'No, I'm fine thanks.'

He nodded and got the fish out of the fridge, already prepped, covered with a marinade and on a tray.

I strolled over, sitting at the breakfast bar so I could watch him work as he padded around the kitchen in bare feet.

'So what did you do, before coming down here?' I asked.

'Still Bright's but other aspects of the business. Buying and selling industrial machines, that kind of thing. It kept me moving about a lot. Terry wanted to lay down roots and I was happy to keep travelling.' He pulled open the fridge and rummaged in the salad drawer.

'Do you cook often?' I asked, as he rinsed some Tenderstem broccoli and new potatoes, tossing them onto the tray with the marinade. A drizzle of oil and salt and pepper and he slid it into the oven.

'Nah, not really. No point when there's only me. You?'

'Same.' I didn't want to admit the only cooking apparatus I owned was a microwave and most of my meals now came out of plastic cartons.

He took a large mouthful of wine and came around to join me on the next stool, spinning around so we were facing each other, our knees almost touching.

'So, how was your day?' he asked.

'Not bad, except the pressing machine had it in for me,' I said, raising my thumb and showing Dan the blister that had formed there, a little bubble protecting the skin healing beneath.

'Ouch, looks painful.' He took my thumb and raised it to his lips, and I held my breath. His gaze was intense and my whole body tingled in anticipation. 'All better now,' he whispered.

I put my glass down and pulled his face towards mine. Dinner forgotten.

34

Dan managed to untangle himself from me long enough to turn the oven off before I dragged him to the bedroom. It was just as Ashley said, Dan was a gentleman, checking I was okay, if I was ready. I'd waited twenty-two years to feel something like the attraction I felt for Dan and now it had arrived, it was a force I couldn't contain. Thankfully he looked nothing like his brother and at no point did my assault cross my mind. The consensual act between Dan and I was so far removed from my time spent in Terry's office it didn't haunt me like I thought it might. My only concern was that Dan didn't spurn my advances like last time. I wasn't sure my ego would survive but he was easily persuaded.

Afterwards I was a little sore, my body used in ways it hadn't been before, but the elation as I stared at the ceiling, skin glowing, made it worthwhile.

'I better put the dinner back on.' Dan laughed, pulling on his boxer shorts and bustling out of the room.

I sighed, a calmness trickling through my veins as I fought the urge to sleep. I could still feel him there, between my legs, the sensation so strange I reached down to check.

'Are you okay? I didn't hurt you, did I?' Dan came back and crawled in beside me, slipping his arm under my head and pulling me in for a cuddle.

'No, it was fine.'

'Wow, what an endorsement!' Dan coughed as I laughed, squeezing his side as he tried to jerk out of my grasp.

'I didn't mean it like that.'

We lay for a while, staring at the ceiling, Dan's fingers twisting a strand of my hair over and over.

'Do we have to get up yet?' I asked.

'The oven timer is set to go off when it's done, so, no, you can snooze for as long as you like.'

'Good.' I closed my eyes for a second, enjoying being held, knowing whatever happened, I'd have this connection to Dan forever.

I dozed off, the clattering of plates in the kitchen brought me round. Initially confused about where I was as the bed was empty.

'Ah, you're awake. Dinner is served.' Dan poked his head around the door.

I blinked rapidly, trying to shake myself out of my stupor. Groggily, I poured myself into my clothes, glancing in the mirror before I left the bedroom, wondering if a more mature Jess would look back. Although I felt different on the inside, like a woman rather than just a girl, there'd been no physical change.

Hurrying to the table I sat down. The sea bass looked delicious, although I was apprehensive whether I'd like it or not. In prison you learn not to be fussy, you eat what you're given, or you don't, simple as that. I ate most things, unless I saw someone spit in the food, which happened on occasion.

Dan poured the wine and picked up his knife and fork. I did the same, steeling myself for the fish. It was one of many firsts tonight.

'Can I ask a personal question?' Dan's eyes were piercing, and I nodded, my mouth full.

'What were you in for?' It was the question I'd been waiting for, the one everyone always wanted to know as soon as they found out you'd been in prison.

I finished my mouthful and laid down my fork. 'I killed someone.'

Dan froze mid-chew, wide-eyed, and I stifled a laugh, which would have been wholly inappropriate.

'Accidentally,' I added, and Dan slowly resumed chewing. Did he think he'd just slept with a cold-blooded murderer?

'Oh, I'm sorry,' he mumbled, like he regretted bringing it up after all.

'I had a car accident, drove into a tree and killed my best friend's boyfriend.' I looked away, the mood dipped, an awkward moment in an otherwise pleasant evening.

Dan put his cutlery down and reached for my hand. 'That must have been awful. For everyone.' His eyes were sincere, and he stroked my palm. His kindness overwhelmed me, and I leaned back in my seat. It gave me the courage to say more, knowing I wasn't being judged.

'I got sentenced to four years. I had the accident when I was seventeen, I'd only been driving a few months, but by the time I was sent down, I'd already turned eighteen. Even I'm not sure it was enough, but that's what they gave me.' I remembered the cold courtroom, the too large blouse they'd given me to wear. How someone in the gallery screamed like a banshee when my sentence was read. An inhuman howl of pain and anguish. I pushed the memory away.

We resumed eating, the silence stretching out for a minute until I tried to lighten the mood.

'You're surrounded by criminals, you know. Doesn't it make you uneasy?' I smiled and Dan feigned a laugh.

'Not really, I don't think of it like that, although I might now!'

The sea bass was lovely, and I cleared my plate with ease. Dan had cheesecakes for dessert in little glass dishes, just enough to give a hit of sweetness after a meal.

I leaned back and rubbed my stomach.

'That was delicious, thank you.'

'You're welcome.'

'Is this all your stuff? Are you waiting for a delivery or something?' I asked, looking around at the sparse room.

'This is it. Terry has some stuff in his garage that was left at my parents, but because I move around so much, I tend to travel pretty light.'

I chewed my lip, realising Dan had little family left alive bar his niece. Guilt gnawed at me from within. He refilled our glasses and took the plates to the sink.

'I can wash up,' I offered.

'No, absolutely not, you're my guest. Anyway, I can think of a much better use of your time.' The corners of his mouth drew up, cheeks a rosy red.

'Oh really?' I said in the most seductive tone I could manage.

* * *

I woke bolt upright at a sound from the street below. Foxes screeching, their mating sound was like nails across a blackboard. I rubbed my throbbing head and swung my legs over the edge of the bed, standing up to search for water. Dan snored lightly behind me, the duvet barely covering his naked body. It looked like I'd stolen the covers.

There was no question whether I should spend the night. It wasn't discussed. I saw from my phone it was three in the morning. Dazed, I stubbed my toe on the corner of the bed and bit my tongue, inwardly howling, and hobbled onward. The bathroom light had been left on, so I drank straight from the tap, lapping up the cool water and soothing my throat.

Sitting on the toilet, I unlocked my screen to see I had four missed calls from Karla throughout the evening, the last one at ten, but she'd left no voicemail. I couldn't call her back now; it was way too late, but I hoped she was okay. I sent a text just in case. If her phone wasn't switched off, she'd probably have it on silent like mine, so I wouldn't wake her. I sent another text to Ashley, just to let her know I was safe and Dan had been the perfect gentleman. Yawning, I finished peeing and made my way back to bed.

I woke early to Dan planting butterfly kisses on my shoulder. Pressed up against me, I could tell he was more than awake.

'Morning,' he said as I stretched my limbs.

'Morning,' I replied, reaching around to stroke him.

Half an hour later, I was pulling my clothes on and tying my hair into a ponytail. Face now devoid of make-up, I looked pale and tired. It was barely seven o'clock and I needed caffeine.

'I'll run you home on the way, is that okay? I've got a meeting at nine with a client, something Terry had booked before he disappeared, taking on more work.'

'Sure, no problem,' I replied, trying not to wince as Terry was mentioned.

The morning was a bit of a rush, which Dan playfully berated me for, as according to him, it was my fault I'd tempted him, and we'd got out of bed late. He drove quickly, the traffic heavy but moving.

'I'll see you in a bit,' he said when we reached my house, leaning across the passenger seat to give me a kiss before I jumped out. I waved as he drove away.

I didn't notice when I put my key in the door, the side was bowed. It wasn't until I had to force the door to get it to move across the carpet, pushing aside a sea of my stuff strewn on the floor, I realised I'd been burgled.

35

My mouth gaped and I gingerly peeked inside to see the bedsit had been turned over. Practically everything I owned had been thrown onto the floor – clothes, books, food from the cupboards. I glanced at the mattress, skewed across the frame of the sofa bed where it had been pushed aside.

The money! Clambering over my clothes, I reached the thin mattress and lifted it. The money had gone, along with the photos of Terry. That's what this was about, the money, and the only one who knew I had it was Karla.

I slumped onto the edge of the bed, lowering my head and thrusting my fingers into hair at my scalp, pulling in frustration. Why? I didn't understand. I said I'd give her the money; she didn't have to break into my fucking home!

'Jesus Christ.' Stuart stood at the door, his voice making me jump. A gust of air rushed in as he pushed it open for further inspection. He was dressed in a shirt and tie, no doubt heading into the office. I should be on my way to work too.

'Someone broke in.' I waved my hand around at the devastation.

'What have they taken?' He cast his eye around the room, deep lines etched on his forehead.

'I don't know yet, not much I don't think.' I wasn't going to admit I had nearly two grand robbed from a dead man hidden under my mattress.

'I'll call the police.' He pulled his phone from his pocket, his fingers moving across the screen.

'No,' I blurted, and Stuart paused, raising an eyebrow.

'The door is damaged, I'll need a crime number to go through the insurance,' he said stiffly.

'I'll pay for the door; it just needs knocking back out. I don't think they've taken anything else.'

Stuart narrowed his eyes and I realised I'd been

too eager to dismiss the police's involvement. He was now suspicious. 'What have you got yourself into, Jess? Because I said to your sister you can only stay here if you keep yourself out of trouble. I don't want you bringing any shit to my door.'

'I haven't, I promise,' I pleaded, looking Stuart straight in the eyes, imploring him to let it go.

The silence stretched out until it was his turn to sigh; shoulders sagging, I watched him relent.

'Okay, this one time, all right! I've got to go to work. I'll pop back and take a look at the door this afternoon. Try and secure it as best you can in the meantime.'

I nodded, awash with relief. My eyes prickled with threatening tears. How had I gone from being on such a high to such a low in a matter of hours? I was going to fucking kill Karla. If anything like this happened again, Stuart would throw me out, then where would I be?

Snatching up my phone, I sent her a text. My fingers pounding the screen.

WHAT THE FUCK!

I called Dan and left a message on his voicemail. Obviously, I was going to be late to work, it was already eight thirty. I pushed the door shut. It closed, but the catch wouldn't stay, so I found something to wedge underneath to stop it from opening. I waded through the remnants of my life that looked like they'd been fired out of a cannon into the tiny space. All the time, my phone remained infuriatingly silent.

None of the new clothes, still with their tags on, had been taken and I hung them back up on the upturned rail. The microwave, kettle, even my half-full bottle of vodka remained untouched. I had one hundred cigarettes sitting on the side from my last supermarket visit. Surely, they would have been taken to sell on if it was a proper burglary. I knew it was Karla. When I didn't answer the phone last night, she must have paid me a visit. A vein pulsed in my forehead, throbbing intently. All Karla caused was chaos.

It took around half an hour to put the room back together. I'd need to borrow Stuart's hoover again as the carpet was a mess, but all my things were returned to where they'd been before.

Fixing the door as best I could, wedging it closed, I left for work, texting Stuart as I walked so he would know how to get in later. Before I could put my phone back in my pocket, Helen rang.

'Stuart said you've been burgled!' she shrieked down the phone.

'Yes,' I replied flatly.

'Why has someone burgled you? Stuart's worried about his house.'

'Nothing of Stuart's was taken, Helen, it's fine, I'm going to pay for the door.' I was trying to remain calm, but the urge to tell Helen to fuck off was growing.

'He says you didn't want him to call the police. You better not be in trouble, Jess, because I tell you, I won't let you back into our lives again.'

I bit the inside of my cheek, sucking air through my nostrils. Who the hell did she think she was? 'Keep your beak out, all right, it's between me and Stuart. He's my landlord, not you. I'm not doing anything.'

'He's really strait-laced, Jess, does everything by the book, so no dodgy dealings, okay!'

'I've just told you I haven't done anything.' I enunciated each word, starting to lose my temper.

'People don't just get burgled for no reason,' she snapped.

'Of course they do, all the time!' I hung up before I let her push any more of my buttons.

I marched to Bright's, ready to give Karla hell. I was no fighter, but inside I raged, convinced when I saw her, I'd scratch her eyes out. However, when I got there, flying straight into the warehouse without clocking in or stashing my things, she was nowhere to be seen. I scanned the stations; Hanna, Laura, Agnes, Natalia and other girls I knew, although not well, were there, but no sign of Karla.

'Where's Karla?' I asked Agnes.

'No idea.' She shrugged and I stormed back to Dan's office, pushing open the door, but Barry sat where Dan should be.

'Well hello there, just the person I wanted to see.' He smirked, sitting upright.

'Where's Dan?' I asked, ignoring him.

Barry frowned and shook his head. He must still be at his client meeting.

'Go and put your stuff away and I'll see you back here in a minute.' Barry pulled my file out of his satchel.

I rolled my eyes and willed my blood pressure to drop. Projecting my temper onto Barry would only serve to put me on his shit list and he'd already made it clear that wasn't a good idea.

'Sure,' I replied and forced a smile, heading out to clock myself in and drop off my things in a locker. I checked the one Karla always used, but it was empty. She'd not replied to my text message either; it looked like she hadn't even read it. 'Sorry, bit of a nightmare morning,' I said on entering Dan's office and flopping into the chair.

'Everything okay?' Barry slipped into the mask of caring probation officer all too easily and I saw how I'd been taken in at first.

'No, just family stuff,' I lied, not wanting to tell him about the burglary. I didn't want him to question why I'd been targeted.

We went through the usual questions, my answers slight variations from last time, elaborating here and there until I could see Barry was satisfied. I wanted to fly under the radar as much as possible.

'Brilliant, Jess, you've settled in well. Now it's head down, nose clean and hope the next five months whizz by.'

We locked eyes for a moment, and I waited to be excused, but he just stared at me. Eventually he closed my file and laid his palms flat on top of it, a tight smile stretched across his face, eyes twinkling.

'So, let's talk about Terry.'

36

I ran my tongue across the front of my teeth. Barry's cold stare making my skin crawl.

'What about Terry?' I said.

'Heard anything else?'

The back of my neck prickled with sweat; he didn't know anything.

'Funny you should ask. Dan told me yesterday the police have had a sighting in Portsmouth.'

Barry leaned back in the chair, clasping his hands behind his head. 'Portsmouth?' he sneered and I nodded. His eyes darted around the room; I could see him trying to recall Terry mentioning the area.

'Can I go now?' I asked, there was only an hour left before lunch and I wanted to see if Karla had shown up.

'Sure. Stay out of trouble, Jess, and I'll see you next week.' He grinned, the mask firmly back in place. I matched his fake smile with one of my own before leaving.

Frustrated I couldn't find Karla, and Dan wasn't back either, I joined one of the girls I barely knew, Natalia, who was working on the dryers. She didn't talk much and that was fine with me. My head felt as though it was going to explode.

Dan bowled in at lunchtime, carrying a sub roll he'd bought from the café, winking as he passed. I wanted to talk to him, but the machine had just finished, and Natalia was already pulling out towels and handing them over to fold.

I went for lunch once we were done, buying myself a roll and loitering in the yard with a cigarette. Ashley sent me a text, dying to hear all the juicy details from last night and I sent her a quick message back saying I'd ring when I could. Next, I tried Karla. Her phone went straight through to voicemail and since she'd made her account private and not yet accepted my friend request, I couldn't see if she'd posted on Facebook. I sent another text with only the words 'Ring me'.

I unwrapped my ham roll and tore a bite out of it. I leant against the side of the building, scrolling through Facebook when I saw Ashley had commented on Eddie Watt's wall. A remembrance post had been put up yesterday. The anniversary of the accident was coming up, the date seared into my mind forever. The date when everything changed. It wasn't until March but looked as though a family member was organising a balloon release to mark the occasion.

I took another bite, chewing slowly as something caught my eye, a flicker of recognition. I moved the screen upwards trying to find it again. There, around ten comments down from Ashley's. Karla Grant had commented on the remembrance post last night at almost midnight.

Love you always

I coughed, choking on a mouthful of doughy bread, eyes streaming as I stared at the screen. Trying to process what it meant. Karla knew Eddie. Knew him well enough to post on Facebook how much she loved him!

A cold sweat ran the length of my spine and I sank against the wall, feeling my legs give out. How did she know Eddie? Could they have been a couple before he got together with Ashley? Did we know her back then? I didn't think so, I had no memory of ever seeing her before my first day at Bright's. Maybe she'd known us, although Ash didn't remember her. Perhaps Karla wasn't her real name?

It dawned on me if she knew Eddie, if she was local to the St Helier estate or had been, she must know I killed him.

'Jess.' Dan's voice interrupted my thoughts and I looked up to see him frowning at me where I'd sunk to the gravel. He wrapped his hand around my upper arm and pulled me to my feet. His fingers digging into the flesh.

'You're hurting me,' I cried, trying to yank my arm away.

Dan's face was contorted, and he led me away from the warehouse doors further out into the yard.

'What the fuck is this?' he spat, shoving a piece of paper into my chest.

My feet scuffed the gravel as he carried me along. I pushed him off as we came to a halt at the edge of the plot, out of earshot of anyone. I peeled the paper away from my chest, glowering at Dan. I'd never seen him angry, but his eyes were ablaze. Holding the paper out, I blinked back tears as I tried to focus, registering where I'd seen it before.

'Where did you get this?' I spoke through gritted teeth. In my hand was the first image of me and Terry that had been put through my door. The one taken by the secret camera, of me kneeling in front of Terry on the night he died. He was still alive in this one. Before he pushed his cock in my mouth, before I bit down. Air rushed out of my lungs like I'd been winded. Even with my head bowed in the picture, Dan had worked out it was me.

'Well?' he said as I looked at him through watery eyes.

'H-have you seen the video?' I stammered.

'There's a fucking video?' He raised his voice, incredulous and my tears erupted.

'It's not what you think.'

'What do I think? That you have a thing for screwing the boss?'

I winced as he snatched the paper out of my hand and stalked away.

I left the yard, tears streaming down my cheeks, until I found a grass verge on a residential street and sat on the kerb. Dan thought I'd tricked him; I wasn't who I said I was. From the photo, he assumed I was sleeping with Terry, that's what was depicted, an act of consent.

I lit a cigarette and tried Karla again, no reply. I had to tell Dan, screw the others, I had to come clean. I smoked quickly, forming the words in my head, and hurried back to Bright's before I lost my nerve.

Laura stared at my stained puffy face as I zipped through the warehouse, whispering behind me, but I didn't care. Dan was in the office with the door shut, but I didn't knock, just barged straight in. He looked up in surprise, eyes wide, his anger subsided, whereas I was seething.

'Who sent you the photo?' I demanded.

'I don't know, it was just here, on my desk.'

I clenched my jaw.

'Look at the picture again,' I instructed, stabbing the desk with my finger.

'What?'

'Tell me what you see, Dan. Hang on, wait, let me tell you what I see. I see a girl on her knees in an office with the blinds closed, in front of her boss. The same boss that has a hidden camera in the corner to take photos or videos of these moments. What you don't see in this picture is my face, the panic in my eyes, how I felt sick when your brother unzipped his fly and forced himself on me.'

Dan's mouth hung open. He looked wounded, as though my words had been bullets, firing into him. Coming to his senses, he looked up in the corner above the shelf.

I sighed. 'It's not there. It's been moved. I don't know by who or where it is.'

'What are you saying, Jess? Are you telling me Terry assaulted you?'

I snorted. 'Not just me, all of us.'

Dan stared, lips moving, but nothing came out. He blinked and gave his head a slight shake, as though trying to dislodge the words I'd placed there.

'No, no.' Dan's voice was quiet, eyes imploring. I knew he didn't want it to be true. Who would?

'Your brother, Terry, was a low-life, a predator, who used us for his own filthy self-gratification,' I said flatly, before walking out of the office.

37

I collected my things and left without bothering to clock out. I was done for the day but didn't want to go home. The bedsit had been tidied; the horror of the morning now gone, but I wasn't sure I'd feel safe there. Also, Stuart might be fixing the door and I couldn't face more questions. The closest thing I had to a friend, bar Ashley, had stolen from me and the man I'd given myself to, had decided I was a slut. It was the latter that hurt the most, it ate me up inside. I'd been a target of sexual gratification. For him to assume I'd welcomed it in any way made me sick.

I balled my hands into fists as I stomped along, the fire in my belly still smouldering. I had no real idea where I was going until a 151 bus came past and I chased it to the next stop. I wanted comfort and there was only one place I'd get it.

The bus took me almost to the door and I jumped off, jogging up the path.

'Mum,' I called out as I unlocked the door, not wanting to surprise her.

'In here,' she called back from the sitting room.

Helen would be at work so I would have Mum all to myself.

She sat in the chair, her slippers on, but she was dressed and even wore a little make-up. Shirley Valentine was on the television and she had a tray of tea and biscuits on the table beside her. My chin wobbled as soon as I saw her.

'What's happened, poppet?' she said, taking one look at my puffy red-rimmed eyes and throwing her right arm open, the left she barely raised off her thigh. I swallowed hard, she'd called me poppet since I was a child. Hearing her say it sent me over the edge.

I drew into her, my knees to the carpet, head in her lap as I sobbed. All the fear, anger and frustration from the past few weeks leaking out. I had no control and Mum let me cry, stroking my hair and telling me it was going to be all right.

Eventually I sat back on my heels.

'Tell me what's wrong,' she implored, the creases damp surrounding her eyes.

'I don't know, Mum. Everything I touch seems to go wrong. I'm tainted, I'll always be tainted. It'll stay with me forever, follow me everywhere.'

'Yes, yes it will. Until you learn to forgive your-self. You had an accident, made a mistake and someone died. That will never change, but you've paid your debt to society. I love you; you know I do, I always will, but it was a mistake to come back here.'

I gasped and she shook her head.

'For you, only for you. There are too many mem-ories, too many people who know your business. How will you ever move on and rebuild with that death looming over you?'

I stood, wiping my tears and gave a solitary nod. Mum was right, she always was.

'I'll stick the kettle on, do you want one?'

Mum shook her head and picked up her small teacup, taking a slurp.

'Has the carer been in?' I shouted from the kitchen.

'No, Helen popped home at lunchtime,' Mum called back.

My jaw tightened, no doubt she'd already reported the burglary to Mum. Maybe she was right, Karla too, once I was signed off from probation perhaps a new start was what I needed. Somewhere nobody knew me, or what I'd done.

Terry's disappearance hung over me like a storm cloud, threatening to break at any second. We weren't in the clear yet, not by any stretch. Dan would have more questions and maybe he'd start joining the dots. I knew I had to be strong, stick to the plan, say nothing to no one. Even if Karla and I weren't on the same side any more, she didn't want to go back to prison any more than I did.

I made the tea and went outside for a cigarette, my head throbbing. I hadn't cried so much in years, not since my first night inside, when realisation hit I'd be in that cell for the next four years. Or the night of the accident where it all started, when they couldn't get a pulse from Eddie and Ashley wouldn't stop screaming.

I rolled the cigarette around between my thumb and forefinger, staring at the overgrown grass. Perhaps I should offer to cut it, but I knew the ground was too wet. In the summer, Mum would be in the garden all the time, soaking up the sun. Well, she used to. Did I really want to leave the area? Leave her behind?

A knock at the door jolted me from my thoughts and I stubbed my cigarette out.

'It's Donna,' Mum called as I passed the sitting room. I'd forgotten she was coming.

'Jess! Hi, how are you?' Donna, Mum's hairdresser, stepped over the threshold and dropped her box of tools, throwing her arms around me. She'd been cutting mine and Helen's hair since we were children and every two months or so without fail she'd perm and highlight Mum's hair, with a trim in between.

'I'm fine thanks, Donna, how are you? You look well.' Donna never seemed to age, her red hair almost reached her backside, hung from a ponytail.

'Good thank you, it's all the yoga I do, you know, good for the mind and body!'

'I'll make tea,' I offered, putting the kettle on again.

I helped Mum onto one of the kitchen chairs and Donna wrapped the black cloak around her. She sprayed her hair with a water bottle, combing it through. It must be only a trim today. Mum and Donna chatted about her eldest son, Matt, who'd started his own business. Pride radiated off Donna, rippling into the atmosphere. Did Mum ever speak about me like that? Doubtful, how could she be proud of me?

'How about you, Jess? If you don't mind me saying, your hair looks like it hasn't been cut in ages.'

'No, it hasn't. If you've got time, I'd love a couple of inches off,' I said, grabbing a handful and brushing the split ends against my palm.

I finished the tea and left Donna and Mum to it, going back outside for a smoke and to check my phone. Karla hadn't looked at my text or tried to ring, but I did have two missed calls from Dan. He could get stuffed, irritation bubbled from the depths of my stomach.

It was almost four and Helen would be back around half five. I was hoping I'd get a trim and be on my way before she returned. With the mood I was in and her poking her nose into my business, I was sure there'd be a fight. I didn't want to put Mum through it.

'Your turn?' Donna poked her head out, grinning at me.

I returned to the kitchen and sat in the chair. Mum had moved to the table, her hair blow-dried to perfection.

'How much off?'

'Good three inches, I reckon. My split ends are terrible.'

'Hmmmm,' Donna agreed. As she sprayed the questions began. What was prison like? Did you make any friends? Was it like *Bad Girls*, that show on ITV years ago?

Like a tennis player, I batted away serves which just kept coming. Trying to be polite to the woman who had known me since I was a child. It wasn't her fault, everyone had questions. Perhaps I should print an FAQ and carry it around with me to hand out as soon as the barrage started?

Thankfully, Mum managed to intervene and

steer the conversation away from prison life and onto the much safer topic of holidays.

I zoned out, watching my phone on the table vibrate. Another call from Dan. His third now.

'Someone's keen,' Donna said.

Mum smiled, her eyes glinting.

'Not any more,' I replied.

38

Donna offered me a lift home, she was heading over to Tesco and it was only five minutes out of her way. Before she could launch into more questions, I asked how Mum had been while I was away.

'Well, she was devastated obviously. You're her baby, you'll always be her baby. She felt it was an injustice, we all did. I mean that Watts kid, he was a nasty bit of work. Between you and me, I think you did the world a favour.' Donna patted my forearm and I smiled weakly. 'Course, when your mum had her stroke, they had it rough for a while. Helen was stressed out, but your mum is doing better, the physio is helping.'

'I wish I could have been there,' I admitted, biting my lip to stop it quivering. I had no more tears left today.

'I know, pet, but she's fine now, see. All she needs is a little bit of extra help. She's still the same, thank God she hasn't lost it up here.' Donna tapped her temple.

As we approached the house, Donna pulled up behind Dan's silver Mazda. I felt a surge of nervous excitement. What was he doing here? Had he come to made amends? If he had, despite admiring the effort, I was too annoyed to entertain it. He opened the door, lingering by it, as I opened mine, thanking Donna for the lift and saying goodbye. I ignored him and walked down the path, my key ready, hearing the sound of Donna's car pull away.

'Jess, wait. I'm sorry.' He was a few steps behind, and I turned around, my hands on my hips.

'I didn't lie to you. Your brother was a monster,' I blurted, louder than I'd intended.

Dan didn't answer, he looked shell-shocked, as though my words were peppered with bullets.

Stuart's front door opened, and he came out, laden with cans for the recycling bin. Eyeing Dan suspiciously, he paused mid step. 'You all right, Jess?' Stuart's voice sounded gruff, deeper than usual, and I almost chuckled.

'Fine. How much do I owe you for the door?' I asked, turning away from Dan.

'Nothing, I fixed it, you're right it just needed knocking out a bit. Let me know if there's a draught.'

'Will do, thanks, Stuart.'

He nodded, dumped the cans and moved back inside.

'Can I come in?' Dan asked.

'I don't think so. I'm pretty tired, I've had an awful day. I got burgled this morning.'

'Yes, sorry, I didn't get your voicemail until later, after, you know...' Dan had the decency to stare at the ground.

'After you practically called me a slut?' I prompted.

'I didn't say that.' He frowned.

'Okay, insinuated then.' I sighed, the fight leaving me.

'Tell me what happened.' His eyes pleaded with mine.

I didn't have the energy to explain to him what an

arsehole his brother was. How we all knew, but couldn't prove, that Barry and he had some kind of arrangement. We were all cattle as far as they were concerned. 'Look, Dan, I don't want to get into it now.'

I unlocked the door and went inside, closing it behind me, leaving Dan out in the cold. I swallowed the lump in my throat and crawled into bed, kicking off my trainers. No inclination to cook, I pulled the duvet over me and closed my eyes.

* * *

The following day when I got to work, Karla was already there, sporting a nasty black eye and split lip.

'I've been calling you, why haven't you answered?' I hissed, dragging her into the yard by the elbow.

'I've been a bit busy,' she gestured at her face and rolled her eyes.

'You broke into my fucking house, Karla!' I snarled, ignoring her bruised face.

'I'm sorry, I had no choice, I had to get the money and you weren't answering your phone.'

My arms springing to life, I shoved her into the wire fence and for a second she stared at me, mouth gaping, before shoving me back.

I launched at her, pushing her to the ground, my hands finding her throat as she thrashed underneath me.

'What the fuck is going on here?' A hand grabbed me by the scruff of the neck and lifted me off Karla as she scrabbled back in the dirt, coughing and shooting daggers at me. Barry held me up like I weighed nothing. 'You two fighting over the boss? I know it's Valentine's Day tomorrow, but I never saw you do that with Terry.' Barry smirked and I wrenched out of his grip.

'Fuck off, Barry,' Karla snapped as she stood and brushed herself off.

'She did that to you?' Barry pointed from me to Karla's face.

'No I didn't,' I interrupted, my tone measured.

'Jess,' Dan called from across the yard. He stood by the shutters, flanked by two men, one in a suit and one wearing a police uniform.

'Shit,' muttered Karla, under her breath, standing close enough for me to catch it.

'What have you done, Jessica?' Barry's voice came from behind me, laced with sarcasm.

I moved towards Dan, glaring at him.

'This is Detective Wimslow and you remember Officer Stokes, they want to ask you a couple of questions about Terry.'

I swallowed hard, smiling tightly at the pair.

Stokes raised his hand in greeting, blinking through his white blond eyelashes. Wimslow was the polar opposite, where Stokes was pale, he was Mediterranean-looking with olive skin, dark eyes and black slicked-back hair. I'd find him more attractive if I wasn't concerned he was about to lock me up.

'Sure.'

They turned and headed back to Dan's office and I followed, Barry left behind.

'Excuse me, I'm Jess's community rehabilitation officer, is there something I should know?' Sweat hung on his top lip where he'd jogged to catch us up.

'It's only a couple of questions Mr...' The detective raised an eyebrow.

'Mulligan,' Barry provided.

'I'll be fine, Barry,' I managed as I started to close the door behind me.

'I'll leave you to it.' Dan hung back to talk to Barry. I was glad he'd stayed out, partly because I couldn't bear to look at him and partly because what I was going to say, he wouldn't want to hear.

I sat across the desk from the detective. Officer Stokes stood behind, there was no chair for him. His hands clasped behind his back, he remained still, as though he was outside Buckingham Palace.

Detective Wimslow slid the black and white image across the desk to me. I was sick of looking at it. Dan had called them, of course he had. Wanting to do the right thing in the face of what I'd told him, but, of course, now it gave me a motive. It gave all of us a motive.

'Do you want to tell me what's going on in this picture, Jess?'

'I think it's pretty self-explanatory.' I crossed my arms, trying to rein in my mouth, but I was pissed off. Karla had robbed me and Dan had sold me out.

'Okay, I'll rephrase. Simple question. Did Terry take advantage of you in any way during your employment at Bright's?'

'Yes.'

'Did he force or coerce you into performing oral sex?'

'Yes.' My eyes prickled, but I refused to blink.

'When did this happen?'

'Shortly after I started.'

The detective leant forward and interlocked his fingers. His hands were massive, and he wore a silver linked watch, the hairs on his wrist pushing through the gaps. 'Did he threaten you?'

'He said money had gone missing and if I didn't do what he wanted, I'd have my probation revoked. He'd get me sent back to prison.' My chest deflated as I said it out loud, like a flurry releasing from my mouth with the words spoken.

'Do you know if it was just you, or anybody else?'

'I think all of us.'

The detective wrinkled his nose. He gazed past my shoulder out of the office window. 'Okay, we'll need you to provide a statement of what happened. I'll have to speak to everyone here. Did you know you were being filmed?'

'No.' I wrung my hands, now there was two of us searching for the camera. I had to hope whoever had sent me and Dan the photos, didn't hand it over to the police. If there was video of what Terry had done to us, then there had to be video of what Karla and I did to him.

'When was the last time you saw Terry?'

'I told Officer Stokes, on the Friday he disappeared, just after five when I was leaving. Has anyone found him yet?' I tried to muster a look of concern, clearing my throat.

'No, not yet. Do you have any idea of his whereabouts?'

I shook my head.

'We need to set up interviews at the station, for all you ladies, I think. Stokes, can you set that up for tomorrow. We need the names and contacts for all employees. Let Mr Bright have the times and he can let them know. We can send a car if need be.'

'Sure thing.' Officer Stokes nodded and, for a second, I thought he might salute.

I pushed my chair back and got to my feet. I needed a cigarette.

'Yes, you can leave, Jess. I'll see you tomorrow.' He tilted his head and smiled, but it didn't reach his eyes. Those were watching me like a hawk.

39

Detective Wimslow had those penetrating eyes you normally only see in TV thrillers, ones where they always have a hunch.

I shook the notion from my head. No one knew anything and I had to keep it that way. Pretty easy, all I had to do was stick to the story. If they hadn't found anything incriminating on the CCTV at Bright's or in Croydon town centre, or inside Terry's car, then we were home free.

Karla's words rung in my head 'no body, no crime'. All things considered, we were in a good position, before Dan had a crisis of conscience. Or was it

more than that? Did he suspect me of doing something to Terry?

Returning to the yard, not caring I hadn't
washed, dried or pressed an inch of fabric today, I lit
a cigarette and sucked in the smoke. Karla was beside me in seconds, a cigarette pulled from the
packet and lit in an instant. She appeared jittery, like
an addict fumbling to get their first fix of the day.

'So?' she said.

'Fuck off.'

'Don't be a dick. What's happened, why do they
want to talk to you?'

'They want to talk to all of us.'

Karla frowned, her chin jutting forward. 'Why?'

'Because someone sent Dan the photo of me in
the office. For all I know, it could have been you.' I
shifted my body away from Karla, who tutted.

'Look. I'm sorry I broke in. I owe money to some
bad people okay, I needed it.' She pointed at the
purple bruise around her swollen eye. Whatever
Karla had got herself into, I didn't want to be a part
of it. I was going to do everything to ensure I
wouldn't be going back to prison.

'Well, you've got it now. I think that's us even,

wouldn't you say?' I raised my eyebrows and she snorted.

'Whatever,' Karla replied, chucking her cigarette as Laura poked her head out of the warehouse door.

'Is no one doing any work today, fucking skivers!'

'Fuck off,' Karla and I said in unison as we made our way back inside.

I finished the rest of my shift, working alongside Natalia, loading tablecloths from a local restaurant. The smell of spices and curried sauce made me salivate.

I half expected Dan to come and find me, but he called a meeting at quarter to five, as we were packing up. He explained to the girls that the police wanted to ask us all some questions about Terry and we should come to work as normal tomorrow. A car would be sent to collect us for individual interviews at the station and bring us back afterwards.

'Yippee, day trip to the cop shop,' Laura mocked.

Dan laughed awkwardly and scratched his chin. 'I'm sure it'll be quick and painless; you'll be back here knee-deep in laundry before you know it.'

I glanced around at the girls as they began to disperse, there was an air of disquiet as they exchanged looks, already wondering how much to say. Some maybe wondering if we should drag Barry into it. Expose him for the fraud he was. I wasn't sure it was something we could prove though, not without Terry, and he wouldn't be making an appearance any time soon.

'Hey, want to go for a drink after work?' Dan's voice was gentle as he approached after the others had moved off.

'Why did you call the police?'

He looked puzzled at my obvious frustration, rocking back on his heels. 'Why wouldn't I?' I looked away, running my tongue across my teeth. I couldn't really blame Dan; he was only doing what he thought was right.

It would be good to go for a drink, I could do with one. Plus, I had to find out what Dan knew, or thought he knew. He waited for me outside his office while I used the bathroom and made myself look presentable.

On the way out, Karla overtook us, smirking, but thankfully she didn't say anything.

Dan locked up and we walked around the back to

the yard. The bitter wind whipped my face and I shrank into my coat.

We didn't talk much on the way to the pub, only to comment on the weather. This time he took me to The Greyhound, which overlooked a large pond. It was picturesque, or would have been in summer when you could sit outside and admire the view. Inside, there was no log fire, but we found a quiet corner to sit in and Dan got us drinks. Half a lager for him, a cider for me.

'I am sorry for my reaction yesterday. I was surprised and appalled obviously.'

'And you jumped to conclusions,' I said.

'Yes, I jumped to conclusions.'

'I'm sorry you had to find out like that. If it were up to me, you would never have known.'

'Why didn't you tell me?'

'How could I? Dan, he blackmailed me, not just me, all of us. I'm sure Barry's got something to do with it. He's dodgy as fuck.' The words spilled out and I took a mouthful of my cider, to stop talking. The amber liquid warming my throat.

'Yeah I don't much like him. I'm so sorry about

my brother. I had no idea he's such a... such a...' he faltered.

'Depraved sexual deviant?' I tried to make light of the situation, but Dan's sombre face didn't change. I couldn't blame him; it wasn't a laughing matter. How would I feel if Helen had been unearthed as a paedo or something? 'I don't know why you called the police though?'

'Because he should be held accountable, if he's done those things, he should pay for them.' Dan gulped his drink, his knuckles white on the glass.

'What do you mean "if"?' My hackles up.

Dan shook his head, backtracking.

I waved him away, downing the rest of my drink. I had to calm down, I felt like a fuse about to blow.

'Anyway, he's not here. All the police are going to do is drag your workforce through the mill, having to explain in detail how they were sexually assaulted by their boss.'

Dan sighed and hung his head in his hands.

I stood to go to the bar to get us more drinks. Dan was scrolling through his phone when I returned, but he put it away when I joined him, carrying on where we left off.

'I'm sorry. I thought I was doing the right thing. For all I know, it could have something to do with his disappearance.'

'How do you mean?' I narrowed my eyes.

'Well, if he's into *that*, he might be mixed up with all sorts of weirdos.' Dan took my hand across the table, his touch warm and inviting. I slid my fingers along his. 'Your hair looks nice by the way.'

I was surprised he'd noticed.

'It desperately needed a cut,' I admitted.

'Do you want anything to eat? I'm kind of hungry.' He picked up the menu and leafed through it.

'Sure, I'm hungry too. We could get a takeaway and go back to yours?' I suggested, wanting to get out of the pub. No longer wanting to talk about Terry. What was done was done, there was little point in holding on to my anger. I wanted things back to the way they were. With Dan I felt happy and safe, he was a good man and besides no one was perfect.

'Why not yours?' Dan quizzed, smiling.

'Because you've got a bigger bed,' I replied, aware my face had turned crimson.

'Sold.' Dan knocked back his drink in one go and waited for me to finish mine.

On the way back to the car, he wrapped his arm around me, and I leant into his side, glad he was no longer interested in talking about Terry. Once inside his car, though, Dan turned on the engine and pulled away before glancing at me.

'Who do you think sent the photo to me? I mean, it was in an envelope on my desk, with my name written on, it didn't come through the post.'

Something niggled at me, something from earlier that hadn't sat right at the time, but there was so much going on I missed it. The photo. When I told Karla the photo had been sent to Dan, she didn't ask which one. She didn't ask if it was the one where Terry was alive or where he was already dead in the doorway of his office. I'd been sent both, had both put through my door. She didn't ask, because she already knew. What the hell was she up to? Did it have something to do with her face today or the money? Could she be being blackmailed? I had to find out what Karla had got herself into before she exposed us both.

40

Hours later, I lay beside Dan staring at the ceiling unable to sleep. He shuffled and rolled over, eyelids fluttering amidst a dream. We'd ordered a Chinese takeaway and opened a bottle of wine before falling into bed. Avoiding the topic of Terry's disappearance, I managed to forget, for a couple of hours at least, what tomorrow would bring.

Watching him sleep sent a rush of guilt through me. I loved spending time with him, his touch tonight was tender, like I was so fragile I might break. I was glad I'd waited. Sex with Dan was infinitely better than any fumble at seventeen with someone my own age. He was older, more experienced, and I felt like an adult.

I worried I was falling for him, unsure how that could ever work after what I'd done to Terry. To have that bigger secret would be like a chasm between us.

He rolled over onto his back, jolting me from my thoughts. I watched the rise and fall of his chest, the dip in the centre and the curve of the muscles. Resisting the urge to stroke him, I rolled away. I needed to think clearly.

If Karla had sent the photos and put Terry's ring in my locker, I had to find out why. Was she planning to frame me for his disappearance? It didn't make any sense when she helped me get rid of his body. Any evidence that implicated me, surely implicated her too. Was she trying to scare me, push me to make a mistake? Had she got herself mixed up in something that was out of her league – stupid when she was so close to being free.

Questions swirled around my head with no logical answers to satisfy them. I slid my phone off the bedside table and sent a text to Ashley, asking how she was. I'd ring her tomorrow, perhaps she'd know what to do. All I could focus on was giving my statement to the police and making sure I stuck to my story. I wasn't sure what they could do, even if we all told the truth about Terry. They could hardly bring a dead man to justice, could they?

I managed a few hours before being rudely woken by Dan's shrill alarm. I jumped out of bed to use the bathroom, nervous energy already making my stomach cramp. When I came back, Dan was stretching, his skin taut over the muscles in his torso. I briefly considering climbing back in.

'Where are you rushing off to?' Dan asked as I pulled on my jeans.

'Home, I need to have a shower and get ready.'

'You okay?' Dan said, rubbing sleep out of his eyes and propping himself up.

'Yeah fine, I'm just nervous about the police interview.'

He narrowed his eyes. 'What do you have to be nervous about?' Did he suspect something?

'I guess you've never had to explain a sexual assault to a complete stranger. It's not exactly going to be pleasant!' I snapped.

'Sorry, sorry. Wasn't thinking.'

I slipped on my trainers, legs buckling. I needed some air.

'I'll catch you later,' I said, grabbing my bag and slinging it over my shoulder.

Outside was crisp and bracing, the sun ebbing higher, full of promise, but it wouldn't be warm. It would be another cold February day ahead, although the shoots of daffodils were coming up on the grass verges. The assurance that spring and warmer weather was to come.

When I reached home, having caught a passing bus which took me halfway, it was already eight. I was pleased to see the bedsit untouched, having pictured all the way home what I would find.

I wasn't inside long, a quick shower, slice of toast and a touch of mascara before heading back out the door.

My pocket buzzed and I fished out my phone as I walked to work, I wanted the fresh air, needing the vitamin D. Ashley's name flashed up on the screen, she was up early.

'Hiya,' she said when I answered.

'Hi, how are you?'

'Good thanks, been up half the night finishing

this essay, I must have rewritten the bloody thing about five times, so I'm knackered.' She yawned. 'What about you?'

'I've got so much to tell you.'

'Did everything go all right with Dan? I've been waiting for you to ring me with the goss!' That wasn't what I'd meant, but I realised popping my cherry had been overshadowed by the photos and the police visit. I hadn't even got around to telling Ashley about it.

'It was amazing, we had dinner, wine, he was gentle. It was perfect,' I reminisced.

'Ah, I'm glad. Told you. He sounds like a keeper,' Ashley said, but my head was all over the place. Making the transition to Dan's girlfriend was the last thing on my mind.

'Listen, you know the girl I mentioned, Karla, you said you didn't know her.'

'Yeah.'

'Well, I think she knows us from old. Karla Grant...' I waited.

'Yeah, I remember you saying, but no, I don't remember her,' Ashley said.

'Well she knows – sorry knew Eddie. She commented on his memorial event.'

'That's weird, hang on, let me look.' I heard some background noise, Ashley humming as I imagined her scrolling through the long list of people who'd commented. 'Shit!'

'What?'

'I can't believe I didn't make the connection before. Karla Grant?'

'Yeah.' My mouth dried up, throat clogging as I waited for Ashley to continue.

'I only knew her as K. It's what everyone called her, I thought her name was Kai or Kay or something. I didn't know her surname.'

'Ash, who is she?'

'She's Eddie's sister.'

I could hear the blood thudding in my ears as a boy on a skateboard whizzed past me and I dropped the phone, it clattered to the pavement.

'Shit,' I mumbled, scooping it up and checking the screen.

'Jess, Jess, you still there?'

'How is she Eddie's sister? I mean, I'm not being

funny, but Eddie was white, pale as me. Karla is mixed race.'

'You don't remember, do you? We used to call the house Barnardo's, there were about ten kids living there, they used to foster. Eddie and K, Karla, were foster kids. The Prices weren't their biological parents, they had a couple of kids of their own but used to foster too. They were lovely people, had fostered for years.'

Goosebumps peppered my skin as I hurried along, trying to make sense of what Ashley was saying. I had a vague memory of the nickname Barnardo's for a house on the estate, but it was long before Ashley and Eddie hooked up.

'So your mate, Karla, is Eddie's sister?'

'It would appear so.'

'Does she know?'

'She must know. I don't see how she can't know. She's been inside, different prison, but got out a few months before me.'

'What was she in for?'

'Drug dealing.'

'Makes sense, someone had their claws into all the kids in that family.'

'Listen I've got to go. I'll speak to you over the weekend.'

I ended the call and lit a cigarette, ignoring the tremble in my hands.

Now I knew why Karla would have a reason to target me. But it still didn't shed any light on why she would firstly help me dispose of Terry, only to try and set me up for the crime. If that was what she was doing? My insides churned; did I have reason to fear my interview with the police today? Was Karla going to grass me up? Would she tell the police what really happened? I had to get to her before her interview.

41

I jogged, slowly at first, but as fear took hold, I sprinted to Bright's, arriving ten minutes before nine, sweaty and with a stitch.

'What happened to you?' Agnes wrinkled her nose at my dishevelled appearance as we crossed paths at the lockers.

'Nothing. Fancied a jog. Seen Karla yet?' I panted.

'No. I've seen rota, we're together today. Pressing machine. Try not to burn yourself this time, eh.' Agnes disappeared around the corner into the warehouse as I put my things in my locker.

I made a pit stop at the ladies' to splash some cold water on my glowing face before joining her.

It'll be fine, Karla will be here soon, and I can talk to her. Make her see sense. Perhaps once it was all out in the open, she'd understand. I'd be able to tell her the truth of what happened in the car, the real version only Ashley and I knew.

'Hey.' Dan caught me around the waist as I hurried to join Agnes, making me jump. He released me quickly before anyone saw, a mischievous look in his eyes. 'I missed you this morning.'

Despite my worries, I broke into a smile; it was nice to feel wanted. I wished I could enjoy it, everything seemed clouded by Terry and Karla.

'Oh, and happy Valentine's Day.' He reached forward and gave me a kiss. I blushed; I'd been so caught up I'd completely forgot.

'Happy Valentine's Day,' I replied, feeling the heat in my cheeks.

'Ready for today?'

'Guess so. Are the police here yet?'

'Yes, and I've swapped you with Hanna, so you're one of the first. As you were nervous, I thought you might prefer to get it over and done with.'

I looked around; a deer caught in the headlights. I had to find Karla now.

'Is Karla here?'

'She's in the car already, I caught her on the way in.'

I nodded and returned to the locker to get my bag, blinking away my dizziness. 'Can you tell Agnes where I've gone, she'll be waiting for me on the pressing machine.'

'Sure. Good luck, see you in a bit.' Dan smiled at me sympathetically, brushing his fingers past mine as I went.

I chewed my lip, pulling open the door to Bright's and seeing the police car waiting outside, its engine running. Karla sat in the passenger seat; I could see her mass of curls past the driver. It wasn't Officer Stokes driving.

In the back, Laura sat chewing her fingernails, her face pale. I guessed for some of us even getting back inside a police car would bring back memories we'd all prefer to forget. I had no idea what Laura had done to serve time, but as she shifted in her seat, it was obvious how nervous she was.

'Miss Strickland?' a voice jolted me back into the present and the driver, a female officer I'd not seen before, called out to me through her window.

I nodded and climbed in the back next to Laura.

She smiled at me tightly and my stomach lurched, even the new-car smell brought back memories. I'd been transported from the hospital once discharged directly into custody, where I was arrested for causing death by dangerous driving, with a mountain of CCTV capturing me swerve along the road and eventually into a tree.

As we pulled away, Karla turned to look at me, her face devoid of emotion, like she was dead behind the eyes. I studied her face for a second, trying to make the connection that I now knew was there. As hard as I tried, I had no recollection of her from the estate. Knowing she was Eddie's sister; I imagined her hatred must have been difficult to hide when she finally met the person responsible for robbing her brother of his life.

The policewoman tried to make conversation with her, raising the topic of the bruising around her eye which was turning green. Karla was giving her the old, 'I walked into a door' routine, which the officer was not buying.

Throughout the journey Laura kept fidgeting and

I stared out of the window for a distraction. Each of us apprehensive about the interview ahead.

When we finally reached the station, the memories came floating back. The interview rooms hadn't changed in four years, the same paint peeling off the walls, the same table and chairs. I went first, keen to get it over and done with, while Karla and Laura waited in the seating area. I should have pushed Laura to go, then Karla and I would have had a chance to talk alone. Now I needed to pray she wouldn't bubble me up. Surely there was too much at stake for her to take the risk. She had to know if she offered me up, there was the possibility I'd drag her down with me.

Detective Wimslow arrived with another lady I didn't recognise; she was in plain clothes and was introduced as Detective Mansfield. No doubt brought in because of the delicate questions likely to be asked.

Wimslow kicked off by asking when I first joined Bright's, what date it was, how I came to get the job. I told them about Barry, our community rehabilitation officer, how he suggested Bright's would be a good fit. I knew I wouldn't need to say any more. They'd connect the dots when all of us had the same story, even if no one cast any shade on him. They'd see the pattern, look at his placements and maybe even take a look at his bank account, or perhaps I'd seen too many movies.

'When was the first time Terry acted inappropriately towards you?'

'It was my second week when he called me in to have a chat about how I was getting on. He told me he liked to look after his girls, bonus schemes, extra hours, basically if I was good to him, he'd be good to me. I got the general idea straight away.'

'And did he make any advances to you then?' Mansfield asked, shuffling forward in her seat. I nodded.

'Of sorts, but I told him to get stuffed and left. When I came back to work the next day, he didn't mention anything, so I thought I'd be left alone.'

'Did you tell any of the others?'

I shook my head.

'Okay, so you didn't tell any of the other employees, what about Barry, did you go to him about it?'

'No.'

'Why not?' Wimslow asked.

'Because the next time Terry called me in, Barry was already there. Apparently, money had gone missing and Barry was warning me how easy it would be for me to get my probation revoked if I didn't toe the line.'

'What money had gone missing?'

'I don't think there was any money, it was just a way to get us to do what he wanted.' I knew that to be true, although I couldn't prove it.

Detective Mansfield smiled at me, her expression warm and comforting, although in my mind all I could hear was *she's police, you can't trust her.*

'Has Terry ever assaulted you?' she asked.

'Yes, he forced me to give him oral sex.' I cringed at the term, but it was better than saying the words 'blow job' to a policeman. I closed my eyes, rubbing my temples. Saying the words took me right back to that claustrophobic office and the clinking of Terry unbuckling his belt. My throat narrowed and I coughed.

'When was this?'

I couldn't remember the exact date, I'd tried to block it from memory, but I told the police when I thought it was.

'Did it happen more than once?'

I shook my head. A lie, but I wasn't going to admit an assault on the night he disappeared, that would be stupid.

'Do you hate Terry?'

I glared at Wimslow. *Here we go.* 'What do you think? Everyone hates him. He's a predator.' I bit, unable to hold back. My cool demeanour vanished.

'Has he ever forced you to have sex with him?'

'No, not me, others.'

'Who?'

'It's not my place to say. It's up to them if they want to share it with you.' I pursed my lips and crossed my arms. Trying to remind myself their job was to make me uneasy and it was stupid to fall into their trap.

'Jess, we're just trying to find out what happened to Terry and build a picture of what sort of man he was.'

This time, I remained quiet; I didn't need to tell them what sort of man he was. The worst kind.

They went on to ask about the camera, did I know it was there, had I seen the photo before? I answered no to everything, praying Karla wouldn't say differently. I hadn't told Dan I'd received two photos through my door. If only I'd had the chance to speak to her. I should have rung her last night; it was stupid of me to be so unprepared. Although it was unlikely they'd be able to tie me to Terry's disappearance.

I shifted in my seat; sure the interview would be near the end. How many more questions could they ask? Wimslow leaned forward, placing his forearms on the table and clasping his fingers together. He looked fixedly at me and I had to stop myself from squirming under his gaze.

'Let's go back to the Friday that Terry was last seen. Can you talk us through the day, your move-ments, Terry's movements, because we have reason to believe you may have been the last person to see him alive...'

42

Shit. How much did they know? Karla could have been here all night, for all I knew, spilling her guts and telling them everything. A cold sweat settled on the small of my back and I flexed my fingers, the chill making them go numb.

Take it easy, they're fishing, they don't know anything. We'd done everything right, left no trace. I was sure of it.

Again, I ran through the events of that day, how I left shortly after five when Terry was still in his office. Afterwards, the questions came about my movements later that evening. What did I do when I left work? I avoided using Karla as an alibi, like we had arranged. I had a feeling she wouldn't be keeping to her end of the bargain. I told them I walked home, alone. They asked what I'd had for dinner? Did I speak to anyone? See anyone? Did I watch any television?

My voice cracked as my throat dried up and I sipped the water they'd provided whilst trying to answer their questions. *Always stick as close to the truth as possible.* Karla had said there was no CCTV in the roads we'd walked through, but how could she have been certain? For all I knew it could have all been a pack of lies? She could have been setting me up from the start.

As the pressure mounted, Wimslow suddenly leaned back in his seat, thanking me for coming. The interview was over.

I sighed inwardly; my entire body sagged.

'When you find Terry, will he be charged?' I asked, trying to deflect the spotlight off me for a moment, so they'd believe I didn't know what happened to Terry.

'We're gathering evidence at the moment, but with many witnesses coming forward, it's likely we'll be able to build a case.'

I smiled tightly and left the room. Fat lot of good it would do now, but Terry got what he deserved in the end, even if it hadn't been delivered by the Crown Prosecution Service.

Back in the waiting area, both Laura and Karla had disappeared. I assumed they were being interviewed. The clock behind the Perspex window displayed five to eleven.

Unable to sit still, I paced the floor, backwards and forwards, stopping momentarily to read the signs on the noticeboard.

Laura came back first, looking visibly shaken, her face as white as a sheet. I wrapped an arm around her briefly and gave her a squeeze.

She leaned into me, whispering. 'That was awful.'

'Did you tell them what Terry did to you?' I asked, not knowing for sure if he'd ever hurt Laura.

She nodded and I knew from the pain in her eyes she'd relived something she'd rather forget.

'Well done, it's over now.'

We flopped into the chairs and Laura chewed the sleeve of her hoody, standing a few minutes later when Karla appeared.

In contrast, she appeared unfazed, her expression rigid. I was dying to know what she'd said to the police, but before I could ask, another uniformed officer was buzzed through from the corridor and announced he was going to drive us back to Bright's.

I texted Dan on the way back, letting him know we'd be there shortly. He didn't reply and when we returned, I saw why. It was all hands on deck as a rush turnaround of towels had come through from a top London hotel.

'Their current supplier has two machines broken down. So, this is our chance to show them what we can do,' Dan shouted across the sound of the washing machine on its full spin. He'd rolled up his sleeves and helped Natalia unload another batch. I'd never seen Terry get stuck in before. Dan's forehead glistened as he worked and I found myself staring, daydreaming about peeling the damp shirt off him. 'Are you giving us a hand or what?' he called, sniggering as he noticed my eyes had glazed over.

I nodded and hurried to put my stuff in my locker. Catching Karla alone, I pulled her to one side along the narrow corridor.

'What did you tell the police?'

'What do you think I told the police?' She frowned at me, but I fixed my stare and waited. 'I didn't tell them anything all right. Can you get off my back?'

'We need to talk,' I said.

'We *are* talking.' Her voice dipped in sarcasm and I had to resist the urge to slap the smirk off her face.

'Guys, Dan's waiting for you.' Natalia popped her head around the corner.

I scowled at her timing.

'After work,' I said to Karla, as we headed back to the warehouse.

The rest of Friday passed in a haze of bright white towels. We got through them all in the end, my arms ached from the lifting and folding. All of us resembled a sweaty, frizzy mess by the time they were collected. As a thank you, Dan bought cold cans of Coke and heart-shaped doughnuts from the café, and we slouched on the floor, enjoying our treat.

I'd not seen everyone in such a good mood before, chatting amongst themselves, smiling and laughing. It was never like that when Terry was in charge. Dan's small gesture had been a morale boost at the end of a hard day. I was sure most were relieved their police interview was over, the ordeal of explaining what Terry had done to each of them no longer a weight on their shoulders.

'We're back,' came Agnes's voice as she peered around the corner into the warehouse, eyes widening at us chilling on the floor, our fingers sticky with icing.

I beamed at Agnes and Hanna as they rounded the corner, the last to return from the cop shop. My smile faded when Detective Wimslow followed behind.

'Ah excellent. I hoped you'd still be here. Miss Strickland, can you come with me please?'

I heaved myself to my feet at the same time as Dan, my muscles rigid and non-compliant.

'What for?' he jumped in as I stared incredulously at the detective.

'We just need to ask some more questions at the station.'

The room was silent, all eyes on me as Dan moved to speak to the detective. My heart began to pound and the vein in my forehead throbbed.

'But why?' he pressed.

'If you could come with me please,' Wimslow repeated.

Had Karla grassed? I shot a look at her. *What have you done?*

She smirked; one eyebrow raised. Her eyes locked on mine and my gut jolted as though I'd been sucker-punched.

It didn't feel real as I walked out to the lockers to collect my things, Dan coming to join me. My legs were like jelly, as though they belonged to someone else.

'They won't tell me what it's about. What's going on, Jess?' He looked concerned, almost panicked, which put me on edge.

'I don't know,' I replied, trying to keep my voice steady. *It's okay, they don't know anything. It'll be fine.*

There was no small talk in the car, Wimslow kept glancing in his rear-view mirror at me, but I ignored him. Instead concentrating on trying to keep as still as possible, no fidgeting, no nerves on show. I wasn't going to give anything away. I wasn't under arrest, not yet anyway. Did I need a solicitor? How would I even go about finding one? My pulse quickened and I silently gasped for air, sucking in rapid shallow breaths.

Calm down, Jess, or you're going to hyperventilate.

On arrival, I was escorted into the same interview room as before. Wimslow sat and was joined by Detective Mansfield again, who smiled as she entered. She fixed the machine to record and once the date, time and occupants had been recorded, Wimslow jumped straight in.

'Earlier we asked you if you knew you were being filmed. You told us you didn't, but we've heard that you had seen the image before, the one that was sent to Daniel Bright.' Wimslow frowned at me, his hands clasped on the desk.

I remained silent, debating whether to stay that way.

'We've been told, Jess, that someone sent a photo to your home address. In fact, not one, but two photos.'

Still I remained quiet, weighing my options. Did I talk or not? Either way, Karla had fucked me.

43

I considered my choices. If I didn't talk, I looked like I had something to hide. If I did talk, I had to be sure I wasn't going to tie myself up in lies I'd already told. Karla had pointed them in my direction, and I had to steer them away.

'I did get sent the photos.'

'Why did you lie?' Wimslow's eyes were like slits, I'd lost his trust now.

'Because I couldn't bear to think of anyone else seeing them, those photos of me, doing... that.' My eyes watered and I let them, a little emotion would do me no harm. 'I got sent two and I was waiting for something else, a message or something,' I continued.

'Did you think you were being blackmailed?' Mansfield asked.

'I assumed so, but I never received anything else. I thought perhaps it was Terry, or maybe Barry.'

Wimslow's chin jutted forwards, ears pricked up. Bingo. 'What made you think that?'

'I believe Terry owed Barry money; I'd heard it mentioned around the warehouse. I'm not sure what for though.' I had to hope Wimslow wasn't going to drop my name to Barry, although I was sure he'd know where it came from. I'd have to worry about it later. All I had in my arsenal was deflection.

Detective Mansfield scribbled on her pad, she was left-handed and had smudges of ink beneath her little finger; I noticed as she brushed her fringe out of her eyes.

'Did you have anything to do with Terry Bright's disappearance?' The question came out of nowhere.

I snorted and Wimslow raised his eyebrows.

'Something funny?'

'Well, have you seen the size of me? I don't know what you think happened, but I had nothing to do with it. I mean even Dan thinks his brother is holed up with some prostitute somewhere.'

'There's been no bank account usage, no phone records since the Friday when you were the last reported person to see him.'

'What Terry did or where he went once I left Bright's, I have no idea.' I leant back and folded my arms, eyes blazing.

They had nothing; I was sure of it.

The detectives glanced at each other, before Mansfield leant forward in her seat, clasping her hands together.

'You see, the thing is, Jess, the CCTV we have of Terry leaving the warehouse isn't great quality. We can't be sure it's him. We're comparing it with other images of him to see if there are any differences.'

The room fell silent, you could hear a pin drop. None of us moved. I froze in my seat as my stomach plummeted. Did they think it was someone else?

Doesn't matter, can they prove it? the voice in my head counselled.

Saliva rushed into my mouth, making me nauseas, all the time trying to conceal how I was feeling. To keep my poker face.

'Well, I'm sorry, I can't help you. I saw him as I left Bright's and that was the last time.' I hoped my bravado would convince them. Why were they even pursuing it? It wasn't as though he'd turned up dead. Was Dan putting pressure on them for results?

'Okay thanks, Jess, you're free to leave. Don't go too far though, eh,' Wimslow said, shuffling some papers, his expression grave.

I wasn't offered a lift and had to make my own way home. I rang Karla three times, but there was no answer; it was gone six and she wouldn't have hung around for me. I had to talk to her about Eddie. She was playing around with my life; my freedom was on the line and I had no damn clue where she lived. Was all this revenge for the accident? I'd paid my dues, done my time. What more did she want?

As I walked along, it hit me around the head like a sledgehammer. Fuck! I hadn't got rid of Terry's coat, hat and boots. They were still in a bag in the corner of the bedsit, by the clothes rail. I sped up, eager to get home. Too full of nervous energy, I didn't bother to wait at any of the bus stops and I ignored Dan's calls. Heart pumping, I walked as quickly as I could, bursting into a jog every so often. How had I been so careless? I'd forgotten about them, sitting there. In-criminating evidence. My DNA would be on those boots, the hat and coat, it would show I'd worn them. That in turn would prove I was the figure on the CCTV. Shit!

Panic rose within and I was light-headed by the time I reached the front door, throwing it open and racing to check the items were still there. The carrier bag remained; some discarded clothes had been thrown over the top, which was why I hadn't noticed them. At least Karla hadn't taken them when she stole the money, tied them up in a bow and delivered them to the police. Perhaps she didn't find them, too busy searching for cash.

I sank onto the bed to untangle my thoughts. What would I do, burn or bury them? What if someone was watching? I shuddered, sure I wasn't enough of a prime suspect, in a crime the police couldn't even be sure happened, to warrant being followed. Images of a dark car parked further down the road flashed into my mind. I had seen too many movies for sure. Whatever I did with them, I needed to get them out of the bedsit.

Scooping the entire bag into my backpack and

squeezing in the enormous camel coat, I just about managed to do the zip up. On my back it was heavy, but I'd resigned myself to the fact that my Friday night would be spent getting rid of evidence.

Before I left, I called Dan back, I wanted my mobile to point at me being at home if it was ever checked. It barely rang before it was answered.

'Hey, how are you? I've been worried.'

'I'm fine, just more questions. I think they believe I had something to do with Terry going missing.' I forced a laugh; it was better for me to tell the truth and point out how ridiculous it was. Easier than Dan thinking it but not wanting to ask.

'Really? How?'

'I have no idea, but they keep asking me the same questions. I think I was the last person to see him that Friday. You'll have to ask them.' I sighed.

'Want me to come and get you?'

'No, thanks, but I'm home now, I'm shattered. I'm going to chill and have an early night.'

'Okay, if you're sure.' Dan sounded disappointed, but I had other things to do.

'Yeah, I'm not great company, to be honest.'

'I know you didn't have anything to do with it,'

Dan said. My throat felt thick and I swallowed the guilt down.

'I'm not sure how they think I'd be able to do anything to your brother, he was three times the size of me.' The line went quiet. Had we been cut off?

'Dan, you still there?'

'*Was*. You said was. You've said it twice now.'

My heart leapt into my throat. 'What do you mean?'

'The day you got burgled, you said to me 'your brother *was* a monster' in front of your place remember?'

Shit. The walls seemed to close in, the backpack weighing me down.

'And you've just said it again. Was.'

'I didn't mean to, you're reading too much into it,' I faltered.

'Jess, is there something you're not telling me?'

44

'Of course not.' I scrunched my eyes tight, my heart shattering into tiny pieces. I knew what I had to do. If I'd learned anything inside, it was attack was the best form of defence.

'Are you sure...' Dan began, but I interrupted him, launching my tirade.

'You know what, you sound exactly like them. How the fuck do you think I could do something to Terry? I'd love to hear your theory. He's bigger, double my weight. You clearly don't trust me at all. Perhaps we're better off stopping this now. After all, shagging the boss is a massive cliché, isn't it?'

Dan was silent on the other end, but I could hear him breathing, slow and steady.

'I'll see you on Monday at *work*.' Laying on the sarcasm. I didn't wait for a response and hung up. Happy fucking Valentine's Day.

How had things gone so wrong? I had the chance to move on, have a relationship. Dan made me happy, he was lovely, a gentleman and seemed to like me too. But we couldn't move forward with Terry between us and if he had any suspicions at all, it made him dangerous. My liberty came first. I'd look for another job, scour the papers and ask around. With Terry gone, Barry couldn't hold me to ransom if I managed to get another employer to take me on.

Wiping my face with the back of my hand and tossing my phone onto the bed, I groaned as I stood. The weight on my back becoming heavier with each passing second. No time to complain, I had a job to do. Ignoring my stomach rumbling, I left the bedsit and started walking. I had to avoid buses, or anywhere there was CCTV. I put up my hood to hide my hair and walked four miles, picking a random direction. I marched with purpose, imagining myself on an army training exercise.

I found a clothes recycling bin in a dark corner of a large Tesco's car park and put Terry's boots in there, the steel toecaps made them ridiculously heavy. By then my shoulders were numb, but my lower back still throbbed.

Once binned, I turned in the opposite direction and walked for another four or so miles. My legs ached and a blister was forming on my heel. All the time, my stomach cramped, hollow, screaming at me to be fed, but I pushed on.

Circling around, I found another bin, this time at Waitrose and tossed in the coat.

Halfway back, I got rid of the hat in a rubbish bin on the edge of a park. The chances of them being found and connected to Terry were slim to none. That's if anyone was looking, which I didn't think they were.

I didn't stop to eat until I was closer to home, not wanting to be caught on any shop cameras and having to explain why I was so far away. I made it to half nine before running into a Londis which was still open and buying some crisps and chocolate. I walked along munching the large packet of Walkers thinking about Dan. The words I'd spoken clomping around my head, the weight of them substantial. At least it hadn't been face to face. Dan would have seen through me straight away.

As I approached home, exhausted, all I wanted was my bed. Kicking off my trainers I lay down and unwrapped a bar of chocolate, shovelling it in at speed. Pins and needles peppered my thighs and lower legs as I willed myself to move. I wanted a cup of tea, but the effort would be too much.

I drifted off in record time, waking up still fully clothed in the dark, my mouth sticky where I hadn't cleaned my teeth. Rolling over, calf cramping, I flexed my toes and pulled my phone out from under the covers. No calls from Dan. My chest twinged; I couldn't blame him. I had been vile on the phone. I did have a text from Karla though, sent three hours ago, at midnight.

Enjoy your stay?

That bitch. I was tempted to text back, tell her I knew she was Eddie's sister, but I didn't. It would be a better conversation face to face and hopefully I'd have a chance to do it at work, although I'd have to wait two days. If only I knew where she was staying, where John lived.

I got up to get a drink and get undressed, my back and legs stiff. I dreamed of the day I'd have my own bath I could sink into with a good book.

Scrolling through Facebook, I looked at Ashley's posts first and then the main feed. There was a vomit-inducing one of Helen and Stuart holding hands in front of the sun setting. At least they were happy. I had a pang of regret when I thought about Dan. That could have been us. I had to snap out of it. He was the least of my problems. Whatever Karla was doing, I had to get her to stop. I couldn't go back to prison and I'd do anything to make sure I didn't.

* * *

Morning came around all too soon, although I slept in until nine. I hobbled out of bed like an old woman, turning the shower as hot as I could stand it. Everything was sore – my legs, my feet and back. I had to see Karla. Make her see sense. With no idea where she lived, if she disappeared and left Bright's,

I'd never be able to find her. I feared the damage was already done.

I text Karla back, perhaps I'd make a joke so she wouldn't think anything was wrong.

Ha ha, very funny. You around today? Shopping? Lunch?

I doubted it would work, but it was worth a try. Karla had well and truly set me up. She held all the cards. I needed to get the footage back; without that, she had no proof of what we'd done. It would be my word against hers. She would only drop me in the shit if she knew her name wouldn't come up. Perhaps that was what she was waiting for or she enjoyed pushing me over the edge?

Devouring a bowl of cereal for breakfast, it wasn't until halfway through I realised the milk had started to turn. I cleared out the fridge and made a list of what I needed, gathering up my washing to take to Mum's. I wasn't looking forward to seeing Helen, knowing she would give me shit about Stuart's door being kicked in, but at least I'd see Mum.

Karla didn't return my text or my calls, but I

wasn't surprised. I spoke to Ashley while I was waiting for the bus. Trying to sound as nonchalant as I could about Dan and I parting company. She saw straight through me, she always could.

'Ah I'm sorry, Jess, perhaps it's not meant to be. If he doesn't trust you, what are you supposed to do with that?' I told Ashley it was a trust issue why we weren't seeing each other any more, not because Dan suspected me of being involved in the disappearance of his brother.

'It's a shame, but you're never supposed to dip your pen in the company ink anyway, eh?' Ashley giggled at my analogy.

'Look, I've got to dash; I'm meeting some friends for lunch, but are you around next weekend? Perhaps you could come here?'

I grimaced; glad she couldn't see my face. I didn't have much money and I wasn't sure if I'd like any of her friends, or rather whether they'd like me.

'Come on, it'll be fun. I know a few cute guys who'd be falling over themselves for you.'

I sniggered; aware Ashley could read my mind.

'Okay, we'll see. I'll ring you in the week.'

The bus came as I hung up and I got on,

squeezing into a free seat with my backpack slung over my shoulder and a black bin bag of dirty washing on my lap. It trundled on and as it weaved in and out of parked cards along Thornton Road, I spotted Karla walking in the opposite direction. Wild curls blowing in the wind, she stared at the ground, her hands in her pockets as she hurried along. Instantly my body reacted, I felt my jaw clench, teeth compacted together, the anger already bubbling to the surface as I slammed my fist on the bell.

45

Without hesitation, I jumped up, swaying as the bus came to a halt.

'Thanks,' I called to the driver as I hopped off, hurriedly trying to close the distance between me and Karla.

Around ten feet away, she must have heard the scuff of my footsteps on the pavement. I was half walking, half limping, the skin on my heels almost rubbed off from last night's mission.

Karla spun around, caught off guard, her lips parted, but it took her a few seconds to speak.

'You following me?' She smirked, but I could see a flash of something in her eyes, fear maybe.

I closed the distance between us and dropped my bags on the ground.

'What the fuck are you doing, Karla? Trying to get me put away for Terry, is that it?'

'Don't know what you're talking about, mate.' Her tone nonchalant.

I nodded slowly. 'Oh really, didn't grass me up to the police then? Didn't send that photo to Dan, or to me? Guess it couldn't have been you who put Terry's ring in my locker either?'

She shrugged, hands still in her pockets. Did she have a knife hidden down there?

'Fuck off, Jess, you're mental,' she said, before turning her back and stepping away.

Seeing red, I launched at her, pulling her back by the shoulder and throwing her to the ground. In the same second, unable to believe I could be violent but having no control over the impulse. All I knew was rage rushed through me, stirred up by the threat of going back to prison. I couldn't. I wouldn't.

We scuffled, throwing punches, some connecting. Karla caught the side of my cheek, a ring on her finger scraping the skin. It stung instantly and blood trickled down my chin. I grabbed her by the hair, and before we knew it, we were rolling around on the pavement as cars drove by. Pain erupted where she'd banged my head on the concrete and for a second everything blurred.

'Oi, you two, pack it in. I've called the police,' shouted a woman in curlers hanging out of a top-floor window. Her voice sobered us instantly and we pulled apart.

'You bitch.' Karla's eye was swelling closed where I'd caught her with my right fist.

My head throbbed and I rubbed it as I staggered to my feet.

'I know you're Eddie's... sister.' They weren't related by blood, only fostered by the same family, but I knew she thought of Eddie as her brother. As I spoke, everything seemed to quiet around us, the air was still, traffic ceased.

Karla's eyes were bloodshot, welling with tears. She wiped her nose on the sleeve of her coat.

I gingerly checked the back of my head for blood, but my hair only contained grit from the pavement.

'I know that's what this is about,' I said, still trying to catch my breath.

'You killed him.'

'It was an accident, but, yes, it was my fault he died. I killed him and I'll always be sorry. You don't know what happened, Karla, you weren't there. I was trying to protect Ashley.'

Karla screwed up her face. 'What do you mean, protect Ashley?' she spat, her hands on her hips.

'They'd had a row; he'd made her ask me to drive them somewhere. I didn't know at the time, but he was going to do a drug deal. A big one. He had loads of money on him and he was going to buy gear to sell around the estate. We were heading to Mitcham when the fight broke out in the back of the car.' I stretched my neck, looking up at the sky. 'He started laying into her, I saw him punch her a couple of times in the rear-view mirror. I shouted at him to stop; I was crying.'

Karla shook her head. 'Bullshit.'

'You know he used to hit her; you must have seen her with bruises. It wasn't the first time.'

Karla's eyes darted around the road, as though she was trying to process some buried memory.

I carried on. 'He pushed her into the footwell, he was going crazy. He stomped on her, in the fucking footwell.' I choked on the words, eyes filling with tears. 'She was crouched in there on her side, so small, curled up with her arms over her head. I didn't know what to do. I panicked and swerved the car, trying to get him to lose his balance, throw him back into his seat. But I lost control and hit a tree.' Tears gushed from my eyes.

Karla was crying too, dirt smudged across her left cheek.

'Fuck you,' she said, her voice practically a whisper. All the fight gone out of her.

'That's why he went through the windscreen. I had my seat belt on, and Ashley was cowering in the footwell. When I hit the tree, Eddie was out of his seat, stamping on Ashley. Teaching her a lesson.' I swallowed hard, the memory of it too awful to relive.

'I don't believe you.' Her voice was weak, as though her words carried no weight.

'Yes, you do. It's not an excuse, Karla. I killed your brother with my driving, and I have to live with that. I'll forever be sorry, and I wish to God it hadn't happened, but at the time of the accident, he was kicking the shit out of my best mate.'

'If it's true why didn't it come up in court. None of this was ever mentioned.'

'Ashley didn't want anyone to know we were going to buy drugs or that he was hitting her. She didn't want Eddie's memory tarnished. I kept her secret.'

'And went to prison?' Karla frowned, she looked dubious.

'I would have gone to prison anyway; I was driving the car. I caused his death.'

Karla and I stared at each other, my bag of clothes and backpack discarded on the pavement behind me. In the distance, we heard sirens and, without another word, Karla turned and ran. I did the same, scooping up my things and hotfooting it across the road to the playing fields.

Hiding on the edge of the woodland scrub for twenty minutes, watching the police drive up and down the road, searching for the girls who'd caused the disturbance, I waited until the coast was clear. Whatever happened, the truth was out in the open now. I'd have to let Ashley know. Guilt weighed heavily on me, but I had no choice. Karla had to know the truth, perhaps now she understood how the accident had happened, she would see reason. It wouldn't change the loss of her brother, I knew that, and I wasn't expecting to be forgiven. I could tell by the mention of Eddie's name how much she loathed me, no doubt of the opinion my sentence wasn't enough for his life.

Had she known who I was as soon as she laid eyes on me? Was it a coincidence we were at Bright's together? I had no idea, but I hoped she would let it go and stop putting me in the picture for Terry's disappearance. Karla made me anxious, she was unpredictable and clearly not afraid to get involved when the police weren't looking in my direction. Did she think she could throw me to the wolves and I wouldn't take her with me?

A lump formed at the back of my head and I was desperate for some painkillers. Satisfied the police had gone, I came out of my hiding place and headed back across the playing fields to Mum's. Pushing my key in and opening the door.

'What the hell happened to you?' Helen said from the top of the stairs.

46

I didn't answer.

Helen's cheeks turned pink and she stormed down, taking one look at my bloody face and the red swollen knuckles on my right hand. 'Have you been fighting?' she asked, incredulous.

'Get out of my face, Helen.' I sighed, carrying my clothes into the kitchen and loading the washing machine, trying to find the right cycle.

'You're going to end up back inside. What is wrong with you?'

I ignored her.

'Stuart's just called; the bloody police have been round.'

I spun to face Helen, eyes wide. 'Round where?'

'To his house! Asking about you, how long you've lived there, how does he know you. That kind of thing. He's not happy. I had to beg him to let you stay. He told you not to bring trouble to his door.'

I closed my eyes, head swimming. I could look for a new job, but not a new place to live too. Not one I could afford anyway.

'I'll call him,' I said, reaching for my phone.

'He's on his way here to pick me up, you can talk to him then.' Helen huffed and put the kettle on.

I rummaged in the cupboard for some painkillers, popping two in my mouth and slurping from the tap before going to see Mum in the sitting room. She was trying to do the crossword in the paper, but her hand was shaking too much to hold the pen steady.

'You okay, love?' She smiled up at me and I had to blink back tears. Her love for me was unwavering, unconditional. It emanated from her in waves. No matter what I did, she would always be there. 'Who did that to you?' she continued, taking in my war wounds.

'Doesn't matter, Mum, just a bad day,' I replied, rubbing her shoulder.

'It will pass. I should know.'

I tried to hold it together, looking away and concentrating on a tiny tear in the wallpaper, where I'd scuffed the handlebars of my new bike against the wall one Christmas. It didn't help, my eyes welled up as my head throbbed in a slow rhythm. Like a backing track to a tragic movie scene.

Helen brought two cups of tea in and put them on Mum's side table. She eyed me curiously.

I can't remember the last time I'd shown any kind of emotion in front of Helen, other than anger. I reserved my tears for when I was alone, or with Mum, but I was tired. Tired of fighting and tired of lying. I didn't want to have to look over my shoulder any more. I wanted this to end.

Mum squeezed my hand, bringing me back to the present as the doorbell rang. 'Go and clean yourself up before you talk to Stuart,' Mum said, her voice low when Helen left the room.

I hadn't even thought about my appearance and took the stairs two at a time, seeking refuge in the bathroom.

The reflection in the mirror startled me. My hair looked as though it had been backcombed and was peppered with dirt. I even found a roll-up caught in a tangle at the back. Dried blood had crusted on my face, and my nose and chin looked like it was covered in soot. I rinsed a flannel under the tap, wincing as I dabbed at the cut on my cheek.

Ten minutes later, my face was clean, hair brushed and plaited, loosely over the bump, and I'd run my knuckles under the water. A tiny bit of Savlon on my wounds and I headed back downstairs.

Stuart was in the kitchen and I stumbled over myself apologising for the interruption the police had caused him this morning.

'Did they want to see me?' I asked.

'No, I don't think so, just asking questions. Why are they asking questions about you?'

'They are investigating the disappearance of my boss.'

Helen and Stuart exchanged glances across the kitchen.

'Which I had nothing to do with,' I lied.

'No more police, okay, Jess, I want a quiet life.

The minute they turn up with a warrant, your rental agreement goes in the bin, okay?'

I nodded. He wasn't being unfair; I could see why any normal person wouldn't want that in their lives.

'Shall we go, babe?' Inwardly, I cringed at Helen's sing-song voice, but Stuart grinned and moved towards her, planting a kiss on her lips.

'See you later,' Stuart said, moving out of the kitchen and popping in to say goodbye to Mum.

Helen gave me a pointed stare and left as the washing machine spun loudly. Our truce hadn't lasted long.

I popped out the back for a cigarette, sitting on the wall and glancing at my phone. No calls from anyone, no texts. I wished Dan would get in touch, even though I knew it wasn't the best thing for me right now. He gave me comfort and I had to resist the urge to text him and apologise. We could go out for dinner and end up back in his bed. It was the only place I wanted to be. Where I felt safe and desired. If only I hadn't fallen for the one person I shouldn't have. A painful contraction reverberated in my chest whenever I thought about Dan. I hadn't understood heartache could be a physical pain before now.

I sat with Mum for a while, finished my tea, which had gone cold. She told me about her week, the physio which seemed to be working for her leg, but her hand coordination was not improving. I could tell by her expression she was frustrated. Her recovery wasn't moving quickly enough. I understood from Helen she'd never fully recover, but I didn't mention it, not wanting to rub salt in the wounds. Instead I asked her to show me the exercises and we did some together. Giggling when she got stuck on the floor and I had to help her up.

Afterwards, I went to get my shopping and came back to make Mum a drink and a snack before I left.

The bus stop outside was empty, any sign of Karla or our scrap further down the road was long gone. On approach, I saw scrawled on the glass backdrop in black marker:

JESS STRICKLAND IS A MURDERER

I dropped my bags, swearing under my breath. No one was around, so I tried to rub it with my sleeve, but it wouldn't budge. Fucking Gilby and those knobs wouldn't let it go. Were they trying to hound me out of town? Did they think I was living at Mum's?

I turned my back on the graffiti, annoyed I was carrying too much to make the journey home on foot. I hated being dependent on buses, but after what happened I never wanted to drive again. How could I possibly be in charge of a two- or three-tonne weapon. That's what a car was after all. I was lucky to have survived the accident, my seat belt and airbag saved my life. I'd walked away with bruises but no broken bones. My scars were on the inside and I'd never be allowed to forget them.

The sky clouded over, and the heavens opened, large fat droplets fell, the smell of spring strangely with them. By the time the bus arrived, I was soaked. I looked around at the faces of the passengers. Why were some staring at me? Then I remembered the fight; I reached up and touched my cheek, the cut still smarting. No doubt the skin around it was turning yellow.

I shuffled to the back and sat to people-watch, the younger passengers scrolling on their phones. A woman in her mid-forties was reading a Kindle and a man, like me, clutched a bag of clothes in one of those large checked holdalls. They were likely going home to their families or partners. Saturday night in front of the television with a takeaway or going home to get ready for a big night out with their friends. Wistfully I imagined all the nights I'd missed, the rites of passage I hadn't taken.

I was going to visit Ashley in Portsmouth next weekend; I'd made my mind up. I needed a distraction, something normal. I could talk to Ashley, tell her everything that had been going on. Everything except the crime we'd committed. I couldn't tell her that, how I'd disposed of a body. I'd never tell another soul. However, I could explain that Karla had my back against the wall. She would know what to do.

I wanted to cut loose. I was twenty-two for Christ's sake and going home to an empty bedsit with only a microwave meal and some children's literature to look forward to. I didn't even own a bloody television. Decision made, I smiled out of the window, watching the houses whizz by, trying to ignore the niggling voice in my head. *If you still have your liberty by then.*

47

By Sunday night, my cheek was an apple green colour but no longer swollen. I also had a graze on my forehead and had to change my parting to the side to cover it. How did Karla look? Would we both arrive at work tomorrow with our faces advertising our falling out? I hoped it was over now. Had I said enough to stop her pursuing my incarceration? I wished we'd had longer to talk as I had no idea where her head was at. I was still in limbo and it made me increasingly nervous.

On top of that I was dreading seeing Dan, my phone had been annoyingly silent all weekend. I hoped he'd call me, and we'd make up. It was foolish though; he probably thought I was nothing more than a silly girl with a crush. It was always going to be like that for me, with him being my first. I couldn't just discard him, but it was different for men. He could have been out at the weekend and hooked up with someone else already. I had no claim on him after all.

On the way to work on Monday morning, my stomach churned, I was jittery. My heels were still sore in my trainers and stupidly I'd forgotten to buy plasters, so I waited for the bus. I would have asked Dan if he had a first-aid box, but that ship sailed as soon as I saw him. Hands behind his head, frowning at his monitor, swivelling from side to side in his office chair. I walked past, looking in through the glass of his office. We locked eyes for a second, but then he looked down at his keyboard. It told me all I needed to know. I'd done enough with my speech on Friday to put him off me for good.

'You okay?' a deep throaty voice came from behind me as I limped towards the lockers.

I turned and saw Detective Wimslow. Inwardly I cringed, forcing a smile. What was he doing here?

Goosebumps dotted my arms and a chill caressed my skin. Where was Karla?

'Yeah, fine thanks, blister,' I explained, slipping my heel out of my trainer to show the bubble on my skin. I didn't want him conjuring up anything else from my limping.

He nodded and I carried on towards the lockers.

'Mr Bright has given us permission to search the premises, but we'll try not to get into your ladies' way.'

I nodded and he smiled tightly, pulling a pair of latex gloves out of his pocket. Mansfield came through the entrance with Officer Stokes, both already wearing gloves. The goosebumps multiplied, my skin turning to ice and I froze, gripped by panic. What would they find? What had Karla planted?

Regaining use of my limbs, I shuffled forwards, finally reaching the lockers. I made to open mine, aware Mansfield was watching from afar, over my shoulder. Without hesitation, I chose the next one along. Swinging the door open, seeing it empty and breathing a silent sigh of relief. I threw my bag in and closed the door. Satisfied, Mansfield turned away to talk to Dan, who'd come out of his office carrying some paperwork. Dan was being overly accommodating, gesticulating wildly. I overheard the mention of an anonymous tip.

Anonymous tip my arse. Karla had to be behind it. Had the truth not done anything to sway how she felt about me?

I slowly opened my locker to retrieve my tabard, checking again that no one was watching. Terry's gold ring caught in the light, almost blinding me. Fuck! I gritted my teeth and swiped it off the floor of the locker, thrusting it in my pocket. I had to dispose of it, but where?

I felt close to hyperventilating. Was it a proper search, with a warrant? Where everything would get torn to pieces? Where would I put the ring? I couldn't keep it on me. If I were arrested, I'd be searched. I'd been strip-searched once before and it wasn't much fun, nor did it leave anywhere to hide. Not anywhere I wanted to put the ring anyway. Chuck it in the drain? Flush it down the toilet? In the incinerator? Where?

I headed into the toilet and locked myself in a cubicle. Pulling the ring out of my pocket, I wrapped it in tissue, then wrapped another layer around it and scrunched it into a ball as though someone had blown their nose on it. As quietly as I could, I climbed onto the toilet and opened the tiny window on the back wall, easing the squeaky lever out of its position and pushing on the wood, where it stuck in the frame.

This side of Bright's faced the road and a tissue would look like it had been discarded. It was the best I could come up with at short notice. I'd collect it later once the police were gone. After one practice go, I flung it to the right, in the direction of the bin, so it hadn't looked like it'd been dropped out of the window. Stepping back down from the toilet, I flushed the chain and washed my hands in the sink. Now I had to deal with Karla.

I found her in the yard, smoking a cigarette even though she'd barely started her shift. Dan was getting too lax; the girls would walk all over him if he let them.

'What the fuck do you want from me?' I shouted from the door, not caring who heard. My temper fast becoming uncontrollable. Her eye was open now, no longer swollen shut, although it was a lovely shade of green like my cheek.

'I want you to go to hell,' Karla shouted back.

I ran towards her before an outstretched arm reached around my middle, scooping me off my feet so my legs swung in the air.

'What's got into you?' Dan hissed. 'The bloody police are here.'

I glowered at him.

'They're here to take her away,' Karla sneered as she sauntered past us back into the warehouse.

It clearly wasn't over.

'Let go of me.'

I pushed Dan's arm away, catching the hurt in his eyes before I thundered after her.

'I thought we were friends! I can't do this any more, Karla, I just can't,' I said to her retreating back, 'and if you make me, I'm going to tell everyone about Eddie.'

She stopped dead in her tracks and spun around, eyes ablaze.

'Go, both of you, get out of here, go for a walk and come back when you've sorted out your differences,' Dan snapped.

I wasn't even aware he was behind us, or anyone

was watching. Karla and I were too swept up in the moment to notice was what going on.

'Everything all right?' Mansfield's attention had been captured.

'Fine, just low blood sugar makes me hangry.' Karla smiled as though butter wouldn't melt. She was a better actress than me.

My nostrils flared.

'Coming to the café, Jess?' Karla asked, and it was as though I'd been transported back to when we first started to work together. Her voice light, eyes expectant. Although any friendship I believed was developing back then was a lie.

'Sure,' I mumbled and followed Karla out the back of the warehouse and into the yard. We walked silently until we were off the premises and around the corner, the animosity between us growing, the lid on a bubbling pan about to explode.

Karla drew out a packet of cigarettes and lit one nonchalantly and I pressed my nails into my palms. It was clear she still thought she had the upper hand and I had to level the playing field.

'I mean it, Karla. If you don't drop this, I'm going to tell everyone what happened the night of the accident. I don't want to do that. I've kept it a secret for this long, for Ashley, but I won't go back to prison.'

'You deserve to rot in there,' Karla whispered, her eyes already brimming.

'I'm sorry,' I cried. 'I'm so, so sorry you lost your brother and I was responsible, but I can't turn back time. Don't you think I've spent years wishing I could? I wrote to your parents, told them how sorry I was.'

'It'll kill my mum if you say anything,' Karla said, cutting me off. 'She thought the sun shone out of Eddie's arse.'

'I don't want to expose him, but I'm not going to take the fall for Terry. If I go down, you're coming with me.' I thrust my hands on my hips.

'Ha! You think? I've got an alibi, sweetheart. The Friday Terry disappeared, John picked me up and brought me straight home. We were there all evening,' she sneered. I'd been right not to say we'd been together.

'Ah, the elusive John? He must be your boyfriend if he's willing to lie to the police for you!'

'What if he is, it's none of your business. He takes care of me.' Her eyes flashed; John obviously meant something to her. I really did know nothing about Karla.

'The police will never believe I got him in that incinerator without help. Your DNA will be in the boot of his Audi, Karla, they'll check if I tell them to. If you say anything, you'll be going back inside too,' I snapped.

We glared at each other for a second, I could practically see the cogs turning in Karla's head. She knew I was right; she couldn't fix me up without getting caught herself.

'I'm going to get rid of Terry's ring and I want that footage. No more fucking around. No more photos or surprise gifts. Just how long were you going to drag it out for?'

'Until I thought you'd suffered enough, then I was going to send the photos of you to the police, that lovely one of you kneeling over his corpse.' A shiver descended the length of my spine. Karla's eyes were steely, her voice cold.

'How?'

'John's got a printer, it's easy to print still images from footage.'

'Does John know what we did to Terry?' My eyebrows shot skyward.

'No, not everything.'

I sighed, feeling my anger slowly dissipate. It was such a mess. 'Terry was a sleaze; he did awful things to us all. We did everyone a favour,' I said, trying a different tack.

Karla snorted. 'I don't feel any guilt about Terry, I helped you because I needed you to trust me. I wanted to mess with your head before sending you back to prison for another murder, but this time you'd get life.' Her words were filled with so much venom and we glared at each other again.

A minute later, she sat on the kerb, staring into the distance. A balloon that had been deflated. I sat beside her, tucking my knees up to my chin.

'It's over now. You had your fun. What did you tell the police?'

'Nothing, I was biding my time, I didn't give you an alibi, thought you might trip yourself up there. I told them you'd been sent photos, but that was it.'

I sighed, rubbing the back of my neck.

A car passed us and beeped its horn, Karla gave them the finger.

'You've got your last appointment with Barry this

week, haven't you? You'll be free of Bright's, go to the coast like you wanted to. If that wasn't a lie?'

Karla shook her head, lighting another cigarette and taking a long drag, blowing the smoke into the air. 'I'll never be free.'

'Why not?' I asked.

'Because I owe a lot of money to some very dangerous people.' Karla looked resigned as she got to her feet. It seemed even outside of prison you could still be trapped, longing for freedom through imaginary bars. It wouldn't be my life; I wasn't going down that path. I just had to find a way out of the mess we were in.

48

Karla and I made our way back to Bright's, an unspoken truce between us. She didn't elaborate on who she owed money to and I didn't want to know. I had enough to worry about.

The atmosphere was sombre inside the warehouse. Laura had her radio switched off and there was barely any chatter. It was stuffy and I perspired as soon as we walked in. An increase of a few degrees outside made all the difference in the warehouse, taking the environment from bearable to stifling.

The police were still searching, moving things around on shelves, checking documents and rummaging through the store cupboard. My heart

skipped a beat when they looked over the incinerator. Karla and I glanced at each other across the
room and I bit my lip until it bled. I thought it had
been used since that night, to burn hospital sheets,
but I still went cold. Mansfield was looking in the ash
drawer, which even though we'd emptied, forensi-
cally there was likely to still be traces of Terry left
behind.

Karla gave the slightest shake of the head and I
concentrated on the towel I was folding.

'What's going on with you two? Is this all over
Dan?' Agnes asked me.

'Sort of,' I replied. It was a perfect cover for
everyone to think we were falling out over a mutual
attraction to the boss. Agnes tutted and rolled her
eyes, before going on to talk at length about the pastries she was going to bake after work.

By lunchtime, the police were finished with the
search and spent some time in Dan's office talking to
him. I wanted to go in afterwards and find out what
was said, but I had no reason to now; no excuse to
breeze in and see what the latest was. He looked at
me stonily as I stared into the office, daydreaming.
Brought back into the present by Hanna tapping me

on the arm and asking if I was okay. She was trying to find out how Karla and I had got our bruises, but I wasn't going to tell her.

Outside later, I retrieved the tissue, well, three which had been discarded between the toilet window and the bin, feeling through them for Terry's ring. One was still wet and sticky. I gagged, wiping my hand on my jeans. Slipping the ring into my pocket, still in the tissue, I saw Dan approaching, probably going to the café for a coffee. Gone was the sullen expression from earlier.

'All right, Tyson,' he said, the smallest smile escaping from his lips. His eyes rested on my cheek.

I couldn't help but laugh. Tyson was the boxer who went mad and bit his opponent, wasn't he?

'Friends again?' he asked.

I nodded and he bumped shoulders with me.

'I'm sorry,' I said, unable to keep up the pretence of being angry any longer.

'Me too. This Terry thing is driving me nuts, that's all. Kim's been on the phone all weekend demanding results. I should never have doubted you.'

I chewed the inside of my cheek, guilt sitting in my stomach like a brick.

'Why were the police here again today?'

'Anonymous tip apparently. They didn't tell me what, just asked if they could search. I told them it was fine as long as they were tidy. Barry came in for his weekly catch-ups and they left with him. No idea what that was about.'

I stifled a laugh. It would be good for Barry to have a bit of pressure for a change.

'Do they think something bad happened to Terry?' I asked.

Dan shrugged. 'It's been weeks now. Kim is still sure he's coming back, tells me Harriet is missing her daddy. Perhaps we'll never know.' I swallowed the lump in my throat.

Dan's mobile rang, and he fished it out of his pocket, giving me a wink and walking away to answer. The knot in my chest seemed to ease now we were talking again. I had to take one day at a time. My freedom wasn't guaranteed, for all I knew Barry might be talking to Detective Wimslow now, trying to throw me under the bus just as Karla had. I was sick of living on the edge all the time, running on nervous energy alone. If I lost any more weight, my jeans wouldn't stay up.

I went for a walk around the block into a nearby housing estate after Dan left. When I came to a drain, I bent to tie my shoelace and dropped the ring between the grate, listening to the plop in the water below. Limbs lighter on my walk back to the warehouse. Inside, I discovered Karla complaining about the lack of air to Dan, trying to get him to raise the shutters to let a breeze through. She'd stripped off to a spaghetti-strapped vest top, her spindly arms on show. Faint bruises swirled across her back and shoulders, aged although still yellow. Not from our recent altercation. She clearly was mixed up with a bad crowd. Was she selling drugs again? It was the only reason I could think of why she owed someone money. Stupid of her to go back down that road after what happened the last time. Had she learnt nothing from her stint inside?

I knew the system wasn't perfect, it spewed out probationers, back into their old lives with little support and it was easy to get involved in the same shit they were locked up for. Karla was smarter than that.

When the day ended, I forced myself out the door, without waiting to see if Dan was going to ask me to hang back. I wanted more than anything for him to ask me over, to spend the evening with him and let him take me to bed. The pull was strong, and it took willpower not to catch his eye as I passed his office, but the two of us together wasn't a good idea. Perhaps once things had calmed down and the police were no longer hanging around.

I didn't understand why they were wasting resources on Terry as a missing person, although I supposed with anonymous tips from Karla, perhaps they suspected foul play. Barry hadn't returned, he'd no doubt be back in tomorrow and I wasn't looking forward to our meeting, remembering how he'd squeezed my wrist when he asked about Terry.

Later that evening, around nine, I was buried in one of the thrillers I'd bought from the charity shop when Ashley called.

'What you up to?' she asked.

'Well I'm not rollerblading down the high street, I've opted for a quiet night in... like *all* my nights currently.' I sniggered, fully aware this was tragic for a twenty-two-year-old, but my limited social circle didn't help.

'I'm in the pub, the Woodman, on the High

Street... I've got a shot lined up for you already.'
Ashley giggled.

'What are you doing there?' I dropped my book
and sat up, glancing at my frightful reflection in the
mirror.

'It's my nan's birthday, I completely forgot until
Mum reminded me she'd booked a family dinner at
Pizza Express. I caught the train down earlier. I'm
staying with her tonight, but my parents have slunk
off back to Chichester already and now I'm all by my
lonesome. I said I wanted to catch up with some *old*
friends... And that, my girl, is you!'

'I bet they loved that,' I said, knowing how Ashley's parents detested me. They always blamed me
for leading her astray.

'I didn't mention you. Anyway, come onnnnnn!
It's Monday night, the place is dead. Let's get
wrecked. I have no lectures tomorrow and my train
isn't until lunchtime. It can be pre-Saturday drinks.'

'Okay, okay, I'm coming. I'll be there in about
twenty.'

49

Ashley was sat at the bar, her glossy long hair covering her back. She wasn't lying when she said she had shots ready. They sat on the bar, an oily film swirled on top. My throat closed automatically.

'Check you out, quick as a flash and still you look fab!' Ashley said, giving me a hug.

I slid into the seat beside her, brushing my hair over my shoulder. I'd got ready in five minutes, a speedy wash, applied a little mascara and lip gloss and ran the straighteners through my hair. I'd even managed to cover my bruise with concealer, so it was barely noticeable. Not bad for someone who twenty minutes ago was rocking slob chic.

My heart raced from the march, combined with excitement of seeing my best friend. Without hesitation, I necked the shot, the liquid burning my throat.

'Jesus!' I cringed.

'Can I get two gin and tonics, the elderflower if you have it? Thanks.' Ashley smiled at the bartender, who, by the way he was blushing, had a bit of a crush. No doubt she'd been chatting him up while she waited for me. It was something I'd never done; it seemed a life so far removed from my own. Like I was watching through a window into Ashley's, to see what awaited me, when I was brave enough to come out of my cave.

'How was your nan's birthday dinner?' I asked.

'Conservative, and a little strained. I told the parents I'm going to stay in Portsmouth once my degree is finished, the place where I did my work experience have offered me a job as a junior lab technician.'

'That's great, congratulations!'

'Thanks. Funnily enough my parents weren't so chuffed.'

'They just worry about you, probably want you to move closer to them. I'm so glad you got out of here though. I can't wait until it's my turn.'

Ashley paid for the drinks and we moved to a table. The pub was quiet, and we were the youngest in the place.

'How long until you're not on probation any more?'

'Beginning of June, another few months yet.'

'So, tell me about Karla,' Ashley said, twisting her silver ring around her finger.

I told Ashley as much as I could without giving away what had happened with Terry. Problems caused at work by Karla and how hostile she was.

'That's awful. She was always a mixed-up girl though, idolised Eddie. You said she was locked up, for drug dealing?'

I nodded. 'I mean, I'm pissed off with her, sure, but I get it. She's devastated, even now, four years later. She still harbours a lot of resentment about Eddie.' It felt good to be gracious about the girl who nearly cost me my freedom.

We chatted about Dan for a while, Ashley thrilled to be finally getting the details of my limited sex life, while I squirmed, my cheeks hot. She flashed her knowing smile, black winged eyeliner drawn to perfect points. I was in awe of her and dowdy by comparison.

'What's the plan for Saturday, you might have to lend me some clothes,' I said, and Ashley launched into a full-on timetable of our afternoon and night out, shifting excitedly in her seat. It was infectious and for a short time I was wrapped up in it too.

'I've got so many people I want you to meet!'

I swallowed, knowing I wasn't the social butterfly that Ashley was. It was only for one night though and I needed out of here.

We drank until closing, staggering out of the door after Ashley unsuccessfully tried to convince the bartender to let us stay for a lock-in. I called a taxi to drop her off first at her nan's, then take me home, crawling into bed worse for wear at quarter to midnight. It felt good to be a normal twenty-two-year-old for one night, having fun with my friend. For a second, I glimpsed the life I could have and almost forgot about Terry.

* * *

The next morning when the alarm went off, I scrunched my eyes up tight and tried to ignore it, throwing my phone across the room in disgust. A stupid move as I had to get up to shut the bloody thing off.

I text Ashley as I waited for the bus, to say thanks for a great night, but she was likely still comatose if her train wasn't until lunchtime. I, on the other hand, had to drag myself to a muggy warehouse to spend eight hours sweating over someone else's dirty bedsheets.

I rubbed the back of my neck, trying to stave off the threatening headache. Gallons of water were needed today, and I got a bacon roll and a bottle of water from the café before heading into Bright's.

'Where's mine?' Dan asked as I walked past his office, already eating as I couldn't wait.

'I ate it,' I said, mid-chew.

He got up and came over, tugging a piece of stray cotton on the sleeve of his polo shirt. 'I... um...' he began.

'Jess, you're first up today. Dan, mind if I use your office,' boomed Barry, who looked more dishevelled than I did. Irritation cloaked his voice and my mouth dried up, the roll hard to swallow. He was angry. Without waiting, Barry made to go into the office as Dan bristled beside me and cleared his throat.

'Actually, Barry, I have some calls to make, so you'll have to find somewhere else for the next hour.'

The two men stared at each other, all bravado, with their shoulders back and chests puffed out in nothing shy of a pissing contest. Barry was bigger than Dan in stature, although he conceded first, giving a little chuckle.

'No worries, mate. Jess, come around to the warehouse, we'll find a *cosy* corner.' Barry left and my shoulders sagged.

'Prick,' Dan muttered.

'Here.' I wrapped up the bacon roll I was no longer interested in eating and handed it to Dan.

'Don't worry, I was kidding.'

'No, honestly, I don't want any more.'

'Are you hung-over?' Dan looked mildly amused.

I nodded and watched his eyes narrow.

'Did you have a date?'

I snorted; the mere suggestion was ridiculous.

'I'll see you later.' I headed to the lockers to put my stuff away, my stomach lurching. Barry was pissed off. He must know I told the police about him. Fuck. I wasn't sure why I'd done that, trying to divert attention away from me, but I hadn't considered the consequences. Karla said as soon as we met, he had us all by the short and curlies.

I rounded the corner and Barry had pulled two chairs opposite each other, in the corner of the warehouse. They were too close together and my knees brushed his as I sat. Inwardly, I shuddered. He gave me a cold stare, eyes penetrating, before looking at the form and running through the usual questions at speed. Once he'd finished, he put the folder on the floor and leaned forward, resting his forearms on his thighs. We were too far away to be overheard by anyone. I inched backwards to avoid the coffee breath leaking from his mouth.

'So, you told the police Tel owed me money?'

I swallowed, shaking my head. My legs quivered, knees bouncing of their own accord.

Barry leaned closer still, entering my personal space. 'Don't fuck around, Jess. I can make life difficult for a little slut like you. Even if you are banging the boss.'

I gasped at the venom in his tone. His cheeks were mottled, blood pressure sky-high.

'So play nice, or I promise you, you'll be back in Bronzefield before you know it.' He squeezed my thigh, which may have looked at a distance as a friendly gesture, but he dug his fingers into the muscle.

I squirmed in my seat, refusing to speak.

'Perhaps I'll find out exactly what Terry liked about you, eh, would you like that?'

My head throbbed as I shook it, Barry's hand inching higher. Finally, he released me, picked up his folder and stalked away, chair screeching back on the floor, leaving me a shaky mess. We weren't free at all, none of us. We might have cut off Terry's head, but another would grow back in its place.

50

I had no time to process my meeting with Barry before Karla came into the warehouse. She was pale, a sheen upon her skin and her hand was covered in a makeshift bandage of a tea towel and masking tape. Dark circles beneath her eyes conveyed a sleepless night.

'What happened?'

The other girls hadn't noticed yet; while I was with Barry, they were helping Dan unload a hospital order. Knee-deep sorting through the sometimes-gruesome sheets, separating what would be burnt and what would be cleaned. It wasn't rare to find more than a drop of blood left behind. Hanna told me stories of entrails she'd found tangled in one sheet.

I steered Karla into the store cupboard, out of sight of the others, and watched as she fell apart. I'd never seen Karla cry properly before, not like this. She was the strong one, armour-plated. I placed my hand on her shoulder and felt her stiffen at my initial touch before slowly melting until I was practically holding her up. We sank to the floor, amidst boxes of detergent.

'They cut my finger off,' she whispered, holding up her hand, the bandage looked like a boxing glove. She shivered, her teeth chattering. Her face looked almost grey.

'Who did?' I asked, eyes wide. My heart rate accelerated. I'd seen a lot of things over the four years spent in prison, bullying, assaults, but nothing of that level of violence.

'Leon,' she said as if I'd recognise the name.

I shook my head, it meant nothing to me. 'Come on, you need to go home.'

'I've got nowhere to go, he knows everywhere,' she sobbed, and I sat awkwardly in the small space unsure what to do.

Pulling myself to my feet, I wiped my forearm across my brow. 'Stay here for a sec, let me get you some water.' I left the room and headed over to Dan, tugging him by the arm out towards the yard.

'What's up?' He'd rolled his sleeves up, the dark hairs on his arms made him look tanned. I bit my lip, hit by a pang of regret those arms might not hold me again.

'Karla's hurt herself. Her hand is all bandaged up, she's come in, but there's no way she can work today. In fact, she needs to go to the hospital.'

'Okay, give me a minute and I'll run her over there, it's only down the road.'

'Great, would you mind if I went with her? Can you spare me?' I turned back to the sheets, hearing Agnes squeal at something she'd found in the folds.

'Sure, we'll manage.'

I reached up and planted a quick kiss on his cheek, watching it instantly flush red.

He laughed, shaking his head. 'You know how to get around me.'

I smiled, perhaps it wasn't over after all?

I took a glass of water to Karla, who looked positively clammy now. Was it shock or did she have an infection? I asked to take a look, but she refused to unwrap the bandage. I had so many questions: when did it happen? How much blood had she lost?

'Dan's going to take you to hospital, I'm going to come with you. Get that properly looked at,' I said, giving her the water to drink.

Fear shot through her eyes and her head whipped up to look at me.

'It's okay, you don't have to tell them anything, you can say you had an accident, chopping tomatoes or something.' Quite why I was helping her after her campaign against me I had no idea, all I knew was she was going to get herself killed if I didn't do something. I couldn't have that on my conscience.

Thirty minutes later, we were waiting in Accident and Emergency at Croydon University Hospital. Dan had dropped us off outside, telling me to ring him when we wanted picking up.

'This used to be called Mayday, I remember my mum telling me,' Karla said, holding her arm close to her chest as though she'd broken it.

'Why aren't you living with your mum and dad?'

'It's not safe for them.' Karla glanced at her hand and back to me. I nodded. So that was the reason

Karla had been sofa-surfing. No fixed abode, she kept moving. Who was after her?

'Do you want to tell me what happened?' I asked softly.

Karla glanced around; the waiting room was packed. Almost every seat was taken, and the low hum of chatter was constant. 'Not here. Later.'

'Karla Grant,' called the triage nurse and Karla stood, waiting for me to join her. I hadn't intended to, I was squeamish at the best of times, but she looked like she needed the support. Despite what she'd done, I couldn't walk away.

She hadn't been lying, her pinkie finger had been hacked off below the knuckle, the end open and sore. The nurse asked how had it happened, what had it been cut with? Karla told her a chopping knife, for tomatoes, but she didn't look convinced. Did she by any chance still have the end of her finger? My throat closed and I had to look away as the nurse examined it.

'I just want to get the doctor to check this over, I'm not sure whether we'll be able to stitch it as it is. You might need a skin graft.' She put a temporary covering over the finger, and we were sent back out to the waiting room.

'Are you okay, do you want some sugar or something?'

Karla nodded; she looked a little green around the gills.

'Be right back,' I said as I went to wrestle with the vending machine at the other end of the room. I had enough change for a Boost and a can of Coke which we shared, only because Karla couldn't eat it all. She pepped up around ten minutes later once the sugar hit her system.

We waited for almost an hour before the doctor called us. By which time it was gone lunch and my stomach grumbled. My hangover was long forgotten, but I still had the munchies. The nurse stitched and bandaged the finger properly, although the doctor advised Karla might require a skin graft. By the time we left, with antibiotics and an appointment booked at another NHS site with a hand specialist, it was mid-afternoon.

Karla fumbled with her lighter until I stepped in, both of us desperate for a cigarette. I hated hospitals, the smell seemed to get on your clothes and in your hair. I always had to wash it off. Karla looked exhausted as we trudged off the hospital grounds.

'Shall we get a cab back to mine?' I asked, not sure if Karla would agree but I knew she was scared. She already said she didn't have anywhere else.

'No, I need to get my bag from Bright's, my duffel bag is in a locker.' Was she carrying around her worldly goods in a duffel bag?

'Sure, I'll ring Dan.'

Dan picked us up around ten minutes later, jumping out the car to help Karla into the front seat. He seemed concerned, making sure she was comfortable, and he'd bought lunch for us in case we hadn't eaten. I found the visceral pull in my gut for him during the drive hard to ignore.

When we got back to Bright's, the girls rallied round, keen to hear Karla's story of what had happened. She mentioned an accident where the knife slipped when cutting a tomato, and I was in awe at how easy the lie spilled off her tongue. I shouldn't have been surprised, she'd been spinning lies since we'd met. Could I believe anything she said now?

While the girls were occupied, I found Dan in his office, gathering up the sandwiches he'd bought

from the café to bring out to us. I stood in the doorway, blocking his exit.

'Thanks for this morning, you've been amazing.' I
tilted my head to the side and jutted my hip out,
seeing his eyes slide to it.

'That's okay, wouldn't be much of an employer if
I didn't look after my staff.'

He made to leave, stopping inches from me when
I didn't move. The atmosphere between us electric. I
leaned forward, brushing my lips across his gently,
before stepping aside to let him pass. His ears were
pink, and I noticed he hadn't shaved today, a dark
shadow ran across his jaw.

'You're a nightmare,' he breathed. He gave the
slightest shake of the head and I giggled as I watched
a grin emerge. 'Come on, you must be starving.'

I followed him back to Karla and sat on top of a
table to eat. Dan passed us a sandwich, a bag of
crisps and a bottle of lemonade. I dove in. We
chatted for a while, although Karla didn't join in
much. Agnes said once the initial order was finished,
nothing else came in, so it had turned into an unusu-
ally quiet day. I knew Karla was shattered, so once I'd
eaten, I crept away and called for a taxi. Dan had run

us around enough and I didn't want to bother him again.

'I've got a taxi coming. She's exhausted, so I'm going to take her home with me,' I said, out of earshot of the others.

'I thought you two had a row?' Dan asked.

'We did.' I shrugged and Dan shook his head like he didn't understand women.

There was no other option but to have Karla stay with me, she had nowhere to go. Not anywhere that was safe anyway. I didn't want to say that she was fearing for her life. I didn't want Dan to know, by taking her home with me, what I'd be getting mixed up in.

51

The taxi ride was silent with both of us staring out of opposite windows. When we got home, I paid the driver and helped Karla out of the car. I lifted out the enormous duffel bag from the footwell, that Karla had hidden in the broken locker nobody used, slinging it over my shoulder as I fished for my keys.

'You'll have to share the bed with me again,' I said flatly, pushing open the door and dropping the bag on the carpet.

'That's fine. Thank you.' Karla lowered herself onto my bed, slipping off her trainers and curling her legs up under her. Her usual icy demeanour gone, almost like she'd run out of steam. I had no doubt it was down to the shock of Leon's attack and not because she'd thawed and we'd suddenly become friends. She needed me and Karla was smart, she did what she had to, to get by.

I checked my phone; it was almost five.

'Tea?' I offered and Karla nodded. I didn't have a lot of milk and would have to pop out later, but for now I wanted to get Karla settled and find out how it all happened. I checked the door was locked, momentarily considering how much danger I was in by having her here?

The ashtray positioned between us, I sat cross-legged facing Karla, each of us sipping our scalding-hot mugs of tea.

'Who's Leon?' I ventured.

'He's a dealer, he's big time, been around for years. He used to sell to my brother.'

The penny slowly dropped.

'Is that who Eddie was going to see when Ashley asked me for a lift?'

Karla nodded.

'He was going to buy drugs to sell around the estate?' I clarified.

'He wasn't going to buy. Eddie already had the drugs on tick, he was going to pay Leon.'

'And Eddie never arrived,' I said quietly.

'I had to work off Eddie's debt.'

I shut my eyes, awash with self-loathing. What did that entail? Selling drugs? Selling herself? I cringed.

'The money in the car disappeared. Ten grand,' Karla continued.

'It was seized by the police as evidence,' I said, hoping she didn't assume I'd walked away from the accident with it.

'I know. Leon lost Eddie and I replaced him. Until I was caught and sent down.'

'You must have cleared his debt by now?'

'I have. With the money you gave me,' she had the good grace to look ashamed of the use of the word *gave*, 'but once you're in, you're never technically out.'

'So what was the finger about?'

'I asked to leave, but apparently I've got interest to pay, it's never-ending.' Karla sniffed, rubbing her eyes with the back of her hand. I'd heard about these gangs; there was only one way out once you were in.

Especially if Karla was a perfect little worker bee, selling drugs for free. 'That's why I've never been home. I can't put my parents at risk. He doesn't know where they live now, as they moved after Eddie died. So I'm on my own.'

'You're not on your own,' I said, patting Karla's knee.

'I don't deserve your help.'

'Maybe not, but I think you need it. I can never make up for taking Eddie's life, but I'd like to help you get away.'

'I can't run, he'll find me,' Karla spluttered, terror etched on her face.

If I didn't do something Karla would end up being left for dead at the side of the road and I'd have another death of the same family on my conscience. 'How much do you still owe?'

'Another grand; it goes up every week,' Karla said miserably.

'Jesus, how are you ever supposed to pay it at a grand a week?'

'That's the point.' She lit a cigarette and offered me one of hers. I finished my tea and took it, opening the front door to let the air through.

We smoked in silence. How could I get Karla out? Perhaps Dan could help, he'd worked all over the place, maybe he knew somewhere remote she could hide. It all seemed so unreal, these were the problems from movies with drug deals and car chases, but if I'd learnt anything from being inside there were many bad people in the world.

'I want to show you something – do you have a laptop?' Karla said.

'I don't even own a TV, Karla, let alone a laptop.' I snorted.

'Fuck.' She pulled out a small SD card from an inside pocket of her duffel bag, holding it up for me to see.

'What's on it?'

'It's from Terry's hidden camera. It's where all the footage is stored. When I took it from the office, I pulled out the SD card but couldn't view it as it's a micro SD card. It doesn't fit into a laptop, you see, it's the wrong size.' Karla held the tiny card up to the light. 'I told John I needed to see what was on it and he ordered me this adaptor. He's quite techy.' She rummaged in the pocket again, but this time retrieved a larger card that the micro SD slotted neatly into.

'I don't understand?' I said, frowning at it.

'Most laptops have a standard-sized slot, for an SD card – that's this one. To view a micro SD card, you have to pop it inside this one, then it'll fit. Get it?'

I nodded.

'How did you know about the camera?' I asked.

'After the first time he, you know, I said no more. He told me that everything in the office was filmed and my *video* would go viral if I didn't play ball. Of course, I told him to prove it and the next day he showed me an image. I knew the camera was some-where up high from the angle, so I searched for it when he was out. There was only one option really, on top of the filing cabinet.'

'What did you do with it?'

'I left it there then, I didn't want him to know that I knew where it was, but after he kicked the bucket, I took it home and smashed it to smithereens.'

Blood drained from my face. All along I was pan-icking about the camera and she'd had it! There was proof on that tiny card, proof we'd all been victims of some kind of sexual assault at the hands of our boss. I sighed, fat lot of good it did us now.

'You should burn that,' I said flatly.

'No, I want to see it.'

'Hiya,' came a voice from the open door. Stuart stood on the threshold.

'Hi, Stuart, this is Karla. Karla, this is my land-lord, Stuart.'

Karla managed a smile.

'Hey, just wanted to see if you were okay, haven't seen you much.' His eyes cast around the room as they always did whenever he popped in. Checking I wasn't trashing the place.

'I'm fine thanks. Actually, Stuart, you don't have a laptop I can borrow for an hour or so, do you?'

Stuart scratched his head. 'Yeah, I've got an old one under the stairs. It's slow though.'

'Slow is fine,' I said, smiling.

He went back next door to check and I raised my eyebrows at Karla, who sniggered.

Twenty minutes later, I'd made another cup of tea, using the last of the milk, and we were sat side by side, with Stuart's laptop resting on my thighs.

'Are you sure you want to see this?' I asked, words hollow.

'Yeah.' Karla inserted the card and it took a

minute or so to register. I double-clicked File Explorer and opened the SD card.

Terry was organised, there were folders for each month, and dated files within each folder. For January and February, the files were unnamed.

'Perhaps the camera dumped all the files here automatically and Terry chose what to keep?'

'Maybe,' I said, steering back, over two years' worth of folders.

Steeling myself, I clicked on the second to last file, which opened in a full-screen window. The day Terry died began to play out.

52

The video was weird, and it took a second for us to work it out. The image was good-quality and in colour, unlike the printouts Karla had sent, but it seemed to jump, as though scenes had been cut and pasted together. Some were long, some barely more than a few seconds. We watched snippets of what looked like an average day. Terry coming in, hanging up his coat, logging on to the computer. Then, after he'd left his office, a second later he was back, carrying a cup of tea. I frowned at Karla.

'Must have been on a sensor, only recording when there's movement in the office. Makes sense, I guess.' She seemed to know more than I did.

As the day crept towards the afternoon, we cringed through Terry shovelling in a bulging foot-long subway that made my stomach roll.

Karla dragged the cursor forward and suddenly I was in the office, on my knees and Terry was undoing his belt. She clicked pause and there we were, frozen. I swallowed bile which rose in my throat and forced myself not to turn away. My hand trembled and Karla gripped it.

'We'll skip it,' she said, going to move the cursor forward.

'No, I need to see it.'

Relenting, Karla hit play and we both concentrated on the screen.

It seemed to happen within a few seconds, Terry forcing himself on me, me biting and him slapping my head away. He clutched his arm and hit the deck. Karla gasped; she obviously hadn't seen it all the way through.

'Did you see him hit his head?' I asked.

'Yeah.'

'I told you. He collapsed; I didn't do anything!'

'Looks like a heart attack,' Karla agreed.

We watched the morbid video, speeded up, us two running around, clearing up. Heaving him into the chair and securing him with tape.

Karla was still holding my hand as the video ended and I breathed a heavy sigh. Seeing it played out on screen, watching Terry fall, his death a natural one, I felt a strange release. I'd almost convinced myself I'd been wrong, that he couldn't have just dropped dead. It didn't change the fact that we'd committed a crime even if it wasn't a murder.

'There's another file,' I said, going back to the folder.

'Definitely motion sensor, look at the dates, nothing over the weekend as no one was in. The last file is on the Monday.'

Karla double-clicked and we watched.

'Who's that?' she asked as two figures appeared.

'Dan and Terry's wife, Kim,' I replied as they entered the office and started looking around. Kim was going through the drawers and cupboards, riffling through paperwork. She looked like a woman possessed. What did she think she'd find? 'Is there no sound on this thing?' I asked, as Dan came back in and a conversation broke out, Kim gesticulating wildly, pointed a red-nailed finger at him.

'Nope, just images,' Karla replied.

I rubbed the back of my neck. It was infuriating not being able to hear them.

We skipped forward, watching Dan and Kim come and go. Then Barry entered, looking over his shoulder as he came into the office. Everything about him was suspicious but particularly the way he moved. He rounded the desk, looking through the contents, as Kim had. His hand moved fast, glancing up at the door every few seconds, to make sure the coast was clear.

'Looking for his money,' Karla said flatly. That much was obvious.

Barry stood to his full height and put his hands on his hips. As though receiving a flash of inspiration, he spun around and reached out to the Kelly Brook calendar. Whipping it off the wall, he revealed a small dark grey panel.

'What's that?' I pointed at the screen and we both squinted.

'A safe. Look, there's the dial.'

We watched as Barry moved the disc backwards and forwards, trying a variety of combinations, eventually getting frustrated and slamming his fist on the metal door. He left soon after, only to be replaced by Karla moving swiftly in, standing on Terry's chair and reaching up to feel around for the camera. A hand closed over the lens and the video ended.

'Terry had another safe hidden in his office. Do you think Dan knows?'

'No idea.'

'What if Barry never got into it? It could have more money in it?'

'I doubt that.'

'We've got to get into the safe!' Karla's eyes came alive, like she was a pirate searching for treasure.

'Yeah, good luck,' I scoffed, getting up from the bed as pins and needles ravished my legs. I didn't want any part of it. 'I'm going to pop out for some milk and cigarettes. Want me to grab anything?'

Karla shook her head, her concentration fixed on the screen.

'I'll be back in a minute, don't break the laptop and don't steal anything!'

'What's that supposed to mean?' Karla frowned.

'It means I don't bloody trust you,' I snapped as I closed the door, letting fresh air wash over me as I strode to the local shop. I scratched my wrists, agitated about leaving Karla alone in the bedsit. I had to be as quick as I could. After all, it wasn't the first time she'd stolen from me and even if we were now allies to a certain extent, it didn't mean she wouldn't stab me in the back the first chance she got.

The shopkeeper, Ali, was Turkish and always smiling, greeting every customer. I smiled as I came through the door and began filling up my basket: bread, milk, crisps and chocolate before heading to the counter to ask for cigarettes.

On the way back, I called Ashley, asking if she remembered a guy called Leon. She was quiet for a second, although I could still hear the chatter of people around her.

'He's bad news, Jess. If Karla's mixed up with Leon you need to stay well away,' Ashley whispered down the phone.

'He cut her finger off,' I said and heard Ashley suck in a breath.

'Fuck, ditch her, Jess. She's not your problem.'

'I can't. She needs help to get away from him,' I said through gritted teeth.

'Why do you always have to play the hero? She doesn't need rescuing, Karla made her bed, she has to lay in it,' she blurted.

'I have to go,' I said and hung up, doubling over like I'd been punched in the gut. Did Ashley think I had a hero complex? I'd saved her, hadn't I, saved her from that violent prick Eddie, kept my mouth shut and spent four years in prison while she had her reputation still intact. I clenched my jaw, teeth knitted tightly together until they ached.

The phone rang repeatedly, and a text message came through with an apology, but I didn't reply. I hurried back to the bedsit, pushing my anger down and chain-smoking my annoyance away.

'Look, look.' Karla was on her knees as I came back in and unloaded my bag of shopping. She was like a kid, desperate to show me a new toy.

'What?' I said, still irritated by Ashley's words.

'I've got the combination; well, I think I have. I've spent the past half an hour looking back through all the videos until I found Terry putting something in the safe. I've zoomed in as close as I can, and I think I can just about make it out. About a week before he died, he put in a large envelope. Three days later, he opens it again, takes some money out, puts it in a jiffy bag and leaves it on his desk.'

'And that's the packet we found on his desk?'

'Yes! Which means there's still money in the safe!'

53

'We don't know that. Barry could have been in since, or Dan even. There's no video to show otherwise,' I said.

'We have to try!'

I turned around, leaning against the counter to give Karla my full attention. 'I'm not a thief, Karla. It wasn't so bad stealing from that pig Terry, but he's gone. We'd be stealing from Dan and I'm not okay with that.'

Karla slumped back on the bed, deflated. 'It could be my ticket out of here,' she said, holding up her bandaged hand.

'Let me think about it.'

'I can do it; I don't need you!' she huffed.

'Oh really? What one-handed? How long is your bandage on for, Karla, a couple of weeks? Is there any point in you going to Bright's in the meantime?'

Karla tutted and closed the laptop lid.

I made tea and beans on toast for both of us before taking the laptop back to Stuart. He kept me chatting for ten minutes about his plans with Helen this coming weekend and did I know if she liked ice skating? He seemed perplexed when I told him he probably knew her better than I did.

'My sister has always been a mystery to me,' I said by way of explanation. He frowned but accepted it, telling me to have a good evening with my friend.

When I returned, Karla was already asleep, on top of the covers. I laid a blanket over her and switched on the lamp before getting ready for bed myself. It was barely eight, but I was shattered and laid down to read an old Christopher Pike book I rescued from the boxed-up stuff at Mum's. Books I read as a kid were always a comfort. Their words taking me back to a better time.

A buzzing sound came from my pillow and I saw Dan had text, checking in to make sure we were okay.

I replied we were, and I'd see him tomorrow. I ended the text with a kiss.

I watched Karla sleeping, her eyelids fluttering as she dreamt. I owed her nothing, I'd paid my dues for the life of her brother, so why was I compelled to help? Was Ashley right? Did I have a hero complex? No, it was guilt. If Eddie hadn't been killed, Karla wouldn't have been roped into working for Leon. It all traced back to me, back to that night and I couldn't stand by and watch another life be destroyed. I had to help.

Perhaps if there was money in the safe, it was never Dan's at all. It could all be Barry's, he never let on how much money Terry owed him or what it was for. I assumed it was something to do with us girls, getting a cut after he delivered a 'good' one, but it was all conjecture and I wasn't sure we'd ever find out the truth. If Barry's money was in the safe, it looked like he didn't know how to get it out. Surely, Dan would know Terry had a safe? What could be inside it? I guess we'd find out if we got in.

* * *

When I woke, Karla was wrapped in my towel, a plastic bag over her hand, having just come out of the shower. I was surprised the noise hadn't woken me up.

'Where are you going?' I asked.

'Work of course.'

I shook my head, rubbing the sleep out of my eyes. 'Why? You're not much use with only one hand,' I said.

'I have my last meeting with Barry today. He's going to sign me off and I'll be free. Plus, I'm going to see what's in that safe if it bloody kills me.'

'Karla, I'm not sure about this.'

'What if Dan doesn't know about the safe, what if Terry never told him? What if the money inside there is what he owed Barry, nothing to do with Dan or Bright's?' Karla said, mirroring my thinking.

'Yeah, but what if it's not?'

She rolled her eyes at me and sprayed my deodorant under her arms.

'Help yourself,' I muttered.

I pulled the covers back, emerging from the bed and scratching my head. I tossed and turned so much, my hair was always a tangled mess when I woke up.

Karla got dressed as best she could one-handed. I had to help her with her bra and the button on her jeans.

'Is it sore?' I asked.

'Yeah, hurts like a motherfucker.' She grimaced.

'What time is it?'

'Half seven. I'll make tea, go and get in the shower.'

I did as I was told. Once I was dressed and had done my hair, we were ready to go.

Outside, it drizzled and we waited in a corner of the bus shelter to share a cigarette.

'So, are you going to distract him, and I'll go in? Or shall we wait until he's left and do it after hours?' Either option wasn't particularly inviting but I didn't want to lie to Dan's face if I could help it. Karla was going to try and get into the safe with or without my help and I knew I owed her.

'I think waiting is better, don't you? I'm sure there aren't any more cameras, only the one out the back in the yard, so if we leave via the front door, we should be okay.' I fidgeted, my stomach fizzing, excited but equally terrified. I'd committed more crimes since coming out of prison than I ever had before I went in, showing the big idea of reform in the justice system didn't work. This was the last time though, in future I'd stay on the right side of the law, be an upstanding member of society. Once this was done, Karla and I would be even, she'd have a chance at a new start with some money behind her and I'd be able to let go of the demons that haunted me.

'Sorry, girls, would you mind smoking elsewhere?' a man in his forties said to us, as our smoke wafted in his face.

'Oh, fuck off.'

'Sorry, sure.'

Karla and I spoke at the same time as I dragged her behind the bus stop, hidden by the advertisement, where we were no longer under shelter.

'I'm getting wet now,' she complained.

The bus arrived soon after and the man threw Karla a look of contempt as he got on, so, on exiting the bus, she stuck her middle finger up at him whilst blowing a kiss.

When we got into Bright's, Dan and Barry were having a heated discussion in his office. Barry was gesticulating and Dan shook his head, palms raised up to the heavens. As we passed, Barry stormed out, muttering 'tosser' under his breath. Dan had a smirk on his face as he leaned against the door frame.

'What's all that about?' I asked.

'Money,' Dan said.

Karla eyes bulged.

'You owe him money?' I asked, before Karla could get a word in.

'Terry does apparently. Ten big ones.'

Karla shuffled off to the lockers.

'I'm not paying him though,' Dan said, his voice lower. 'He won't tell me what it was for. Well, he says it was an investment, but I think it's dodgy.'

'Hmmmm,' I agreed.

'Want to get a drink later this week maybe?' Dan asked as I made my way to the lockers.

'Maybe. Are the police done with this place now?' I didn't mean it to sound like a dig, although Dan looked pained.

'I'm not sure. Detective Wimslow is popping in this morning to give me an update but nothing was found in the search to my knowledge.'

I nodded, turning away as I cleared my throat, feeling the hair prickle on the back of my neck.

'You hear all that?' I whispered to Karla, and she bobbed her head as she struggled to put her tabard on.

'Oh, Karla, let's have a chat, yeah, about your duties. We need to look at what you can do without causing any further damage.' Dan appeared at the narrow entrance to the lockers.

'Sure,' she replied and followed him back to his office.

54

I got stuck into a load of hotel sheets alongside Natalia and we chatted about what had been on television; well, she did, I listened. She was amazed when I told her I didn't own one yet.

'What do you do when you're at home?'

'I read, although I try not to be there too much. It's one room so can be kind of claustrophobic at times.'

'I hear you, I'm at my mum's and in the box room, which is basically the dumping ground for the house. Can't wait to get my own place one day.'

Karla returned with a clipboard; she'd been tasked with doing a stock check to see what needed ordering. It was nice of Dan to give her something to do. We didn't get sick pay, so if we didn't work, we didn't earn. She rolled her eyes at me, brandishing the clipboard as she disappeared into the store cupboard. Secretly I think she was relieved Dan hadn't told her to go home. The rest of us were picking up the slack but it was good to be busy.

While we waited for the sheets to finish in the dryer, Natalia popped to the café for a takeaway latte and I headed around to the office. Detective Wimslow filled the doorway, his head nearly touching the top of the frame and the shoulders of his blazer skimming the sides. He was an imposing sight. I moved around to the lockers, catching the end of the conversation.

'When he's found, he'll have a number of alleged offences he'll be required to assist us with. We'll keep looking but the tip off in Portsmouth was a dead end and we've currently got very little to go on.' Wimslow's throaty voice carried and he coughed before continuing.

'His phone records and financial activity prior to his disappearance don't appear unusual. There's no CCTV after him leaving his car in Croydon town centre. We've turned up nothing here or at his home and the local hospitals have had no admissions that match his description.'

'Have you spoken to Kim?' Dan asked.

'I'm going to visit her now. I'll be in touch if anything new comes in and please let me know if Terry tries to contact you.' They said their goodbyes and shook hands. I came around the corner just as Wimslow was leaving, an ashen-faced Dan staring after him.

'What's happened?' I asked, rushing forwards, but Dan looked at me through absent eyes before turning back into his office and collapsing into his chair. A cold unease seeped into my skin as I waited for him to speak.

'I can't believe it. They've tracked girls that used to work here. All have the same story, years of abuse, pretty much since we started Bright's. I can't even, I can't get my head around it. Fuck.' Dan rested his head in his hands. I leant across the desk and wrapped my fingers around his arm, trying to comfort him, my chest heavy.

'You weren't to know, Dan. This has nothing to do with you.'

'What sort of fucking man was he?' Dan glanced up at me, eyes watery. I chewed my lip. There was no need for me to answer, he knew what sort of man his brother was now.

'I hope he never comes back,' Dan said bitterly, standing up and grabbing his coat. 'I need to get some air, I'll be back in a bit.' He rushed straight out of the building without another word and I went back to the warehouse, my legs like lead, wishing I knew how to ease Dan's anguish.

At lunchtime, Karla and I queued to get a roll at the café. I could tell she was chomping at the bit to confirm arrangements and, feeling the pressure from Leon, I knew she'd want to do it tonight. However, Agnes was in the queue too so we made polite conversation. Clutching our lunch, we hung back in the yard to smoke a cigarette and I watched Karla pace, the gravel crunching beneath her trainers. My mind wandered to Dan, he still wasn't back.

'So tonight then. Do you think we should hang back and wait until Dan leaves?'

'Surely he'd check the place before locking up?' I said.

'We can stay in the store cupboard and if he checks, we'll say we didn't realise the time.'

'That's lame.' I laughed but it sounded hollow.

'Got a better idea?' Karla scowled at me and threw her cigarette to the ground before stomping off.

'Hey, how'd your meeting go with Barry?' I called, hurrying after her.

'He signed me off, but he was a prick about it.'

Karla didn't have to explain, unfortunately I knew only too well.

I spent all afternoon chewing my thumbnail until it was sore, the skin surrounding it shredded. I struggled to contain my anxiety, unable to avoid multiple trips to the bathroom and blaming the dodgy chicken wrap from the café when the others asked if I was okay. The excuse went with the sheen on my skin from constant perspiration. Karla scowled at me at every opportunity, mouthing at me to get my shit together. She didn't know I had other things on my mind, not just what she was planning. I thought about telling her to shove it. After all, I was only doing it for her. Just one last thing and then we were done, as far as I was concerned the score would be settled.

When it got to quarter to five and the girls were clearing their stations, preparing to go home, Karla and I slipped inside the store cupboard. We'd got our bags earlier to bring with us in case Dan checked to see if any lockers were still in use. Gradually it grew quieter until we heard lone footsteps come into the warehouse and then leave again. My heart thudded in my ears as we remained still, scared to touch any-thing and make any noise.

Ten minutes later, I got a text from Dan. He'd only come back to work an hour ago and I hadn't had a chance to talk to him.

How about that drink? Meant to catch you after work but think I've missed you

A door slammed in the distance which sounded like it could be the front entrance. We didn't emerge from the store cupboard for another ten minutes, just to make sure everyone had left.

'Reply to him then, make sure he's gone.' Karla

nudged my arm and my trembling fingers flew across the screen.

Sorry. Hope you're okay? Tomorrow? X

We listened, but there was no sound, so we crept around the corner, thankful for the little natural light left streaming through Dan's office window. The sun was setting, and I didn't want to use a torch. We'd be in and out in five minutes anyway.

'Okay, let's hurry. I hope he hasn't locked the door,' I said.

Karla tried the handle to the office, and it opened. A rush of endorphins sped through my veins. She hurried forward into the office, whipped the calendar off its hook and threw it onto the desk, bending over to squint at the dial. I leant on the door frame, reluctant to fully enter. Karla didn't look like she needed much help as she swivelled the dial right, and left, then right again, her tongue stuck out over her bottom lip. I heard her tut and mutter something unintelligible as she tried the dial again. Dots of sweat appeared on my back. Something was wrong.

'It's not working!' Karla said, standing up to stretch her legs, checking the numbers she'd written on her wrist, hidden by the bandage. 'Fuck's sake!' She went back to the dial again as I rubbed the back of my neck. Jittery, like bees were buzzing inside my head.

'Let's go,' I tried, but Karla ignored me.

My phone buzzed loudly, causing both of us to jump. I pulled it out of my pocket, Dan again.

I'm fine. Tomorrow sounds good. Just heading back to the office, left my bloody laptop.

'Karla!'

She turned immediately, hearing the panic in my voice.

'Dan's on his way back,' I said.

'Shit!'

I rushed forward and Karla and I both grabbed the calendar, ripping part of it before it fell to the floor. Bending, we knocked heads as we grabbed for it at the same time. Karla awkwardly returning to her feet, waving her bandaged hand around.

'Let me do it, go and wait by the door. Shout if you hear him.'

Karla did as I asked, and I turned the pages of the calendar back to February. As I did, something caught my eye, a scribble above Kelly Brook's head on the cover, three numbers 34-26-36. Kelly's measurements. They had to be written as a reminder. Jesus, Terry was such a sleaze!

I quickly turned the dial and the safe clicked open. Pulling back the door, a large envelope was the only item inside. I grabbed it as I heard Karla call out.

'I think he's here, hurry!'

I pushed it closed, spun the dial and returned the calendar at lightning speed before rushing out of the office and closing the door. Joining Karla, we ran back towards the store cupboard, adrenaline coursing through our bodies. A second later, we heard the front door open and faint footsteps.

'What have you got there?' Karla whispered as we huddled on the floor of the store cupboard in the dark.

'Sshhhh,' I hissed, terrified of getting caught with my hand in the till.

We strained our ears, listening for the main door to be closed again. It came a minute later, but

we still held our breath for what felt like an
eternity.

'I think he's gone,' I whispered and allowed my
body to relax. I crossed my legs and leant back on the
shelves, positioning my phone to use as a torch.

'What did he come back for?'

'Forgot his laptop apparently. Thank God he
mentioned it!'

'How did you get in the safe?'

'Numbers were written on the calendar, Kelly's
body measurements!'

Karla pulled up her bandage and I saw she was
two digits out from what she'd written on her wrist.

I turned over the envelope and looked at it, then
back at Karla. On the front written in black marker
was Barry's name.

'Told you! It's Barry's money that Terry owed
him. He must have taken a bit out for something
else, gambling probably.'

I stared at the envelope, I'd never stolen anything
before I'd been to prison, now I'd done it twice. I
wasn't proud of what we'd done, but Karla needed
the money. It was a means to an end.

Karla rolled onto her knees and leaned over to

take the envelope, pulling the opening apart. A wodge of cash sat inside. She gasped and handed it to me to look. I ran my finger over the notes and sucked in air like a marooned fish. It was around the same amount as last time.

Karla sank back on her heels, her body limp, and she sobbed. Shaking with heaving moans, she placed her good hand over her face. 'I'm free,' she whispered through snot and tears.

55

Eventually, Karla's sobs retreated and she looked at me. 'Let's go, I'm desperate for a ciggie.' She hauled herself up.

'I need a wee,' I admitted. Still feeling the rush from almost getting caught but equally glad it was over. I handed over the money to Karla. I didn't want any of it. 'Let me talk to Dan about somewhere for you to go, he's been all over the place, he's bound to know somewhere quiet, where you can disappear. We're going out for a drink tomorrow, I'll ask him then.'

'You two a thing now then?'

I shrugged and Karla grinned, her mood having dramatically improved now.

'I don't know.' It was the truth; I didn't know where I stood with Dan any more.

We made our way out of the warehouse with a quick stop for me to use the toilet before leaving. For a second, I panicked Dan might have double-locked the door, but the push-release button worked as it always did.

Outside, the sky was full, heavy rain came in sheets and the air was thick with the smell of wet trees.

'Can I crash at yours again?' Karla raised her voice over the howl of the wind.

'Yeah,' I replied. Where else could she go? At least my place was safe and I could keep an eye on her there. I wanted to check in on Dan but it would have to wait.

The bus stop was deserted, so we smoked freely under the shelter while waiting for the bus to make its way down the road from Croydon town centre. We'd missed the beginning of rush hour and the traffic was free-flowing instead of the usual crawl. I relayed what

I'd overheard Detective Wimslow say to Dan which added to Karla's celebratory mood. It looked like we were in the clear. 'I fancy an Indian takeaway. Let's treat ourselves, we deserve it.' Karla's eyes lit up as she patted her bag, containing the money. Her whole face had changed, she seemed younger and brighter without the world sitting on her shoulders.

I nodded in agreement, although I wasn't hungry. I watched her bounce from foot to foot. How could Karla go from utter hatred for me to where we were now? In a kind of semi-respectful, mutually agreed truce. Unless it was an act? No, not now, not after everything that had happened. I pushed the thought aside.

It took twenty minutes for the bus to arrive and Karla talked about how she'd love to live by the sea. When we got back, the first thing she did was pull out the money and start counting, licking her thumb as she fingered through the notes, a running total in her head.

'There's almost another five grand here!' Karla's eyes were wide, she looked like she'd won the lottery.

I didn't answer. I wanted a shower, my skin felt grimy and I wanted to scrub it away.

'You don't approve?' Karla asked.

'Of stealing,' I replied.

'This will save my life, literally!' Karla waved some notes in the air.

'I know, I helped, didn't I? Feel guilty, that's all.'

'Why? It's money Terry owed Barry, nothing to do with Dan. It's from before.' Karla felt the need to explain, but I understood.

'When are you going to pay Leon?' I asked.

Karla shrugged, piling up the notes and putting them back in the envelope. 'Maybe I won't, maybe I'll do a bunk.'

I shuddered; the image of Karla's cropped finger still fresh in my mind. I was sure he'd take more than that if he knew what she was planning.

'Don't look so worried,' Karla said, reading my expression, but I couldn't help it. Leon wasn't going to let her go that easily.

* * *

The following morning, I woke first, assaulted by the smell of last night's curry leftovers. Karla was full on snoring, with her mouth hanging open, and I had to resist the urge to take a photo. If it was Ashley, I might have put it on Snapchat for a laugh, but Karla and I didn't have that kind of friendship.

In my Facebook notifications, I saw Ashley had tagged me in a photo of a new top she'd bought which she was going to wear on Saturday night. It was black, off the shoulder and glitzy, laid out on her pink dotty duvet cover. *Can't wait to get smashed with my oldest friend!* she'd written underneath. I hadn't responded to her text after we'd argued about Karla, so I commented underneath to say I couldn't wait either. It was true. An opportunity to get out of here and go out properly on a Saturday night to a pub or a club would be too good to miss. I used to dream about all the partying I'd missed out on. We went out before, of course, but most of us were underage. If we could, we'd sneak into the Moon on the Hill, but Gilby would always get too loud once he'd had a drink and we'd be thrown out.

When I first went away, I'd planned to come out guns blazing when I got paroled, but I'd grown up since then and here I was now, almost two months later. There had been no party, just Helen waiting for me to convey the message I wasn't welcome at home and to escort me to Stuart's.

Karla woke when I opened the front door to smoke on the step, letting the smell of curry out at the same time. She rolled over and yawned, stretching her knobbly knee out of the covers.

'Morning,' I said, yawning myself. We'd had a few drinks with the takeaway and I was a little fragile. In comparison, Karla looked fresh-faced and ready to take on anything as she leapt up to stick the kettle on before joining me.

'When I move, you'll come and visit me, won't you?' Karla asked in a rare glimpse of vulnerability.

'You want me to?' I asked, incredulous.

'Yeah, I do,' Karla replied matter-of-factly.

'Well, I guess I can come for my holidays.' I smiled, feeling for the first time there was hope of forgiveness. We'd have to regain each other's trust first, but if we could, and we managed to move on, I'd be absolved of my part in Eddie's death.

* * *

When we got to work, I delivered Karla like the walking wounded to Dan's office, where he was already sat behind the desk. He gave Karla another mundane admin task to do, shredding all the old personnel files of employees no longer with us. There was a cabinet full of them, all files containing a photo. I remembered the one Barry took of me at our first meeting.

'Most prospective employers want to see what their applicants look like. It'll work in your favour,' Barry had said, eyes twinkling. Little did I know he was auctioning us off to Terry. It made my throat constrict and I swallowed the sickly feeling.

'There's loads of them,' I whispered, running my hands across the files tucked neatly in the cabinet. How many women had he abused?

'Terry had a high turnover of staff. It was one of the first things I noticed when I checked Payroll, loads of people on there haven't been removed from the system,' Dan explained.

'Well, you know why now,' Karla said, without a hint of embarrassment.

'Karla!' I snapped, but Dan shook his head.

'It's okay. I'm sorry, Karla, I had no idea what he was up to.'

She gave Dan a solitary nod and started to pull out the files one by one.

I edged towards the door, I had to get started on the laundry, but I wanted to talk to Dan first. He looked like he'd been sucker-punched.

'Time for a quick cigarette?' I asked, hoping he'd come outside where we could talk.

'Sure.' He headed for the front door and I followed, bracing myself for the cold wind. I lit a cigarette and sucked in the smoke, blowing it out through my nostrils.

'Are you okay? After yesterday?' I asked.

'I'm fine.' Dan clenched his jaw and looked away, obvious he didn't want to talk about Terry.

'Still on for a drink tonight?' he asked, happy to change the subject.

'Sure. I need your help with something.'

Dan's eyebrows shot up. 'Go ahead.'

'You said before, you've moved around a bit. I'm looking for somewhere quiet, not necessarily remote, a small village perhaps. Does anywhere spring to mind?'

'For you?' he asked.

'Uh-huh.' Looking away so he couldn't read the lie on my face. I wasn't sure why I didn't tell him the truth; childishly I wanted to see if he cared. I also thought the fewer people that knew Karla was leaving the better.

'Okay, I can think of a couple of places.'

'Great, you can tell me about them tonight,' I replied, flicking my cigarette into the road and heading back inside.

By getting Karla out safely, out of Leon's clutches, I'd have paid my penance. The guilt I felt for causing Eddie's death would hopefully rescind over time and I'd be able to put it behind me and move on. I owed her, by killing Eddie I'd made Karla his replacement in Leon's eyes. Her debt was down to me. I couldn't turn back now, I had to see it through to the end.

56

The roles had reversed between Dan and I. Dynamics shifted to a more level playing field. I wasn't the timid virgin hankering after my older boss any longer. Even though there was an age gap between us, it seemed to have shrunk in the past few weeks. I believed Dan regretted questioning me about Terry and wanted to make amends, especially now the full extent of his violations had been exposed.

I felt his eyes on me as I joined the other girls. We stood in a semicircle and Dan informed us we had a busy couple of days ahead with a new gym trialling Bright's. Karla was still out of action and we'd have to carry on without her. If it got too much, he'd get a temp in. It was important we did well in the trial as a contract could be awarded for the daily turnaround of their towels. Dan had been pushing hard at getting new business in. He was a natural salesman, charming and attentive. Unlike Terry who was slimy and too big for his boots.

I was paired with Agnes and made the effort to have a two-way conversation as opposed to letting her chat away, oblivious to the fact I wasn't listening. Her mother had finally gone back to Poland and she was having a rest from running around after her as well as the children. The surgery on her knee was not going ahead on the NHS, who'd figured out Agnes's mother was only visiting England and was not a resident, so she'd packed up and flown home.

The towels that came in were cheap, low-quality and some of the fibres got caught, leaving strings we had to trim off once they were dry, which slowed everything down. But still the towels were packaged to go back by four and Dan was pleased we'd turned the order around quickly.

I hadn't seen much of Karla, but when I stopped by the office, her and Dan were sat across the desk from each other, photos scattered all over. So many looked alike, slight, pale, blonde, with the exception of a few dark-haired girls. I caught Dan holding my photo, twirling it in his fingers. He lowered it as soon as I clocked it was me, his ears turning pink.

'He used to call me his Caramel Queen,' Karla said, referring to her darker skin. I shuddered and Dan and I exchanged a horrified look. At least we'd never have to put up with Terry's abuse again. Karla had received months of it before I arrived, it was no wonder she seemed cold and bitter. It had to be a protective shell.

Later, on the way out I asked Karla if she was staying with me again.

'Can I? Leon knows where John lives, and I'd rather stay out of the way in case he decides to pay him a visit. I have got to go and get the rest of my stuff though. Pack it up in case I have to leave in a hurry,' Karla said, and I nodded.

We got the bus home and I got ready for my evening out. Karla left for John's to collect her things. I warned her to be careful, to keep her eyes peeled and make sure Leon wasn't about.

'Can you trust John?'

'Oh yeah, he's kind of like my sugar daddy.'

I cringed. How was a girl like her ever going to be able to get back on her feet without help? How were any of us?

I met Dan at the Woodman in Carshalton, the same bar I'd met up with Ashley. It was busier this time, the difference between a Monday and a Thursday evening. He was freshly showered, dark hair still damp, and wearing a deep blue shirt. As I kissed his cheek on arrival, I was floored by the scent of his aftershave, a delicious citrus aroma which made me want to consume him.

'You look nice,' I said as he pushed a glass of what looked like Coke across the table towards me.

'So do you. It's got vodka in it by the way.' He gestured at the glass as I took a sip. 'I feel like I've barely seen you this week,' Dan continued.

'It's been really busy,' I replied, wanting to say more but knowing I shouldn't. I didn't want Dan getting caught up in Karla's problems. He had enough of his own, as did I.

'And you're thinking about moving away?' He frowned at his pint, refusing to meet my eye. My stomach swirled.

'Maybe, Karla and I might. She wants to live by

the sea. Any recommendations?' I felt mean, I had no intention of going anywhere, but I was intrigued to see Dan's reaction to my sudden departure. He seemed more bothered by it than I thought he would.

'You two back friends again then?'

'Yeah, we sorted it.'

'Seemed pretty serious. What happened?'

'Oh, just bitching behind my back, girl stuff. Gossip flying around,' I lied, thinking on my feet.

'Right, and you're sure you want to move in with her?' Dan said, incredulous.

'Maybe.'

'I thought you had to stay here for the length of your probation period?'

'I can move, I just need to let them know, get a new officer.'

'Oh.' Dan wiped the condensation off his glass with his thumb, staring at it.

'But I'll probably stay, and join Karla when my six months is up,' I replied.

'When's that?'

'I've got another four months' yet.'

Dan nodded and finished his pint, standing to go

back to the bar. He gestured to see if I wanted another, but I shook my head, I still had half a glass.

I checked my phone to see if Karla had been in touch, but I had no notifications at all. Dan slid into his seat and I put my phone back in my bag.

'What about you? You won't stick around forever, when your six months is up on your lease, you'll move on, I guess?' My voice seemed unnaturally high. The atmosphere strangely fragile, both of us on eggshells. I wished I was brave enough to tell him how I felt.

'I don't know, maybe. I can't leave the business with anyone and if Terry isn't back I'll have to stay or sell up.' His tone was sharp. Was he feeling abandoned?

I glanced around at the other punters, deep in conversation, a few scrolling on their phones, giggling over who knew what. There was an awkward silence, followed by a sigh from Dan.

'I'm sorry about before, everything was great until I brought up Terry. Now it's all... fucked.'

I reached over and put my hand on his forearm. 'It's not that. I like you; I do. I'm worried I'm going to get hurt when you leave and I'm not sure I want to stay. Everything feels up in the air and I don't know where I am.'

'Let's just see what happens? With Bright's, with moving, all of it.' Dan looked up at me through his lashes and I melted. Who was I kidding, I'd already fallen hook, line and sinker! I was fooling myself I could move on like nothing had happened between us.

'Okay,' I whispered, a grin emerging.

The atmosphere evaporated instantly and a minute later we were laughing about the pissing contest Dan had with Barry over using the office.

'So, small villages, for Karla, preferably by the sea, somewhere I could go too, one day?' I reminded Dan, steering him back onto topic.

'Oh yeah, ummm, I was thinking Middleton-on-Sea is nice, quiet, towards Bognor way.'

I nodded, committing the name to memory.

'I have a friend who lives down that way. I'll ask her if there's any rentals she knows going cheap.'

My ears pricked up. 'Her?' I blurted, shoulders stiffening.

Dan chuckled, eyes glinting. 'One of my mother's

oldest friends. Not really my type, to be honest, she ruffled my hair when I was last there.'

I snorted, almost choking on a mouthful of my drink. 'Well, some men might be into that sort of thing.'

'Not me, I have everything I need right here.' He winked and I blushed.

'Smooth, real smooth.' I laughed.

'I was talking about my beer.' Dan raised his pint to his lips. 'You know, I have a lasagne in the fridge with your name all over it.' He leaned closer across the table and the tiny hairs on my arms stood to attention.

'A ruse to get me back to your place, is it?' I said, raising an eyebrow and finishing my drink.

'Maybe.' He flashed me a dazzling smile and I stood. 'I knew the lasagne was a winner,' he said, getting to his feet.

'I'm going to the bathroom.' I stalked away, unable to keep the smile from my lips. It was the banter I loved, Dan's flirting which tied my stomach in knots.

I knew as soon as I'd walked into the bar and saw

Dan sat at the table, I'd be going home with him. He didn't have to know though.

I used the facilities and checked my reflection in the mirror, the blush in my cheeks was becoming. I looked alive, and it was how I felt whenever I was with Dan.

'Come on then, I'll let you cook me dinner,' I said, as though I was doing him a favour.

Dan returned our glasses to the bar and put on his jacket. On the walk to the car, Dan pulled me into an embrace.

'I've missed this,' he said, tucking my hair behind my ear.

'Me too.'

57

We ate late, the lasagne took ages to cook as it wasn't in the fridge at all, it was frozen. A Marks & Spencer's special for two, bought with me in mind apparently, confined to the freezer after our fight. I sat, wearing Dan's blue shirt I'd removed not long after we got back.

'What will you do, seriously, with Bright's?' I asked.

'I don't know, everything's changed. I'm waiting for the world to stop spinning so I can figure out what I want. There's a reason Terry ran the business and I moved around.'

I waited patiently for Dan to continue, laying my fork across my plate.

'He was better at the business side, he put down roots with Kim, had a kid. I didn't want the same thing, day in, day out, no one was going to catch me. Do you know what I mean?'

How would it feel to be so free-spirited? I was anything but. I nodded. 'I get that, but you're so good at it.'

'The selling, yeah maybe, but I'm not a natural leader. I don't think I'm great at managing people.'

'The girls love you,' I replied.

Dan looked away; he knew the reason. Anyone would be better than Terry.

'So, about us? Are you happy to go with the flow, see what happens?' I asked, biting my lip, drawing Dan's attention back to me.

'Yeah, I like you. A lot. I'm always smiling when I'm with you.' He blushed, ears tinged pink and my face glowed.

When we'd both finished eating, I washed up the plates and Dan dried beside me. He'd tried to object when I started filling the sink with soapy water, but I told him to stop being silly. I didn't need him waiting on me hand and foot, I was no pampered princess and told him so.

'I'd like to think we're a team,' I said, drawing closer and wrapping my arms around him.

'You're the boss,' he answered before pressing his lips to mine.

* * *

'Are you sure you need to go home?' Dan asked later, as he watched me getting dressed.

'Yes, my taxi will be here in a minute. Karla's staying with me and I forgot to give her a key.' It was already eleven and Karla had text ten minutes before because she couldn't get in.

Overcome with guilt, I told her I'd be fifteen minutes and called a taxi straight away. I pulled on my jeans, fingers fumbling to do up the buttons.

Dan rolled onto his side, his arm propping his head up, naked chest on display. I wanted nothing more than to climb back in beside him. 'What's she running away from?'

'What we're all running away from,' I stated, standing up straight and pulling my hair out the back of my top.

'And what's that?' Dan looked at me quizzically.

'The past.'

* * *

Karla was leaning against the front door, smoking a cigarette. She kept setting off Stuart's security light and I was surprised he hadn't come out to investigate the disco going on in his front garden.

'I'm sorry.' I hurried along the path after paying the driver. At Karla's feet sat two bulging carrier bags, stuffed to the brim. 'Got the rest of your stuff then?' I asked as I slid the key in the door, looking Karla over to make sure she was in one piece.

'Yeah, John got it together for me, we went out for pizza and had a few drinks.'

I pushed open the door and we headed inside. Noting the time, I went into the bathroom to wash my face and when I came out, Karla was already undressed and in bed.

'Do you think you can trust John? He won't tell Leon where you are?'

'John doesn't know exactly where I am. No one does,' she snorted.

'What about where you work?'

'Jeez, girl, you are paranoid!'

'I'm not the one with nine fingers,' I shot back, and Karla tutted, rolling away from me. I hoped Karla had been smart and not given anything away. Ashley warned that Leon wasn't to be messed with.

I lay awake thinking about Dan, acutely aware of the ache in my groin. Was I in love? Whatever it was, it was bound to end in disaster. There wasn't a happily ever after for us here. Not in this town where I could never escape from my past and definitely not with the man whose brother's body I'd got rid of.

* * *

In the morning while I was getting ready, I received a call on my mobile from Mum which made my heart stop. She rang me so scarcely, I immediately panicked, launching across the bed to snatch up my phone and making Karla jump.

'Mum, are you okay? Where's Helen?' I asked breathlessly.

She laughed down the line. 'I'm fine, Helen's upstairs. I just wanted to see if you were okay, you haven't been in touch for a few days.'

I sighed, Mum was checking in. I'd been selfish not to let her know I was okay.

'Sorry, Mum, yes I'm fine. It's been a busy week and I've got a friend staying with me.'

'Ashley?'

'No, not Ash, Mum, I'm seeing her tomorrow though. I'm going to Portsmouth.'

'That's great, send her my love, won't you.' I heard shuffling in the background and Helen's voice. 'Helen wants to talk to you; I'll see you later.'

I rolled my eyes.

'Bye, Mum.' More shuffling.

'When are you next round, we need to talk.' That was Helen, no pleasantries required.

'You do know where I live, don't you, right next to your boyfriend.'

'Can you come around after work, I'll cook dinner.'

'Sure.'

Helen hung up and Karla eyed me curiously.

'Families,' I said with a shrug.

She gave an exaggerated shake of the head. 'Wouldn't know.'

58

It played on my mind at work as I folded the towels fresh out of the dryer, the fabric almost nuclear in my hands. What could Helen want to talk about? Was she going to ask me for money? Did Stuart want me to move out and was frightened to tell me? My head whirled with questions. Although I was grateful to have something to take my mind off Karla who'd told me, on the way in to work, she was going to visit Leon tomorrow night and pay her out-standing debt.

'I'm going to see what he says, play it by ear. I won't mention moving,' she'd said.

'I wouldn't,' I'd agreed. Leon didn't sound like

someone who would graciously let Karla leave his empire, especially when it transpired what a good seller she was. Karla had been moving sizeable amounts around the St Helier estate since her release six months ago, which made sense why I'd seen her a couple of times near Mum's house. I imagined Gilby was one of her best customers.

'I'm not going to be around, remember, I'll be at Ashley's on Saturday night.'

'It's fine, John said I can stay there, he's going to come with me to Leon's.'

'He knows him well enough to go with you?'

'John smokes a lot of weed!' Karla had laughed as though that was explanation enough.

Natalia sang along to Laura's radio, quite content. I was oblivious, too wrapped up in my own thoughts for conversation. Dan called round to our station to say hello, he'd bought in a box of Krispy Kreme doughnuts and everyone was allowed a break to eat before washing their hands.

'Icing on the bed sheets won't go down well with the Hilton,' Dan said.

I hung back as the girls dispersed, queuing to get into the bathroom.

'That was a lovely gesture,' I said, reaching up to kiss him on the lips, sticky from the icing.

'I'm going for boss of the year.' He winked and licked his lips approvingly before pulling me against him. 'So, when am I going to see you next? Free tonight?'

'No, I've got to go to Mum's, Helen's cooking dinner, and tomorrow I'm visiting an old friend in Portsmouth. I probably won't see you until next week.'

'Okay, well give me a call if anything changes. I'm going to check out the rugby club tomorrow morning, see if they'll have an old man like me,' Dan said, sticking his non-existent belly out and patting it.

'I'm more than happy to keep you fit if that's what you want?' I said, grabbing a fistful of his shirt and planting a long kiss on his lips.

'Definitely. Although I might have to count on the rugby this weekend.'

* * *

After work, I jumped on the bus home with Karla. The bedsit looked like a bomb had hit it. Karla had pulled all her stuff out of the duffel bag and clothes were strewn over the bed.

'I'll tidy up,' she said, catching the look on my face.

'I'm going to have a quick shower and go over to Mum's. You staying in?' I asked and she nodded, waving her bandaged hand around the room.

'You won't recognise it when you get back.'

'Hmmmmm.' I rolled my eyes. 'Don't overdo it,' I said, gesturing to her hand.

I decided to walk to Mum's as the sun was shining. The temperature had crept up, making the warehouse muggier than usual, and outside you could get away with a denim jacket or a thick hoody. Despite worrying about Karla and what Helen was going to say, I was in a good mood. Dan and I were back on track, for the time being at least. Plus, I couldn't wait to see Ashley tomorrow. She'd texted this morning with the time of the train I should catch and let me know she'd be waiting for me at the station.

I heard Helen's voice before I got to the front door. The sound of clattering pans and obscenities floated through the open kitchen window and for a moment I was transported back to being fifteen again. Walking home from school, having stopped at the bus stop for a sneaky fag. Mum would be in the kitchen, baking scones or biscuits for Ashley and me to feast on.

The atmosphere couldn't have been more different as I let myself in.

'Mum, I can't find the fucking saucepan,' Helen shouted from the kitchen. I glimpsed Mum wincing through the door to the sitting room.

'All right, chill out,' I said, helping Helen search through the cupboards. Eventually I found it in the corner cupboard, being used as a storage for potatoes so old they had stalks.

'I'm telling you, she's losing it,' Helen whispered as I handed her the pan to wash.

'So, what's up? Why the summons?' I asked, dismissing her comment about Mum. She loved to overreact.

'Go and say hello to Mum first.'

I did as I was told, stooping to give Mum a kiss. She sat in her chair, newspaper open on her lap, trying to change the television channel.

'Here, let me help you. What do you want on, Mum?' I asked, taking it out of her hand.

'*A Place in the Sun*, it's on Channel Four.'

I put it on and noticed Mum's hand was shaking more than usual. I clasped it in mine. 'Are you all right? Had a good week?'

'No, everything aches this week. Cramps and spasms are getting worse. I'm going to go back to the doctors, see if they can up my medication or something.' I nodded, searching for the right thing to say but finding myself at a loss. Instead I patted her hand and laid it back on her lap, her bony knees accentuated by the baggy leggings she wore. My mood dipped and an ache stabbed my chest. I was helpless.

'I'm going for a cigarette, coming?' Helen poked her head around the door.

'Sure.'

'Dinner's on, Mum. Shepherd's pie, and I'm doing you some green beans.'

'Thanks, love.'

I followed Helen out the back and sat on the wall, accepting the cigarette she held out to me and lighting it.

'I'm moving in with Stuart,' Helen announced once she'd lit hers, blowing a stream of smoke from her mouth along with the sentence.

'What? That's a bit soon, isn't it?'

'Jess, my life has been on hold for the past few years. I've had to look after Mum, remember.' The dig didn't go unnoticed. Helen was about as subtle as a brick.

'Okay, I'm sorry, *again*, that I wasn't around to help.' I sighed, throwing my hands up in the air.

'Well, now you are, so I have a suggestion. Move in here.'

'What?'

'I'll move out, you move in. Simple.'

'I'm not sure,' I stammered, the rug pulled out from under my feet. Did I want to move back in here? Two months ago, yes, but now I was used to living on my own with only myself to look after. Was that selfish? Yes, it probably was.

I could read Helen like an open book. She was passing the reins to me; she'd done her time as Mum's soul carer, and I owed her after all. I looked away, no choice but to accept the arrangement. It would mean cheaper living but less freedom.

Helen narrowed her eyes. 'Brilliant, that's decided then.' She flicked her ash and rolled back on her heels.

'When?' I asked.

'This weekend, no reason to delay.'

'Hang on, I'm in Portsmouth tomorrow.'

'Well, when you're back Sunday, you can move your stuff in here. Stuart will run you back and forth, I'm sure.'

'I have someone staying with me,' I tried.

'Does Stuart know? I'm not sure he'd be too happy about that?' Helen put her cigarette in the plant pot and stood up. 'Right, come on, dinner is almost ready.'

I hung back, teetering on the step. Annoyed I'd been railroaded but also a sinking guilt because, besides what she thought, I didn't begrudge Helen happiness even if it was at the expense of my own.

59

Mum was surprised but pleased with the news as Helen announced she would be moving in with Stuart. She used terms like 'nothing will change', 'fantastic support network' and 'two daughters to look after you now'. I smiled sweetly and played along, even though my heart was caving in.

What right did I have to complain? My mother needed looking after and I would make sure she had the best possible care. It went without saying. Even if that forfeited nights with Dan and visiting Portsmouth to see Ashley regularly. Family came first and Helen, as much as I hated to admit it, was right. She deserved to make a go of it with Stuart, even if it was all way too soon. It was none of my business, as Helen reminded me.

'I hope I'll get to meet that man of yours, Jess,' Mum said as a wobbly spoonful of Shepherd's pie made its way from the plate to her mouth.

'I'm sure he'd love to visit.' I smiled tightly, trying to ignore Helen, who was fidgeting in her seat.

When we washed up later, Helen told me about the carer, Grace, the buxom Nigerian woman I'd met already, who came in four times a week. She'd recently upped her visits and Mum seemed to like her. Occasionally she would stay and play checkers or gin rummy if she had time.

'Mum's very fond of her. Grace doesn't suffer fools gladly, she'll put you right if you step out of line.'

'I don't need spying on, Helen. I'm perfectly capable of looking after myself and Mum,' I said, scowling.

'Ha, we'll see.' She was getting off on it, I could tell, so I made my excuses and left, using the long walk home to let it sink in.

I rang Dan as I walked, who tried to make me see the positives. More spare cash, time spent with Mum, the home I grew up in and the potential for boyfriend sleepovers. He slipped the last one in under the radar, but I hadn't failed to notice the use of the B word. He'd never referred to himself as my boyfriend before. I was glad he couldn't see me beaming.

'Thank you. I'm sorry – it's a lot to take in. I'm further away from you, from work and however I look at it, it feels like I'm going backwards not forwards.'

Dan said he understood. We chatted about my trip to Portsmouth and I could tell he was uneasy about me going. Did he think I was going to hook up with someone else?

'Just beware those university boys, okay, they're too damn smart for their own good.'

'Smart, but no common sense,' I threw back and he chuckled.

When I got home, Karla had spruced up the bedsit and it smelt of antibacterial wipes and Dettol spray mixed with the vanilla candle that must have been burning for hours. She lay in the middle of my bed, scrolling through her phone, a smug grin on her face.

'See, I can be clean and tidy.'

'Thanks, it looks great!' I didn't have the energy to go into what happened at Mum's or tell Karla that pretty much from Sunday she'd be homeless again. I'd forgotten to mention it to Dan when we spoke, so I sent a quick text to see if he'd been in touch with his friend in Middleton-on-Sea. It looked as though Karla might need to leave town sooner than I'd anticipated if she was visiting Leon tomorrow. I worried she'd need a quick escape.

During the train ride to Portsmouth, Ashley bombarded me with photos of clothes and links to bars she was going to take me to, clearly excited at the prospect of my visit. I tried to relax and get into the spirit of our upcoming night out, but I had the world on my shoulders again. I desperately wanted to shake it off and enjoy, for once, being twenty-two. As hard as I tried, I couldn't push Karla from my mind. I chewed my nails to the quick, apprehensive at the idea of her visiting that monster after what he'd done to her last time. Praying John would keep her safe.

The journey took around two hours, with a change of train at Horsham. I shivered on the platform, even in the bright sunlight and slowly rising temperatures. Anxiety about meeting Ashley's friends was starting to kick in. What would they think of me? The jailbird, the girl from the estate with a criminal record and dodgy past. Had Ashley told them about me?

I needn't have worried as Ashley jumped up and down in her leopard-print Converse high tops when she caught a glimpse of me through the window as the train pulled in. Immediately a rush of love exploded as I raced off the train with my backpack and we collided together.

'Missed you,' she exclaimed, squeezing me tight.

'You too!' I breathed in her perfume, nestled into her shoulder. 'So, what's the plan?' I asked, pulling away.

Ashley hooked her arm through mine as I adjusted my backpack on my shoulder and led me towards the exit. 'Back to mine to work out clothes, get our glam on, then a few of the gang are coming over for pre-drinks. I thought we were going to head into town, but apparently there's a massive party down the road. So that's even better – we can stagger home later.'

Home, as it turned out, was a rented house shared by students near the university. A small mid-terraced three-bedroom with five occupants. Ashley had a double bedroom that she shared with her roommate, Fiona, who was on the same course. Luckily Fiona had gone back to London to visit her parents for the weekend and apparently had given permission for me to use her bed. The house was lived in, plates in the sink, empty bottles of beer and wine lined the counters ready to be taken out for the recycling, but I envied the space, which felt massive compared to my single room.

Ashley's bedroom walls were covered in artwork. I recognised her swirly pencil strokes and bold primary colours.

'I still don't know why you chose science; you could easily have taken art,' I said, dumping my backpack on the floor.

'Not great job prospects though for a hopeful artist. Plus, I like the black and white of science. It's about fact, evidence, not how you might interpret what something is. It either is or it isn't.'

I shrugged, smiling at Ashley's enthusiasm. I barely remembered school now, it seemed a lifetime ago.

Throwing open the doors to her wardrobe, Ashley began pulling out dresses and sparkly tops, all more suited to her than me. 'Don't panic, I'm not going to give you anything with sequins. I thought this would be good for you, or this?' she suggested, pulling out a floaty red sheer top with a camisole underneath and a green high-necked, backless top which I much preferred.

'That one.' I gestured to the green. It might even go okay with the jeans in my bag.

When Ashley was finished, the only items I wore that were mine were underwear and shoes. She'd tried to get me in heels, but knowing I was going to be drinking, I preferred to keep my trainers on.

'Very cool.' Ashley appraised me as she finished her mascara.

The doorbell rang and we went downstairs. Within minutes, the lounge was full as Ashley hurried to introduce me to everyone. Yvonne, Harry,

Mia, Philip and another girl I didn't catch the name of, all toasted my arrival with Prosecco which Ashley pulled from the fridge.

I was intimidated by them, her cool, university friends. They seemed so elite, confident, and my social anxiety peaked. I tried to fade into the background, but Ashley stuck close to me as we made our way to the party, holding my hand for support.

On arrival at the large double-fronted house, I'd been cornered by Harry in the kitchen as he was fixing me a drink. He waffled on about being on the debating team and how he loved a woman with opinions, trying to draw out what I thought about cannabis being legalised.

Ashley rescued me promptly, chiding Harry for trying to keep me all to himself. Every space was occupied – the house belonged to a lad called Paul, whose parents were on holiday in Antigua, so it was customary for a party to be held. It had more rooms than I'd ever seen and twice I almost got lost trying to find a bathroom. I bumped into Paul on the way back through a room with floor-to ceiling shelves full of books. We chatted for a while about our favourite novels, one subject I was at ease talking about.

Alcohol flowed and I drank more than I ever had before, happy for my head to loll on my shoulders. I floated around the house, trying to be more sociable, buoyed by Prosecco and grateful to be anywhere else but at home. Happily distracted from my worries of Karla and Leon. I enjoyed play-acting as someone else as the night wore on, even flirting a little with Harry whom I had no interest in.

Ashley had been lost in the conservatory, snogging Philip, who, I saw instantly when he'd arrived, she had a thing for. The glint in her eyes was unmistakable; she always found it difficult to hide how she felt. I remembered her looking at Eddie the same way, right up until he died.

My thoughts turned back to that night, the alcohol dulling my normal ability to bury the memory. It had been raining, not too hard, but the windscreen wipers of my car needed replacing, so they smeared the rain back and forth. The sun had set, and I was home having my dinner when Ashley text me, asking if I could give her and Eddie a lift to Mitcham at around eight. It wasn't far and she hadn't learned to drive yet. I was only too happy to go for a drive. I'd had my licence for three months and my mum had helped me buy a beaten-up Vauxhall Corsa, so I'd have my independence.

Eddie was older than us, around twenty-three, but I never felt comfortable around him. He had a reputation on the estate, a vicious temper, but Ashley defended him, telling me he was sweet to her, most of the time at least. That night, Eddie had a flat tyre, but he had to pay his dealer and Ashley offered my services. My car stank of marijuana when we got going; they were smoking a joint when I picked them up and brought it with them. Eddie was already in a mood about his car and Ashley accidentally burnt a hole in his jacket as they smoked in the back seat.

That's when the fight started; he smacked her around the head, not hard, but she said she'd had enough. He wasn't to hit her any more or she was going to dump him. I'd never seen him hit her before, but I had spotted bruises; she always brushed me off when I approached her about Eddie. I should have pushed her to talk about it, made her see that it wasn't right. No man should ever hit a woman, for any reason. If I had, she might have left him sooner and that fateful night might never had happened.

Her threats sent him over the edge and as I drove

down the busy high street, he started to attack her in the back of the car. The windows were all steamed up, the radio too loud, playing drum and bass. I tried to keep driving, looking over my shoulder as they struggled and shouting at Eddie to leave her alone.

Ashley was screaming, her arms shielding her head, pleading with Eddie to stop hitting her. She cowered in the footwell as he kicked and punched, raining blows down upon her, his face contorted with rage.

'You'll never fucking leave me,' he roared as he stamped on her. Seconds later, I threw the Corsa around a bend too fast, terrified to stop, but trying to knock Eddie off his feet. We lost control on wet tarmac, tyres screeching. I tried to brake, but my foot missed the pedal and I accelerated head-on into a tree at the side of the road.

I started to hyperventilate; panic caused by the flashback overwhelming. The room began to spin, and I vomited in a plant pot. At that point, I decided it was time to leave.

60

Outside, in the back garden, sucking in lungfuls of fresh air, I checked my phone, blinking at the screen, trying to focus. Eight missed calls from Karla. Shit! What had happened? I stabbed at the phone, trying to call her back, but it rung out. I tried again, dropping the phone as I fumbled for a cigarette in the packet Harry held out to me after following me outside.

'Something wrong? You look like you've seen a ghost.' He picked up the phone, brushed off the dirt and handed it back to me.

'I don't know. I can't get hold of my friend.'

'Ashley's copulating with Phil upstairs, I believe.'

Harry nodded his head in time to the music playing. A song I didn't recognise, the beat was too fast, my chest vibrated from the bass rippling through me. Was I going to be sick again?

I sank to the floor, sitting cross-legged on the patio, looking out at the expanse of lawn which seemed to go on for miles. It was almost midnight; time had run away with me. So, this was what a university party was like; this was what I'd been missing out on. It hadn't met my expectations; cheap alcohol consumed by the gallon, music that didn't make me want to sing or dance. I didn't get these people, they were different, and even though it was likely my own insecurities, I felt stupid in their company.

As my head whirled, I realised I wanted to go home. Trying Karla again, the line rang and rang. Frustrated, I launched my phone into the flower bed.

'What's going on?' Ashley appeared; her make-up smudged but with a rosy glow.

'I can't get hold of Karla. She went to see Leon tonight. She's rung me about ten times.'

'Jess, I told you, drop her, she's only going to drag you down,' Ashley slurred.

'What, like me? Dragging you down?'

Her mouth dropped open, and her hand moved to her stomach, as though she'd been winded. 'That's not fair. I didn't drop you. You went to prison!' she shrieked.

Eyes of those on the patio turned to us, unable to hear our exchange over the music but obvious from Ashley's body language that we were having a row.

'Great! Fuck this, I'm going home,' I said, grabbing my phone from the flower bed and storming out through the house.

My stomach rolled. I needed food, something to soak up the alcohol, and I staggered on the gravel driveway and out onto the road. Looking both ways but convinced we'd come from the right, I walked in that direction, realising I had no idea where Ashley lived or even where the train station was from here.

A minute later, the pavement echoed with slaps of footfall and I turned around to see Ashley running after me in bare feet, her heels swinging from her hand.

'Oi, pisshead, you can bloody pack that in,' she shouted, reaching me and panting. 'You're my best mate, you'll always be my best mate. The past doesn't matter, you know that.'

'I'm nothing like them.' I thumbed behind me like I was hitching a lift.

'I know, neither am I, but I put on a good show, don't I!' She cackled, bending to catch her breath.

I shook my head and laughed. Linking her arm through mine again, like she did when I got off the train, Ashley pulled me along.

'Did Karla send you a message?' she asked.

'No, just called a bunch of times. I'm worried.'

'Well, there's nothing you can do from here. I'm sure she'll be fine.'

'I hope so,' I said, although a gnawing feeling in my gut told me otherwise.

'Come on, let's get a kebab.'

'I thought you'd never ask,' I replied, my stomach growling.

* * *

Half an hour later, we sat on the floor of Ashley's room, two bottles of water and a feast of doner kebab, chips and chilli sauce spread out between us.

'Lush.' Ashley licked her fingers and I groaned with satisfaction. I'd regret the chilli in the morning, but the food tasted good. 'You need to make sure you drink all that before you go to sleep.' Ashley pointed at the bottle as I chewed.

I nodded, shovelling more pitta bread in before I'd even finished my mouthful.

We chatted until the early hours of the morning, about university, her secret fling with Philip because his mother wouldn't approve. I opened up about Dan, it felt good to get it off my chest.

'I think I might be falling for him, but I'm scared I'm going to get hurt. He normally moves around a lot with work but has swooped in to sort out Bright's. I don't know how long he'll stick around for. I mean, is it just a fling or something more? He's older, more experienced, and I don't know if I feel this way because he's my first, you know.'

'Have you told him any of this?'

'No, not yet.'

'Well you should, tell him how you feel and that you just want him to be straight with you. Is he going to be staying in Croydon and does he want a relationship?'

I nodded, relieved to be able to talk about it with someone.

'If he's decent he'll be honest with you.'

As time went on and we sobered up, talk moved on to the St Helier Estate and Eddie.

'I know you think I'm being harsh about Karla, but Leon isn't someone to be crossed. I'm worried about you.'

I explained how Karla had been repaying Eddie's debts and Leon had forced her to resume selling drugs on his behalf as soon as she was out of prison.

'Sounds like she's a great influence for someone wanting to stay the right side of the law! Why don't you go to the police?' Ashley asked.

I snorted. 'Everyone is corrupt, Ash; my probation officer is as bent as they come. They are all in each other's pockets.'

'Sounds like a Netflix movie.' Ashley laughed, trying to inject some lightness into the conversation.

I yawned, barely able to keep my eyes open.

'Will you come back again?'

'Of course. You ain't getting rid of me that easily.' I bent over to kiss the top of Ashley's head before throwing on the T-shirt I'd travelled in. Climbing in her roommate's bed, I wriggled beneath the covers, watching Ashley do the same.

'Night, Jess.'

'Love you.'

'You too.'

* * *

My eyes stung the following morning as I was assaulted by the bright sunlight streaming in through Ashley's window. She was up already, her bed neatly made as though it had never been slept in. I licked my dry lips, head throbbing a little. It would have been so much worse if I hadn't guzzled a bottle of water, in an attempt to wash down the kebab. My fingers greasy and hair stinking of smoke, I rolled out of bed to remove the sheets.

If I was Ashley's roommate, I wouldn't like to come home to a bed reeking of kebab.

'What are you doing?' Ashley came in, just out of the shower and wrapped in a towel.

'I thought I'd change the sheets or strip them at least.'

'Okay, I'm sure she won't be bothered, but throw them in the corner and I'll sort them later. How are you feeling?'

'Not bad actually.' I stopped to run my fingers through my hair. 'I need a shower though.'

'Here's a towel, it's the next door on the right, shared by five of us, but I think we're the first up. It's pretty early for a Sunday morning here.' Ashley chuckled and began combing her hair.

'What time is it?'

'Just after nine.'

I finished the sheets and left Ashley to get dressed while I had a long hot shower, borrowing someone else's shower gel and shampoo, hoping they wouldn't mind. Afterwards, I felt much more human.

Back in Ashley's room, she was dressed and putting on mascara.

'We might have time for breakfast, when's your train?'

'Eleven,' I replied, suddenly remembering Karla and my appetite vanishing.

I snatched up my phone and sat on the bare mattress, listening to a garbled voicemail that had come through overnight. Karla sounded hysterical. Blood drained from my face and I wheezed like I was suffocating.

'You look like you've seen a ghost, Jess. What's happened?' Ashley was at my side, rubbing my back as I gulped.

'Karla,' I managed.

Ashley swore, shaking her head, but she didn't move.

I dialled Karla's number, but it went straight to voicemail. Leaving Ashley sat on the bed, I paced. It was pointless, I was too far away and unable to get back quickly.

'I need to check if there's an earlier train, can you look for me, Ash?' I asked as I kept redialling Karla's number, hoping to get a different outcome.

A few minutes ago, I was a regular girl waking up with a moderate hangover on a Sunday morning. I'd forgotten all about Karla. For a second, I wasn't an ex-convict, a girl whose friend was part of a drug-dealing gang. I was normal and hankering after a fry-up, although I knew I'd be sick if I ate anything at all.

'There's one in forty minutes, if you get dressed now you might just catch it.'

I chucked the phone and threw on my clothes, quickly plaiting my wet hair so it would be out of my face.

Ashley didn't try to talk me out of it, or bad-mouth Karla while I got ready. She saw from the look on my face I was scared.

'All set?' Ashley said five minutes later.

'Yep,' I agreed, although I was apprehensive to leave. I had no idea what waited for me on my return.

61

The university was a ten-minute walk from the station, although we did it quicker, with long strides.

'Christ, at least I'm getting my exercise today,' Ashley huffed.

'A brisk stroll in the morning is good for you,' I said, pumping my elbows in a comedy fashion.

When we arrived at the entrance, Ashley threw her arms around me and held me tight. 'Take care, let's do this again real soon. Perhaps next time I'll come to you?'

'Well, it looks like I'm moving back in with Mum, so there'll be plenty of space and I know she'd love to have you.'

'You didn't say!' Ashley said accusingly. I'd failed to mention it last night.

'I know, I guess I wanted to forget about it, for the night at least.'

'How come you're moving back?' Ashley asked.

'Helen is moving in with Stuart, my landlord. Who'd have known! It's my turn to take care of Mum, it seems. She made it clear she'd served her sentence while I was serving mine.'

Ashley tutted, mirroring my outrage. She'd never warmed to Helen and always thought she was stuck-up. 'Okay, well at least you'll get to spend more time with your mum. Go on, or you'll miss your train.'

We had another quick hug and I climbed the stone steps.

'See you in a couple of weeks,' she called after me as I waved.

Once safely on the train, which was already at the platform as I hurtled down the stairs, I texted Karla.

I'm on my way back, be there about twelve

I had no idea what had happened or what state

Karla would be in when I got there. I only knew she didn't have any keys to the bedsit, so I fully expected to find her on the kerb or propped up against the front door. As I stared out of the window, the train pulled away and soon we were whizzing past people's back gardens. It was almost warm, without a cloud in the sky and finally it seemed as though winter was a distant memory.

My phone vibrated and I answered it quickly, believing it would be Karla.

'When are you bringing your stuff round?' Helen barked down the phone.

'Helen, it's fucking barely ten o'clock. I know you're excited and all that, but I'm on my way back from Portsmouth on the train. It'll be this afternoon.'

'Okay, keep your hair on, Stuart just wanted to know as he was going to give you a lift.' Should I have been grateful? It was clearly what Helen wanted to hear, but as I was moving out grudgingly, I didn't really care.

'It'll have to be later; I haven't packed or anything. You literally dropped this on me on Friday and I told you I was in Portsmouth this weekend. I'll move when I'm bloody ready,' I snapped and hung up, gritting my teeth until my jaw ached.

I had more important things to worry about than inconveniencing Helen's move to the love nest this weekend. I guessed Karla would have to stay with me at Mum's. That would be something else Helen would moan at, but with no warning, what did she expect?

I relaxed back in my seat, staring out the window again at the houses. Ashley and I had a great night, even though I got a little too drunk and had a bit of a wobble about fitting in. It didn't matter in the end; Ashley had seen through it all. In fact, she was living the same way. Did everyone morph to suit their surroundings? Like a chameleon? Perhaps they did.

My phone buzzed again: a text from Dan. The photo when loaded made me chuckle. Dan was wearing a rugby shirt with a gumshield in, he looked sweaty, his shiny skin covered in mud. Accompanying the photo, he'd messaged:

Can barely walk today, getting old. Miss you. Xx

I typed back:

Take it easy old man. xxx

The bus home came past the station as I emerged from the platform and I chased after it. Glad to be back in the cooler air, than on the stuffy train, which had started to smell anything but fresh as it filled up with people.

When I got home, I half expected Stuart to be hanging around outside waiting for me to return, car keys jingling in his hand, but all was quiet. Karla was nowhere to be seen. All her stuff was gone but thankfully mine remained untouched. My pulse galloped, running through the different scenarios and where she could be. I tried her phone again, but it went straight to voicemail. I left yet another message, must have been my third. Perhaps she was out of battery? Maybe Leon had killed her, and she was lying in a ditch somewhere? No, this wasn't a Netflix thriller, Ashley was right.

After I'd paced around for ten minutes, I began to pack up my things, more to keep busy than because I wanted to. I moved around the room, collecting books and folding clothes to put into the holdall and small red suitcase. It started neatly, but the more disgruntled I became about being forced to move, the more things were stuffed in haphazardly. I stripped my bed, folding up the duvet and cleared underneath it. In the end, it was exactly like leaving prison, my life packed into bags in barely twenty minutes.

I walked around the bedsit, mentally saying goodbye to my first ever adult home, unable to shake the feeling I was going backwards.

Just as I was about to leave, my phone rang. I fumbled getting it out of my pocket, desperately trying to answer.

'Hello,' I said breathlessly.

'They beat John up, he's battered, Jess. They won't let me go.' Karla sobbed. She was hysterical, rambling down the phone.

'Calm down, what happened?' I asked, keeping my voice steady. It appeared my worst fears about Karla seeing Leon had been confirmed but I had to keep it together.

'We went to see them to pay the debt. I gave him two grand, more than I owed but figured it would sweeten him up. John and Leon were having a laugh at first; Leon said we were all clear now. But when

John asked if he could take me away, let slip we were thinking of moving; Leon went ballistic.'

I lowered myself onto the sofa. 'Then he beat him up?'

'With a baseball bat, he's in hospital. I've been with him since last night. At least we're safe here.'

I sighed and Karla sniffed, a muffled sound as though she wiped her hand across her nose. 'Shit. Are you okay, did they hurt you?'

'I'm fine.'

'Okay listen, when you leave, come to my mum's address, you know which one it is, don't you?'

'I'm not leaving John here, I can't.'

'Are you sure it's safe?'

'Yes.'

'Okay, come in to work tomorrow. I'll get the details from Dan about a new place. He suggested Middleton-on-Sea.'

'Okay.'

I heard a siren in the background.

'I better go back inside.'

We said our goodbyes and I got up to pace. I hoped Dan had been able to pull something out of the bag, as the sooner Karla disappeared, the better. God, why was life so complicated?

'Knock, knock,' came a chirpy Stuart from the door he'd pushed open.

'Oh hi,' I mumbled.

'All done, I see, fantastic. Looks as good as new. Here's your deposit and the last month's rent. You gave me two last time, remember?' Stuart handed me a brown envelope and looked at his shoes.

'Thanks.'

'Right, want a lift? I think Helen's keen to get settled in tonight.' The look on the lovesick puppy that was Stuart made me want to vomit.

I rolled my eyes and picked up the bulging holdall, passing my suitcase and backpack full of books to Stuart. Unprepared for the weight, he staggered a little and I stifled a laugh.

In the car, Stuart clicked his seat belt into place and turned the engine on. Patting the steering wheel, he looked at me and over my shoulder to the bedsit. 'A new chapter,' he said, grinning.

'Problem is, I've already read the book,' I replied.

62

Helen was the most hyper I'd ever seen her, hugging me when I arrived, which she didn't even do on the prison steps. Lined up neatly along the hallway were suitcases and boxes of Helen's belongings. I imagined they'd been there since six a.m.

'How's Mum?' I asked.

'She's fine. In fact, I think she's looking forward to being bossed about less.'

'I bet, no dictatorship here,' I mocked, looking over my shoulder.

'Ha ha.' Helen flicked her hair and stalked out of the kitchen.

I followed and found Mum stretching on the carpet.

'Hello, sorry you caught me doing my stretches. I could feel my leg was seizing up.' She flexed her calf, pointing her toe but unable to keep the tremor still.

'I'm just going to show Jess the folder,' Helen said. That sounded ominous.

A minute later, we sat side by side at the kitchen table, Helen flicking through the pages of a blue ring binder.

'So that's her meds, two of each, twice a day. Stretching exercises here. I've written all her appointments so far this year on the calendar. She has physio tomorrow, but Jeff, the driver, collects her and brings her back. He has the key safe code. Grace's details are here and there's the telephone number to her department. Last page is miscellaneous house info, bin days, fuse box, et cetera.' She closed the folder and grinned at me; her eyes manic.

I tried to absorb everything in the folder, but I knew I'd be calling on it for days to come. Helen was thorough, if not overbearing, but her system with Mum had worked so far and I couldn't deny she was well looked after.

Less than half an hour later, Helen and Stuart departed and the house all of a sudden seemed too big. Helping Mum back into her chair, it struck me again how frail she was. At fifty-five, I had visions of her running around with her future grandchildren, pushing them on swings and chasing them around the park, but that would never be. My chest tightened as I tucked a blanket over her legs.

'Cup of tea and a slice of cake, Mum?'

'Ooh that would be lovely,' she said, her eyes lighting up at the mention of cake.

Once Mum had a hot cup of tea and a slice of cherry almond loaf to nibble on, I took my mug out into the garden to have a cigarette and phone Dan.

'Hey.' Dan sounded pleased to hear from me when he answered.

'It's so good to hear your voice,' I said, a little overwhelmed.

'Are you okay? You at your mum's?'

'Yes, I'm here now. I'm going to spend the rest of the day getting Mum settled in.'

'Okay, no worries. Good time in Portsmouth?'

'It was okay, a house party, full of mostly dull

people, but I drank more than my weight in Prosecco and am feeling rotten today.'

'I bet!'

'How was rugby, any bruises?'

'A few, I could do with some nursing.'

I giggled.

'Have you managed to get in touch with your "lady" by the seaside?'

'I have, she's got a couple of places she knows are available. She sent me the details. I'll show you tomorrow.'

'Ready to move into now?' I pressed.

'Yes, I believe so, why?'

'It's kind of become urgent.' I didn't want to say any more.

'Understood.'

I steered the conversation back to the rugby match. Dan said he came home muddy and a bit battered but loved every minute.

'So, what time does your mum go to bed?' Dan flirted.

'About nine-ish according to my sister's folder,' I quipped.

'Text me the address and I'll see you for a good-night kiss then.'

My insides quivered. 'Okay.' I hung up as my cheeks flushed.

Dinner was earlier than Helen's normal timing, partly because I was being belligerent and partly because I was starving. Other than cake at lunchtime, I hadn't eaten a thing all day. Too busy running around. My stomach squirmed around four and I put the prepared casserole into the oven. Slicing up bread to go with it, I considered the positive that life would become calmer from now on. Dan and I could take it slow, I had Mum to look after and she had to be my main priority. Perhaps I could even do a course at the college; it was only down the road. They had evening classes; I could learn something which would help me get a better job.

More buoyed than I had been since the news of moving back had been announced, I joined Mum in the front room for a game of rummy. I hadn't played in years. My first cell mate at Bronzefield, Maria, liked to play and we were happy to while away the hours, but she was only on remand and was quickly replaced by Darcy, the tattooed hairdresser who had a thing for petite blondes.

Brushing the memory away, I declared rummy and laid my run of spades.

'Jammy.' Mum laughed and held her cards out to me so I could deal another round.

When the casserole was ready, I buttered the bread and we both ate in front of the television. Mum dipped her spoon in, leaning over her little table, and I sat with a tray on my lap. We laughed at old episodes of *Frasier*.

It darkened outside as I washed up. Once finished, Mum beckoned me over.

'Listen, love, I never wanted either of you girls to care for me. I told Helen to try and get me assisted living or something.'

'Don't worry, Mum, we'll look after you.' The notion of us putting her in any kind of home was ridiculous. After what I'd put Mum through, taking care of her was the right thing to do. She needed me and I'd missed four years of life with her already. I'd never be able to get that back, but I could use this time to make amends.

'I don't want you wasting your life looking after

me. You should be out living it.' Mum's face was scrunched up in frustration, her hands balled into fists.

I didn't know how to answer, so I gave her a hug. My heart broke at how selfless she was and at how selfish I'd been.

'We'd never put you in a home, Mum, never.'

Mum sighed and pulled me back in for another hug.

She was subdued at bedtime, maybe she was missing Helen. I had nowhere near her caring skills, although she was more like a bustling matron than a carer. I tucked Mum in, pulling the curtains closed and put on the radio. Mum liked to listen to LBC at bedtime for some background noise.

'Night, love. I'm glad you're here,' Mum said.

'Night, Mum.'

No sooner as I'd checked my reflection in the bathroom mirror, I heard the lightest tap on glass. My nerves tingled, knowing Dan would be downstairs waiting for me. There was nothing I could do for my pale, lacklustre hung-over face and I had to hope he didn't notice.

'I'm here to fix your washing machine,' Dan

smirked as I opened the door, dressed in navy overalls and carrying a toolbox.

'Are you for real?' I pulled back the door, doubled
over laughing.

Dan came in and went straight into the kitchen. I
automatically put the kettle on, as I did whenever we
had guests.

While I was rummaging in the cutlery drawer for
a spoon, still chuckling to myself, Dan pressed himself against me, his breath warm on my neck after he
pried my hair away. Goosebumps rippled all over my
body and I arched my back, reaching a hand behind
to grip the fabric of his overalls.

'Turn around.'

63

We giggled over a cup of tea; our cheeks still flushed from the sex we'd had against the counter. Dan hadn't been joking when he'd suggested he come over for a goodnight kiss, wearing the overalls for comedy effect. I couldn't deny he was the best-looking handyman I'd ever seen.

'It's a nice place,' Dan said, seeing past the antique pine dresser and dated wallpaper.

'It's a bit of a time warp. I think Mum was getting ready to do it up before I got sent down and it all fell apart after that. The stroke wasn't far behind,' I said, my focus on my mug.

Dan nodded, eyeing me sympathetically, then taking a sip of his tea.

'I think I need to make Karla leave tomorrow. It's not safe for her here any more.'

'What's happened?'

'The less you know, the better.'

'I feel a bit like a gangster's moll here!' Dan chuckled, chewing his lip. He didn't look much like one in those overalls.

'Do you think one of the places your lady friend suggested will work?'

He rubbed the back of his neck as he considered. 'There's an old boathouse, near the beach. A one-room sort of thing.' I nodded as Dan told me about the location. The boathouse was owned by Natasha, Dan's contact in Middleton-on-Sea, and she was looking for someone quiet to rent it, all bills included. It was a quick-turnaround renovation, which was going to pay for her own mortgage apparently. 'It's available immediately, so I can ring Natasha in the morning and say to expect Karla shortly. I'll have to vouch for her as she won't have any references, but as long as she's got a deposit, it'll be fine.'

'She's got money,' I said and Dan smiled, squeezing my knee.

'Well that's sorted then.'

He stayed for a little while longer, until ten, and I locked up before climbing the stairs to bed.

Helen's room, which was our old room and now a sole occupancy, was barren. Normally there would be an abundance of discarded bottles, make-up containers and scrunched-up tissues adorning the bedside table. Her messiness used to drive me around the bend when we shared the space, but without her stuff, it was too big. I wasn't sure me and the contents of my holdall and suitcase could fill it.

It took me even less time to place my belongings around the room in an attempt to make it more homely than it had to pack up the bedsit. The first things I unpacked were my books, which had grown considerably with every trip to the charity shop. There was still plenty of space on the shelf for more and I'd run out of things to read. I'd have to dip into Mum's collection to see if she had anything other than *Flowers in the Attic*, which I'd read a hundred times.

As I lay on the bed, a text came through from Dan:

Night sweetheart xx

I texted back to say goodnight, aware of the warm glow growing in the pit of my stomach permeating through me. Even with everything going on, I was happy.

Karla texted to say everything was fine and John was being taken off the ventilator as he was able to breathe by himself.

Absent-mindedly, I scrolled through the photos on my phone, laughing at a selfie from last night of me and Ashley I didn't remember taking. I sent it on to her with the caption 'look at these beauties', to which she replied quickly, cringing at how drunk we were before thanking me for visiting and asking if I had as bad a hangover as she did? I replied I did and she asked me how Karla was. I told her I hadn't seen her but heard she was all right.

Full and content, I rolled onto my side to get into the covers. Maybe everything would work out after all.

* * *

I got up early, before my alarm. My period had arrived with a vengeance and stomach cramps were in full swing. A cup of tea and toast for me and Mum before I jumped in the shower to get ready for work. I helped her downstairs after she'd had a wash and got dressed. Grace was coming in at midday and would fix Mum's lunch; she was looking forward to it as she had two crossword puzzles for them to do. Once she was settled in the chair, she held my hand, drawing me close.

'I love you, Jess, and whatever you may think, I'm proud of you.'

My eyes welled up at the unexpected affection.

'Have a lovely day.' She turned away, flicking through her magazine and I took my cue and left.

A few minutes later, I was across the road at the bus stop, basking in the glorious sunshine and deliberately ignoring the graffiti that was still there. I'd have to check in with Grace later; make sure Mum was all right. Glad I'd remembered to programme her number into my mobile.

Today was going to be good, I could smell it in the air. Stuart was right, although a cliché, it was a new chapter and I had to make it work. I'd decided to talk to Dan, I didn't want to pretend to be happy coasting along. Unable to bear to think about him with anyone else, I wanted exclusivity. Not that I believed he was putting it about when he didn't see me, but I needed to feel secure as my affection for him grew. He'd mentioned the boyfriend word in a passing joke, and I hoped he'd make it official. A little stability in my life wouldn't go amiss.

Dan was in the office on his phone when I strolled past, so I blew him a kiss before automatically heading to the lockers. I was a little early and wasn't sure what time Karla would arrive. If she'd been at the hospital with John all night, it wouldn't be early. Her Facebook account had been deleted and I could see she was trying to remove her presence online in preparation for running. I messaged her quickly to see if she was okay and got one back quickly with only the word 'shattered'.

I was looking forward to inspecting the old boathouse with Dan, online at least, and excited to see what Karla would make of it. She looked too cool, perhaps dressed a bit too street, to go unnoticed in a small seaside village. Maybe she'd change her look to try and fit in?

Hanna and Laura were already unloading a delivery and I jogged to help them, still fixing my tabard as I went. Damp, smelly towels from the gym, sweating in giant sealed bags made my throat constrict.

'Grim!' Laura heaved and I clapped a hand over my mouth, enveloped by the odour as we pulled the bags apart.

'What's that honk?' teased Dan, shouting from the back of the warehouse.

'You disgusting men!' Hanna shouted back.

We all laughed, and he didn't come any closer.

In ten minutes, we'd filled three machines full of towels and raised the shutters to let some fresh air in, to clear the stink.

Barry arrived and called on me first for our meeting. He looked as though he was going to burst. His cheeks were mottled, neck a blotchy pink, and I was sure any moment his eyes would bulge. It was unnerving, but I remained passive. Barry spoke in a measured tone, keeping everything professional but the silence lingered between questions and I had to fight the urge to fill it. I became increasingly uncomfortable, shifting in my seat as the tension became palpable. He gripped his pen so hard his knuckles were white, asking only the questions necessary and promptly filling the form as we went.

He leant back in his seat once the form was complete, crossing his arms and awarding me a fixed stare. I swallowed, feeling my pulse spike. What was the matter with him?

'Well, what else has been going on?' he asked, his foot tapping in a slow, steady rhythm. He waited expectantly as I gathered my thoughts.

I began to babble, telling him about my change of address and how I was now caring for my mother. He suggested looking on the internet to see if we could claim any financial aid from the government, although I was sure Helen would be up to date with that.

'Are you okay, Barry?' I asked as the meeting came to a close, unable to stand the atmosphere any longer.

He ran his tongue across his teeth, the simple act

seemed menacing. Picking up his pen from the table and twirling it in his fingers, he spoke. 'I'm being let go. Someone has reported me to my employer. It's been suggested I take bribes and rough up the girls. Some would go so far as to say trafficking.' An icy smile grew on his lips and I shivered.

64

My knee shook, and I briefly considered making a run for it, but Barry's eyes held me frozen.

'You look like a rabbit about to get flattened by my BMW.'

I swallowed, my mouth filling with saliva as he sneered.

'So, what do you know, Jess? Was it you telling tales?'

'I'm sorry, Barry, but I have no idea what you're talking about. I haven't contacted your employer.' My voice came out in a squeak, like a mouse, and I gritted my teeth.

'No, I didn't think so. It's safe to say we both know

who did though. I'm looking forward to seeing that raggedy little bitch today. I trust she'll put in an appearance.' His jaw clenched and I stood, my lungs in a vice unable to take a breath. 'I hope you girls know what you've let yourselves in for, because, if you didn't know, I'm one of the nice ones,' Barry mocked as I left.

Who had told the rehabilitation company? I didn't even remember which one he worked for. I only remember Barry telling me they were contracted by the Probation Service. How on earth had Karla fitted in snitching on him with everything else going on? Like Barry, I couldn't imagine it being anyone else, though. Maybe she had her own list that she was ticking off before leaving? Either way, I was lighter knowing I wouldn't have to meet with Barry again. I hated the slimy ginger prick. Without Barry, Terry would never have had access to us. He was an enabler to the worst kind of man.

I headed outside to the yard for a cigarette, calculating in my head the number of meetings I'd have to endure with whoever turned up next week. I'd toe the line, play by the rules and keep my head down. I hadn't forgotten Karla and I had pretty much got away with disposing of Terry. Detective Wimslow hadn't been back, nosing around and he said himself their leads had dried up. The pressure had eased and it seemed they were more interested in Terry's crimes against women, perhaps assuming that was why he'd done a runner. Whatever their theories, they couldn't prove anything and without a body, the case would remain a missing person.

Soaking up the vitamin D as I leaned against the wire fence, I composed a text to Helen. I reasoned there was no point in staying pissed off and wrote I hoped she'd had a great first night at the Helen and Stuart love nest, and that Mum was fine this morning. I knew she'd appreciate my sarcasm like no one else.

Barry came out to smoke, thankfully staying the other side of the yard as he was on the phone. I took the opportunity to send a message to Karla, to warn her Barry was on the warpath. Dan knew she might be late and as I'd told him she'd need to leave today, I didn't think he was counting on her working a shift. Thankfully since the towels, nothing else had come in and it looked to be a slow day.

Hanna, Laura, Natalia and Agnes were standing

around station five, by the pressing machines, deep in conversation when I went back in. It sounded as though Hanna was trying to teach them some Slovakian swear words. I waved as I went past, wanting to find Dan. It would be lunchtime soon and I wanted to catch him before I went to the café. He was in his office, squinting at his monitor, a can of Coke at his lips. I watched him for a few seconds before he looked up and saw me approach, waving me in.

'Hey,' he said, his smile wide and infectious, making the lines around his eyes crinkle.

'Hi.' I walked around to his side of the desk and perched on the corner, leaning to brush my lips on his.

I had the urge to straddle him as I recalled the image of him in his overalls from last night. 'No overalls today?'

'Didn't think they were suitable for the office.' He laughed, reaching up to weave his hand into my hair and pull me in for a longer kiss. The stirring in my stomach making me wish we were somewhere more private. 'Right, enough of that, I've got work to do. Oh, have you seen Karla yet? I'm going to put an advert on Indeed for her replacement once I've spoken to her.'

'No, not yet,' I replied.

'I'm here,' came a voice from behind us, and I turned to see Karla looking smaller than ever in the doorway.

'Are you okay? How's John?' I asked, jumping up.

'He's stable, that's the main thing. They brought him round, the swelling on the brain has come right down. When he woke up, he told me to go.'

Karla looked on the brink of tears and I led her to the chair in front of Dan's desk and sat her down.

'You look like shit. Have you eaten anything? Do you want a cup of tea?'

'Coffee, if you're making,' she replied, rubbing her eyes.

Dan moved his monitor around so Karla could see the screen.

'This is the place we've found.' He tapped his keyboard. I hurried to the kitchen to make a strong coffee, relieved the photos were still up when I returned.

'It looks perfect,' I said to Karla, leaning over to look at the photos.

Dan told her the monthly rent; Natasha had re-
duced it as a favour. As long as Karla could find
work, she'd be able to afford it. With the leftover
money after paying Leon, she had enough to keep
her going.

'And I can move in today?' She seemed in shock
as Dan and I both nodded vigorously. Karla clapped
her hands over her mouth and tears filled her eyes.
She was much changed from the girl I'd met three
months ago. The streetwise firecracker who wouldn't
take any shit from anyone. Karla looked tired, worn
out and ready to collapse, her already tiny frame appeared fragile with the pounds she'd lost in the past
two weeks. I worried she'd drop from the stress of
it all.

Dan and I beamed at each other, both of us
knowing we'd helped in our small way, that in a
matter of hours Karla would be living another life. It
hadn't got past me that Dan had no idea what Karla
had been involved with; he'd sought out Natasha and
arranged the rental on the boathouse all because I'd
asked him to. Trusting my word was enough. My
chest swelled and I squeezed his shoulder. Pulling
my phone from my pocket, I noticed I had a missed

call from Helen. I'd ring her back, swiping instead to Google Maps and typing in Middleton-on-Sea.

'Is it far enough away? It's only an hour and a half.'

'It'll be fine,' Karla said, looking at her own phone. 'It's a train to Bognor and a short bus ride apparently,' she added, and I noticed her duffel bag at her feet. She was packed and ready to go.

The office fell quiet for a second, the atmosphere serious.

'Try not to miss me too much.' Karla's mouth twitched and for a second the girl was back, filling the room with her exuberant personality. The spark not quite extinguished from her eyes.

'Believe me, I won't. You're a pain in the arse!' I replied, pulling her to her feet. I hugged her, the exchange feeling awkward and although she stiffened initially, she wrapped her arms around me and squeezed me tight.

'Right, let's get you out of here before Barry sees you.'

65

We all left the office, exiting Bright's by the front door, the sun glaring down at us. There wasn't a cloud in the sky, and I raised my face to bathe in it. A vibration came from my back pocket – Helen again, checking up on Mum. Jesus, she was relentless! Why move out if she was going to call every five minutes? I'd ring her back once Karla was safely on her way to the station.

'Can I give you a lift?' Dan offered.

'Nah, it's fine. I can get the bus; the train isn't until two thirty. There's plenty of time.'

'And you'll be okay? You have enough money?' I asked.

'Yes, Mum!' Karla smirked and I tutted.

'Natasha will meet you at the property at five, that'll give you plenty of time to get there, but here's her number and the boathouse details.' Dan handed Karla a printout of what we'd viewed online, including the address and telephone number.

She took it, nodding, and folded it, slipping it into her duffel bag.

'Thank you, for everything.' She looked from me to Dan, and back again. The sincerest I'd ever seen her.

I bit down on my lip; it wasn't the time to joke about what a nightmare she'd been ever since I'd met her. All the dodgy dealings, the backstabbing, lies and hatred between us now pushed aside. I'd never be able to make up for killing Eddie and I owed her for coming to my rescue with Terry. Even if she did have an ulterior motive at the time. Hopefully now the scales were even.

We stood awkwardly, as though no one wanted to be the first to say goodbye. Dan scuffed the kerb with his shoe, and I chewed my nail. My phone buzzed again. Scowling, I pulled it from my pocket. This time it was a text from Helen.

Ring me. Urgent

My heart lurched as I swiped to call her back. What was so urgent? Shit, why hadn't I bloody answered the phone?

My stomach flipped like I was on a coaster as I waited for Helen to pick up, then I saw Karla's face pale.

'Fuck,' she breathed, and her eyes closed for a second. Before I could turn around to see what was behind me, a voice boomed over the noise of the traffic.

'Finally decided to show up, have you?' Barry strode over, his eyes wild, rubbing his hands together.

I ended the call as Helen picked up. It would have to wait; I knew Barry wanted to tear Karla limb from limb.

'Hi, Barry,' Karla said flatly, her face giving away the annoyance at his interruption.

'Little smoking break, is it?' He lit a cigarette and glanced around at each of us, waiting for a response that never came.

I followed suit, pulling a cigarette from the pack in my back pocket and handing one to Karla.

'Well, this is nice,' Barry said, glaring at us.

Dan and I exchanged a look, in which I tried to convey I wanted him to stay. However, he must have misread my signal because with a slight nod of the head towards Bright's, he said: 'I better get back. See you later, Karla, take care, okay,' and he was gone.

Alone with Barry, who looked like a boxer gearing up for a fight, my heart hammered in my chest, making my ears buzz.

He looked from me to Karla and back again. 'You know I've been wondering what's going on between you two? Why Karla was so keen for me to be your rehabilitation officer, Jess. I had to pull in a few favours of course. I don't normally cover new releases from HMP Bronzefield. Why was she so eager to have you working at Bright's?' Barry paused, waiting for an answer, his eyes narrowing when none came.

Karla and I exchanged looks. I'd guessed when I found out she was Eddie's sister that she might have been keeping an eye on my release date, that much was obvious, but she'd managed to engineer me coming to Bright's? What had she promised Barry to make that happen? I closed my eyes. It was in the past now, but it still burnt to know how intent she'd been on ruining my life.

'At first, I thought you two might have been friends, that's what she told me, but after seeing you at each other's throats I realised that wasn't the case. It must be important; she paid in kind after all,' Barry sneered, and I felt my throat close up.

Karla looked at the floor, her skin pasty, like she was about to throw up.

Barry stepped towards Karla, blowing smoke out of his nostrils. 'Well come on, I can't just go without solving the mystery, not now you've got me the fucking sack.' His booming voice reverberated through me. He looked deranged, eyes dark and malicious. A loose cannon and I had no idea how far he'd go.

It didn't matter now, whatever Karla had done, however I'd ended up at Bright's. Things had changed; Terry had gone and Karla and I had made our peace as best we could.

'Karla's just leaving,' I said, taking a protective step towards her.

'She's not going anywhere,' Barry countered, reaching out and grabbing a hold of Karla's wrist before she could turn.

It all happened so fast. I lunged at Barry, to try and loosen his grip on Karla's arm. She tried to twist away, shouting at him to let her go. We were all so caught up in the moment, the three of us tugging at each other, that none of us saw the black 4x4 mount the kerb. There was no time to move or even a chance to react as it ploughed into us all.

Barry was tossed up in the air like a rag doll, taking the brunt, as I bounced on top of the bonnet. The car sprawled us out like bowling pins across the pavement before speeding away. I landed awkwardly, searing pain, like I'd never experienced, shot up my arm and shoulder as I skidded across the concrete, smashing my head on the bin. I stayed conscious long enough to see Barry hit the deck, his eyes wide with shock as he face-planted the pavement, his limbs at awkward angles, before the world went dark.

* * *

Blinking away sleep, I struggled to regain focus beneath the bright lights. Helen leaned over me, her face tear-stained, and a tissue she'd been twisting wrapped around her finger. For a second, I thought I was dead, my head throbbed and I had a dull ache along my right side.

'Karla?' I asked, throat stinging. I hadn't seen Karla after the car ploughed into us, had she been flung into the road?

'She's fine, been discharged. She had a mild concussion. The other guy who was with you, he's in intensive care, fractured skull.'

'Where's Dan?' I tried to sit, and Helen flapped, getting me to lay down again. Why was she crying? Had I been badly hurt? Lifting my head, I tried to look at myself, but my eyes wouldn't focus. The beeping machines sped up as I tried to untangle myself from the wires.

'Jess, stop, you're fine. A broken arm that's all, maybe concussion but otherwise okay. They've operated on you already; you've got a pin in your arm and you'll have to wear a cast for six weeks.'

I tried to lift it, the cast heavy on my arm, but I had no strength.

'I've got something to tell you.' Helen's chin wobbled, like it always did when she was upset. The memory of missing her calls flashed into my mind.

'Mum?'

She nodded slowly. 'When Grace arrived, Mum had brought all her pills down from the bathroom and taken every single one. They told me she would have been unconscious when she passed, her heart simply stopped.'

I let out a half sob, half howl and tears came in an avalanche.

Helen lowered her head and reached out for my hand, gripping my fingers as we cried together. It was my fault, my first day caring for Mum and I'd failed her.

'She left a note, explaining she didn't want us looking after her. She missed her independence and didn't want us to waste our lives. Apparently, she was happy to go.' Helen heaved, great wracking sobs which made her entire body shake.

'I'm so sorry,' I said, my words seeming weak, unable to even scratch the surface of our grief.

We cried together for a while and, worn out, sat in silence as I stared listlessly up at the ceiling tiles and ultraviolet lights. The machine attached to me had returned to a rhythmic monotonous beep.

'Where's Dan?' I asked again. Why wasn't he here? What time was it?

'He was here before you went for your op. He'll be back soon.'

'What time is it?'

'Eleven?'

My mouth gaped, eleven at night! 'Helen, go home. I'm okay. You must be exhausted. Where's Stuart?'

'He's outside.' Helen let go of my hand and stood, brushing my hair away from my face. 'I am tired,' she admitted. 'I'll come back in the morning, soon as I can.' She smiled at me, her eyes awash with pain. I smiled back and watched as what was left of my family walked out the door.

66

It was surprisingly easy to drift back into sleep. Anaesthetic was an amazing thing, although I woke again hours later, the lights now dim, with the driest mouth I'd ever had. It took me a few minutes before I noticed a sleeping Dan, curled up in the chair Helen had sat in, his jacket over him like a blanket.

'Hey,' I croaked, and he opened his eyes straight away, jumping up. I pointed to the water jug on the bedside table and he filled a plastic cup. I drank it in one go and nodded again for more.

'How are you feeling?' he asked, his face a mask of concern.

'Okay.'

'I'm so sorry about your mum, Jess.'

As soon as he mentioned Mum, my eyes filled again. He dabbed at them with a tissue and stroked my hair, kissing my forehead every so often until I stopped crying.

'Where's Karla?'

'She's fine. After the accident, you and Barry were taken in an ambulance, but Karla barely had a scratch, amazingly she got up and brushed herself off. The paramedics wanted her to go and get checked over in case of concussion, so I drove her to the hospital. There were loads of witnesses to the incident, other drivers and pedestrians, they got the number plate. Leon's been arrested already.'

'How do you know about Leon?'

'Once she was discharged, Karla and I had a long drive down to Middleton-on-Sea,' he said by way of explanation. 'She told me everything. I had no idea what she was mixed up in.'

My teeth clamped together, surely he didn't mean everything. She wouldn't have told him about Terry, would she? 'Everything?'

'Leon, Eddie, the drugs. How many years she'd spent hating you.'

I coughed and Dan let me have another drink before continuing.

'As soon as she told me she knew who was driving the car, once she'd been checked over and you were taken to theatre, she said goodbye to John and we jumped in the car.'

'What about the police?'

'We spoke to them before we left, they came to the hospital to take statements, having already spoken to witnesses at the scene. They had the number plate and Karla didn't want to name names. Leon is clearly a dangerous man. He made a direct attack on Karla's life with no regard for you or Barry.'

'How is Barry?'

Dan shook his head, looking past me out towards the corridor. 'Not good, they're trying to control his internal bleeding.'

I closed my eyes, head swimming. Barry was a twat, but I didn't want him dead. If anything, he'd saved mine and Karla's lives, even if it was only because he'd been in the wrong place at the wrong time.

'I'm so sorry I dragged you into this,' I mumbled.

'You didn't, we're a team and I'm not going anywhere.' He took my hand in his and kissed it.

'How are we doing here?' A nurse pulled back the curtain, a wide smile and striking gap between his two front teeth.

'Okay,' I said, my throat still feeling sore.

'Do you need some more pain medication?'

'Yes please,' I replied, wanting nothing more than to float away and forget everything.

EPILOGUE

Sand tickled in between my toes as I padded along the shore, the tide slowly going out as the sun set way off in the distance.

'Water's bloody freezing,' Dan said, his jeans rolled up, dashing away from the surf. Karla giggled, as did I.

It was mid-June; I'd been without my cast for over a month, although my arm still looked pale and spindly. Hidden beneath a hoody, I rubbed at it, the ache never went away.

Dan's hand reached for mine and we walked together, Karla in front. I'd been desperate to visit but wanted to let her get settled in her new home. I'd spoken to her every week since she moved, our bond cementing slowly over time. We didn't talk about Terry and it was as though what we'd done never happened. Karla seemed to have changed, the attitude had disappeared, and she sounded optimistic about her future in the small seaside village. She'd got a job, at a dental practice, looking after the admin and patient records and was keeping on top of the rent.

She came back to Croydon for the anniversary of Eddie's death in late March. With Leon on remand, she felt able to reunite with her foster parents, who welcomed her with open arms. They let off blue balloons to mark the occasion at a playing field close to the crash site. There was quite a turnout as in death, Eddie had become a legend of the estate. The secret of what happened in the car that night remained buried. I'd kept my promise to Karla, there was no point in dredging up the past.

Ashley had been invited to attend, but she politely declined, wanting to close the door on that chapter of her life and now that Karla knew the truth about what happened, she understood. Now on the final stretch of her degree, Ashley was eager to start her job as a junior lab technician. We've already met up since I last went to Portsmouth and hopefully our nights out will be a monthly fixture moving forward.

Dan had booked a hotel for the weekend, knowing we couldn't all fit into Karla's small boathouse but when we'd arrived, she had a surprise. Her tiny bump was obvious at once, she was so skinny and I saw her face light up as she patted it, confirming what I'd guessed. She was twelve weeks pregnant. A lump grew in my throat and I hugged her tight, whispering my congratulations into her curls.

John came down every weekend and was in the process of selling to move in with Karla permanently. They planned to buy a house together, maybe even get married. I couldn't get my head around Karla being anyone's wife, but it suited her, I'd never seen her look so happy and vibrant. It was lovely to have some good news after the hell we'd lived through.

Helen and I were still grieving. I'd moved back into the bedsit, unable to bear living alone in Mum's house, incapable of stopping the visions of her in the chair every time I came into the sitting room. It might have been comforting for some, but it highlighted my guilt. Helen was doing her best to rid me of it and I was grateful she didn't hold me accountable. Mum's letter had seen to that. We were selling the house, having done the painful task of going through everything.

We'd laughed over our baby pictures and school reports. Cards we'd made Mum from school, Easter bonnets and Christmas gifts. Mum had kept everything, so we boxed it up and took it with us. Almost everything else was given to a charity who cleared houses. They removed the furniture and gutted the place ready for sale. I was worried that sitting empty, it'd be vandalised but there'd been no more visits from Gilby or his friends. No graffiti or windows smashed. I had a feeling I had Karla to thank for that although she never mentioned it.

Once sold, I intended to move out of the bedsit into a flat with my half of the proceeds, although Helen and I seemed to get on well as neighbours. I'd miss popping over for a cup of tea after work. Mum's death had brought us closer together than I'd believed possible, although I missed her terribly. She had been cremated and her ashes lived with Helen for now, so in a sense I saw her most days too.

Dan offered for me to move in with him when I said I couldn't go back to Mum's, once discharged from the hospital. We'd been getting on so well, I didn't want to jinx it, so politely declined. He didn't renew the lease on the maisonette but put an offer in on a terraced house nearer Bright's. Deciding to put down roots after all. We had a conversation about his future plans when I came out of hospital, when he told me he'd thought of us as exclusive after the first night we spent together. I needn't have worried about whether I was his girlfriend or not.

The workers at Bright's were happy, Dan was doing a fantastic job running the laundry. The girls were all were quite taken with him, forever telling me how lucky I was, and since Karla had left, no one had handed their notice in, even the ones who'd finished with their probation. He'd pledged a safe working environment with better pay and bonus incentives that didn't include sexual favours. In turn, they worked hard and stayed loyal, the memory of Terry's reign now fading.

He was still a missing person, but the trail had gone cold. Wimslow hadn't been back to Bright's, I don't think they were looking too hard for him. Dan kept in touch with Kim regularly and saw his niece every few weeks. She'd started seeing a guy she'd met on Hinge, a dating app. I thought it was a bit quick, but Dan wasn't perplexed. He said, despite appearances, she'd told him Terry had treated her like shit anyway. So if anything, she'd had a lucky escape.

I'd had my final probation meeting. The new guy, Dave, signed me off and wished me well. He spurred me on to find an evening course, where I could pick up my A-Level English again. I'm due to start in September. Dan is helping me search for another job. As much as I love working with him, I have bigger dreams to chase. I haven't been successful yet but have had two interviews for office jobs. Practice makes perfect and I don't think it'll be too long before I'll be moving on to pastures new. Barry had been wrong about his replacement; Dave was one of the nicest guys I'd ever met. He told us that Barry had spent six weeks in hospital and then discharged to fully recover at home. Apparently, he'd recently got a night job as a security guard. Dan admitted it had been him who'd blown the whistle on Barry, not Karla, after realising he couldn't get justice for Terry's crimes, but he could punish his enabler.

The night I was signed off we spent celebrating my freedom, Dan bought a bottle of champagne and we toasted to our future on his balcony, looking out on the stars. For the first time in a long while, I finally had a future to look forward to. I wasn't one of Terry's bad girls any more.

A red glow simmered over the horizon as we walked back towards the boathouse. 'I have something for you,' Karla whispered as Dan stooped to pick up a pebble and launch it into the sea. She fell in step with me, took my hand and pressed the SD card into it. 'I want you to burn it.' I stopped dead in my tracks, staring down at the grey card in my palm.

'You kept it?' I asked, incredulous.

'I guess I wanted insurance, just in case, but I don't need it any more. Take it.' Karla stared at me, her deep brown eyes earnest.

A seagull swooped down, squawking, and I saw Dan looking at us, his brows knitted together as though he knew ours was a conversation he wasn't supposed to be privy to. I was glad he was far enough away not to hear us over the sea breeze. We resumed walking side by side, pebbles crunching beneath our flip-flops.

'It's the only thing left that ties us to Terry.' Glancing over her shoulder as she spoke in a low voice.

Karla finally trusted me, and she was letting me know that I could trust her too. The three of us bound together with secrets. Two of us tied in a crime we could never reveal. I squeezed my fingers around the card, feeling the edge dig into my skin.

Karla's mobile rang and she veered off to answer it. From the tone of her voice it was John on the other end. I looked out at the receding sea, dragging pebbles back beneath the surf, taking them prisoner. Dan slipped into the space beside me where Karla had been and put his arm around my shoulders as we carried on walking. I thrust the card into my pocket.

'You okay?' he asked.

'Yeah, you?' I replied.

'I'm good.' We walked along in silence, listening to the snatched conversation Karla was having with John who was due to arrive tomorrow.

'You know, I think this would be a perfect spot,' Dan said before he stopped and faced the sea, letting out a heavy sigh. His hand found mine, warm and soft around my icy fingers.

'For what?' I asked, frowning. He turned to smile at me, a flash of sadness in his eyes.

'A bonfire.'

ACKNOWLEDGMENTS

Firstly, thank you to my Mum and Denise Miller, who are my *go-to* readers as soon as I have something new for them. They spur me on with their appetite for more chapters and then I know I'm on the right track.

Thanks to my lovely editor, Caroline Ridding, as well as the entire Boldwood Books team who are always on hand for advice or to answer my questions. They are taking the world by storm! I've now seen my books in a shop, which has always been a dream of mine. I'm getting that bucket list ticked slowly but surely!

Jade Craddock, thank you once again for your

editing prowess, fantastically eagle-eyed and a dream to work with.

A massive thanks to Ian Gilbert from Addfield Environmental Systems Limited who was readily available to answer many gruesome incinerator questions and never tired of my emails. Your advice was invaluable to the book.

More thanks to Hazel Manuel who gave me an insight on what it was like to work in an industrial laundry. Also Athers Philips who supplied me with information on the Probation Service.

The Savvy Writers' Snug on Facebook is where I've found so many supportive authors, as well as the fabulous Gangland Governors group, who have the most wonderful readers with wicked senses of humour. I'd be lost without you all, thank you for your time, advice and for reading my books.

Lastly, thank you to Dean, Bethany and Lucy for being part of Team Rogers.

MORE FROM GEMMA ROGERS

We hope you enjoyed reading *Bad Girls*. If you did, please leave a review.

If you'd like to gift a copy, this book is also available as an ebook, digital audio download and audiobook CD.

Sign up to the Gemma Rogers mailing list for news, competitions and updates on future books:

http://bit.ly/GemmaRogersNewsletter

Explore more gritty thrillers from Gemma Rogers.

ABOUT THE AUTHOR

Gemma Rogers was inspired to write gritty thrillers by a traumatic event in her own life nearly twenty years ago. *Stalker* was her debut novel and marked the beginning of a new writing career. Gemma lives in West Sussex with her husband, two daughters and bulldog Buster.

Visit Gemma's website:

www.gemmaroger-sauthor.co.uk

Follow Gemma on social media:

f facebook.com/GemmaRogersAuthor

🐦 twitter.com/GemmaRogers79

📷 instagram.com/gemmarogersauthor

BB bookbub.com/authors/gemma-rogers

ABOUT BOLDWOOD BOOKS

Boldwood Books is a fiction publishing company seeking out the best stories from around the world.

Find out more at www.boldwoodbooks.com

Sign up to the Book and Tonic newsletter for news, offers and competitions from Boldwood Books!

http://www.bit.ly/bookandtonic

We'd love to hear from you, follow us on social media:

facebook.com/BookandTonic

twitter.com/BoldwoodBooks

instagram.com/BookandTonic

Lightning Source UK Ltd.
Milton Keynes UK
UKHW040250300421
382869UK00003B/181